RESURRECTIONIST

You don't send a gentleman to catch vermin – you send Hawkwood...

A new term at London's anatomy schools stokes demand for fresh corpses, and the city's 'resurrection men' vie for control of the market. When a grave robber is brutally murdered and his body displayed as a warning to others, Bow Street Runner Matthew Hawkwood must venture into London's murkiest corners to hunt down those responsible. Nowhere, though, is as grim as Bedlam, notorious asylum for the insane and scene of another bizarre killing. Sent to investigate, Hawkwood finds himself pitted against his most formidable adversary yet – an obsessive genius hell-bent on advancing the cause of science at all costs.

RESURRECTIONIST

Resurrectionist

by

James McGee

Magna Large Print Books
Long Preston, North Yorkshire,
BD23 4ND, England.

British Library Cataloguing in Publication Data.

McGee, James
        Resurrectionist.

        A catalogue record of this book is
        available from the British Library

        ISBN   978-0-7505-2758-3

First published in Great Britain in 2007 by HarperCollins Publishers

Copyright © James McGee 2007

Cover illustration © Paul Young by arrangement with
HarperCollins Publishers

James McGee assserts the moral right to be identified as the author of
this work

Published in Large Print 2007 by arrangement with
HarperCollins Publishers

Magna Large Print is an imprint of Library Magna Books Ltd.

Printed and bound in Great Britain by
T.J. (International) Ltd., Cornwall, PL28 8RW

PROLOGUE

When he heard the sobbing, Attendant Mordecai Leech's first thought was that it was probably the wind trying to burrow its way under the eaves. On a night such as this, with rain lashing the windows like grapeshot, it was not an unusual occurrence; the vast building was old and draughty and had been condemned years ago. Only as Leech turned the corner at the foot of the broad stairway leading to the first floor, candle held aloft, did he realize that the weeping was not emanating from outside the building but from one of the galleries on the landing above him.

The galleries were long with high, arched ceilings and sound had a tendency to travel, so it was hard to tell the exact source of the distress, or even whether the sufferer was male or female.

Probably the bloody American, Norris, Leech thought, as another low moan drifted down the stairwell. It was followed by a long-drawn-out howl, like that made by a small dog. Judging from the intensity of the ululation, it sounded as if the poor bastard was in mortal torment, in the throes of another of his regular nightmares. But then, Leech reflected in a rare moment of compassion, if I were chained to the bloody wall by my neck and ankles, I'd probably be suffering bad dreams too.

The howl gave way to a keening wail and Leech

9

cursed under his breath. The ruckus was liable to disturb the wing's other inhabitants, and once they'd picked up the din and joined in it would sound like feeding time at the Tower menagerie, which was a guarantee that no one would get a wink of sleep. God rot the mad bastard!

Reluctantly, Leech prepared to mount the stairs, only to be startled by the harsh jangle of a bell. Suddenly he remembered that was why he'd come downstairs in the first place – in answer to a summons from someone outside, requesting admittance. Leech reached into his jacket pocket and consulted his watch. It was a little after ten o'clock. He didn't need to look through the inspection hatch to see who it was.

As he was reaching for the bolts on the inside of the door, Leech noticed that the wailing had stopped. It was as if the sound of the bell had triggered the silence. He breathed a sigh of relief. Maybe it would be a quiet night after all.

The door swung inwards to reveal a slender figure dressed in a black, rain-sodden cloak and wide-brimmed hat, dripping with water. A woollen scarf, wrapped round the visitor's neck and lower face as a protection against the inclement weather, hid his features.

Leech stood aside to let the man enter. 'Ev'ning, Reverend,' He whispered. 'I was wondering if the bloody rain would keep you away. Beggin' your pardon,' Leech added hurriedly. His voice remained low, as if he was afraid he might be overheard. Members of the clergy were not welcome here. That was the rule, by order of the governors.

The clergyman untied his scarf, revealing his

clerical collar, and lifted his head. 'I was detained; a burial service for one of my parishioners and a host of other duties, I'm afraid.'

In raising his head and thus elevating the brim of his hat, the clergyman's countenance was revealed. It was neither a young nor an old face. But there was wisdom there, in the eyes and the crow's feet and the deep furrows etched into the cheeks and forehead. There were several scars, too, along the jawline: small and round, hinting at a brush with some variation of the pox. High along the priest's right cheekbone what looked suspiciously like a wound from a blade had created a shallow runnel.

Leech had often wondered about the scar and the priest's background, but he had been too wary to ask the man directly and no one he had mentioned it to knew the circumstances of the disfigurement; or, if they did know, they chose not to impart information on the subject. So Leech remained ignorant and more than a mite curious.

The priest removed his hat and cloak and shook them to expel the rain. 'How is he?'

Leech shrugged. 'Wouldn't know, Reverend. I don't have a lot to do with 'im. You probably see more of 'im than I do. I make sure 'is door's bolted and that he gets 'is victuals, an' that's as much as I 'as to do with it. An' that suits me just fine. Anything else, you'd be better askin' the apothecary. How long's it been since you've seen 'im?'

'We played our last game a week ago. I was soundly beaten, I'm afraid. His command of strategy is quite formidable and, alas, I was rather

11

a poor adversary. However, he was exceedingly magnanimous in victory.' The priest patted Leech's arm. 'Let us hope this evening's contest proves more rewarding.'

Another low moan drifted down from on high and the keeper tensed. 'Buggeration. Er ... sorry, Reverend.'

The slam of a metal door from deeper inside the building echoed through the darkened wing. It was followed by the sound of heavy footsteps and an angry warning. 'God damn it, Norris! If you don't keep it down, I'll be in there tightening the bloody screws!'

As if at a given signal, the threat was answered by an uneven chorus of raised voices in varying degrees of excitement. This was followed, in quick succession, by a cacophony of high-pitched screams, a peal of hysterical laughter and, somewhat incongruously, what sounded like the opening chant of some religious exultation.

'Hell's bleedin' bells!' Leech spat. 'That's gone and done it.'

The priest shook his head. 'Poor demented souls.'

Poor souls, my arse, Leech muttered under his breath. Aloud, he said, 'Come on, Reverend, I'll take you to him. Quickly now, stay close to me. And I'd be obliged if you'd put your 'at back on and keep your scarf high. Don't want any pryin' eyes spottin' your collar. Wouldn't want either of us to get into trouble.' The attendant jerked a thumb skywards. 'Then I can go and help deal with that lot upstairs.'

Casting a wary eye around him, Leech turned

12

and led the way along the dimly lit corridor. The priest hurried in his wake. Gradually, the noise from the first floor began to recede as they left the stairs behind them.

Not for the first time, the priest was struck by the speed at which decay was spreading through the building. There were wide cracks along the edges of the ceiling. Rainwater was running down the walls in streams. Many of the window frames were so far out of alignment it was clear that some sections of the roof were too heavy for the bowed walls to support. The entire edifice was crumbling into the ground.

Leech turned the corner. Ahead of them a long corridor led off into stygian darkness. A blast of rain splattered loudly against a nearby window. The sound was accompanied by a groan like that of an animal in pain.

Leech grinned at the priest's startled expression. 'Don't worry, Reverend, it's only the rafters. Used to be in the navy,' the attendant added, 'I knows a bit about ship building. Got to give the ribs room to breathe. Same with this place. Mind you, the stupid buggers only went and built her on top of the city ditch, didn't they? Know what we're standing on? About six inches o' rubble. Below that there's naught but bleedin' soil. We ain't just leakin', we're bloody sinkin' as well!' Leech looked up. 'Anyways, we're here.'

They were standing in front of a solid wooden door. Set into the door at eye level was a small, six-inch-square grille, similar to the screen in a confessional. At the base of the door there was a gap, just wide enough to admit a food tray. Both the grille and the gap were silhouetted by the pale yellow glow of candlelight emanating from inside the room.

Leech reached for the key ring at his waist.

'You know what to do, Reverend. Pull on the bell as usual. It'll ring in the keepers' room. I'll be off at midnight, unless the buggers upstairs are still awake, but old Grubb'll be on duty. He'll be waitin' to unlock the door and see you out.'

The priest nodded.

Leech gave the door a wary eye. 'You'll be all right?'

The priest smiled. 'I'll be perfectly safe, Mr Leech, but thank you for your concern.'

Leech rapped the key ring on the door and placed his mouth against the metal grille. 'Visitor for you. The Reverend's here.'

Leech waited.

'You may enter.' The voice was male. The soft-spoken words were measured and precise. There was something vaguely seductive in the tone of the invitation that caused the short hairs on the back of Mordecai Leech's neck to prickle un-comfortably. Slightly unnerved by the sensation, though he wasn't sure why, the keeper unlocked the door, pushed it open, and stepped back.

In the corner of the room, a shadowy figure rose and moved slowly towards the light.

The priest stepped over the threshold. Leech closed and locked the door, then waited, head cocked, listening.

'Good evening, Colonel.' The priest's voice. 'How are you this evening?'

The reply, when it came, was low and indis-

14

tinct. Leech tipped his ear closer to the door but the conversation was already fading as the occupants moved away into the room.

Leech stood listening for several seconds then, realizing that it was pointless, he turned on his heel and made his way back down the corridor. As he approached the stairwell his ears picked up the sounds of discordant singing and he groaned. Sounded as if they were still at it. It was going to be a long night.

Half an hour after midnight, the bell rang in the keepers' room. Amos Grubb sighed, wrapped the blanket around his bony shoulders, and reached for the candle-holder. Attendant Leech had warned him to expect the summons. Even so, Grubb felt a stab of resentment that he should have to vacate his lumpy mattress in order to answer the call. The wing was quieter now, after the recent disturbance. It was quite astonishing the effect a bit of laudanum could have on even the most obstinate individual. One small drop in a beaker of milk and Norris was sleeping like a baby. Most of the others, nerves soothed by the resulting calm, had swiftly followed suit. A few were still awake, snuffling and whispering either among or to themselves, but it was relatively peaceful, all things considered. Even the rain had eased, though the wind was still whistling through the gaps around the window frames.

It was bitterly cold. Grubb shivered. He'd been hoping to get his head down for a few hours before making his early-morning rounds. Still, once the visitor was on his way, Grubb thought

15

wistfully, he could look forward to his forty winks with a clear conscience.

The elderly attendant swore softly as he squelched his way along the passage.

He halted outside the locked door and rattled the keys against the grille.

There was the sound of a chair sliding back and the murmur of voices from within.

Grubb unlocked the door and stepped away, holding his candle aloft. 'Ready when you are, Reverend.'

Grubb saw that the priest was already wearing his cloak. He'd donned his hat and scarf, too. The clergyman turned on the threshold. 'Goodbye, Colonel, my thanks for a most convivial evening. And very well played, though I promise I'll give you a good run next time,' he said, wagging an admonishing finger.

Stepping through the door, the priest drew himself tightly into his cloak and waited as Grubb secured the door behind him.

Together, they set off down the passage. Grubb led the way, candle held at waist height, on the hunt for puddles. He was conscious of the priest padding along at his side and glanced over his shoulder, trying to steal a look at the clergyman's face. Leech had asked him about the scars a month or two back. Grubb had confessed his ignorance and was as curious as his colleague to learn their origin. He couldn't see much in the gloom. The priest's head was still bowed as he concentrated on watching his footing, his face partially obscured beneath the lowered hat brim, but Grubb could just make out the scars along

16

the edge of the jaw. The attendant's eyes searched for the jagged weal across the priest's right cheek. There it was. It looked different somehow, more inflamed than usual, as though suddenly suffused with blood.

As if aware that he was being studied, the priest glanced sideways and Grubb felt the breath catch in his throat. The priest's eyes were staring directly into his. The obsidian stare made Grubb blanch and lower his gaze. The old attendant sensed the priest raise the scarf higher across his face, as if to repel further examination.

Wordlessly, Grubb led him to the front hall and waited as the clergyman adjusted his hat. Then he unlocked the door.

Across the courtyard, almost obscured beyond the veil of drizzle, Grubb could just make out the entrance columns and the high main gates.

'Can you see your way, Reverend, or would you like me to fetch a lantern?'

The priest stepped out into the night then paused, his head half turned. When he spoke, his voice was muffled. 'Thank you, no. I'm sure I can find my way. No need for both of us to catch our death. Good night to you, Mr Grubb.' He set off across the courtyard, head bent.

Grubb stared after him. The priest looked like a man in a hurry, as if he couldn't wait to leave. Not that Grubb blamed him. The place had that sort of effect on visitors, particularly those who chose to come at night.

The priest vanished into the murk and Grubb secured the door. He cocked his head and listened.

Silence.

Amos Grubb drew his blanket close and mounted the stairs in search of warmth and slumber.

It was the pot-boy, Adkins, who discovered that the food tray had not been touched. An hour had passed since it had been placed in the gap at the bottom of the door, and the two thin slices of buttered bread and the bowl of watery gruel were still there. Adkins reported the oddity to Attendant Grubb, who, shrugging himself into his blue uniform jacket, went to investigate, keys in hand.

Adkins wasn't wrong, Grubb saw. It was unusual for food to be ignored, given the long gap between meal times.

Grubb banged his fist on the door. 'Breakfast time, Colonel! And young Adkins is here to take your slops. Let's be having you. Lively now!'

Grubb tried to recall what time the colonel's visitor had left the previous evening. Then he remembered it hadn't been last night, it had been early this morning. Perhaps the colonel was in his cot, exhausted from his victory at the chessboard, although that would have been unusual. The colonel was by habit an early riser.

Grubb tried again but, as before, his knocking drew no response.

Sighing, the keeper selected a key from the ring and unlocked the door.

The room was dark. The only illumination came courtesy of the thin, desultory slivers of light filtering through the gaps in the window shutters.

Grubb's eyes moved to the low wooden-framed

cot set against the far wall.

His suspicions, he saw, had been proved correct. The huddled shape under the blanket told its own story. The colonel was still abed.

All right for some, Grubb thought. He shuffled across to the window and opened the shutters. The hinges had not been oiled in a while and the rasp of the corroding brackets sounded like nails being drawn across a roof slate. The dull morning light began to permeate the room. Grubb looked out through the barred window. The sky was grey and the menacing tint indicated there would be little warmth in the day ahead.

Grubb sighed dispiritedly and turned. To his surprise the figure under the blanket, head turned to face the wall, did not appear to have stirred.

'Should I take the slop pail, Mr Grubb?' The boy had entered the room behind him.

Grubb nodded absently and slouched over to the cot. Then he remembered the food tray and nodded towards it. 'Best put that on the stool over there. He'll still be wanting his breakfast, like as not.'

Adkins picked up the tray and moved to obey the attendant's instructions.

Grubb leaned over the bed. He sniffed, suddenly aware that the room harboured a strange odour that he hadn't noticed before. The smell seemed oddly familiar, yet he couldn't place it. No matter, the damned place was full of odd smells. One more wouldn't make that much difference. He reached down, lifted the edge of the blanket and drew it back. As the blanket fell away, the figure on the bed moved.

And Grubb sprang back, surprisingly agile for a man of his age.

The boy yelped as Grubb's boot heel landed on his toe.

The food tray went flying, sending plate, bowl, bread and gruel across the floor.

Amos Grubb, ashen faced, stared down at the cot. At first his brain failed to register what he was seeing, then it hit him and his eyes widened in horror. He was suddenly aware of a shadow at his shoulder. Adkins, ignoring the mess on the floor, his curiosity having got the better of him, had moved in to gawk.

'NO!' Grubb managed to gasp. He tried to hold out a restraining hand, but found his arm would not respond. His limb was as heavy as lead. Then the pain took him. It was as if someone had reached inside his body, wrapped a cold fist around his heart and squeezed it with all their might.

The old man's attempt to shield Adkins' eyes from the image before him proved a dismal failure. As Attendant Grubb fell to the floor, clutching his scrawny chest, the scream of terror was already rising in the pot-boy's throat.

1

There were times, Matthew Hawkwood reflected wryly, when Chief Magistrate Read displayed a sense of humour that was positively perverse. Staring up at the oak tree and its grisly adornment, he had the distinct feeling this was probably one of them.

He had received the summons to Bow Street an hour earlier.

'There's a body...' the Chief Magistrate had said, without a trace of irony in his tone. '... in Cripplegate Churchyard.'

The Chief Magistrate was seated at the desk in his office. Head bowed, he was signing papers being passed to him by his bespectacled, round-shouldered clerk, Ezra Twigg. The magistrate's aquiline face, from what Hawkwood could see of it, remained a picture of neutrality. Which was more than could be said for Ezra Twigg, who looked as if he might be biting his lip in an attempt to stifle laughter.

A fire, recently lit, was crackling merrily in the hearth and the previous night's chill was at last beginning to retreat from the room.

Papers signed, the Chief Magistrate looked up. 'Yes, all right, Hawkwood. I know what you're thinking. Your expression speaks volumes.' Read glanced sideways at his clerk. 'Thank you, Mr Twigg. That will be all.'

The little clerk shuffled the papers into a bundle, the lenses of his spectacles twinkling in the reflected glow of the firelight. That he managed to make it as far as the door without catching Hawkwood's eye had to be regarded as some kind of miracle.

As his clerk departed, James Read pushed his chair back, lifted the rear flaps of his coat, and stood with his back to the fire. He waited several moments in comfortable silence for the warmth to penetrate before continuing.

'It was discovered this morning by a brace of grave-diggers. They alerted the verger, who summoned a constable, who...' The Chief Magistrate waved a hand. 'Well, so on and so forth. I'd be obliged if you'd go and take a look. The verger's name is...' the Chief Magistrate leaned forward and peered at a sheet of paper on his desk: 'Lucius Symes. You'll be dealing with him, as the vicar is indisposed. According to the verger, the poor man's been suffering from the ague and has been confined to his sickbed for the past few days.'

'Do we know who the dead person is?' Hawkwood asked.

Read shook his head. 'Not yet. That is for you to find out.'

Hawkwood frowned. 'You think it may be connected to our current investigation?'

The Chief Magistrate pursed his lips. 'The circumstances would indicate that might indeed be a possibility.'

A noncommittal answer if ever there was one, Hawkwood thought.

'No preconceptions, Hawkwood. I'll leave it to

you to evaluate the scene.' The magistrate paused. 'Though there is one factor of note.'

'What's that?'

'The cadaver,' James Read said, 'would appear to be fresh.'

The oak tree occupied a scrubby corner of the burial ground, a narrow, rectangular patch of land at the southern end of the churchyard, adjacent to Well Street. Autumn had reduced the tree's foliage to a few resilient rust-brown specks yet, with its broad trunk and thick gnarled branches outlined against the dull, rain-threatening sky like the knotted forearms of some ancient warrior, it was still an imposing presence, standing sentinel over the gravestones that rested crookedly in its shadow. Most of the markers looked to be as old as the tree itself. Few of them remained upright. They looked like rune stones tossed haphazardly across the earth. Centuries of weathering had taken their toll on the carved inscriptions. The majority were faded and pitted with age and barely legible.

At one time, this corner of the cemetery would probably have accommodated the more wealthy members of the parish, but that had changed. Only the poor were buried here now and single plots were in the minority. The graveyard had become a testament to neglect.

And a place of execution.

The corpse had been hoisted into position by a rope around its neck and secured to the trunk of the tree by nails driven through its wrists. It hung in a crude parody of the crucifixion, head twisted

23

to one side, arms raised in abject surrender.

Small wonder, Hawkwood thought, as his eyes took in the macabre tableau, that the gravediggers had taken to their heels.

Their names, he had discovered, were Joseph Hicks and John Burke and they were standing alongside him now, along with the verger of St Giles, a middle-aged man with anxious eyes, which Hawkwood thought, given the circumstances, was hardly surprising.

Hawkwood turned to the two gravediggers. 'Has he been touched?'

They stared at him as if he was mad.

Presumably not, Hawkwood thought.

A raucous screech interrupted the stillness of the moment. Hawkwood looked up. A colony of rooks had taken up residence in the graveyard and the birds, angry at the invasion of their territory, were making their objections felt. A dozen or so straggly nests were perched precariously among the upper forks of the tree and their owners were taking a beady-eyed interest in the proceedings below. The evidence suggested that the birds had already begun to exact their revenge. They'd gone for the tastiest morsels first. The corpse's ragged eye sockets told their own grisly story. A few of the birds, showing less reserve than their companions, had begun to edge back down the branches towards the hanged man's body in search of fresh pickings. Their sharp beaks could peck and tear flesh with the precision of a rapier.

Hawkwood picked up a dead branch and hurled it at the nearest bird. His aim was off but it was close enough to send the flock into the air in a clamour of indignation.

Hawkwood approached the tree. His first thought was that it would have taken a degree of effort to haul the dead man into place, which indicated there had been more than one person involved in the killing. Either that, or an individual possessed of considerable strength. Hawkwood stepped closer and studied the ground around the base of the trunk, careful where he placed his own feet. The previous night's rain had turned the ground to mud. But earth was not made paste solely by the passage of rainwater. Other factors, Hawkwood knew, should be taken into consideration.

There were faint marks; indentations too uniform to have been caused by nature. He looked closer. The depression took shape: the outline of a heel. He circled the base of the oak, eyes probing. There were more signs: leaves and twigs, broken and pressed into the soil by a weight from above. They told him there had definitely been more than one man. He paused suddenly and squatted down, mindful to avoid treading on the hem of his riding coat.

It was a complete impression, toe and heel, another indication that at least one of Hawkwood's suspicions had been proved correct. Hawkwood was an inch under six feet in height. He placed the base of his own boot next to the spoor and saw with some satisfaction that his own foot was smaller. The depth of the indentation was also impressive.

Hawkwood glanced up. He found that he was standing on the opposite side of the tree to the

25

body. The first thing that caught his attention was the rope. It was dangling from the fork in the trunk, its end grazing the fallen leaves below. The noose was still secured around the neck of the deceased.

In his mind's eye, Hawkwood re-enacted the scene and looked at the ground again, casting his eyes back and to the side. There was another footprint, he saw, slightly off-centre from the first. It had been made by someone planting his feet firmly, digging in his heel, taking the strain and pulling on the rope. The indication was that he was a big man, a strong man. There were no other prints in the immediate vicinity. The hangman's companions would have been on the other side of the tree, hammering in the nails.

Hawkwood stood and retraced his steps.

He looked up at the victim then turned to the gravediggers.

'All right, get him down.'

They looked at him, then at the verger, who, following a quick glance in Hawkwood's direction, gave a brief nod.

'Do it,' Hawkwood snapped. 'Now.'

It took a while and it was not pleasant to watch. The gravediggers had not come prepared and thus had to improvise with the tools they had to hand. This involved hammering the nails from side to side with the edge of their shovels in order to loosen them enough so that they could be pulled out of the oak's trunk. The victim's wrists did not emerge entirely unscathed from the ordeal. Not that the poor bastard was in any condition to protest, Hawkwood reflected grimly, as the body was lowered to the ground.

Hawkwood stole a look at Lucius Symes. The verger's face was pale and the gravediggers didn't look any better. More than likely, their first destination upon leaving the graveyard would be the nearest gin shop.

Hawkwood examined the corpse. The clothes were still damp, presumably from last night's rain, so it had been up there a while. It was male, although that had been obvious from the outset. Not an old man but not a boy either; probably in his early twenties, a working man. Hawkwood could tell that by the hands, despite the recent mauling they had received from the shovels. He could tell from the calluses around the tips of the fingers and from the scar tissue across the knuckles; someone who'd been in the fight game, perhaps. It was a thought.

'Anyone recognize him?' Hawkwood asked.

No answer. Hawkwood looked up, saw their expressions. There were no nods, no shakes of the head either. He looked from one to the other. No reaction from the verger, just a numbness in his gaze, but he saw what might have been a shadow move in gravedigger Hicks' eye. A flicker, barely perceptible; a trick of the light, perhaps?

Hawkwood considered the significance of that, placed it in a corner of his mind, and resumed his study.

At least the manner of death was beyond doubt: a broken neck.

Hawkwood loosened the noose and removed the rope from around the dead man's throat. He stared at the necklace of bruises that mottled the cold flesh of the victim's neck before turning his attention to the rope knot. Very neat, a professional job. Whoever had strung the poor bastard up had shown a working knowledge of the hangman's tool. In a movement unseen by the verger and the gravediggers, Hawkwood lifted a hand to his own throat. The dark ring of bruising below his jawline lay concealed beneath his collar. He felt the familiar, momentary flash of dark memory, swiftly subdued. Odd, he thought, how things come to pass.

Placing the rope to one side and knowing it was a futile gesture, Hawkwood searched the cadaver's pockets. As he had expected, they were empty. He took a closer look at the stains on the dead man's jacket. The corpse's clothing bore the evidence of both the previous night's storm as well as the brutal manner of death. The back of the jacket and breeches had borne the brunt of the damage, caused, Hawkwood surmised, by contact with the tree trunk as the victim was hoisted aloft. He had already seen the slice marks in the bark made by the dead man's boot heels as he had kicked and fought for air.

There were other stains, too, he noticed, on the front of the jacket and the shirt beneath. He traced the marks with his fingertip and rubbed the residue across the ball of his thumb.

Hawkwood examined the face. There was congealed blood around the lips. Had the rooks feasted there, too?

Hawkwood reached a hand into the top of his right boot and took out his knife. Behind him, the verger drew breath. One of the gravediggers swore as Hawkwood inserted the blade of the knife between the corpse's lips. Gripping the dead man's chin with his left hand, Hawkwood used the knife to prise open the jaws. He knelt close and peered into the victim's mouth.

The teeth and tongue had been removed.

The extraction had been performed with a great deal of force. The ravaged, blood-encrusted gums told their own story. Hawkwood could see that a section of the lower jawbone, long enough to contain perhaps half a dozen teeth, was also missing. A bradawl had been used for the single teeth, Hawkwood suspected, and probably a hammer and small chisel for the rest. Hard to tell what might have been used to sever the tongue; a razor, perhaps.

The verger's hand flew to his lips, as if seeking reassurance that his own tongue was still in situ. He stared at Hawkwood aghast. 'What does it mean? Why would they do such a thing?'

Hawkwood wiped the blade on his sleeve and returned it to his boot. He looked down at the corpse. 'I would have thought that was obvious.'

The three men stared back at him.

Hawkwood stood up and addressed the verger. 'Your most recent burial – where was it?'

Verger Symes looked momentarily confused at the sudden change of tack. His face lost even more colour. 'Burial? Why, that would be... Mary Walker. Died of consumption. We buried her yesterday.' The verger glanced at the two grave-diggers, as if seeking confirmation.

It was the older man, Hicks, who nodded. 'Four o'clock, it were, just afore the rain came.'

'Where?' Hawkwood demanded.

Hicks jerked a thumb. 'Over yonder. Top o' the pile, she was.'

A sinking feeling began to stir in Hawkwood's belly.

'Show me.'

The gravedigger led the way across the burial ground towards a large patch of shadow close to the boundary of the churchyard, and pointed to a dark rectangle of freshly turned soil.

'How deep was she?' Hawkwood asked.

The two gravediggers exchanged meaningful glances.

Not deep enough, Hawkwood thought.

'All right, let's take a look.'

The verger stared at Hawkwood in disbelief and horror.

'I'd step away, if I were you, Verger Symes,' Hawkwood said. 'You wouldn't want to get your shoes dirty.'

Blood drained from the verger's face. 'You cannot do this! I forbid it!'

'Protest duly noted, Verger.' Hawkwood nodded at Hicks. 'Start digging.'

Hicks looked at his partner, who looked back at him and shrugged.

The shovels bit into the soil in unison.

At that moment Hawkwood knew what they would find. He could tell from the expressions on the faces of the gravediggers that they knew too. He had the feeling even Verger Symes, despite his protestation, wasn't going to be surprised either.

In the event it took less than six inches of top-soil and a dozen shovel loads to confirm it.

There was a dull thud as a shovel struck wood. They used the edges of the shovels to scrape the soil away from the top of the coffin. What was immediately apparent was the jagged split in the wood halfway down the thin coffin lid.

'Good God, have you no pity?' The verger made as if to place himself between Hawkwood and the open grave.

'If I'm wrong, Verger Symes,' Hawkwood said, 'I'll buy your church a new roof. Now, stand aside.' He nodded to Hicks. 'Open it up.'

Hicks glanced at his partner, who looked equally uncomfortable.

'Give me the bloody shovel,' Hawkwood held out his hand.

Hicks hesitated, then passed it over.

The three men watched as Hawkwood inserted the blade of the shovel under the widest end of the lid and pressed down hard. His effort met with little resistance. Other hands had already rendered the damage. The cheap lid splintered along the existing split with a drawn-out creak. Hawkwood handed the shovel back to its owner, grip̃ d the edges of the shattered lid and lifted.

Thᵉ verger swallowed nervously.

Hawkwood knelt, reached inside the coffin and lifted out the crumpled fold of cloth.

The burial shroud.

Burial plots were at a premium in London and mass graves were common in many parishes. It was often impossible to dig a fresh grave without disturbing previously buried corpses. The pit at St Giles in the Fields was a prime example where, for years, rows of cheap coffins had been piled

31

one upon the other, all exposed to sight and smell, awaiting more coffins which would then be stacked on top of them. The depths of the pits could vary and coffins weren't always used. A year or two back, in St Botolph's, two gravediggers had died as a result of noxious gases emanating from decomposing corpses. Graves were often kept open for weeks until charged almost to the surface with dead bodies. In many instances the top layer of earth was only a few inches deep so that body extremities could sometimes poke through the soil.

Which made it easy for the body stealers.

Hawkwood left the gravediggers to fill in the hole and retraced his steps back to the murder scene. He looked down at the corpse and then at the grubby shroud in his hand.

Strictly speaking, bodies were not considered property. Burial clothing, however, was a different matter. Steal a corpse and you couldn't be done. Steal clothing or a shroud or a wedding ring and that was a different matter. That carried the punishment of transportation. Whoever had ransacked this grave had been careful.

Which begged the obvious question.

Why leave the dead man's corpse behind? Why wasn't this one bound for the anatomist's table as well? The dead man was relatively young and, other than the obvious fact that he was lifeless, he appeared to be in good physical shape. He should have been a prime candidate for any surgeon's anatomy class. The corpses of well-built men were always in demand, for, with the skin stripped away, they could be used to display muscles to their best advantage. To any self-respecting body stealer, this wasn't just a cadaver, this was serious cash-in-hand.

There was the soft pad of footsteps from behind. It was the verger.

'How many?' Hawkwood asked.

The verger bit his lip. 'Four in the last two weeks, including the Walker woman. The other three were all male.'

Hawkwood said nothing and reflected on the speed of the corpse's transformation from Mary Walker to *the Walker woman.* 'What about a night watchman?'

Verger Symes shrugged. 'It's true we have employed them in the past, and it makes a difference for a time. The snatchers go elsewhere: St Luke's or St Helen's. But then the watchman becomes complacent and relaxes his vigilance, usually with the aid of a bottle, and the stealings begin again. We are not a wealthy parish, Officer Hawkwood.'

It was not an uncommon story.

The number of graveyards in the capital that had escaped the attention of the sack-'em-up men could be counted on the fingers of one hand. Deterrents had been tried – night watchmen, lamps, dogs, even concealed spring guns – but to little avail.

The wealthy could inter their dead in deeper graves, in family mausoleums and private chapels or beneath heavy, immovable headstones, encasing the remains in substantial coffins, either lead-lined or made entirely of metal. The poor could not afford such luxuries. They did their best, mixing sticks and straw with the grave soil for example, in the vain hope that the resulting fibres would choke the stealers' wooden shovels. Paupers' graves were easy targets.

'Can I ask you a question, Officer Hawkwood?' The verger looked pensive. 'When I enquired earlier why anyone would do such a terrible thing – murder a man, then cut out his tongue – you said it was obvious. I don't understand.'

Hawkwood nodded. 'Same reason they didn't take this body away with the other one. It was left here for a purpose.'

'Purpose?'

Hawkwood returned the verger's gaze.

'It's meant as a warning.'

'You think that's why they left the body? As a warning?'

James Read asked the question with his back to the room. He was gazing out of the window, looking down into Bow Street. It was early. The Public Office on the ground floor was not due to open for over an hour. Outside, however, the roads were already busy with morning traffic. The click-clack of hooves and the rattle of carriage wheels could be heard, along with the cries of street vendors as they made their way to and from Covent Garden, barely a stone's throw away round the corner at the end of Russell Street.

The fire, still crackling in the grate, had raised the room's temperature considerably since Hawkwood's last visit. James Read did not like the cold so he was studying the oppressive late November sky with no small degree of despair. He suspected that the weather was about to take a turn for the worse. There was a sullen quality in the air that hinted of yet more precipitation, possibly sleet, and that probably meant the early arrival of winter snow. He sighed, shivered in resigned acceptance, and turned towards the fire's warming embrace.

'That was my first thought,' Hawkwood said.

Knowing James Read's propensity for an open fire, Hawkwood had wisely left his coat in the ante-room under the eye of Ezra Twigg. He was glad he had done so. He would be roasting otherwise.

'You base that on the manner of death and the removal of the dead man's tongue, I presume?'

Hawkwood nodded. 'The gravediggers and the verger got a good look. It'll be all round the parish by midday. If it isn't already.'

'I would have thought the crucifixion would have sufficed,' James Read said. 'The tongue seems rather excessive. Not to mention the teeth. You have thoughts on the teeth?'

'Waste not, want not,' Hawkwood said dispassionately. 'The body and the tongue were left as a warning. The teeth were taken for profit.'

A fine profit, too, if one had the stomach for it. Most body stealers had. It was a lucrative sideline. Many resurrection men removed the teeth from corpses before delivering their merchandise to the anatomists. A good set could fetch five guineas if you knew your market.

'As I said: excessive.'

'Not if you really want to put the fear of God into your rivals,' Hawkwood said.

The Chief Magistrate frowned. 'Which would

35

indicate a serious escalation in violence.'

'They're making their mark,' Hawkwood said. 'Staking their territory. The Borough Boys will be looking to their laurels.'

The Borough Boys had long been the capital's most notorious team of resurrectionists. They plied their trade mostly around Bermondsey but supplemented their incomes by regular forays north of the river. Up until now they had ruled the roost, but a rivalry had begun to develop. There were rumours of a new gang based along the Ratcliffe Highway, whose members had a mind to deter all the other body stealers from entering their domain by whatever means necessary. Fear and intimidation were their watchwords. Unbeknownst to the majority of respectable citizens, deep in the city's shadows and the gutters a vicious war was being waged.

'What about the deceased?' Read asked. 'Do we know his identity?'

'There's a possibility his name is Edward Doyle.'

The Chief Magistrate raised an eyebrow.

'Hicks, one of the gravediggers told me. He denied knowledge at first, but then had a change of heart after he'd taken a closer look at the face second time around, so he said.'

James Read kept his eyebrow raised.

'I wasn't satisfied with his first answer. I pressed him on it.'

'I've always admired your powers of persuasion, Hawkwood,' Read said drily. 'So, you think he was involved?'

Hawkwood shook his head. 'In the murder? No,

his shock was genuine. In planning the removal of the woman's body? Maybe. Proving it might be difficult.'

'So your thought is that he tipped off Doyle there was a newly buried body. Doyle turned up to collect it and ran into a rival gang who stole the body, killed Doyle and left *his* body on display?'

'I'd say so,' Hawkwood agreed.

That James Read expressed no concern at the gravedigger's alleged involvement came as no surprise to Hawkwood. It was common knowledge that most resurrection men plied their business with the connivance of those connected to the burial trade, be they undertakers or gravediggers. It wasn't unheard of for those who dug the graves to be personally involved in exhumations. After all, they knew where the bodies were buried, literally. A common ruse was for gravediggers to let slip to interested parties that certain cadavers, by prior arrangement, were not in the coffins that had been recently buried but left instead on top of the casket, hidden under a thin layer of loose earth just below the surface, ready for retrieval.

'What else do we know about Doyle?' Read asked.

'Hicks thinks he may have been a porter, one of the Smithfield lot.'

'And?'

'And nothing. That was all he knew.'

Read sucked in his cheeks. 'What does that leave us?'

'Not much,' Hawkwood admitted. 'But it's all I've got. If he does work out of Smithfield, the odds are he'll have had a regular watering hole close by, maybe one of those drinking dens up on Cow Street. And if he was a resurrectionist on the side, it's even more likely. From what I've heard, most of the bastards spend their takings on rotgut.'

The Chief Magistrate bit his lip. 'I take it you intend paying the area a visit?'

'I thought I might,' Hawkwood said. 'Ask around. See what I can dig up.' Hawkwood kept his face straight.

'Thank you, Hawkwood. Most amusing.' The Chief Magistrate returned to his desk and took his seat. 'But, before you do, I've another pressing matter that requires immediate attention. I'm afraid to say this is turning out to be a most memorable morning. While you were investigating the incident in Cripplegate, I received word of another murder, a most curious occurrence, not to mention a most intriguing coincidence, given your recent encounter with death and divinity.'

Hawkwood wasn't sure if this was another example of the Chief Magistrate's mordant wit, or how he was expected to respond, if at all. He decided to wait and see.

'The conveyor of the information was in a severe state of agitation, understandably. As a result the details are somewhat incomplete. We do know the victim is a Colonel Titus Hyde.'

'Army?' Hawkwood frowned.

The Chief Magistrate nodded. 'Indeed, which is why I felt it appropriate that an officer with your background should initiate the investigation. Bizarrely, we were also provided with the murderer's identity, and his address. The perpetrator would appear to be a man of the cloth; a Reverend Tombs.'

'A parson?' Hawkwood couldn't mask his surprise.

'I've dispatched constables to the parson's house. It's doubtful he'll be there, of course. Most likely he's gone to ground somewhere, but it's the logical place to start looking for him. I'd like you to visit the scene of the crime.'

The expression on the Chief Magistrate's face told Hawkwood there was more to come. 'Which was where?'

The Chief Magistrate pursed his lips. 'Ah, again, that is another perplexing factor. The killing took place last night, or rather in the early hours of this morning, in Moor Fields. The exact location...' the Chief Magistrate paused '...was Bethlem Hospital.'

And there it was. Hawkwood stared at the Chief Magistrate. Save for the ticking of the clock in the corner and the crackle of burning wood in the grate, the room had gone uncannily silent.

Because not many people called it that.

In the same way the Public Office was known, at least to the personnel who worked there, by a nickname, the Shop, so too was Bethlem Hospital; and not just by its staff, but by the entire city, if not the entire nation. Bethlem had been its founding name, but it had another: a single word synonymous with incarceration, misery and madness.

Bedlam.

2

Hawkwood stared stonily through the railings at the state of the building he was about to enter. Despite having dominated the area for centuries and become ingrained in the public consciousness, the place still held a morbid fascination, even if it was collapsing into ruin.

The original façade had been some five hundred feet in length, modelled, so it was said, on the Tuileries Palace in Paris. In its prime, the building must have been a magnificent sight.

Not any longer. The place had been falling apart for years, subsidence and rot having taken its toll. The east wing had already been demolished, following a damning surveyor's report. Only half of the original building remained and that was little more than a shell. It was no longer a palace but a slum, as shoddy and as run down as the houses and secondhand furniture shops that occupied the narrow streets around it.

Hawkwood had never visited the hospital, though he'd lost count of the times he'd walked past the place, and he couldn't recall a single occasion when he hadn't experienced a dark sense of foreboding. Bethlem had that effect.

He glanced up. Above him, surmounting the posts either side of the entrance gates, were two reclining stone statues. Both were male, naked and badly eroded, victims of more than a century's exposure to wind and rain and the capital's filthy air. The wrists of the right-hand figure were linked by a thick chain and heavy manacles. The statue's head was tilted, the carved mouth was open in a silent scream of despair, as if warning passers-by of the cruel reality concealed behind the gates.

He heard laughter, the happy sound at once at odds with the cheerless surroundings. He looked over his right shoulder. There'd been a time when Moor Fields had been counted among the capital's greatest visitor attractions, its landscaped lawns and wide walkways framed by neat railings and tall, elegant elm trees inspiring tributes from artists and poets.

Most of that had long since disappeared. What had once been a smooth, green, manicured meadow was now a meagre desert of bare earth and weeds. What remained of the railings were bent and broken. The trees that lined the pathways looked listless and unkempt in the dull morning light. Parts of the encompassing lawn had suffered from chronic subsidence, creating, after stormy nights, rainwater-filled depressions. It was from the edge of one of these shallow ponds that the laughter had originated. Two small boys were playing with a toy galleon, re-enacting some naval engagement, totally immersed in their imaginary battle, oblivious to the incongruity of the moment.

Hawkwood turned away. Climbing the steps, he entered the courtyard and made his way across to the hospital's main entrance. There were niches either side of the door. In each one there stood a painted wooden alms box. One was in the shape of a male youth. The other was a bare-breasted female figure. Above them was an inscription encouraging the visitor to make a contribution to the hospital funds. Ignoring the carved inducement, Hawkwood pulled on the bell, and waited.

A small hatchway was set in the door. The hatch cover slid back and a pair of hooded eyes appeared in the opening.

'Officer Hawkwood. Bow Street. Here to see Apothecary Locke.'

The face disappeared from view and the hatch slammed shut. There was the sound of a bolt being released and the door swung open.

Inside, the building was pungent with the smell of piss and shit and damp straw. Hawkwood had skirted Smithfield on his way to the hospital and the reek from the piles of horse, cattle and sheep dung left behind from the previous day's market hung in the air, strong enough to make the eyes water. For a moment he thought he might have tracked something in on the sole of his boot and he lifted his foot to check. Nothing; the fetid odour must be part of the building's fabric.

The door closed heavily behind him.

A cleaning operation was in full spate. Mops and pails were in liberal use in a bid to restore some semblance of order after the night's storm. Judging by the amount of dark seepage still trickling down the walls and across the uneven floor, it looked like a losing battle. Despite the activity, the atmosphere appeared subdued. Most of the workers were toiling in silence. Present among the cleaning gang were several unsmiling

42

men in blue coats. Hospital staff, Hawkwood supposed.

The porter who had let him in, a thin man with a long nose and lugubrious expression, stepped away from the door. 'Apothecary's in 'is office. I'll have someone take you up.' The porter caught the eye of one of the blue-coated men and beckoned. 'Mr Leech? Officer Hawkwood. He's from Bow Street.'

The blue-coated attendant nodded. 'Been expectin' you. Follow me.'

Hawkwood fell in behind his guide as he climbed the stairway to the first-floor landing. Conditions here didn't look to be any better than those at ground level.

The upstairs gallery ran the full length of the building, divided at intervals by floor-to-ceiling openwork grilles. The left-hand side of the gallery was occupied by cells, so the grey morning light could only enter by the windows along the opposite north wall. It barely supplemented the inadequate candle glow.

The smell was worse than down below and when he passed one of the open cell doors and saw what lay in the cramped room beyond, Hawkwood understood why.

There was a low wooden cot with a straw-filled mattress. Seated upon the mattress was a man, or at least what appeared to be a man. He was desperately thin. His face was as pale and as pointed as a shrew's. A soiled woollen blanket covered the lower half of his body except for his feet, which protruded from beneath the filthy material like two pale white slugs. It was clear that beneath the

43

covering the patient was naked from the waist down. He was wearing a grey shirt and yellow handkerchief around his neck but it was his head-wear that caught Hawkwood's attention: a red skullcap, beneath which was wrapped a loose, once-white bandage. Hawkwood found himself transfixed, not just by the man's expression, which was one of abject misery, but by the iron harness fastened around his chest and upper arms and the iron ring around his throat. The ring was attached by a chain to a wooden pole that ran vertically from the corner of the cot to a bracket in the ceiling. As the blanket slipped off one scabby leg Hawkwood saw that there was another strap around the man's ankle, attached by a second chain secured to the edge of the cot. It was clear from the state of him that the man was sitting in his own waste.

The attendant spotted the revulsion on Hawkwood's face and followed the Runner's gaze. A sneer creased his lip. 'What you lookin' at, Norris?'

Hawkwood watched as a single tear trickled slowly down the shackled man's emaciated cheek.

The attendant seemed not to notice but turned abruptly and continued along the gallery. Hawkwood tore his eyes away from the open door and followed his guide.

Most of the cells they passed were occupied, with the majority housing more than one patient. It was clear that Norris wasn't the only one who was chained up. Even in the darkened interiors Hawkwood could see that a number of patients, both male and female, were similarly restrained. Several more blue-coated keepers were in attend-

44

ance, some supervising patients or else engaged in cleaning duties.

The attendant led Hawkwood along the wing, finally stopping outside a door with a brass plate upon which was etched *Apothecary*. Leech knocked on the door and awaited the summons from within. When it came, he opened the door, spoke briefly to the occupant then indicated for Hawkwood to enter.

It was an austere room, darkly furnished and, like the rest of the building, it carried an overwhelming air of dampness and decay. There were a great number of books. On the wall immediately behind the desk were tier upon tier of shelves, filled with rolled documents. Patients' records, Hawkwood assumed.

Apothecary Robert Locke was not the authoritative figure Hawkwood had been expecting. He had envisioned someone middle-aged, with an academic air. Locke, on the other hand, looked to be in his mid thirties, stocky, with a studious countenance and a slight paunch. His youthful face, framed by a pair of small, round spectacles, looked pale and drawn. He turned from the window where he had been standing in thoughtful pose and greeted Hawkwood with a formal, yet hesitant nod.

'Your servant, Officer Hawkwood. Thank you for coming. I've asked Mr Leech to remain, by the way, as it was he who admitted the Reverend Tombs into the hospital last night.'

Hawkwood said nothing. He looked from the keeper to the apothecary. Both eyed him expectantly.

'Forgive me,' Hawkwood said. 'I was wondering why I was instructed to ask for the apothecary. Why am I not seeing the physician in charge, Dr Monro?'

A look passed between the two men. Apothecary Locke pursed his lips. 'I'm afraid Dr Monro is unavailable. His responsibilities cover a rather broad – how shall I put it? – canvas. He has other duties that also demand his attention.'

What might have been a smirk flickered across Attendant Leech's face.

'And yet he's in charge of the hospital, and therefore of the patients' welfare, is he not?'

Locke nodded. 'That is so. However, he is by title only the visiting physician and thus is not required to attend the premises on a daily basis. He oversees prescriptions to patients two days a week and attends the governors' subcommittee meeting on Saturday mornings.'

'And the rest of the time?'

There was just the slightest hesitation, barely noticeable, but it was there nevertheless.

'I understand the majority of his time is spent at his academy, commissioning and, er ... setting up his exhibits.'

'His what?' Hawkwood wondered if he'd heard correctly.

'His paintings, Officer Hawkwood. Dr Monro is a respected patron of the arts. I understand Mr Turner used to be one of his many protégés.'

'Turner?'

'The artist. He has received many plaudits for his works. His forte is landscapes, I believe.'

'I know who Turner is,' Hawkwood snapped.

46

The apothecary stiffened and blinked. The look that flickered across the bespectacled face suggested that Locke's expectation of a Bow Street emissary had probably run to a ponderous, black-capped, blue-waistcoated conductor of the watch with an ingratiating manner and a pot-belly. Patently what the apothecary had not made provision for was an arrogant, long-haired, scar-faced, well-dressed ruffian with a passing knowledge of the arts.

For his part, Hawkwood recalled Locke's initial response to his question. The apothecary's turn of phrase had seemed a little odd at the time, as had the emphasis on the word 'canvas'. All was now becoming clear. He hadn't imagined Attendant Leech's smirk. The unmistakable whiff of resentment hung in the air. There might be more to this timid-faced apothecary than he had first thought. And that was certainly an avenue worth exploring.

'Forgive me, Doctor, it just seemed curious to me that the hospital's chief physician would appear to spend rather more time with his paintings than his patients. However, there's another doctor on the staff, I believe: Surgeon Crowther? Or have his duties taken him elsewhere, too?'

Hawkwood allowed just the right amount of sarcasm to creep into his voice. His tactic was rewarded. This time, the apothecary's reaction was less restrained. He flushed and coughed nervously.

Over his shoulder, Hawkwood heard Attendant Leech shift his feet.

Locke's eyes flickered towards the sound. 'I'd be obliged, Mr Leech, if you would be so good as to wait outside.'

The attendant hesitated then nodded. Locke waited until the door had closed. He turned back to Hawkwood. Removing his spectacles, he extracted a handkerchief from his pocket and began to polish each lens. 'I regret that Surgeon Crowther is...' the apothecary pursed his lips indisposed.'

'Really? How so?'

Locke placed his spectacles back on his nose and tucked away his handkerchief.

'The man's a drunkard. I haven't seen him for three days. I suspect he's either at home soaking up the grape or lying in a stupor in some Gin Lane grog shop.'

This time there was no mistaking the edge in the apothecary's voice. It was sharp enough to cut glass. 'Which is why you are talking to the apothecary, Officer Hawkwood. Does that answer your question? Now, perhaps you would care to see the body?'

Attendant Leech led the way.

As they were going down the stairs, the apothecary paused as if to collect his thoughts. Allowing Leech to get a few steps ahead of them, he took a deep breath. 'My apologies, Officer Hawkwood. You must think me indiscreet. I fear I rather let my tongue run away with me, but it has been somewhat difficult of late, what with the surveyors' final report and the notice and so forth.'

'Notice?' Hawkwood said.

'The building's been condemned. Hadn't you heard?' The apothecary made a face. 'Some would say not before time. You saw that the east wing's already gone? That used to house the male patients. Since its destruction we've had to move the men into the same gallery as the women; not the most suitable arrangement, as you may imagine. It's fortunate we're not operating at full capacity. When I started there were double the number of patients there are now. Hopefully we'll have more room when we move to our new quarters, though goodness knows when that will be.'

They descended a few more steps, then Locke said, 'A site has been procured, at St George's Field. Plans have been agreed, though there's been some doubt about the funding. You may have seen the subscription campaign for donations in *The Times?* Ah, well, no matter. Unfortunately, attention has been diverted to the New Bethlem very much at the expense of the old one. We have been abandoned, Officer Hawkwood. Some might even say betrayed. Which accounts for the deplorable state of repairs you see before you.'

They reached the bottom of the stairs. A few of the keepers nodded as the apothecary passed. Most of them ignored him and continued to swab the floor.

'I've a hundred and twenty patients in my care, male and female, and less than thirty unskilled staff to tend them. That includes attendants, maidservants, cooks, washer-women and gardeners – though God knows there's scant need for *their* services. I'm required to sleep on the premises and to make rounds every morning, dispense advice and medicines and direct the keepers in

49

the management of the patients. Note that I said "direct", Officer Hawkwood. I have no authority over them, save in the supervision of their daily schedule. I'm not permitted to dismiss or even discipline the keepers, despite the fact that many of them are frequently the worse for drink. My complaints continue to fall on deaf ears. Wait, did I say "deaf"? Absent would be a better word.'

They had left the rattle of mops and pails behind them. The damp smell, however, seemed to follow them along the corridor.

The apothecary's nose twitched. 'Is this your first visit, Officer Hawkwood?'

Admitting that it was, Hawkwood wondered where the question was leading.

'And what was the first thing that struck you when you walked through the door? I beg you to be truthful.' As he spoke, the apothecary side-stepped nimbly around a puddle.

'The smell,' Hawkwood said, without hesitation.

The apothecary stopped and turned to face him. 'Indeed, Officer Hawkwood, the smell. The place reeks. It reeks of four centuries of human excreta. Bethlem is a midden; it's where London discharges its waste matter. This is the city's dung heap and it has become my onerous duty to ensure that the reek is contained.'

Hawkwood knew it was going to be bad. He'd seen it in the pallor on Locke's face, in the expression of dread in the young apothecary's eyes, in the quickening of his breath and the faint yet distinct tremor in Leech's hand as the keeper had unlocked the door.

The window shutters were open but, as the morning sky was overcast, the room was suffused in a spectral half-light. When he entered, Hawkwood felt as if all the warmth had been sucked from his body. He wondered whether that was due to the temperature or his growing feeling of unease. He'd seen death many times. He'd witnessed it taking place and had visited it upon his enemies, both on the battlefield and elsewhere, and yet, as soon as his eyes took in his surroundings, he knew this was going to be different to anything he had experienced.

He heard the apothecary murmur instructions to Attendant Leech, who began to move around the room lighting candle stubs. Gradually, the shadows started to retreat and the cell's layout began to take form, as did its contents.

It was not one room, Hawkwood saw, but two, separated by a low archway, as if two adjoining cells had been turned into one by removing a section of the intervening wall. Even so, with its cold stone floor and dark, dripping walls, the cell resembled a castle dungeon more than a hospital room. Hawkwood recalled a recent investigation into a forgery case which had taken him to Newgate to interview an inmate. The gaol was a black-hearted, festering sore. The cells there had been dank hellholes. The design of this place, he realized, looked very similar, even down to the bars on the windows.

In the immediate area, there were a few sticks of rudimentary furniture: a table, two chairs, a stool, a slop pail in the corner, close to what looked to

51

be the end of a sluice pipe, and a narrow wooden cot pushed against the wall. On top of the cot could be seen the vague shape of a human form covered by a threadbare woollen blanket.

The apothecary approached the cot. He straightened, as if to gather himself. 'Bring the candle closer, Mr Leech, if you please.' He turned to Hawkwood. 'I must warn you to prepare yourself.'

Hawkwood had already done so. The pervasive scent of death had transmitted its own warning. At the same time he wondered if the dampness in the cell was a permanent phenomenon or solely a consequence of the previous night's deluge. He could hear a faint tapping sound coming from somewhere close by and concluded it was probably rainwater dripping through a hole in the ceiling.

Locke lifted the corner of the blanket and pulled it away. Even with Leech holding the candle above the cot, in the dim light it took a second or two for the ghastly vision to sink in.

Hawkwood had seen the injuries suffered by soldiers. He'd seen arms and legs slashed and sliced by sword and bayonet. He'd seen limbs shattered by musket balls and he'd seen men turned to gruel by canister. But nothing he had seen could be compared to this.

The corpse, dressed only in undergarments, lay on its back. The body appeared to be unmarked, except for one incontrovertible fact.

It had no face.

Hawkwood held out his hand. 'Give me the light.'

Leech passed over the candle. Hawkwood

crouched down. From what he could see, every square inch of the corpse's facial skin from brow to chin had been removed. All that remained was an uneven oval of raw, suppurating flesh. The eyelids were still in place, as were the lips, though they were thin and bloodless and reminded Hawkwood of the body he'd examined first thing that morning. Unlike that corpse, however, this body still possessed its tongue and teeth.

Beside him, the apothecary was staring at the corpse as though mesmerized by the epic brutality of the scene. Reaching for his handkerchief, Locke polished his spectacles vigorously and perched them back on his nose. 'From what I can tell, the first incision was probably made close to the ear. The blade was then drawn around the circumference of the face, with just sufficient pressure to break through the layers of the epidermis. The blade was then inserted under the skin to pare it away, separating it from the underlying muscle in stages.' The apothecary grimaced. 'It would be rather similar to filleting a fish. Eventually, this would enable him to peel and lift the entire facial features off the skull, probably in one piece, like a mask...' Locke paused. 'It was skilfully done, as you can see.'

'Where the devil would a parson pick up that sort of knowledge?' Hawkwood said.

The apothecary looked puzzled. 'Parson?'

'Priest, then. Reverend Tombs – isn't that his name?'

The apothecary stiffened. He turned and threw a glance at the keeper, his eyebrows raised in enquiry. The keeper reddened and shook his

53

head. The apothecary's jaw tightened. He turned back. 'I fear there has been a misunderstanding.'

Hawkwood looked at him.

Locke hesitated, clearly uncomfortable.

'Doctor?' Hawkwood said.

The apothecary took a deep breath, then said, 'It wasn't the priest who perpetrated this barbaric act.'

Hawkwood looked back at him.

'Reverend Tombs was not the murderer, Officer Hawkwood. He was not the one who wielded the knife. He couldn't have done.' Locke nodded towards the body on the cot. 'Reverend Tombs was the victim.'

3

The apothecary looked down at the corpse and gave a brief shake of his head, as if to deny the bloody reality that lay before him.

'I confess, we took it to be the colonel's body at first. It seemed the obvious conclusion in the light of Mr Grubb's assurance that he'd escorted Reverend Tombs out of the building, or at least the person he assumed to be the reverend. It was only when I made a closer examination that I became aware of the deception. Unfortunately, we'd already sent word to Bow Street by then. I had thought, wrongly, that Mr Leech had informed you of the error upon your arrival.'

Locke lifted the corpse's arm by the wrist and traced a path across the unmarked knuckles. 'The colonel had a scar across the back of his right hand, just here. He told me it was the result of an accident during his army service. It was quite distinct and yet, as you can see, there is no scar.' The apothecary let the arm drop back on to the cot. 'This is not Colonel Hyde.'

'But it *is* the Reverend Tombs? You're sure of that?'

Locke nodded solemnly. 'Quite sure.'

'Did he have scars too?'

Hawkwood couldn't help injecting a note of sarcasm into his enquiry. To his surprise, Locke showed no adverse reaction to the retort but

55

stated simply, 'As a matter of fact, he did.' The apothecary met Hawkwood's unspoken question by pointing to his own cheeks and jaw, the areas of the corpse's face that had been excised. 'The worst of them were on his face. Here and here. The minor ones are still visible there behind his left ear, if you look closely.'

Hawkwood turned to Leech. 'You escorted Reverend Tombs to the room? What time was this?'

'It'd be about ten o'clock,' Leech said. 'It were still rainin' cats and dogs.'

'After you left him, what did you do?'

Leech shrugged. 'Finished me rounds, went back upstairs.'

'And the key?'

'Left it on the 'ook in the keepers' room with the rest of 'em.'

'And this ... Grubb, he'd have taken the key to let the priest out?'

Leech nodded. 'That's right.' The attendant pointed to a bell cord hanging in the corner of the room. 'Soon as he 'eard the bell ring, he'd have been on 'is way.'

'And Grubb noticed nothing untoward?'

Leech shook his head. ''E never said. I saw 'im when I came on again this morning, before Adkins told 'im about the colonel's tray not bein' touched. Asked him how things had gone and 'e said there'd been no problems. The parson rang the bell. Grubb collected him and escorted him out.'

'I'll need to speak with Attendant Grubb,' Hawkwood said.

Locke nodded. 'Of course, though he is still convalescing.'

'Convalescing?'

'He suffered a seizure when he discovered the body. Fortunately it was not as serious as we first feared. He is feeling rather frail, however, and has not yet returned to his duties. I can take you to him.'

Hawkwood nodded and looked around the room. 'Has anything been moved, Doctor?'

'Moved?' Locke frowned.

'Put back in its place. Is this how it was when Grubb found the body?'

'I believe so, yes.'

Hawkwood stared at the iron rings set into the wall above the bed. He had a sudden vision of Norris, the patient chained to the wall by his neck and ankles. He walked towards the table. In the centre of it lay a chessboard. From the position of the pieces, the game was unfinished. Hawkwood picked up one of the figures – a white knight. It was made of bone. Hawkwood had seen similar sets before, carved by French prisoners of war imprisoned on the hulks. It wasn't uncommon for such items to appear in private homes. There were agents, philanthropists who acted on behalf of some of the more skilful artists, offering to sell their carvings on the open market for a modest, or in some cases not so modest, commission. He wondered about the provenance of this particular set as he took in the rest of the items on the table: two mugs and an empty cordial bottle. He picked up the bottle. 'Curious there's no sign of a struggle.'

Locke blinked.

'Look around, Doctor. Not a chair overturned,

not so much as a bishop upended or a pawn knocked out of its square. Doesn't that strike you as odd? You think the man just stretched out and allowed himself to be butchered? He was already dead before that was done to him. He had to be.'

Locke looked pensive. 'I found no obvious signs of injury to the body – other than the trauma ... damage ... to the face, of course – which suggests the cause of death could have been suffocation. A sharp, swift blow to the stomach, perhaps, to incapacitate, followed by a pillow over the face. Death would occur in a matter of minutes; less, probably, if the victim was already gasping for air.'

'So he smothered him, then mutilated him? Well, that's certainly a possibility, Doctor. So tell me: where did he get the blade?'

The question seemed to hang in the air. Locke went pale.

'I'm assuming there are rules about patients owning sharp objects, knives and such?' Hawkwood said.

Locke shifted uncomfortably. 'That is correct.'

'Not even for cutting up food?'

'That is done by the keepers.'

'And razors? What about shaving?'

'The difficult patients are secured. Those of a more ... placid ... disposition are looked after, again by the keepers, usually with a pot-boy in attendance.'

Hawkwood saw that the apothecary was clenching and unclenching his hands.

'What is it, Doctor?'

Locke, clearly agitated, swallowed nervously. 'It's possible that *I* may have ... ah, inadvertently,

58

provided Colonel Hyde with the opportunity to procure the ... ah, murder weapon.'

'Oh, and how is that?'

Cowed by the look in Hawkwood's eyes, the apothecary started to knead the palm of his left hand with his right thumb. It looked as if he was trying to rub a bloodstain out of his skin. 'There were occasions when I was called upon to attend the colonel in my ... ah, medical capacity.'

'Really?'

'Nothing too serious, you understand: a purgative now and again, and there was the lancing of an abscess a month or so ago.' The apothecary's voice faltered as he realized the significance of the confession.

'So you'd have had your bag with you?'

'Yes.'

'Which would have contained what, exactly?'

'The usual items: salves, pills, emetics and suchlike.'

'And your instruments?'

There was a moment's pause before the apothecary answered. When he did so, his voice was close to a whisper. 'Yes.'

'Your surgical knives, with their sharp blades? Because you'd need a knife with a sharp blade to lance an abscess, wouldn't you, Doctor?' Hawkwood said.

The apothecary glanced towards Leech, but there was no sympathy on the attendant's face, merely relief that someone else was in the firing line.

Hawkwood pressed home his attack. 'That's what happened, isn't it? At some time during one

59

of your visits to remove a boil from the colonel's arse, he managed to steal one of your damned scalpels.'

Locke's face crumpled.

'And you're telling me you didn't even notice the loss?'

Locke's expression was one of abject misery.

Hawkwood shook his head in disbelief. 'I've half a mind to arrest *you*, Doctor, though, frankly, I wouldn't know what to charge you with – complicity or incompetence. I'm beginning to wonder what sort of place you're running here. Good Christ, who's in charge of your damned hospital, the staff or the lunatics?'

Locke's cheeks coloured. His eyes, magnified by the round spectacle lenses, looked as big as saucers.

Hawkwood was aware that Attendant Leech was staring at him. Word of the apothecary's dressing down would be all over the hospital the moment Leech left the room. He nodded towards the body and the ruin that had once been a man's face. 'How long would it have taken to do that?'

Locke took a deep breath; his lips formed a tight line. 'Not long, if the murderer knew his trade.'

There was a pause.

'Well, go on, tell me,' Hawkwood said, wondering what else was to come.

'Colonel Hyde was an army surgeon. He operated in field hospitals in the Peninsula. His treatment of the wounded was, I understand...' Locke bit his lip '...highly regarded.'

60

'Was it indeed?' Hawkwood digested the information. Then, taking a candle from the table, he stepped through the archway into the other half of the cell.

There was another table upon which stood a jug and a washbowl. Against one wall sat a mahogany desk, a folding chair and a large wooden chest bound with brass. Looking at them, Hawkwood felt an instant stab of recognition. As a soldier he'd seen desks and chests like these more times than he cared to remember. Enter any officer's quarters, be it in a barracks, or even a battlefield bivouac, and it would be furnished with identical items; they were standard campaign equipment. He even had a chest of his own, strikingly similar to the one here, back at his lodgings in the Blackbird tavern. It had been acquired during his time in the Peninsula, at an auction following the death of the chest's former owner on the retreat to Corunna.

The room and its contents were at complete odds with the bare functionality of the sleeping quarters and a world apart from the conditions in which the other patients, or at least the ones he'd seen, were being kept. Those had bordered on the inhumane. By contrast this accommodation was verging on the palatial. Why should that be? Hawkwood wondered.

By far the greatest contrast lay in the collection of books and the drawings that covered the walls; several score, by Hawkwood's rough estimate. So many, they would not have disgraced a small library. Hawkwood held the candle close and ran his eye over the serried ranks of leather-bound

61

volumes. None of the authors' names meant anything: Harvey, Cheselden, Hunter. Others were evidently foreign. Vesalius and Casserio appeared to be Italian, while some, like Ibn Sina and Massa, sounded vaguely Oriental. The ones in English were all similar in tone: *Anatomy of the Human Body, The Motion of the Heart, The Natural History of the Human Teeth.* There were others with titles in Latin. Hawkwood assumed they were medical texts, too.

The etchings and engravings that filled the spaces on the cell walls were in a similar vein, literally. Each and every one of them showed representations of the human body in anatomical detail, skeletal and musculature, both whole and partial, from skulls and torsos to arms and legs. A couple, which to Hawkwood's untutored eye resembled the root system of a tree, were, he realized upon closer examination, diagrams of veins and arteries. Some were close to life size, others were smaller and looked as if they might have been torn from the pages of books or old manuscripts. Many of the renditions depicted the moving parts of the body, such as the neck and the joints at wrist, elbow and knee; all were remarkably and gruesomely intricate. The illustrations had an unsettling quality. Looking at them, Hawkwood realized why he was experiencing disquiet. The drawings reminded him of the horrific wounds and the amputated limbs he'd seen in the army's hospital tents. The smell in the cell brought it all back to him. The only things missing were the blood and the screams; the screams, at any rate.

He sensed a presence at his shoulder.

'The miracle of the human body,' Locke said softly. 'Men have strived for centuries to learn its mysteries.'

An illustration caught Hawkwood's attention. It was nightmarishly graphic, depicting the lower half of a human torso from stomach to mid-thigh. The skin of the lower belly and pelvic area had been opened and peeled back layer by layer to reveal the interior of the abdomen. The upper legs were shown severed at mid thigh. The end of each thighbone could be seen encircled by densely packed layers of muscle and flesh. Each limb looked disturbingly similar to the cuts of meat he'd seen hanging from hooks above the Smithfield butchers' stalls he'd passed on his way to the hospital. He found himself transfixed. The figure did not appear to possess genitalia, which seemed odd, given the artist's exceptional eye for detail. He looked closer, raising the light, and realized what he was looking at and what it meant. The figure was female.

'Van Rymsdyk,' Locke said behind him. 'A Dutch artist; dead now, but much in demand by anatomists for his expertise in capturing the human form. The Hunters, Cheselden, they all made use of his services.'

The names still meant nothing, although there was no doubting the skill of the illustrator. The detail was astonishing.

'Convincing, aren't they?' the apothecary murmured. 'Too vivid, some might say. Yet without van Rymsdyk and the rest, medical science would be becalmed, like a ship awaiting a breeze. If I may continue with the analogy, surgeons are the navigators of our times. Like Magellan and Columbus before them, they search for new worlds. To navigate, you require a map. If no map is available, you create your own, so that others may follow in your wake.' Locke spread his hands. 'These are surgeon's maps, Officer Hawkwood. Anatomical charts of the human body. The more accurate the chart, the less danger there is of running aground.'

The apothecary blinked owlishly and fell silent, as if suddenly overcome by his own loquacity.

Hawkwood's attention was drawn to the far corner of the cell, the part of the room in deepest shadow. He moved closer. The drawing was similar to the rest: a standing female figure, explicitly nude. The figure's right hand was raised to conceal its right breast. The left hand was held lower, covering the groin area. The belly was shown cut open, revealing the organs beneath. Each organ was marked with a letter. The figure was framed by four smaller insets, each differentiated by a Roman numeral, showing the progressive, layered dissection of the stomach wall.

The apothecary followed his gaze. 'Ah, yes, a Valverde engraving, one of his studies on pregnancy.' Locke stared at the wall, lost in thought.

Hawkwood had seen enough. He wanted to be out of there, away from the disturbing images and the darkness and the dripping stonework and the smell of death. He wanted to be where there was sunlight and fresh air, not in this ... slaughterhouse.

He turned and led the way back into the sleeping area and the waiting Leech. 'Keep the room locked. No one enters. There'll be someone along to collect the body for examination by the coroner's appointed surgeon.'

Who was about to have a very busy morning, Hawkwood reflected wryly, what with this *and* the dead man in the graveyard.

He turned to the apothecary. 'Take me to Grubb.'

Locke nodded and ushered him into the corridor, plainly relieved at being able to leave the cell and its grisly contents behind.

The elderly attendant was in his room, huddled in a chair, a blanket covering his legs. A bowl of thin broth and a lump of soggy-looking bread sat on a table beside him. His face was pale and drawn and he gazed apprehensively at his visitor as Locke made the introductions.

The attendant's hands shook as, with a faltering voice, he relived the events of the previous night, confirming that he'd noticed nothing unusual when he'd gone to collect the parson.

'You didn't see his face?' Hawkwood asked.

Grubb shook his head. 'Not properly. 'E was already wearin' 'is 'at and scarf when I let 'im out of the room. I did take a quick gander when I was walkin' 'im to the door, but 'e caught me at it and pulled 'is scarf up. Mind you, it were a bitter night.'

'Did he say anything?'

Grubb thought back. His chest rose and fell. The breath wheezed in his throat. ''E said goodbye to the colonel, when I let 'im out of the room.'

'But the colonel didn't reply,' Hawkwood said. 'Did he?'

Grubb shook his head. 'I thought I 'eard them talkin' before I unlocked the door, but I couldn't make out the words.'

Hawkwood heard Locke gasp and threw the apothecary a warning look. Hawkwood knew it had been part of the colonel's plan, talking with himself to trick whoever was outside the door into believing that both occupants of the room were alive. Similarly, by posing as the priest and halting on the threshold to bid his unseen host good night, he had fooled Grubb into thinking the colonel was acknowledging the farewell, perhaps with a nod or a wave of his hand.

'Did he say anything else?'

'Said good night when I let 'im out the front door. I offered to see 'im to the main gates, but he said he was all right on his own.'

There was no doubting the man's nerve, Hawkwood thought. It had been a simple ruse. It had relied on one elderly keeper, probably with fading eyesight and encroaching deafness and a time of night when the corridor would be in semi-darkness, lit only by dull candlelight. As an escape plan it had been astonishingly well executed. The rain had been a bonus.

Hawkwood could see that Grubb was tiring. There was a vacant look in the attendant's eyes and his breathing was becoming harsh and un-even. He nodded to Locke, indicating it was time to go. The apothecary bent and drew the blanket over the attendant's waist.

'We need to talk, Doctor,' Hawkwood said, when they were back in the corridor. 'I think it's time you told me all about Colonel Hyde.'

4

The apothecary took a deep breath, as if to compose his thoughts. 'Truthfully, have you ever seen *anything* like this?'

'No,' Hawkwood admitted. *No one had.*

He'd investigated killings, of course, seen scores of murder victims, usually as a result of drunken brawls, burglaries that had gone wrong or family feuds that had gotten out of hand, even crimes of passion, but this was different, a new experience. It wasn't the manner of death but the mutilation of the victim that set this murder apart. The excising of the priest's face had not been the result of a blood-crazed, frenzied attack. The skin had been removed with great precision. Peeled away like a mask, the apothecary had said. And so it had been; deliberately and specifically removed for the purpose of aiding the colonel's exit from the hospital. Which indicated the escape had not been a spontaneous act but the culmination of a carefully thought-out strategy. And that, Hawkwood knew, opened up a whole slew of possibilities, not one of them palatable.

'Why was the colonel here?' Hawkwood asked.

They were back in the apothecary's office. Locke was seated at his desk. Hawkwood was standing by the window. Thankfully, there were no bars and no illustrations of any description on the walls. Even the view over the well-trodden ground of Moor Fields was a consolation after the claustrophobia of the colonel's cell.

A shadow moved across the apothecary's face. 'Warriors survive the battlefield bearing many scars. Not all are caused by damage to the flesh. There are other wounds that run much deeper. The effect of war on the human mind is a fascinating concept and one that has occupied me for some time. It's not an interest shared by the majority of my fellow physicians, despite the increasing number of poor souls committed to hospital asylums by the Transport Office and the Navy's Sick and Wounded Office each year.'

The apothecary paused, then said, 'Am I right in thinking you've knowledge of such matters? It occurred to me when we met that you have the look about you; that scar beneath your eye, for example, and the distinct mark of an ingrained powder burn above your right cheek. You were a military man; the army, perhaps? Am I right?'

Hawkwood stared at his inquisitor. The burn mark was a legacy most musketeers and riflemen carried with them; a rite of passage, caused by flecks of burning powder blowing back into the face when their weapon was discharged.

'I was a soldier,' Hawkwood said.

'May I ask what regiment?'

'The 95th.'

'The Rifles! I've heard great stories of their exploits.' Locke put his head on one side and nodded thoughtfully. 'Though you were not of the rank and file, I suspect. You were an officer? You commanded men in battle?'

'Yes.'

'And saw many of your comrades die?'

'Too many,' Hawkwood said truthfully.

'So you know the nature of war, the horror of it.' It was a statement not a question.

Hawkwood thought of the times he'd woken in the dead of night, drenched in sweat, with the smell of death in his nostrils and the screams of men and the crash of cannon fire ringing in his ears; sounds so real he'd thought he had been transported back in time to the blood and the mud and the flames.

War wasn't glorious, despite the pageantry, the colourful uniforms, and the fifes and drums. War was, without exception, nothing short of hell on earth. There were moments of extraordinary bravery and heady triumph, as sweet as honey on the tongue, but mostly there was fear; massive, gut-wrenching, knee-jerking fear. Fear of being killed, fear of being wounded or crippled, fear of being thought a craven coward by your comrades, fear of dying alone on some bleak, godforsaken foreign hillside with no one back home to mourn your passing. That was the real horror. That was the truth of it.

He hadn't had the dreams for a while, but that didn't mean they weren't there, waiting to emerge unbidden, like demons in the darkness.

'I apologize,' Locke said. The eyes behind his spectacles glinted perceptively. 'It was not my intention to stir up unpleasant memories. In answer to your question, Colonel Hyde was admitted to the hospital a little over two years ago. According to Dr Monro, the colonel's admission was due not to mania, as you might suppose, but

69

an acute state of melancholy.'

'Melancholy?'

'Correct. You saw the carvings above the entrance, I take it?'

Hawkwood recalled the naked stone figures and nodded.

'They are known as Raving and Melancholy Madness. I'm sure you can guess which was which.'

Hawkwood said nothing. He was remembering the manacles and the silent scream.

Locke went on, 'There was a time when diagnosis was considered that simple. If the patient was not obviously suffering from one, he or she was inevitably a victim of the other. It is not, however, as you may have surmised from my discourse, as simple as that. Melancholy comes in many forms. Take the unfortunates contained within these walls, for example. For every ten patients suffering the effects of drink and intoxication, I could show you twenty who suffer from excessive jealousy. For every fifteen stricken by religion and Methodism, I can list thirty whose minds have been addled by syphilis or smallpox. Pride, fright, fever, even love; the causes of insanity – melancholy in particular – are numerous, Officer Hawkwood. But by far the most common are misfortune, trouble, disappointment and grief.'

'You're trying to tell me that the colonel was *disappointed* about something?' Hawkwood said. 'Hell's teeth, if he removed a man's face because he was disappointed, what the devil's he going to do when he's angry?'

The apothecary ignored Hawkwood's retort,

but continued in the same calm manner. 'My understanding is that it was the commissioners' judgement that the colonel's experiences working amongst the wounded and the dying precipitated a state of chaos within his brain. It was as if his attempts to mend the broken bodies of his patients had a debilitating effect on his own sanity; a terrible price to pay for years of dedicated service. I can only imagine the horrors that he witnessed, trying to make whole the shattered bodies of men, but there's little doubt Colonel Hyde arrived here in a state of severe distraction.'

Locke pursed his lips, and then continued.

'As with all patients, he was reassessed after twelve months. I was not involved in the colonel's case, you understand, it was before my time. Regrettably, it was the commissioners' collective opinion that the colonel was incurable. The usual procedure is that incurables are discharged unless their family or friends are unable to provide care. He has no living family. There was a child that died, a daughter, though he did not talk about her. So, grief, too, has undoubtedly played a significant role in his state of mind. Fortunately, it appears he had friends who were willing to stand surety for him, on condition that he remained in our charge. It was at that juncture that he was transferred to our incurable department.'

'Was he ever restrained?'

Locke looked nonplussed. 'Restrained?'

'Like Norris.'

'Ah, yes, Norris. You saw him?'

'Briefly,' Hawkwood said.

An expression of sympathy moved across the

71

apothecary's face. 'He's an American, a seaman. Came to us almost twelve years ago. He's attacked his keepers on at least two occasions.' Locke gave a wan smile. 'But I assure you, he is an exception. The vast majority of our incurables are perfectly harmless. You may even have heard of a couple of them. There's Metcalfe, for example, who thinks he's the heir to the throne of Denmark; the Nicholson woman; and Matthews, of course.'

Clearly the apothecary was expecting Hawkwood to recognize the names. He didn't. He took a stab at one.

'Matthews?'

'Possibly a little before your time. He was the one who accused Lord Hawkesbury of treason on the floor of the House of Commons. In his defence, he told the court that an influencing device controlled by French Revolutionaries was manipulating his mind. The Air Loom, he called it. Fascinating case. He's still here. In fact, believe it or not, he actually submitted plans for the new hospital. His talent for architectural drawing is considerable and yet he's a tea planter by trade. Who'd have thought it? He's undoubtedly one of our more ... interesting patients. There are many others I could tell you about.'

The apothecary smiled again. 'There are those who would tell you the colonel was in good company. But restrained, you ask? No, he was not shackled, despite the irons on the wall.'

'And yet he had his own quarters, separate from the others. Isn't that unusual?'

Locke shrugged. 'Not especially. A number of patients have their own rooms. Certainly, those with a tendency towards violence, like Norris, must remain segregated at all times, and chained. There are others, however, who, through good behaviour, have been granted the privilege of privacy. Matthews is one example. And there are those whose comfort is maintained by the generosity of their friends and family.'

'And the colonel?' Hawkwood prompted.

'Up until now, he was considered to be one of our most obedient patients.'

'You make him sound like some sort of lap dog.'

Locke smiled thinly. 'Sickness is a strange beast, Officer Hawkwood, and none is stranger than sickness of the mind. There are those patients who thrive on the companionship of others and there are those who shrink from human contact. In either case, the patient's welfare can also be affected by the circumstances of his or her confinement.' Locke raised an eyebrow. 'You look at me as if *I* were mad. I assure you the theory is nothing new.

'Colonel Hyde is no drooling imbecile. He's a well-born, educated man, a former army officer, and a surgeon to boot. He is not some prancing fool in a cap and bells. Indeed, I'd put it to you that, had you met and talked with him about the general turn of things, there's every possibility you'd have considered him to be as sane as you or I.'

'Does *he* know he's mad?'

Locke sat back in his chair. He was silent for several seconds before voicing his reply.

'You pose an interesting question. There are doctors who consider madness to be a sickness of

73

the soul, a spiritual malaise. My own theory is that madness is in fact a physical disease, an organic disorder of the brain, which manifests itself in an incorrect association of familiar ideas, ideas that are always accompanied by implicit belief. In my view, the reason people see objects and hear sounds that aren't there is not because their sight or hearing is deficient, it is because their brains are not functioning properly. Nor is their intelligence necessarily at fault. On the contrary, they will frequently reason correctly, albeit from a false premise. In their own minds they are being perfectly rational. And so it is with Colonel Hyde. He is perfectly lucid and articulate. He does not think of himself as either sane or insane. One could argue that is the nature of his delusion.'

'I'm sorry, Doctor,' Hawkwood said. 'I still don't understand. If you're telling me that he was admitted into the hospital due to – what was it, melancholy? – what made him change? What made him commit murder?'

'To answer that, one would have to know how his delusion arose in the first place.'

'And *do* you?'

The apothecary shrugged. 'In the colonel's case, I'm not privy to the full facts of his admittance. It was Dr Monro who oversaw his arrival. I can only generalize.'

'Maybe it's Monro I should be talking to,' Hawkwood said.

'That is certainly your privilege, though, judging by Dr Monro's preoccupation with his extracurricular interests, I would submit that you would be unlikely to learn much. I doubt he has had one moment's contact with Colonel Hyde since he was admitted. I can assure you, Officer Hawkwood, without fear of contradiction that I am far more conversant with the colonel's mental health than Dr Monro, who rarely attends the hospital, even for the Saturday meetings. But you must do as you see fit. There is also Dr Crowther, of course, though I doubt you'd find him sober, let alone lucid. When he is here, he does little except administer purgatives and emetics. That, Officer Hawkwood, is the sum total of *their* lamentable involvement. In their hands, treatment here amounts to little more than meaningless gestures. Purgatives are given to constipated patients. Syphilitics are prescribed mercury. Emetics are given to patients to make them vomit. It's a way of ensuring that fluids move through the system. All other afflictions are prescribed laudanum. Do you know one of the side effects of laudanum? No? Well, there's no reason why you should, but I'll tell you anyway. It's constipation. You see my point? Oh, and if the purgatives and the emetics don't work, we bleed them or give them a cold bath. That way, they'll either die from the flux or pneumonia. Purging, bleeding and inducing patients to vomit may be the recognized methods of mad doctoring, Officer Hawkwood, but they are not the way to treat patients like Matthews or Colonel Hyde.'

'You're telling me there's another way?'

'I believe so, yes. It involves a number of techniques, acquired after lengthy experience of dealing with such cases, but they all have one goal and that is for the doctor to gain ascendancy over the patient, similar to breaking in a horse or...' The apothecary paused expectantly.

'Training a dog,' Hawkwood said. He wondered if his moment of enlightenment would result in Locke rewarding him with a treat, a biscuit or a bone, perhaps? But it wasn't to be. Locke continued, uninterrupted.

'Exactly. The patient must never think he or she is in control. It is not the patient who must set the agenda. It is the doctor. One must not confuse this with punishment, however. Corporal punishment, even severe chastisement, must always be considered a last resort. I do not believe it is possible to gain ascendancy over patients whose thoughts are constantly consumed by their plots to escape. I can safely say that by using understanding and kindness I've never yet failed to obtain the confidence and respect of insane persons.'

'Or their obedience?'

The apothecary inclined his head. If he resented the barb in Hawkwood's question, he did not let it show. 'Indeed. Honey, not vinegar, is the answer.'

'So that's why he has his own room, his own belongings?'

'In part. And, as I mentioned, the colonel is not without benefactors. It is, however, more than anything, a matter of providing stimulation.'

'Stimulation?'

'You recall I mentioned the wound below your eye?' The apothecary pointed with his finger. 'May I ask if you have suffered any other injuries; to a limb, an arm or a leg perhaps?'

Too many to remember, Hawkwood thought, though the most recent, the knife wound in his

76

left shoulder, had been sustained not on the battlefield, but in the swirling darkness of the Thames riverbed. It wasn't a memory he enjoyed revisiting.

He nodded warily and wondered where this was going. The apothecary was too damned perceptive, he thought.

'And during your recovery period, the more you used your arm, the quicker the wound healed; would I be right?'

Hawkwood nodded again. Though, if truth were told, the damned shoulder still ached with a vengeance if he slept awkwardly.

'And so it is with the brain. It is like a muscle. The greater the activity, the more exercise it receives, the healthier it is likely to remain. That is why the colonel was allowed his study area, his books and his drawings and his paper and pens. D'you see?'

Hawkwood nodded.

'They also proved most useful as a reward.'

'Reward?'

'For adhering to the hospital routine. It's an established practice. We make the patient aware that if there are any infringements, privileges such as access to writing materials, personal possessions and so forth, may be withdrawn. For someone with the colonel's intellect the removal of such privileges would be a very serious matter and, in the long term, likely to be detrimental to his health. A patient he may be, but with his military background he is a man who understands only too well the consequences of not observing protocol. It has proved a most effective system with a number of our patients.'

'Really?' Hawkwood said. 'From where I'm standing I'd say the colonel didn't give two figs for your so-called routine, or your damned protocol, and that makes me wonder just how well you knew him.'

'On an intellectual level, I would say I knew him tolerably well. I've spent a number of hours in his company. We would talk of all manner of things: literature, politics and science ... medicine, of course. We are, after all, both doctors, though our backgrounds are somewhat different. My family comes from modest stock. The colonel's family were land owners. We both studied abroad, however. I studied in Uppsala before going on to Cambridge. The colonel attended the university at Padua. He was – is – a learned man. You saw his library. I even consulted with him on several occasions, seeking his advice on the treatment of some of my patients. His understanding of anatomy far exceeds my own and his knowledge of medicine in general is far superior to that of Dr Monro and that drunken sot, Crowther. I found his assistance invaluable. Some of his opinions were rather ... innovative. It made for interesting discussion.'

'You sound as if you liked him,' Hawkwood said.

Locke reached for his handkerchief and spectacles. It was a tactic Hawkwood had come to expect. It allowed the apothecary a few seconds to compose his reply.

'Perhaps I did. But then, you've seen the calibre of the staff. Is it any wonder I sought out *his* company?' The apothecary held up his spectacles

78

and squinted through the lenses. Satisfied that he had removed every smear, he tucked the handkerchief into his waistcoat pocket and placed his spectacles back on to his nose. He looked, Hawkwood thought, not unlike a self-satisfied barn owl.

'When I asked you if you knew how the colonel's delusions arose, you said you could only generalize,' Hawkwood prompted. 'How?'

The apothecary placed his hands palm down on the desk, and nodded. 'From my study of other patients in my immediate care, I believe it's as if every event in their lives, even those that might appear trivial to someone else, carries a hidden significance. It is as though their brains are under attack from a never-ending whirligig of possibilities. Thoughts swirl through their heads in a maelstrom until one thought eventually forces its way to the surface and breaks free of the maelstrom's pull. Suddenly everything becomes wondrously clear, as if the mind has been set free to soar above the clouds. From that point, every germ of thought becomes indelibly linked to that blinding moment of enlightenment.

'I believe that sense of awakening is so intense that the fabric of the delusion begins to expand backwards and forwards in time, forming a kind of framework, an explanation, if you will, for events that took place long before it existed, perhaps as far back as childhood. It's the same going forward. Whenever a new experience is received, that too is perceived to be an intrinsic part of the framework.'

Hawkwood's head was starting to ache. It occurred to him that the colonel wasn't the only one whose brain was spinning. 'So to the colonel this moment of enlightenment would have been like some kind of...' he searched for the word '...revelation?'

'That's as good a definition as any.'

'And this revelation gave him the idea to escape?'

'I see that you have begun to follow my reasoning.'

'So to us, killing the parson was cold-blooded murder, but to the colonel it would have made perfect sense.'

'Yes.'

'Cutting the priest's face off made sense?'

'To Colonel Hyde, yes.'

'So escaping may not have been his sole ambition. It was only the beginning. And unless we discover the nature of this ... revelation, we won't know the form of his delusion or what he might be planning to do next?'

'That is so, broadly speaking.' Locke leaned forward, his face earnest. If he was impressed with Hawkwood's apparent grasp of the situation, he gave no indication. 'And that, of course, is the problem, for the colonel's delusion is *his* reality, no one else's. Only he does not know that. You recall, I told you about Matthews and his Air Loom, the thing that he believes controls people's minds?'

Hawkwood nodded.

'Let me show you.' Apothecary Locke opened a drawer in his desk and took out a sheaf of documents. He began to sift through them. Hawkwood moved to the desk to look over Locke's shoulder.

'Here,' Locke said. Extracting four sheets from the bundle, he spread them out on the desk.

Three of them were clearly architectural drawings.

'These are Matthews' plans for the new hospital. As you can see, they are of a very high standard. And this–' Locke said, passing over a fourth sheet '–is his Air Loom.'

Hawkwood stared down at the drawing in front of him.

It looked like a piece of furniture, a large box with a set of four large organ pipes protruding from the top. On the left-hand side stood three barrels which were connected to the box by flexible hoses resembling the tentacles of some strange sea monster. Seated in front of the mechanism was the figure of a man. His arms were manipulating two huge levers. Three other human figures were also shown, one standing, the other two lying down. Each one appeared to be transfixed by what looked to be a beam of light radiating from the device. The drawing, like the other two, had been very skilfully fashioned. Each component of the device had been designated a letter of the alphabet. The key to the letters was written in a neat copperplate.

'What are these?' Hawkwood pointed at the beams, which were tinted a pale yellowish-green.

'Magnetic rays. They are controlled by the man you see seated at those levers. He is using the beams to manipulate the thoughts of his victims.'

'And he really believes all this?' The whole thing was preposterous, Hawkwood thought.

'Most assuredly, and yet this is the same man

who produced these splendid architectural drawings. If you knew nothing of Matthews' circumstances, and someone else had shown you these plans, I'd wager that you'd never for one moment suspect the artist was of unsound mind. Am I right?'

Hawkwood stared down at the designs. There was little else he could do except agree.

'You understand what I am saying?' Locke said.

'I think you're telling me,' Hawkwood said, 'that, unless you happen to know the colonel's history, to look at him there's no way to tell that he's mad.'

Locke nodded. 'Essentially, yes. He can formulate ideas and arguments, but in his case it's as though – how can I put it? – his thoughts and feelings, even his memories, have been taken over by an outside force. To the colonel, it would be as though messages are being forced into his brain.'

Hawkwood hesitated, trying to grasp the implications. 'Messages? You mean he thinks people are talking to him, telling him to do things? Like ... what? Voices in his head?' Even as he posed the question, he thought the idea sounded ludicrous, but to his surprise the apothecary nodded.

'And these ... voices ... told him to murder the priest?'

Locke made a face. 'A simplification, but, yes, I do believe that might account for his actions. Not unlike Matthews and his revolutionaries.'

'Tell me about the priest,' Hawkwood said.

The apothecary's face seemed to sag. He suddenly looked older than his years. 'There you have me. The Reverend Tombs was here because

I chose to disregard the hospital's regulations.' He looked up. 'Ironic, wouldn't you say?'

'What are you telling me, Doctor?'

Locke sighed. 'A hundred years ago, the superintendent thought it would be a good idea if visiting days were introduced, allowing the public to interact with patients. The scheme proved very popular. The crowds flocked, the patients flourished. But then the gawkers began to arrive, and with the gawkers came the pedlars and the pickpockets and the pulpit bashers, not to mention the doxies. Come to Bedlam, pay tuppence and watch the lunatics perform. What fun! It wasn't long before Bethlem became just another attraction, like the Tower and the Abbey. So, the visits were stopped. No more sightseers, no more pedlars, and no more preachers. It was the governors' fear that their sermons were as likely to inflame the patients as pacify them.'

'But you didn't agree?'

Locke steepled his fingers. 'On the contrary. At the time, they were probably right. It's hard enough trying to keep the poor devils quiet as it is, without having some irate Wesleyan ranting up and down the corridors. But there are preachers and there are preachers. I am not a particularly God-fearing man, Officer Hawkwood, but I'm quite prepared to believe in the efficacy of prayer and contemplation as a means of calming the fevered mind. Not that it works in every case, of course. But, in certain instances, I would consider the taking of counsel to be very therapeutic. And they do say, after all, that confession *is* good for the soul, do they not?'

'They might also say that ten o'clock at night was an odd time to be hearing someone's confession.'

The apothecary flattened his palms on the desk. 'The governors' ruling still applies. Although I personally saw no harm in the Reverend Tombs' visits, I felt that a certain amount of discretion was advisable. At that time of night there are fewer staff around, not so many eyes to see or mouths to spread idle tittle-tattle. Though I understand that on this occasion Reverend Tombs was a little later than he had intended. He told Attendant Leech he'd been attending to parish matters. A burial, I believe it was.'

'His parish is St Mary's, correct?'

The apothecary nodded.

'We dispatched constables to his house,' Hawkwood said. 'Not that it's done any good, seeing as we sent them after the wrong bloody man.' Hawkwood paused to let the point sink in. 'Which prompts me to ask you how the two of them came together in the first place. How did they meet?'

'It was purely by chance. We had an application, about a year and a half ago, to admit a patient who was suffering from the most distressing and quite violent fits. His family arranged his admittance, as they were no longer able to cope with his condition. They were fearful the poor devil would harm his children. The commissioners accepted the petition and we took him in. He was later transferred to our incurable department. Sadly, his condition continued to deteriorate. When it became clear there was no further hope, the family asked that he might receive visits from the Reverend Tombs. The patient had been one of his parishioners and it was hoped that, in his final days, he might derive some comfort from the reverend's presence. I took it upon myself to arrange for the Reverend Tombs to visit him. I do believe it helped. Towards the end, there were moments when he was able to converse in quite lucid terms and bid his family goodbye. It was a very sad case for all concerned. The patient, incidentally, was a former soldier, an infantryman who'd fought in the Peninsula. It was my suspicion that his condition also harked back to his time on the battlefield. Not that it could be proved, of course, though Crowther's examination of his brain did at least confirm it had suffered morbid damage.'

'You examined his *brain?*'

The apothecary blanched and said hurriedly, 'Not I, Crowther. At least we can be thankful that the man was sober on *that* occasion. He–'

'I don't care who wielded the damned knife, Doctor. You're telling me the hospital cuts open its dead patients?'

'Not all of them.'

Not all of them. Good Christ, Hawkwood thought. What sort of place is this?

'You look shocked, Officer Hawkwood,' Locke said, his composure restored. 'Dissections are a necessary procedure if we are to advance our knowledge. As I've told you, I believe there's a direct correlation between diseases of the brain and madness. My own research has convinced me, for example, that the lateral ventricles in the brain are greater in maniacs than those who are sane. I–'

'I'm sure that comes as a comfort to the grieving widows,' Hawkwood growled, not having the slightest clue what the apothecary was talking about and unable to keep the bite from his voice. 'You were telling me about the Reverend Tombs.'

For a moment it appeared the apothecary was about to attempt further justification for his argument, but Hawkwood's demeanour obviously made him reconsider. Clearly the Runner was in no mood to engage in a bracing discussion about ethics.

'Indeed,' said Locke. 'I understand the colonel heard of the Reverend Tombs' visits from one of the keepers, a passing reference perhaps and mention made that the patient had been a military man like himself. Whatever the circumstances, I do recall that after some consideration I decided there'd be little harm if the Reverend Tombs were to accept Colonel Hyde's request to call upon him. That would have been about six months ago. Since then the reverend has been a regular visitor to his room, usually once a week.'

'So the priest *was* here to hear the colonel's confession?'

The apothecary shook his head. 'You misinterpret the situation. Besides, Reverend Tombs was an Anglican. No, although on this latter occasion he was here to play chess, I'm sure their conversations touched upon a variety of topics: medicine, philosophy, history, the war...' The apothecary frowned and added pointedly, 'I did not place my ear against the door.'

'Did they *ever* tell you what they talked about?'

The apothecary shrugged. 'Only in the most general terms.'

'So you weren't aware of any recent disagreement the two of them might have had?'

Locke pursed his lips. 'No, not at all. As far as I was aware they always parted on the best of terms.'

There were plenty of men who'd come to blows over a game of hazard, Hawkwood mused. Why not chess? But even as the notion entered his mind, he dismissed it as so unlikely, it bordered on the ridiculous.

'What about the colonel's mood? Did you notice any changes recently?' Even as he posed the question, he was reminded that the colonel had been diagnosed as incurably mad. The man had probably suffered more mood changes than there were fleas on a dog. How could anyone, even a mad-doctor, differentiate one from the other?

But Locke shook his head. 'None. There was nothing in his manner to suggest his state of mind had been ... transformed in any way. In any case, the colonel was never one to display emotion. Indeed, that was one of his characteristics. In many respects it made him an ideal patient. His demeanour was always calm, one might even say tranquil, accepting of his lot, if you will. You've seen his room. It was a place of order, of study and contemplation.'

Hawkwood considered the implications. If there had been no obvious disagreement or falling out between the two of them and the colonel had displayed no startling changes of personality, that left ... what? He needed more information; a lot more.

'I want to see your admission documents on Colonel Hyde,' Hawkwood said. 'And I need a description. We know what he was wearing when he left, but we need to know the rest – his height, hair colour and so forth – if we're to hunt him down.'

'Very well.' The apothecary paused before continuing. 'I can tell you that Colonel Hyde is forty-nine years of age. His hair is still dark, though it is receding and he has some grey around the temples. He is of slender but not slight build and he has a military bearing which can make him look taller. If truth were told, his physique is not dissimilar to that of the unfortunate Reverend Tombs.'

How convenient, Hawkwood thought. 'Other than his madness, is he well ... physically?'

Locke blinked, as if the question had been unexpected. 'Indeed he is. The colonel enjoys excellent health. In fact, he made a point of maintaining his physical condition through a routine of daily exercises. I recall it was the cause of some amusement among the staff.'

Hawkwood frowned. 'What sort of exercises?'

'He told me once that he learned them from his regimental fencing master. I believe that, during his military service, the colonel was considered an excellent swordsman.'

'Scalpels *and* sabres,' Hawkwood said. 'My, my.'

Locke coloured.

'Anything else we should know?'

88

Before the apothecary could reply there was a sharp rap on the door. Locke started in his seat. He turned, a look of mild annoyance on his face. 'Come!'

The door opened. Mordecai Leech stood on the threshold.

The apothecary's eyebrows rose. 'Mr Leech?'

'Beggin' your pardon, Doctor, there's a Constable Hopkins from the Foot Patrol down below. Wants to see Officer Hawkwood. Says it's urgent.'

But the constable wasn't down below. He was behind Leech's shoulder, presumably having shadowed the lumbering attendant up the stairs without the latter's knowledge. Young, and dressed in an ill-fitting blue jacket and scarlet waistcoat, he looked dishevelled and was breathing hard, as if he'd been running. He elbowed the startled Leech aside and thrust his way into the room. His gaze settled on Hawkwood and his eyes widened in recognition. 'We have him, Captain! We have the parson!'

It was on the tip of Hawkwood's tongue to ask what bloody parson, when it struck him that Hopkins had been one of the constables dispatched to St Mary's earlier that morning by James Read and that, as far as they and the Chief Magistrate were concerned, Reverend Tombs was still the man they were looking for.

As though suddenly mindful of his surroundings, the constable removed his black felt hat and held it behind his back. The removal of the headgear revealed a mop of unruly red hair and prominent ears that would have made a fine pair of jug handles.

'Where?' Hawkwood was already heading towards the door, aware that both Locke and Leech were staring at the constable as though the latter had sprouted a second head.

'The church. We tried the vicarage first. Knocked on the door.' The words came out in a rush. 'But there weren't no answer. Then we heard someone movin' around inside, so we called out that we were from Bow Street, under orders from the Chief Magistrate, and that he was to let us in on account of questions we wanted to ask him about a murder.' The constable fought for breath. 'We couldn't see anything, so Conductor Rafferty left Constable Dawes and me at the front and went round the back to see if he could look through the window and find out what was going on. That was wh–' The constable paused, transfixed by the look on Hawkwood's face.

'Rafferty?' A nerve flickered along Hawkwood's cheek. 'Edmund Rafferty?'

The constable blinked at the growl in Hawkwood's voice and nodded again, nervously this time.

'God's teeth!' Hawkwood rasped. He swung back to Locke. 'Don't stray too far, Doctor. It's likely I'll need to talk with you again. You, too, Mr Leech.'

Locke nodded dully.

But it was a wasted gesture. Hawkwood, with Constable Hopkins at his heels, had already left the room.

5

Ignoring the startled expressions on the faces of both attendants and patients, Hawkwood ran for the stairs, thinking that it didn't make any bloody sense.

What on earth had possessed the colonel to take shelter in the house of his victim? Stealing the priest's face had been an essential part of the colonel's plan to trick the authorities into thinking the parson was the murderer. If he'd truly believed that his subterfuge was going to work, even for a brief period, he must have known that the priest's house would be the first place the police would visit.

The only explanation that Hawkwood could come up with was that Hyde would have had need of food, probably clothing and money as well. Armed with the parson's address – presumably obtained during their many dialogues – there would be no need to prowl the streets or break into someone's house. He had a ready-made bolthole just waiting for him, courtesy of his victim. It wasn't as if the parson was going to return home unexpectedly and disturb him.

But the colonel must have known he'd be racing against the clock. So why had he not simply taken the provisions he required and made his getaway?

The simplest explanation, of course, was that

91

Colonel Hyde was as mad as a March hare and there didn't have to be a logical reason for any of his actions.

And Rafferty! Bloody Rafferty of all people.

Conductor Edmund Rafferty, an overweight Irishman of bovine disposition and larcenous tendencies, was, in Hawkwood's opinion, about as much use as a two-legged stool. Their last encounter had not ended on the best of terms. The light-fingered Rafferty had attempted to pilfer a gold watch, part of a hoard rescued from a gang of pickpockets. Hawkwood had spotted the wily rogue making the snatch and had threatened to cut the Irishman's hands off if he saw him doing it again. Rafferty had lost that round and the watch had been restored to its rightful owner. Since then, Rafferty had kept his head down. It probably explained why he'd sent the constable instead of coming himself, although it had to be said that Conductor of the Watch Rafferty was in no shape to engage in any form of strenuous physical activity, like running to deliver a message, for example. So it was probably just as well he'd remained behind.

And this was the officer Magistrate Read had sent to apprehend a murderer? Hawkwood thought bitterly. If he'd known it at the time, he'd have remonstrated with James Read, demanding that he send someone else. Though, to be fair, when the constables had received their orders, it had been thought that the killer was a lowly vicar who, with any luck, would surrender the moment the law landed on his doorstep. They certainly wouldn't have been expecting to be confronted by an insane army surgeon who had removed said vicar's face with a razor-sharp surgical blade.

By the time Hawkwood reached the stairs, the constable had caught up and was alongside, his cap in his hand. His face was still red.

'You said Rafferty went to the back of the house?' Hawkwood realized his low opinion of the Irishman was probably audible in his tone.

The constable nodded. 'That's when the parson made a run for it. We 'eard Conductor Rafferty yell and ran to see what was happening. The parson was attackin' him with a knife. Tried to slice his neck, he did. He had the woman with him.'

'Woman?' Hawkwood stopped dead. 'What bloody woman?' They were at the foot of the stairs.

Taken by surprise, the constable had to side-step smartly to avoid a collision. 'Dunno, sir. He was dragging her towards the church. By the time we got there, the vicar had locked the door behind 'im. He warned us not to try and get in, else he'd knife her. That's when Conductor Rafferty told me to come and get you, while he and Constable Dawes stood watch.'

'Was Rafferty hurt?'

'No, but he was fair shook up,' panted Hopkins. ''E was pretty quick for a big 'un!'

Pity, Hawkwood thought, turning back towards the entrance. The porter was hovering.

'Open the bloody door!'

Hearing the cry and seeing the two men bearing down upon him like charging bulls, the porter fumbled for the bolts. The door was barely ajar before Hawkwood and the constable were push-

93

ing past him. Leaving the porter and assorted residents and staff gaping after them, Hawkwood and Hopkins dashed from the hospital entrance and sprinted towards the main gates.

St Mary's lay to the south, close to the river, and was probably less than half a mile as the crow flew. On foot it was closer to a mile, if they stuck to the main streets, but they could shave a quarter off that distance by using the back alleyways. With the constable in step behind him, Hawkwood ran to catch a killer.

In the shadow of St Mary's, Conductor of the Watch Edmund Rafferty was reflecting on life, chiefly his own, and how close he had come to losing it.

It had been a close shave, literally. Just thinking about it brought the Irishman out in a cold sweat. In his mind's eye he saw again the knife blade scything towards his throat. He had surprised himself at his own agility. He was a stout man and ungainly, but the desire for self-preservation had lent power to muscles he hadn't known he possessed, enabling him to jerk his head aside at what had seemed the last second. He could have sworn he had heard the whisper of the blade as it flashed past his neck. It was only later, as he struggled to get his breath back, that he lifted a tentative hand to his throat and saw the thin smear of bright red blood on his fingertips. Curiously, he hadn't felt a thing when the blade made contact. He tried to recall the weapon. It had been a very slender blade, he remembered that much; as thin as a razor. And the skill with which the dark-robed priest had handled the knife had been completely unexpected.

But what had chilled Rafferty's blood even more than the attack itself was the look on his assailant's face. The parson's expression had not been one of panic, as might have been expected from someone who was cornered and fearful of imminent arrest. During the brief moment their eyes met, Rafferty had seen a vision of Hell, a malevolence that went beyond anything he had seen before. Had the devil or any of his acolytes been able to take on human form, there was no doubt in Conductor Rafferty's mind that he had been face to face, if not with Beelzebub, then certainly one of his minions.

The look on the woman's face had been just as memorable. There had been no colour in her complexion, only the sickly pallor of abject terror. Rafferty had seen her eyes widen momentarily as she had been pulled through the door, probably in recognition of his police uniform and the hope, swiftly suppressed, that rescue was at hand. Rafferty barely had time to register her predicament before being forced to defend himself from attack. He had heard her scream as he had thrust himself aside, the high-pitched shriek dying in her throat as the priest's hand clamped itself around her neck, dragging her ungainly, protesting body towards the church. Rafferty, lumbering to his knees, heart thumping, had watched helplessly as the heavy wooden door slammed behind them.

Which was when Hopkins and Dawes had arrived on the scene.

The three police officers had approached the

church door apprehensively, Rafferty slightly behind his colleagues, and limping. Having just survived one nerve-shredding encounter, the Irishman was, understandably, proceeding with no small degree of caution.

To Rafferty's relief, the church door was locked. It was Hopkins who hammered on the door, repeating the announcement that had been made earlier at the front door of the house; namely that they were there on orders from Bow Street, to initiate enquiries pertaining to a murder at Bethlem Hospital.

The response had been a scream that rooted the three men to the spot. It was a sound Edmund Rafferty had no wish to hear repeated. It had raised goose pimples along his arms and sent a cold tingle rippling down his spine. Beside him, the two constables were staring at the door like mesmerized rabbits.

The woman's screams had continued for what seemed like minutes, though in truth it had probably been only a few seconds, before fading into an uneasy silence. Then had come the warning; an excited male voice calling out to them not to force an entry or the woman would die.

Rafferty had waited for the short hairs on his forearms to lie back down before pressing his ear to the door. The door was old and the wood was thick and he hadn't been able to hear much. Mostly it had sounded like a woman sobbing. But there had been another sound too, a low murmuring noise, as if someone was praying. There had been an eeriness about the barely audible words and phrasing. It had sounded more like an incantation than a prayer.

'What do we do now?' Dawes asked nervously. Older than Hopkins, he was a lanky, unambitious man and had no intention of attempting anything remotely valiant.

'You go round the back. See if there's another door. If there is, you stand guard. I don't want no heroics.'

Rafferty turned to Hopkins.

Earlier that morning, when he'd been told the name of the Runner assigned to the case, Rafferty had known his day was unlikely to be a happy one. Hawkwood. The name alone had been enough to cause palpitations. In Rafferty's opinion, a harder bastard never drew breath. Just the thought of being confronted by those blue-grey eyes and having to admit that he'd been threatened and outwitted by a bloody vicar was enough to shrivel Rafferty's balls to the size of redcurrants.

However, if there was one maxim Rafferty lived by, it was that even middling rank had its privileges. Rafferty knew that, in sending Hopkins to track down Hawkwood at Bethlem rather than going himself, he was merely delaying the inevitable, but at least it gave him a little more breathing space. There was always the possibility that in between Hopkins' departure and Hawkwood's arrival, the vicar might see the error of his ways and surrender. Well, it was a church. Miracles *could* happen.

No sooner had the two constables departed on their respective missions than another uncomfortable realization wormed its way into Rafferty's sub-conscious: he needed to take a piss.

Rafferty knew if he left his post and the vicar made a run for it, and got away, Hawkwood would have his guts – literally, if their previous run-in had been anything to go by.

Rafferty eyed the church door. No voices could be heard, though he thought he detected scraping sounds, as if someone was dragging furniture across a stone floor. Rafferty tried peering in through one of the windows, but the lower sills were too high, even standing on tiptoe. In any case, the windows were composed of stained glass so viewing anything through them was impossible.

The need to empty his bladder had suddenly become all-consuming. The Irishman eyed the nearest grave marker, a tall, moss-encrusted stone cross. Nothing else for it. He'd have to piss and keep an eye on the church at the same time.

It was only as he was performing the act that he realized it wasn't as easy to do both as he had first supposed. There was the danger that if he concentrated only on the door, he'd very likely end up watering his breeches. The irony of the situation was not lost on Rafferty. The thought occurred to him, as he let go over the base of the cross, that Hawkwood hadn't yet arrived on the scene and here he was, already in danger of wetting himself.

His bladder emptied, Rafferty, relieved in more ways than one that the tricky moment had passed without incident, prepared to do up his breeches.

'Oi!'

Caught, if not with his breeches down then

certainly unbuttoned, Rafferty swung round, cock half in hand, heart fully in mouth. Stumping towards him was a small, round-shouldered, sour-faced man of about sixty, brandishing a long-handled hoe.

'What's your bleedin' game?'

Hastily, Rafferty shoved himself back in his breeches.

'I asked what your game was,' the man snarled again. He lifted the hoe, holding it across his body like a quarter-staff.

Modesty restored, Rafferty was wise enough to follow the old adage that attack was the best form of defence. 'Police business. And who might you be?'

'Quintus Pegg, and I'm the bleedin' sexton, that's who. An' since when did police business give you the right to piss all over the bloody gravestones?' The hoe carrier nodded towards the dark tell-tale stains on the stonework at the foot of the cross and the thin wisps of steam rising up from the grass.

Rafferty frowned at the unexpected and ferocious response. Avoiding the natural inclination to follow the sexton's irate gaze, he drew himself up. 'Sexton, is it? Well, cully, when I'm on police business, I'm thinking that I can piss just about anywhere I damned well choose and that includes down your neck, if I've a mind to. Now, is there a back door?'

The sexton blinked at the change of subject. 'What?'

'You heard. The church; is there another door round the back?'

The sexton looked confused. 'Aye, course there is, but it's locked an' there ain't no key. Why you askin'?'

It explained why Dawes hadn't returned, Rafferty thought. Having found another door, the poor bugger was probably soiling himself at the thought that someone might actually come through it. But at least he was staying at his post.

'Sweet Mother–' Rafferty rolled his eyes at the sexton's question. 'Because the vicar's locked himself inside, that's why, and–'

'Stupid bugger!' the sexton snorted.

Cut off by the remark, Rafferty blinked. Then the thought struck him that Sexton Pegg, having no knowledge of that morning's events, was assuming the vicar had locked himself in the church by accident.

He was about to set the record straight when the sexton raised an eyebrow. 'Who was it raised the alarm? Was it the wife?'

'The wife?' Rafferty repeated. A dark thought beckoned.

Unconcerned by the Irishman's delayed response, Sexton Pegg nodded towards the house behind them. 'She's 'is 'ousekeeper. That's why I 'appened along. I was away gettin' this sharpened.' The sexton indicated the hoe. 'Thought I might be back in time for a bite o' breakfast. Mind you, she weren't around earlier; probably at 'er sister's place. Thick as two fleas, those two are. Spends more time with 'er than she does with me, moody cow.'

Rafferty hesitated, though he knew the question had to be asked. 'Your wife ... what does the good lady look like?'

The sexton sniffed and held his left hand up, palm down. ''Bout this tall, face like a shrew, nose you could pick a lock with.'

Rafferty knew then, beyond any shadow of doubt, the identity of the woman in the church. He suspected that her current disposition was probably a long way from moody.

'Why do you want to know?' the sexton asked, suddenly wary.

Rafferty, irritated that the sexton seemed to be asking all the pertinent questions, told him.

The sexton stared aghast at the sturdy wooden door. The hoe slid through his fingers. 'Bleedin' 'ell. What are we going to do?'

We? Rafferty thought. Then he remembered that he was a police officer and therefore supposedly in charge of the situation.

'We wait.'

'Wait?' The sexton looked doubtful. 'What for?'

'Reinforcements,' Rafferty said sagely. 'They've already been sent for.'

Let Captain bloody Hawkwood sort this one out.

Sexton Pegg didn't look too convinced by the Irishman's reply.

'And 'ow long's that goin' to take?' The sexton nodded towards the church. 'Can't leave herself in there with 'im. You just told me 'e had a go at you, and you're a bleeding police officer. There's no knowin' what he might do to 'er. What 'appens if 'e decides to 'ave 'is way with 'er?' The sexton, in contrast to his earlier uncharitable remarks, was now looking distinctly queasy at the prospect of his wife becoming the victim of a serious sexual assault by a vicar.

Hell would probably freeze over first, Rafferty thought. He turned, only to discover that the sexton was no longer at his side. His ears picked up a thin, intermittent, trickling sound. He followed the source and found that the sexton had discarded the hoe and was busy relieving himself against the same tomb marker.

Nerves, Rafferty supposed. He was about to pass a barbed comment, when the sexton lifted his nose and sniffed the air. 'Can you smell that?'

Rafferty threw the sexton a look.

Sexton Pegg buttoned himself up and wiped his hands on his breeches. 'No, not that. More like … something burning.'

Both men turned towards the church. They were just in time to see the first bright tongues of flame rise into view behind the stained-glass windows.

And the screaming began again.

They had left the hospital behind them and cut down along Little Bell Alley, which wasn't so much an alley as a six-foot-wide, effluent-flooded, rat-infested passageway. They were attracting stares and catcalls as they ran, but Hopkins' uniform was proving valuable in clearing a path, and the determined look on Hawkwood's face as he pushed his way through made it clear to all that it would be unwise to try and impede their progress.

Hawkwood was breathing hard. He was also wishing he hadn't worn his riding coat. It was flapping like a cape and seemed to gain weight with every stride he took. Tradition had it that

Runners had gained their sobriquet because of their fleetness of foot. Another half mile of this, Hawkwood thought, and they'll be calling us Bow Street Crawlers. He wondered how Hopkins was faring. He could hear the constable's boots pounding along the street alongside him.

There was no immediate profit, Hawkwood knew, in telling Hopkins that the Reverend Tombs was dead and the man they were pursuing was in fact an inmate of the country's most notorious lunatic asylum. The constable, Hawkwood recalled, was new to the job and looked excited enough as it was. There was such a thing as too much information. But the lad had stamina, that was for sure.

Hopkins was thinking the same thing about Hawkwood, as he hastened to keep up.

The constable had managed to avoid Hawkwood's eye since leaving the hospital. He suspected that Hawkwood was aware of his nervousness and that only served to make him more jittery. He'd shot the Runner a few surreptitious glances along the way, taking in the severe features, the scar below the left eye and the ribbon-tied hair, and wondered how much of the captain's fearsome reputation was fact and how much was hearsay.

He'd heard that Hawkwood was a man who did not suffer fools gladly, so the last thing Hopkins wanted was to appear foolish, especially this early in his career. He'd also heard it whispered that Hawkwood lived by his own rules, with unique contacts within the criminal underworld. Hopkins wasn't sure what that meant exactly, and he wasn't about to ask, but it certainly added to the air of menace that seemed to attach itself to Hawkwood's shadow. The mere mention of his name had been sufficient to drain the blood from Conductor Rafferty's face when he learned the identity of the officer in charge of their assignment.

In the short time he'd been attached to Bow Street, Hopkins had soon picked up on some of Conductor Rafferty's less than enviable character traits, sloth and deviousness being the most prominent. Rafferty also liked to throw his weight around among the new recruits. Susceptibility to intimidation, therefore, was not one of his most obvious weaknesses. So Hopkins had been intrigued to discover what it was about Hawkwood that had Conductor Rafferty quaking in his pants.

Now he knew.

A thunderous rumble broke into the constable's thoughts. He looked up, just in time to see the carriage bearing down on him. He leapt aside awkwardly, nearly losing his footing in the process. The horse's heaving flank missed him by less than an inch as the carriage pummelled its way past, but he was too late to avoid the wave of water thrown up as the chaise's wheels trundled heavily through one of the muddy puddles left by the night's rain. The constable cursed as his breeches fell prey to the deluge. Recovering his balance and what remained of his dignity, the hapless and waterlogged constable hurried to make up ground.

They were nearly there. Hawkwood could smell the river; a pungent mix of cordage, tar, wet mud, rotting fish and shit from the night-soil barges heading downstream. Calvert's Brewery was less than a mile away and the smell of fermenting hops also hung heavily in the air. The locals, Hawkwood thought, would have no need to visit a tavern for their pleasure. Simply opening their windows and inhaling would have them intoxicated in no time.

The streets were narrower here, and the buildings more decrepit. City commerce had given way to riverside industry, and instead of chaises and phaetons they found themselves dodging drays, barrows and handcarts as they raced towards the church.

When his ears picked up the ringing of the bell, Hawkwood's first thought was that it was coming from one of the merchant ships off-loading at a nearby wharf. It was only when the clanging tones intensified that he knew they were signalling an event far more urgent than a change of watch.

And then he saw the smoke.

Struck by a quickening sense of dread, Hawkwood lengthened his stride. He sensed Hopkins coming up behind him. The two men emerged from the alley simultaneously, and stopped dead.

'Bloody hell!' Constable Hopkins stared wide-eyed at the scene, his soggy breeches forgotten.

The church of St Mary's was being consumed.

The church was smaller than Hawkwood had expected; plain and rectangular in shape, with the bell tower at the northern end. He'd seen chapels that were more impressive. The outside walls looked relatively untouched, but the stained-glass windows, illuminated by a backcloth of dancing flames deep within the building, glowed like

105

jewels. There was a series of splintering cracks like distant musket fire. Gathering onlookers cried out as rainbow-tinted shards of glass, forced from their frames by the heat, showered the ground like hailstones. Plumes of black smoke billowed from the newly ruptured panes, spiralling skywards as if seeking refuge in the grey clouds above. Small fiery eruptions, hesitant at first but quickly growing in confidence, leapt from the body of the church. Hawkwood watched as lizard tongues of flame began to lick the edges of the roof.

At first glance the tower appeared as though it might be immune to the devastation being wrought below. Gradually, however, drifts of smoke could be seen issuing from the louvred window shutters at the tower's summit. The building, its lead spire outlined against the sky, began to take on the appearance of a brightly lit altar candle. The bell continued to toll loudly, drowning the cries of alarm from the watching crowd.

There was a sudden commotion at the entrance to a nearby alleyway. Half a dozen men jogged into view hauling a wooden cart. The fire brigade had arrived. Dutifully, the crowd parted to let them through. Bringing their contraption to a halt, the men stared balefully at the burning building. At first Hawkwood thought they were looking for the fire mark indicating the building was covered by the insurance company that employed them. If no plaque were visible, in all likelihood the brigade would return from whence they came. But the mark was displayed on the wall to the right of the door where the firemen could not help but see it. Hawkwood realized

106

they had stopped because they were completely overawed. It wasn't hard to see why. Their crude equipment was spectacularly inadequate for a blaze of this scale.

Hawkwood spotted Rafferty hovering uneasily at the edge of the throng.

Sensing someone observing him, the Irishman turned. Panic flared momentarily in his eyes as he watched Hawkwood's approach.

'What the devil happened here?' Hawkwood demanded.

It was almost comical the way the Irishman shook his head, immediately defensive. 'It weren't me, Captain. Honest, I had nothing to do with it, swear to God. The parson locked himself inside the bloody place before we had a chance to stop him.'

'He's still in there?' Hawkwood stared aghast at the flames. Drifts of steam were now rising from the shallow guttering along the edges of the roof as rainwater, trapped in the aftermath of the night's storm, was brought to boiling point by the fire below.

Rafferty nodded uneasily.

'Hopkins said there was a woman.'

Rafferty raised his hands in a gesture of hopelessness.

'Has anyone tried to force an entry?'

Rafferty certainly hadn't but he wasn't about to admit that to Hawkwood. Instead he nodded towards the tower. 'He's blocked the door, barricaded himself in. Mad bastard,' he added.

If you only knew, Hawkwood thought.

Hawkwood caught sight of a small, thin, poorly

dressed man squatting on a nearby gravestone, holding his head in his hands.

'The sexton,' Rafferty murmured, following the direction of his gaze. 'It's his wife what's inside.'

There was a shout. Grit and determination having triumphed over doubt, the fire fighters were attempting to unravel their hose. Hawkwood wondered why they were bothering. Even a blind man could see there was little hope. But the fire crew seemed intent on going through the ritual anyway.

'Haven't got a prayer,' Rafferty muttered. 'Poor beggars.'

For once Hawkwood was inclined to agree with him.

Having unloaded their leather buckets from the wagon, the firemen ran to a horse trough by the alley entrance and began filling them at the pump. Two of the men armed themselves with axes. As if reading Hawkwood's thoughts, one pulled a handkerchief from his shirt, soaked it in the water trough and tied it round the lower part of his face. Gripping his axe tightly, he headed for the church door. He was halfway there when he paused, frozen in mid stride, and looked up.

It was then Hawkwood realized he could no longer hear the bell.

The crowd had also fallen silent. All that could be heard was the crackle of the flames, followed by several sharper reports as more windowpanes cascaded on to the ground. The firemen were looking around them anxiously. Hawkwood knew they were worried in case the fire spread; if it did, they had no hope of controlling it. Fortunately, the church was isolated from its immediate neighbours by the graveyard. And in the event that a stray spark should be carried on the breeze, it would struggle to ignite timber still sodden from last night's downpour.

A high-pitched scream caught everyone by surprise. The crowd looked up, following the woman's pointing finger. There was a collective gasp of horror.

The louvred shutters at the top of the bell tower had been flung wide open. The figure of a man, dressed in the black robe of a priest, stood framed in the opening.

'Sweet Jesus!' Conductor Rafferty crossed himself hurriedly.

The fireman, en route to the church door, was transfixed by the sight. The axe slid through his fingers. As one, the crowd took an involuntary step backwards.

Wreathed in smoke, the black-clad apparition turned its face to the sky. A tortured cry rose high above the crackle of the flames.

'O Lord, let my cry come unto thee!'

There was a moment of stunned silence, suddenly broken by a lone male voice, slurred with drink. 'It ain't Sunday, Vicar! Bit early for the sermon, ain't it?'

'Shut it, Marley, you ignorant sod!' The sharp warning was accompanied by a muffled grunt of pain and the sound of a bottle shattering on the cobbles.

Ignoring the altercation below, the figure at the window, face still raised, opened his arms in supplication.

'I stand before you, Lord, a miserable sinner!'

As the words rang out, a stick-thin figure, seated at the foot of a nearby gravestone, slowly raised its head.

Hawkwood was suddenly conscious of movement to his right as a small body thrust itself to the front of the onlookers.

'You murdering bastard!'

Heads swivelled to stare at the accuser.

'You killed my Annie!' The sexton, his face contorted with rage, jabbed an accusing finger towards the smoke-framed silhouette.

Hearing the outburst, a murmur began to spread through the crowd. All eyes turned heavenwards once more.

'Mother of God,' Rafferty said hoarsely.

The onlookers, Hawkwood realized, were not close enough to see that the robed man was not the person they took him to be. All the crowd could make out with any certainty was the black attire. They saw only what they were meant to see. Colonel Hyde was continuing with his deception and distance was lending credibility to his ruse. His appearance had even fooled the sexton.

The black-clad figure called out once more. It was the anguished, beseeching wail of a soul in torment.

'I heard Satan call my name! In my foolishness I answered! And by the Devil's tongue I was corrupted into darkness!'

'That's the spirit, Vicar!' The drunken heckler was back and in fuller voice. 'You bloody tell 'em!'

'Chris'sakes, Marley, will you bleedin' shut your mouth, or so help me–'

110

The strident voice rose once more to the heavens. 'I beheld that pale horse, Lord, and his name that sat on him was Death, and Hell did follow with him!'

'Horse?' Rafferty said, brow puckering. 'What bleedin' horse? What in the name of all that's holy is the beggar on about?'

There was a nervous cough from behind. 'Er ... I know,' Hopkins said. A blush had formed across the young constable's earnest face. Whether it was from the heat coming off the burning building, or from embarrassment at suddenly being the focus of attention, it was difficult to tell. 'It's from the scriptures.'

Hawkwood turned and stared at him.

'Book of Revelation; chapter six, verse eight...' Hopkins hesitated, and then added, somewhat sheepishly, 'My pa's a vicar.'

The young constable's gaze suddenly shifted and his eyes widened. Hawkwood turned. Above him, the figure in the tower, hands clasped together in prayer, was sinking to his knees, head bowed. The voice boomed out once more.

'But in the guiding light of thy glory, o Lord, I have seen the error of my ways and I do earnestly repent my sins!'

'Uh, oh,' Rafferty murmured. 'He's off again.'

Hawkwood stared up at the tower. Smoke was continuing to vent from the opening. It was as if the priestly figure was kneeling at the entrance to the pit of Hell. Bathed now in the glow of the flames, the black robe shimmered like velvet.

Abruptly the figure lifted its head.

'I hear you, Lord! Blessed are they who have

111

seen the way of righteousness! I deliver my soul to your bosom in the knowledge that I may be cleansed of all my transgressions!'

Above them, the dark silhouette rose unsteadily to its feet, bowed its head and slowly lowered its arms, palms outwards. Then, as if reciting a benediction, it spoke. The words rang out loud and clear.

'All that are with me, salute thee! Greet them that love us in the faith! Grace be with you all...'

Raising his right hand to shoulder height, the figure made the sign of the cross.

'Amen.'

Then, in a move that was as swift as it was shocking, the robed figure turned, spread its arms wide and pitched forward into the rising flames.

Shrieks of horror erupted from the women in the crowd. There were loud gasps and exclamations of astonishment from the men.

As the body disappeared from view, a single mournful clang echoed around the churchyard. Several people jumped. The body must have hit or become entangled with the bell rope on the way down, Hawkwood guessed. Either that or some unearthly force had used the bell as a means to summon the dead man's soul into the afterlife.

Beside him, Hawkwood heard a groan of dismay. He turned. The constable's face was ashen. 'Why?' Hopkins whispered, staring at the church tower, now wreathed in smoke. 'Why did he do it?'

'He was mad,' Hawkwood said bluntly.

The constable removed his hat. His lips began

to move in silent prayer. Hawkwood could see that others in the crowd were similarly engaged. A number of the more devout had fallen to their knees. Hawkwood didn't think it was the time or place to tell them that their prayers for Reverend Tombs were both misplaced and many hours too late.

Hawkwood's eyes were locked on the tower and the empty window. The frames and shutters had caught alight and were burning fiercely. At the foot of the building, the fire fighters had been forced to admit defeat. Along with everyone else, they were standing in a state of disbelief, watching the church's disintegration. Bathed in the glare, their faces glowed bright crimson. The heat was intense.

'What?' Hawkwood said absently, vaguely aware that the constable had spoken.

Hopkins blinked. 'The Reverend's last words. They were what my pa used to say.'

'Is that so?' Hawkwood said, not particularly interested.

Hopkins nodded, mistaking Hawkwood's response for polite enquiry.

'Know them off by heart. Drummed into me, they were. It was the blessing my dad used to give at the end of every Sunday service. St Paul's Epist–'

A crash from inside the burning tower drowned out the rest of the constable's words, all except one. Upon hearing it, Hawkwood felt as if the rest of the world had suddenly stopped moving. He turned slowly. '*What* did you say?'

Hopkins looked embarrassed, intimidated by

113

Hawkwood's tone. 'I was saying that I knew the reverend's last words too.'

'I heard that part,' Hawkwood snapped. 'What did you say after that?'

The constable hesitated, awed by the look on Hawkwood's face.

'Um ... that it was the last verse?'

'No,' Hawkwood said softly. 'You said a name.'

The constable swallowed nervously. He realized his mouth had gone completely dry, as if his tongue had been dipped in ash.

As a child, Constable George Hopkins, like many young boys of an enquiring mind, had been an avid collector of butterflies and beetles, impaling their tiny thoraxes with pins and preserving them for posterity in small glass cases for the amusement of family and friends. When he felt those blue-grey eyes upon him, the constable had the distinct impression that this was how the beetles must have felt. He took a deep breath, found his voice.

'It's from St Paul's Epistle, the Book of...'

The constable paused, intimidated by the look on Hawkwood's face.

'...Titus.'

Over the constable's shoulder the church of St Mary continued to burn as brightly as a wrecker's torch.

Apothecary Robert Locke stood at his window and stared out across the city's rooftops. The clouds were the colour of gunmetal and it was difficult to see where the slates ended and the sky began.

Locke's mind took him back to the horror that had been the colonel's cell. He closed his eyes. A vision of the Reverend Tombs' corpse swam into view. He saw again the shabby undergarments, the pale limbs protruding from them, and the bloody atrocity that had once been the parson's face. He shuddered. It was a vision, he suspected, that would haunt his dreams for some time to come.

His thoughts turned to his recent visitor. Not your usual law officer. Well dressed – Locke knew good tailoring when he saw it – though the long dark hair tied at the back with a ribbon had been an interesting affectation, and there had been an arrogance and perceptiveness that Locke had found vaguely unsettling. Indeed, there had been times when Locke had found it hard to meet the man's penetrating gaze. Brains as well as brawn. But then he had been a fighting man, an officer in the Rifle Brigade, no less; one of the most respected regiments in the British Army. Locke congratulated himself on his intuition at picking up on that aspect of Hawkwood's background and wondered what had turned such a man from soldier to police officer.

Soldier. His thoughts drifted again.

From the violence of the American, Norris, to James Tilly Matthews' bizarre conspiracy theories, Locke had seen many forms of madness. Now he was witness to another.

Colonel Titus Hyde: soldier, surgeon, priest killer.

His eyes dropped to his desk and Matthews' representation of his Air Loom. Gazing at the

115

illustration, Locke's thoughts returned to the anatomical drawings in the colonel's quarters. That the colonel should have such items on display was not unusual, given his medical background. Similar charts and diagrams could be found in any physician's consulting room or any one of the city's dozen or so anatomy schools. For centuries drawings of this nature had been the standard reference for physicians and surgeons. What Locke had found unusual – although it wasn't an observation that he had thought to share with Hawkwood – was the one salient feature all Hyde's selection of illustrations had in common. It had both intrigued and disturbed the apothecary, though he didn't quite know why.

All the figures gracing the cell's walls had been female.

6

In a corner of the smoke-filled taproom two customers were competing for the favours of a whore. Though she was well past her prime, overweight and heavily rouged, the duo engaged in the tussle for her ample charms were drunk on gin and, viewed through an alcoholic haze in the muted candle glow, her imperfections were less apparent than they might have been in the cold light of day.

The woman leaned across the beer-stained table. A pair of enormous milk-white breasts strained provocatively against her low-cut bodice. Placing her mouth against the ear of one of her companions, the whore dropped her hand on to the leg of the other and began stroking his inner thigh.

The drunk into whose ear she had been whispering lewd enticements grinned expectantly. Sliding a hand inside her gaping blouse, he began a vigorous kneading of her right breast. The whore pulled away, shrieked playfully and slapped the hand down, deflecting his crude advances with an admonishing finger, at the same time throwing his companion a knowing wink.

Interpreting the wink as a gesture of encouragement, the second man lifted his mug to her lips, encouraging her to take a sip. She did so, tipping her head back. Draining the mug, she wiped her chin with the back of her hand and licked her lips with relish.

The whore, whose name was Lizzie Tyler, had been playing the drunkards against each other for a good ten minutes. It was a game at which she had become an expert. She'd certainly had enough practice over the years.

It was an unfortunate fact that accommodation, no matter how squalid, did not come free, and with the long winter nights drawing in, Lizzie had no intention of walking the cold, dark streets any longer than she had to.

There had in the past been times when, finding herself a copper or two short of the rent, Lizzie had been obliged to pay in kind for the roof over her head. But her landlord, an odious individual by the name of Miggs, whose rat-infested doss-house nestled on a corner of Field Lane, had chosen to interpret this arrangement as his personal conjugal right. And that was an option Lizzie had no wish to pursue. A lady had her dignity and a right to a man's respect, after all, even if she was a whore.

So, Lizzie had taken to plying her trade among the public houses and grog shops around Smithfield and Newgate, enduring humiliation, insults and beatings in a continuing struggle to keep the cold and Landlord Miggs at bay and her lice-ridden head above water.

The advantage of catering for gin-guzzlers was that, more often than not, once they got you into the alley, rammed up against the wall, they were too far gone to do the business. If she was particularly inventive, a girl could wrap the tops of her thighs round a man's cock and, by dint of a little panting and moaning, fool him into thinking that he had outperformed Casanova himself. And in that particular sphere of deception, Lizzie Tyler was as adept as a conjurer's assistant. Whether the customer could rise to the occasion or not, money still had to change hands. But so far all Lizzie had managed out of this pair was a leery smirk and two swallows of rotgut. So, even as she submitted herself to their unco-ordinated fumbling, Lizzie was on the lookout for an alternative source of remuneration, just in case.

One customer had caught her attention. She'd seen him enter the tavern a while earlier. Tall and dark-haired, he was wearing a long black coat over a shabby grey jacket and what looked like a pair of old military breeches. The yellow seam down each leg was faded and worn. His boots, she noticed, also looked old but appeared to be of good quality, which struck Lizzie as odd, given the run-down appearance of the rest of his attire. In her time as a moll, she had seen a variety of men and a bewildering array of footwear from, it had to be said, just about every conceivable angle; it was Lizzie's avowed opinion that you could tell a lot about a man by the boots he wore. And this one intrigued her, seated alone in a booth on the opposite side of the room, his back to the wall, his face now cast in semi-shadow. She'd seen the way he carried himself and the scar below his eye, which, along with the remnants of uniform, suggested he was most likely a wounded veteran, down on his luck, who'd come to the pub looking for employment. Given that

119

the Black Dog doubled as a house of call, it seemed the most obvious explanation.

If you required the services of a professional, a lawyer or an actuary, you paid a visit to Lincoln's Inn or Bartholomew Lane. If you had need of someone at the tradesman's end of the job market – a tailor, shoemaker, or perhaps a weaver – you went to the Green Dragon. If you wanted someone more menial – a chimney sweep, rag picker or suchlike, there was the Three Boys. But if you were seeking someone for the really dirty jobs – a gravedigger or a shit shifter on one of the night-soil barges – then chances were you'd find him in the Dog.

Lizzie eyed the tall man and wondered what sort of work he was after. Already two or three of the other girls had sidled up to his table, jiggled their titties and trailed a hand across his shoulders, in a less than subtle attempt to engage his interest. All of them had received the same response. A brief dialogue had ensued, followed by a shake of the head and an intimidating look that said, *All right, you've tried me once, now don't bother me again.* And so they hadn't.

A sharp tweak of her right nipple jerked Lizzie out of her reverie. The drunk at her elbow was trying to cadge another free feel. Lizzie decided she'd had enough. The charade was over.

'That's it, darlin',' she snapped, slapping the hand away. 'You want Lizzie to take you to paradise, you gotta pay the fare.' She turned to the second man. 'You, too, sweet'eart. What's it to be? Lizzie ain't got all bleedin' night.'

Both men blinked myopically. Lizzie sighed and

looked across the room. The dark-haired man was still seated by himself, nursing a mug. Lizzie considered her options, which were not numerous. Well, she thought idly, it might be worth a try...

Hawkwood sensed he was being watched. He raised the mug to his lips as if to take a sip and quartered the room. It was the plump moll in the corner. He watched as she slapped away the roving hands of her table companions and registered the speculation in her gaze as her eyes met his.

Ignoring her come-on, he lowered the mug and looked around. Similar scenes were being enacted around the room. The molls were out in force. They had good reason to be. It was Saturday evening and it was payday.

In a partially curtained-off alcove, beyond a low archway to the left of the counter, a small knot of poorly dressed men was lining up before a bald, unsmiling, bullet-headed man seated at the pay-table. In front of him sat a ledger and a sack of coin. Behind him stood two younger men, well built, in waistcoats, with the sleeves of their shirts rolled up to display an impressive expanse of well-toned muscle. Each was armed with a thick wooden cudgel.

Hawkwood watched as one by one the waiting men stepped up to the table to sign or make their mark, in exchange for coin. Having collected their earnings, they made straight for the counter and the gin, their faces etched with a combination of resignation and despair. Hawkwood had seen the same haunted look in the eyes of French prisoners of war. It was the look of defeated men with uncertain futures.

The bullet-headed paymaster was called Hanratty and it was his alehouse. The men guarding his back were his sons. Hanratty had been landlord of the Dog for longer than anyone could remember, and the Dog had been an employment agency for a good deal longer than that.

Although the Dog catered for a variety of low-ranking occupations, its primary source of labour derived from its geography. The pub was less than a stone's throw from Smithfield. It was inevitable, therefore, that it also catered for the meat market. Hanratty had been a butcher before he became a publican and he still had contacts in the trade, so if you had need of porters, butcher's boys, tripe-dressers, and the like, the Dog was your first port of call.

Acting as middleman between masters and workers, Hanratty ran his labour exchange with a rod of iron. It was an effective and – for the canny publican, at least – a very lucrative arrangement.

For the men seeking employment, there was a price to pay. If you wanted work, you had to sign on. If there was no work to be had, Hanratty would give you credit to buy food and victuals – but only at the Dog. When he found you work, Hanratty would pay the wages on the employer's behalf – first deducting any money he was owed. Too bad if the debt exceeded the wage, which it usually did. Whichever way a man turned, Hanratty had him by the balls. The pale, drawn faces coming away from the paytable said it all.

For most of them, the only way to alleviate the misery, even if it was just for an hour or two at the end of the day, was drink. Hanratty always made sure he had an abundance of that particular panacea in stock. And it was no coincidence that wages were paid in the evening.

If it wasn't drink, it was likely to be whist or cribbage. A number of games were in session that evening, and a couple of tables along several punters were engaged in a noisy round of dominoes. The click-clack of tiles slamming on to the tabletop accompanied the raucous laughter of the players.

Hawkwood viewed the proceedings with weary fascination. Cards and alcohol: an unholy alliance if ever there was one. It was a bad combination even in the rich gaming clubs along St James'; in this neighbourhood, it was a licence for trouble. Especially if there were molls on tap as well. But Hanratty had his boys on hand in case things got rowdy. If a man was foolish enough to start anything, he'd be taken outside into the alley and shown the error of his ways. A harsh enough punishment in itself, but not as bad as having your name removed from the ledger. Once your name was scratched out, you didn't earn. And if you didn't earn, you starved. So did your family.

It was Hawkwood's first visit to the Dog, though it wasn't his first visit to a house of call. There were a dozen similar establishments within a square-mile of the market and the Dog was the fourth on Hawkwood's list following the gravedigger's tip-off that Edward Doyle, the man hanged in Cripplegate and currently occupying a cold dissection room, may have frequented one of the Smithfield watering holes. So far, however,

123

he hadn't discovered a damned thing.

Hawkwood could think of three reasons for his lack of success: genuine ignorance, concern over self-incrimination, and fear of reprisal. There had been more than a hint of the latter in the responses he'd received, even though his enquiries had been covert. It probably meant that word of the crucifixion had spread and people were too scared to point the finger.

All he could do for the moment was continue working his way down the list of taverns in the hope that something would eventually present itself to him. That didn't mean, of course, that he couldn't indulge himself in a small libation at the same time. Besides, after the day he'd had, he decided he'd earned it. And in a place like the Dog, if he hadn't got a drink in front of him people would have noticed.

It was also one way of taking his mind off the God-awful stench.

The smell had hit him the moment he entered the pub and it hadn't taken long for him to realize that it wasn't emanating from any one source. It was all around him, seeping from every pore of the building, all the way from the foundations, the bricks in the walls, right up to the rafters above him. It oozed from the unwashed bodies and the clothing of the drinkers, and it rose like a thin mist from the blood-stained cellars and killing yards that had, in various reincarnations, been an integral part of the surrounding neighbourhood for the best part of six centuries. Here, the sickly aroma of putrefying flesh and the corrupting smell of death was a living, breathing entity.

On market days, the streets and alleyways around Smithfield foamed red with the blood from the slaughterhouses. Pavements would be slick with discarded entrails, while residue from the mounds of waste products tossed aside by butchers, sausage-makers and cat-gut manufacturers would be left to rot in the shallow, fat-lined gutters.

Inside the Dog, the carpet of sawdust had managed to soak up most of the day's blood, but the pieces of mashed intestines and foot-trodden globules of animal matter tracked into the bar on the heels of the customers had helped churn the once-white dust into a stinking, black molasses that made the cracked flagstones look as if they had been smeared with dog shit.

The smell in Bedlam had been bad enough, Hawkwood thought, raising his mug, but this was far worse.

Inevitably, thinking about the hospital, his mind went back to the fire and the colonel's fiery demise.

Constable Hopkins had asked why. Hawkwood was aware that his terse response, while accurate, still left many questions unanswered.

Apothecary Locke had said that the colonel was originally committed to Bethlem because his mind had been tortured by his experiences in the Peninsula. Hawkwood knew only too well the horrors the man would have witnessed in his capacity as a battlefield physician: tables awash with blood, his fellow surgeons elbow-deep in gore as they cut, probed and cauterized shattered flesh in a desperate attempt to make whole the bodies of soldiers maimed by musket shot, hacked by sabre, or shredded by cannon fire.

Hawkwood remembered his visits to the hospital tents all too well. It wasn't only the sight of the wounded and the dying that remained with him but the sounds they'd made. Soldiers spitting out the leather strap and screaming in agony as the dull-bladed saw was dragged across bone; the whimpering of a drummer boy as the forceps searched for that elusive fragment of lead ball, the heart-rending wail of a dying ensign calling for his mother's comforting hand as his innards cascaded like bloody tripe across his belly. While outside the tents, in the heat and the dust, the sickly-sweet smell of gangrene from the towering piles of amputated, fly-blown limbs would drift on the wind like rotten apples. Small wonder the colonel had lost his reason, Hawkwood reflected.

Many would have called the colonel a saviour, a man of compassion who had dedicated himself to the preservation of life. Who could have foreseen that a dark, malignant force lurking deep within the recesses of the colonel's brain would drive him to commit two savage acts of murder?

Was it possible that, alongside that hidden malignity, there had still burned a tiny spark of conscience? Not only had he murdered a priest, but he'd also killed an innocent woman. Had the guilt finally caught up with him? It looked that way. In the end, overcome by remorse, the colonel had taken his own life.

He'd even used the church bell to summon witnesses to his suicide and cremation.

Hawkwood thought back. What was it Apothecary Locke had said? Confession was good for the soul? By his actions, the colonel clearly thought fire would have the same cleansing effect, even if they were likely to be the flames of Hell and everlasting damnation.

Though perhaps that had been the point.

Either way, the case was closed. Chief Magistrate Read had expressed his satisfaction at that. As he had announced when Hawkwood had returned to Bow Street to advise him on the outcome, it meant that all his attention could now be focused on the Cripplegate murder.

So, in the fetid interior of the Black Dog tavern, Hawkwood sat with his back to the wall, sipped his porter and watched the room.

Lizzie had decided it was time to give her two suitors the heave-ho. Both were virtually comatose. One was already face down on the table. His breathing had become increasingly ragged and Lizzie knew it was only a matter of time before he'd begin to snore. The other was leaning over the side of the bench, looking as if he was about to disgorge the contents of his stomach over the blood-soaked, sawdust-streaked flagstones.

Lizzie sighed. Using her considerable weight, she prised herself from between the two men. As she did so, one breast made an energetic bid for freedom. With nonchalant ease, Lizzie tucked the escaping mammary back into its proper place and squeezed out from behind the table.

The dark-haired man hadn't moved from his seat, Lizzie saw. Perhaps a closer, more intimate approach was called for, rather than her previous long-range attempt to attract his attention. Undeterred by the possibility of rejection, Lizzie reached inside her bodice and pushed up her already spectacular bosom. In her experience, a frontal attack usually did the trick.

Hawkwood watched the moll extricate herself from her companions' clutches. He had an inkling she would soon be heading his way and, judging by the determined expression on her face, unlike the other members of her sisterhood, this one might have a hard time taking no for an answer. He prepared to repel boarders. Unless she had the information he was after, of course; nobody knew the seamier establishments and the people who frequented them like the city's molls.

Hawkwood had made good use of working girls in his career as a peace officer. The advantage being that he very rarely had to make the running. He would wait for the molls to come to him. The tactic had nothing to do with vanity. He just knew that if he hung around in one place long enough the women would invariably make the first move. They'd flirt, some more brazenly than others, and make their play, usually accompanied by a generous view of the goods on offer. And in the course of their inducements he would solicit *them* for information.

So it was with the Doyle enquiry. In each of the drinking dens he'd visited, Hawkwood had casually dropped the name on the pretext that he was an old acquaintance and there was a job in the offing with a chance for both of them to earn a few shillings. But the responses, so far, had all been the same. No one knew the man. Or if they had known him, they weren't talking. Not yet, anyway. The only thing he'd received from the girls so far had been looks of disappointment, genuine and feigned, as they'd deserted him for someone who *was* prepared to pay for their company.

Hawkwood eyed the moll. She was definitely on her way over. He took a sip from his mug, and braced himself.

Lizzie had her prey in her sights when she sensed the presence at her shoulder.

'Find your own, darlin'. That one's mine.'

The voice was soft and seductive and threaded with a raw huskiness that spoke of a lifetime of hard liquor and a throat roughened by cheap tobacco fumes.

Lizzie felt the short hairs along her arms and the back of her neck prickle. She turned slowly and found herself confronted by a pair of midnight-blue eyes set in a pale, elfin face framed by a cascade of jet-black ringlets.

'Sal!' Lizzie swallowed nervously. 'Didn't know you was in tonight.'

'Is that right, Lizzie? And there was I thinking you were avoiding me.' The corner of the young woman's mouth lifted, but there was no humour in her tone. The dark eyes were totally without warmth.

Lizzie felt herself shrink under the piercing gaze.

'Just tryin' to make a livin', Sal,' she said quickly. 'You know how it is. A girl's got to earn a crust.'

The young woman nodded slowly, hands on

129

her hips, as though giving Lizzie's response due consideration.

'Might be worth trying to earn it someplace else then.' Though softly spoken, the threat was there.

Lizzie blanched. 'Didn't mean no harm, Sal, honest.'

'Course you didn't, Lizzie. I know that.' The girl smiled silkily and laid her hand on Lizzie's arm.

Lizzie felt her skin crawl. She prayed that nothing showed on her face.

'You won't tell Sawney, will you?' Lizzie blurted, hating herself for the tremor in her voice.

The girl's eyes narrowed momentarily. They reminded Lizzie of a cat that had once been house-broken but had reverted to a feral creature, cunning and savage. She felt her arm gripped, as if by sharp talons, and winced.

'Now why would I do that?' The voice was quiet, almost a whisper, yet still audible. 'This is just you and me having a quiet chat. Tell you what, why don't you run along like a good girl and we'll say no more about it? How's that?'

Lizzie was conscious of a hollow thumping sound and realized it was the pounding of her heart. She wondered if the other woman was aware of it. Probably; the fingers still holding fast to her wrist were close to her pulse. She nodded and felt a bubble of sweat beading between her shoulder blades burst into what seemed like a thousand droplets of moisture. The back of her dress clung to her body as if it had been drenched with warm water.

'Thanks, Sal. It won't 'appen again. Promise.'

The girl released her grip. 'Course it won't. Go on, now. Off with you.' Slender fingers patted Lizzie's arm reassuringly. 'And take care, now, Lizzie. You hear?'

Lizzie nodded again. Turning hurriedly and sucking in her breath, she headed for the door. She was a yard or two away when the door opened, admitting a blast of cold air and half a dozen fresh customers; more men with empty pockets and low expectations, already casting longing looks towards the counter and the pay-table in the alcove. Most would be looking for a drink. More than a few wouldn't have the money to pay for it, but if their name was in the ledger they knew Hanratty would give them credit. Just for tonight, tomorrow could look after itself.

Had it been any other time, Lizzie would have executed a swift about-turn, fluttered her eye-lashes, hoisted up her bosom and set to work, but not tonight. Ignoring the gauntlet of crude in-ducements and wandering hands, Lizzie pushed her way through the new arrivals and out through the open door.

It was only after she had emerged into the street that Lizzie realized she was still holding her breath. She let it out slowly, emitting a soft in-voluntary moan of relief as she did so. She looked down at her hands and found they were shaking. She clenched her fists, straightened, and moved into the shadows by the side of the building. Leaning against the wall, she waited for her heartbeat to settle. She heard footsteps approach-ing out of the gloom; two more men on their way into the pub. They didn't notice her at first. When they did, they looked surprised not to receive a proposition. Lizzie, her cheek pressed against the damp brickwork, remained silent and let them go.

It occurred to Lizzie, as she waited for her breathing to return to normal, that she had still not earned her rent money. She looked back at the pub's entrance, weighing her options. There was always the George or the King of Denmark. The night was growing colder. The street suddenly looked dark and forbidding and there was a new hint of rain in the air. Lizzie shivered. Pushing away from the wall, she set off towards Field Lane. Tonight, she wanted to be in her own bed. And if that meant submitting to the lecherous demands of Luther Miggs, on this occasion, it was a price she was more than willing to pay.

Hawkwood had seen the exchange between the two women. The expression on the face of the older moll had been intriguing. In the murky interior of the taproom, with shadows playing across washed-out, alcohol-ravaged features, it was sometimes difficult to read a person's face or mood. But there had been no mistaking the look of apprehension in the big moll's eyes when she had turned and seen the younger woman standing beside her.

There was a pecking order in all strands of society, Hawkwood knew, and that applied to the oldest profession as much as it did to any other. Whoring was, by nature, territorial. Molls guarded their patch zealously. It didn't matter if the location was an archway in Covent Garden,

132

an alleyway in St Giles' or the taproom of the Black Dog, the same unwritten rule applied: trespassers would be dealt with. It was clear that in the Dog some sort of boundary had been crossed. What had been surprising, from Hawkwood's perspective, was the absence of histrionics. There had been no hysterical altercation, no screaming or scratching of eyes. There had been only quietly spoken, though evidently very persuasive, words. It hinted at some kind of severe warning.

Curious that it had been the older woman who had given way. In the normal scheme of things, Hawkwood would have expected the younger whore to beat a retreat, but that hadn't been the case. Given that other whores were plying their trade in the Dog, why had the older moll been singled out for chastisement?

She'd strayed from her traditional haunt, Hawkwood surmised, and had chosen the Dog because it was warm and because it was payday and maybe there'd be enough men with money in their pocket or credit to go around. The reason for the older molls' abrupt departure was probably that simple. She'd just made an unwise choice of hunting ground and had been sent on her way by the Dog's matriarch, who, having emerged victorious from the encounter, was now weaving her way through the tables towards Hawkwood's side of the room.

Watching her progress, Hawkwood noticed the way the other whores seemed to give way before her. He wondered if it was his imagination, for it appeared as if most of them were trying to avoid eye contact, acknowledging her superiority within the pack. She'd seen off one weaker rival and the other girls knew it; judging from their collective demeanour, they heartily resented her for it.

Unlike most of the others, she had the looks; there was no disputing that. There was a swagger about her that suggested she revelled in it. The obligatory tight, low bodice accentuated her pale skin and slender curves to their best advantage, but it was her face that drew the attention, the dark eyes especially. She'd have been a pretty child, Hawkwood suspected, and had probably traded on that to get her way. There was certainly self-awareness in her manner. It spoke of someone who'd experienced a catalogue of despair and degradation at the hands of men and had, by force of character, risen above it, most likely at the expense of others. In this sort of place it was sometimes difficult to gauge a person's age, male or female. Somewhere in her mid twenties, he guessed, though she could have been younger.

Even when she stopped at his table, it wasn't easy to tell. He realized then what the confrontation had been about.

She looked down at him and grinned. 'You're a lucky man, sweet'eart.'

'Is that right?' Hawkwood said. 'How come?'

'I just saved your arse. Another ten seconds an' Fat Lizzie would've been all over you like a bad rash. An' she's 'ad more than a few of those in her time, I can tell you. She likes to pass 'em on, too, if you know what I mean.' The girl winked suggestively.

'Lucky I had you watching over me, then,' Hawkwood said.

'Glad I could help, darlin'.' She placed a hand on his shoulder and leaned forward. In the well of her unlaced top, the dark valley between her breasts beckoned invitingly. 'My name's Sal.' Her gaze moved suggestively to Hawkwood's groin. 'Nice breeches.' Her eyes drifted back to his face. 'What brings you to the Dog? You lookin' for company?'

'Not tonight,' Hawkwood said.

At that moment a customer at the adjacent table rose unsteadily to his feet, fumbled at the flap of his breeches and cast an eye towards the back of the room and the doorway leading to the privy. He was barely out of his seat when the girl reached over, grasped the empty chair and pulled it towards her. Spotting the move out of the corner of his eye, the man turned to remonstrate. 'What the bleedin'–?' Then his eyes fell on the culprit and his red-veined cheeks paled.

'Don't mind, do you, Charlie?' the girl said, taking her seat. 'Only I noticed you weren't usin' it.' Her dark eyes glowed.

For a second the man looked as though he was about to speak. Indecision moved across his face. Then his shoulders sagged and he shook his head. 'Nah, that's all right, Sal,' he said hollowly. 'Best be goin', anyway.' Turning quickly to avoid the embarrassed looks of his companions, he left the table and teetered off across the sawdust-smeared floor.

The girl turned back to Hawkwood as if nothing had happened. 'Now, where were we? Oh, yeah, you said you weren't lookin' for company.' She arched an eyebrow. 'You sure? We could call

135

one of the other girls over. They've got rooms out the back. We could have some fun, the three of us. How's that sound? You up for it? I know I am.' She gave Hawkwood the eye once more. 'I'm always up for it.'

'Another time,' Hawkwood said. 'I'm waiting for someone.'

The girl placed her right forefinger between her lips, sucked on it suggestively and ran its moistened tip along Hawkwood's sleeve. 'Been waitin' a while, though, 'aven't you? You sure they're going to turn up?'

'He'd better,' Hawkwood said. 'There's money in it if he does.' He took a sip from his mug. 'Maybe you've seen him around? He said he'd be here. His name's Doyle, Edward Doyle.'

The girl's brow furrowed. 'Can't say as I know the name. What's 'e look like?'

Like death, Hawkwood thought, but didn't say so.

The girl listened to Hawkwood's description of what Doyle would have looked like if he'd had a pulse and all his teeth, and then shook her head. 'Sorry, sweet'eart. Still don't ring any bells. You sure 'e meant the Dog? There's the Dog and Dray over the other side of Long Lane. Maybe you've got the wrong place.'

'Bugger,' Hawkwood said. He clicked his tongue. 'Just my luck.'

'What sort of work was it, if you don't mind me askin'?'

'There's a man wants some hog carcasses delivered. Only a morning's lifting and carrying, but there's a shilling or two in it.' Hawkwood

136

frowned and added glumly, 'Looks like I'll have to find somebody else.'

'There's plenty in 'ere who'd be up for it.' The girl jerked her head towards the counting table.

Hawkwood followed the gesture. 'You're probably right. Maybe I'll try a couple of the other places first though, seeing as we're mates. What was that place you mentioned? The Dog and Dray, was it? If he doesn't turn up there, I might come back.'

'I'll look forward to that. Meantime, I can ask around, if you like. If I hear anything an' you come back, I'll pass it on. What's *your* name, by the way? You never said.'

Hawkwood took a sip of grog. 'Matthews.' He kept his face straight.

'What do they call you?'

'Jim.' Hawkwood took another swallow. The porter tasted as if it had been laced with fulminate. He tried not to grimace.

She smiled at him again, indicating that the attempt had not been a total success. 'You sure I can't tempt you, Jim Matthews? 'Cos you were definitely lookin' a bit lonely sittin' here on your own.'

'The answer's still no,' Hawkwood said.

The girl hesitated, then shrugged philosophically, pushed back the chair and stood up. 'Ah, well, can't blame a body for tryin'. Your loss, sweetheart.'

Blowing him a kiss, she headed towards the back of the room. Hawkwood watched her disappear beyond the veil of tobacco smoke and the tightly pressed bodies. He sensed she knew he was watching her by the exaggerated sway of her hips, though she did not turn back to check.

There was a definite easing of tension at the next table, he noticed. The stilted conversation became more animated. A couple of the men were giving him curious looks, presumably wondering why he wasn't following the girl out. Let them wonder, Hawkwood thought. He considered the girl's prospects. He recalled a story he'd been told about sharks, sea predators that had to keep moving and eating to stay alive. He thought about the girls plying for trade. Their lives seemed very like the shark's: every day spent in an endless trawl for prey. In that regard, each of them was as lost in hope as the men lining up at Hanratty's table.

Following their brief encounter, Hawkwood doubted the girl would be without company for long. She had the looks and she had the wit, and there were plenty of customers in attendance, so the queue for companionship wasn't about to shorten any time soon.

Hawkwood took a look around. A new batch of woebegone souls had begun to file past the pay-table. Another half an hour, he decided, and he'd call it a night. He caught the eye of a serving girl and held up his mug. He'd convinced himself that the grog wasn't too bad. In any case, once the first swallow was out of the way, it didn't really matter because he wouldn't be able to feel the inside of his mouth anyway.

7

Sawney was in the cellar, stacking bodies by the light of a lantern, when he heard the heavy tread on the stair.

'His 'Oliness 'as turned up, Rufus. Didn't know we was expectin' 'im.'

Sawney cursed savagely. The body he'd been trying to prop against the wall was wrapped in a filthy sheet, but the ends of the sheet had come loose and the grey-faced corpse, which was beginning a slow emergence from its state of rigor mortis, was proving to be a bit of a handful.

'Rufus?'

'I heard you, Maggsie. I'm not bleedin' deaf.'

Sawney tried again. This time, he managed to get the corpse's arm to stay inside the sheet. Lucky it was a female. A male would have been heavier and more difficult to manoeuvre.

'Come 'ere. 'Old this,' Sawney snapped. 'Bleedin' sow's all over the place.'

A hulking shape appeared over Sawney's shoulder. 'What do you want me to do?'

Sawney nodded towards the arm, which had flopped loose for the third time. 'Just keep the bloody thing tucked in while I wraps 'er up. And mind what you're doin'. I want to make sure we deliver 'er in one piece.'

'What do you think she'll fetch?'

Sawney reached for the corner of the sheet.

'Four maybe.' He clicked his tongue and looked around the room. 'Not a bad night's work.'

Abel Maggett grunted. 'Too right. Mind you, gettin' 'er over that bleedin' wall was a bitch. Damned near done my back in.' The big man pressed a meaty hand against the base of his spine and winced.

Sawney studied his companion with a jaundiced eye. He was by no means a small man himself, but Maggett towered over him by at least a foot and he was big with it. A slaughter-man by trade, Maggett was capable of hefting pig carcasses three at a time. The thought that the big man had put his back out lifting a woman's cadaver over a five-foot wall was laughable. That was Maggett for you: a real caution.

The knot in the sheet secured, Sawney stood back and admired his handiwork. All told, there were five bodies awaiting delivery: two grown males, a male child and two females. Definitely a good haul.

Sawney knew they'd have to move them soon, however. The wintry weather was a boon, the cellar was ice-cold. Even so, it wouldn't be long before the bodies would start to turn. Sawney was already having doubts about the child's corpse. He thought he'd detected some leakage when he'd wrapped the thing. The quicker they passed the bodies on, the better. Once decomposition started, prices would drop significantly. True, they could always chop the bodies into bits and sell the parts separately, but it was a messy business and he didn't want to go down that road except as a last resort.

He turned to Maggett. 'Where is he?'

'Upstairs.' The big man nodded towards the five sheet-entwined bodies. They reminded Maggett of caterpillar cocoons. 'When do you want to move 'em?'

'It'll have to be before sun-up. Maybe later tonight. Can't risk carrying them through the streets in broad daylight. We'll use the cart.'

Maggett grunted in acknowledgement. His massive chest strained against the material of his shirt and the buttons of his dark moleskin waistcoat.

Sawney lifted the lantern from its hook. 'Right, let's see what the bugger wants.' Taking a last look around the cellar, Sawney led the way up the stairs and entered the room with Maggett at his back. He frowned at the sole occupant, who was pacing the floor like a cat in a cage. 'I thought we 'ad an agreement. You weren't to come callin', 'less you was invited. I don't recall sendin' word that I wanted to see you.'

Verger Lucius Symes stopped pacing and blinked nervously. Lit by the candlelight, his face bore an unhealthy waxen sheen.

'Well?' Sawney rasped. 'I ain't got all bleedin' night. What is it? You after your cut, is that it? I told you it was on the usual terms. You'll get yours when we get ours, and that won't be until later. I'll get one of the Ragg boys to drop your share round in the morning.'

Sawney turned to Maggett, shook his head and blew out his cheeks. 'Christ, all that lifting's done my head in. An' I could murder a wet. I've got a throat as dry as a witch's cunny. Verger looks like he could do with a tot of somethin' as well.

141

Maggsie, you're forgettin' your manners. Get some mugs and open a bottle.'

Maggett frowned. 'We ain't got no mugs, Rufus. Ain't got no booze neither.'

'Bloody hell.' Sawney raised his eye to the ceiling. 'We're in a bleedin' pub, for Chris'sakes. Use your noggin.'

Maggett's wide brow furrowed at the change of tone.

As if to illustrate Sawney's point, a burst of gin-soaked laughter sounded from the other side of the wall, reminding them that the busy, smoke-filled taproom was only a few feet away.

Sawney sighed. 'Go and get some, and tell Hanratty to put it on the slate.'

For someone of his stature, Maggett could move remarkably quietly. Sawney watched him steal out of the room and shook his head again, half in amusement, half in weary exasperation. Maggett was a staunch companion with many excellent qualities, brawn, loyalty and obedience being chief among them. But there were times when he could make a fence post look intelligent.

As Maggett disappeared, there came the sound of a second person's footsteps and the swish of skirts from the passage outside. There followed a brief murmured exchange and then another, smaller figure appeared in the open doorway. The verger's eyes widened momentarily.

Moving into the room, the girl slipped an arm round Sawney's waist.

''Ello, darlin',' Sawney said. He turned and nodded towards the verger. 'Look who's come to visit.'

The girl stared at the verger. There was no welcome in her expression.

The verger stared back then his eyes moved to Sawney. 'You didn't have to do it.'

'Sorry, Verger – do what?' Sawney looked at the girl and raised his eyebrows as if to ask her if she knew what the verger was talking about. The girl shrugged.

'Kill him like that,' Symes said.

'Ah,' Sawney nodded sagely, running a tongue over yellowing teeth. 'You mean young Doyle.'

'Why?' The verger repeated, his voice dropping to a whisper.

Sawney put his head on one side. He looked like a stoat studying a rabbit. 'Because I could.'

The verger blinked.

'Well, what the 'ell did you think was going to happen to 'im?' Sawney rasped. 'You think I was just going to give 'im a tap, tell 'im he'd been a naughty boy and send 'im on his way?' Sawney shook his head. 'Couldn't have him 'arbourin' ideas above 'is station, could I? Should've remembered he was playin' with the big boys. He knew the rules and he broke 'em. In my book, that meant he 'ad to pay. Had to set an example for the rest of them, else there'd just be bleedin' chaos. Can't have that, might disrupt business. And right now business is good.' Sawney paused. 'And you should know,' he added pointedly. 'So don't come whining to me 'cause you don't like my methods.'

Releasing himself from the girl and taking a step forward, Sawney wagged his finger. 'You knew what you were getting into, just as much as

143

Doyle. You're a paid-up member, Verger, and it's us who pays *you* – handsomely, as I recall.'

The verger paled.

'Not to mention the perks,' Sawney continued. 'Like young Sal here, tootin' your flute whenever you drops by.'

The verger's gaze flickered to the girl. Her expression was just as dark as Sawney's and the verger's throat constricted. There was an unblinking intensity in those midnight-tinted eyes that seemed both feline and wild. As he stared at her, he knew, despite the threat in Sawney's tone, that it was the girl who was undoubtedly the more dangerous.

'What?' Sawney said mockingly. 'Don't tell me you want out. Jesus, that's it, ain't it? You're here to tell us you've had your fill. Well, sorry to disappoint you, but it don't work like that. You ain't out till I tell you you're out. This ain't a bleedin' – what do they call it? – Democracy. Besides, the season's only been up and running for a month. We've still got another five to go. The schools are open, terms have started and they'll be wantin' bodies. It's our job to supply them, as fresh as possible. That's what they pay us for.'

Sawney gazed at the verger, who was looking like a man who'd lost a guinea and found threepence. 'No, wait, you weren't actually thinkin' of *leavin'* of your own accord? You ain't that naïve, surely? When will you learn? We own you, Symes. We pay you, so we own you. You ever wondered what might happen if the vicar and the parishioners got to know about your little hobbies? I know you're not strictly what they call a man of

144

the cloth, but you're close enough. What do you think they'd say if, durin' next Sunday's service, young Sal here interrupts the sermon to tell everyone that she sucks your cock of an evening in a back room of the Black Dog pub? You really want to go down that road? No, I didn't think so. And I'll tell you this, so there's no misunder-standin': dropping the word to the vicar and 'is parishioners will be the *best* thing we do to you.' Sawney leaned in close so that his face was inches away from the verger's. His voice dripped quiet menace. 'You get my drift?'

A rattle of tin mugs and the clink of glass from the doorway interrupted the moment.

'I got us a bottle, Rufus,' Maggett announced. 'On the slate, like you said.' The big man appeared oblivious to the tension in the room.

Sawney straightened. 'Did you now, Maggsie? Well done. Just what the doctor ordered. How about you, Verger, a drop of grog to wet your whistle?'

The verger remained silent. Sawney sighed theatrically. 'Jesus, don't tell me there's more?'

'You crucified him.' The verger's voice trembled.

Sawney took the bottle from Maggett's hand and poured three fingers of gin into one of the mugs. He took a sip and smirked. 'Just my little joke.' He raised the mug to his lips once more and paused. 'No, 'ang on, in fact it was Sal's idea.' He turned to the girl. 'That's right, ain't it?'

The girl did not reply. Turning her head in the verger's direction, she stretched out her arms and raised them to shoulder height.

'Bloody rotten way to spend Easter,' she said,

then giggled.

The verger stared at her in horror.

'I tell you, Verger, she's a wag,' Sawney said. 'Has me in stitches, so she does, seein' as it's closer to Christmas than Easter.' Sawney held out the bottle. 'Here you go, Sal, get your tongue round that. You sure you don't want a snort, Verger? You're looking a bit peaky.'

'You took out his teeth and tongue.'

'Too right,' Sawney said. 'There's good money in teeth, especially sound teeth, and young Doyle's teeth were sounder than most. There's plenty of toffs out there who'll pay good money for a new set of canines. It's all the rage. Did I ever tell you about that time I broke into the vault of that meetin' house in Shoreditch? Can't recall how many stiffs they 'ad down there, but I do know it took me three hours to get the teeth out of 'em. Earned myself sixty quid, though. It beats shovellin' shit. An' I'll tell you another thing: there's not a tooth-puller in London that ain't been supplied with teeth dug up from an 'ospital field.' Sawney waited for the information to sink in before adding, 'An' I'll guarantee there's more than one politician sportin' teeth taken from some poor bastard lying dead on a Spanish battle-field. I should bleedin' know.'

'The police said the tongue was cut out as a warning.'

'Did they now? Well, there's truth in that, I'll not deny it. And I'll wager it'll do the trick, too. We're the top dogs here, not Naples and his bleedin' Borough Boys. Us. The sooner they start takin' us seriously, the better. There's a good living to be made for all of us, you included, Verger. So long as nobody rocks the boat...' Sawney paused. 'You said it was the police who told you it was a warning?'

The verger nodded. 'I had to raise the alarm. It would have seemed odd if I hadn't.'

'You did your duty, Verger. Wouldn't expect anything else from a fine, upstandin' citizen like yourself. Don't worry about it. Bloody Charleys couldn't find water if it was rainin'.'

'The man they sent wasn't a Charley. He was some sort of special constable.'

Sawney shrugged, unconcerned. 'Amounts to the same thing. They ain't much better.'

'This one might be,' Symes said. 'He's next door.'

It was often the little things in life that gave the most satisfaction and, for the verger, having borne the brunt of Sawney's scorn for the last few minutes, watching the look of incredulity steal over the latter's face was as pleasurable as hearing a peal of church bells on a Sunday morning.

'He's here?' A nerve quivered in Sawney's cheek. 'Christ, you led him here? He *followed* you?'

The verger swallowed. The pleasure of the moment withered, to be replaced by a creeping dread.

'I didn't lead him anywhere,' Symes said defensively. 'He was here already.'

Sawney frowned. 'Then how...?'

'One of the gravediggers told him they thought they'd seen Doyle drinking in one of the local pubs. He's probably visiting them all, looking for information.'

'Shite!' Sawney swore. 'Did he see you?'

Symes reddened. His new-found boldness was disintegrating by the second. He took an involuntary step backwards. 'I don't think so.' The verger hesitated, and then nodded towards the girl. 'He was talking to her.'

The room went very quiet.

Sawney pivoted slowly. His look was murderous.

'He was *what?*'

'That's what I was coming to tell you,' Sal said quickly. She turned to the verger. 'What was his name?'

'I can't ... no, wait, it was Hawkwood, Officer Hawkwood.'

'*Officer?*' Sawney repeated, frowning.

Sal bit her lip. 'He told me his name was Matthews. Said he was a pal of Doyle's and he was looking for him 'cos there was chance of work for the two of them.' Sal paused. 'Didn't look like a bloody constable. Bastard!'

'He still here?' Sawney asked.

Sal shrugged. 'Don't know. I left him to come to you.'

'What do we do?' Maggett asked. There was a fresh light in the big man's eyes, promoting him instantly from low-witted bruiser to competent lieutenant awaiting orders.

'If he's still here, I want a look at him,' Sawney said. He put down his mug and moved to the wall. Maggett and Sal followed. Symes brought up the rear.

There were several candle brackets set in the walls, all at eye level. Sawney moved to the middle one. Reaching up, he extinguished the candle flame with his finger and thumb, then tilted the bracket to one side. He stepped back, allowing access to the small two-inch aperture left in the plaster, and nodded at the verger. 'Take a look. If he's there, you point the bugger out. You got that?'

Symes stepped up and placed his eye to the hole.

'Well?' Sawney pressed.

Symes couldn't see a thing at first. So poorly was the taproom lit that it took several seconds for his eye to focus and his brain to register what he was seeing. He was aware that the room was still crowded but in the gloomy interior, with tobacco smoke hanging over the counter like a bank of sea fog, it was hard to make out faces. Gradually, however, his eye grew accustomed to the light and individual features began to take shape.

'Chris'sakes!' Sawney breathed. 'How long's it bleedin' take?'

The verger bit his tongue and continued to search the room.

Suddenly he stiffened. He backed away from the wall. 'He's in the corner booth, to the right: the tall one, with the coat and the long hair. He's wearing military breeches, a yellow stripe down the seam.'

Beside him, Sawney heard Sal draw in her breath.

'You're sure it's him?' Sawney said.

Symes nodded. 'He's dressed rough, but yes, it's the same man. I'm certain of it.'

Sawney pushed the verger aside and took a look

149

for himself. When he stood back, his mouth was set in a grim line.

'What?' Maggett said.

'Sal was right. He don't look like a constable. My guess is it's because he ain't. Verger said he called himself Officer Hawkwood. I'm bettin' he's a bleedin' Runner.'

'Bloody hell!' Maggett said, alarm in his voice. 'What's he doin'?'

'He ain't doing anything. Just sittin' there, nursin' a wet.' Sawney stepped away from the wall, his face thoughtful.

'Let me see.' The girl moved to the wall. She had to stand on tiptoe to reach the eye-hole. There was a pause and then she said, 'Yeah, that's him. A few of the girls asked him if he wanted some company before me, but he turned us all down. He's not bad lookin' – for a Runner.'

She stepped away and found Sawney giving her a hard stare. His eyes narrowed. 'Don't you even think about it. You do, I'll slit your gizzard.'

Seeing the look on Sawney's face, the girl's expression faltered. 'I was only jokin', Rufus.'

'I wasn't,' Sawney said softly. 'What did you tell him?'

'Nothing. Said I'd never heard of Doyle. I told him he'd probably got the wrong pub. He should try the Dog and Dray.'

Symes had registered the flash of fear in the girl's eyes. A chill moved through him. There was an awkward silence. 'What should we do?' he asked.

Sawney's gaze moved from the girl to the verger.

'Rufus?' Maggett said. He was over by the wall, taking a look at the individual who was causing all the fuss.

'Hold on,' Sawney said, 'I'm thinkin'.' He took a drink, swilled the grog around his tongue and swallowed. He poured out a fresh mug, then looked at the verger. 'You're positive he didn't see you?'

The verger shook his head firmly, more confident now. 'I'm sure.'

Too busy gawpin' at Sal's tits, Maggett thought to himself. *And who could blame him?*

Sawney mulled over the verger's reply. After a few seconds he nodded. 'Then I don't reckon we've got anything to worry about. There's no one here's going to talk. They know what's good for them. The bastard'll be old news in a week. I'd say we're in the clear.'

Sawney straightened. 'Right, worth a drink, I reckon.' He looked at Symes. 'How about it, Verger? Not much point us fallin' out, not when we've more work lined up. What's done is done. Tell you what, we'll get some more booze in. Good stuff, not this rotgut. Come on, Maggsie, let's see if we can't find ourselves a couple of those bottles Hanratty keeps under the counter for the special customers.'

Maggett frowned. He was wondering what bottles. He was also wondering which special customers Sawney was talking about.

Sawney rolled his eyes at his lieutenant's expression then turned to Symes. 'Be best if you hung around, anyway, Verger, at least until that bastard Runner has slung 'is hook. Go on, have a

151

seat, take the weight off. Sal here'll look after you. How'd that be? Sal, entertain the man. That's an order.' Sawney winked. 'We'll be back in ten minutes. Give you two a bit of privacy. Come on, Maggsie.' Sawney ushered the still-frowning Maggett towards the door. He turned. 'An' you be gentle with him, Sal, y'hear?'

Sal grinned and poked her tongue out. 'Don't you worry. I'm always gentle with Lucius.' She turned to the verger and chuckled. 'Ain't that right, sweet'eart? Go on, sit yourself down.' She nodded towards the chair. 'Make yourself comfortable.'

Sawney and Maggett left the room. Symes watched them, a worried expression on his face.

'Don't worry about them,' Sal whispered, as the footsteps retreated. 'It's just you and me. We've got the place to ourselves.'

The verger hesitated. Sal tugged gently on his sleeve. 'You know you want to.' She dropped her gaze. 'I can tell.'

The verger coloured, but he did not resist when she led him to the wing-backed chair and pressed him down into the seat. She leaned over him, placed both hands on the arms of the chair, and gazed at him from beneath her dark lashes. 'Will it be the usual, then, sir?' she asked teasingly.

Symes closed his eyes, cursing himself for his weakness. He kept them shut as Sal knelt down and began to undo his breeches. When she had done so, she reached for him. Symes caught his breath as he felt the touch of her palm.

Sal grinned as she took hold. 'Toot-toot,' she said softly, as she lowered her head.

The verger's eyes were still clamped shut when Sawney re-entered the room. Symes was breathing heavily. His left hand was on the arm of the chair. His right hand was resting on Sal's shoulder. Sal's head was bobbing up and down in his lap. Neither of them seemed aware that Sawney had returned. A yellow-toothed grin creased Sawney's face as he studied the verger's rapt expression. Sal increased her rhythm. The verger's breathing grew ragged. Without altering her position, Sal looked up, caught Sawney's eye, and winked. Sawney felt himself stiffen. He reached down and adjusted himself through his breeches.

The verger was close to the point of no return. He emitted a low moan as Sal increased the pressure of her lips. She was still looking at Sawney and continued to gaze up at him as he leaned over the back of the chair. Suddenly the verger grunted. At the moment of release Sawney, with exquisite timing, looped the cord round the verger's throat and pulled tight. Caught in that moment of confusion between pleasure and pain, the verger shuddered. As the realization of what was happening struck him, his eyes shot open and he clawed at the cord encircling his throat. Legs kicking, he flailed from side to side in a vain attempt to free himself. Scrambling away from the verger's thrashing limbs, Sal rose and spat the contents of her mouth into the nearest mug. Sawney's forearms bulged. Gradually, the verger's struggles grew weaker, then stopped. Sawney waited for half a dozen seconds before releasing the cord. A strong faecal smell filled the room. He gazed down at the verger's inert body with a look of disgust. 'Bloody sod shat himself.'

Sal rubbed a hand across her lips and grimaced. 'Bleedin' took you long enough.'

'The bugger was spryer than 'e looked.' Sawney tossed the cord aside, reached for the bottle and picked up a mug. He was intrigued to discover his cock was still semi-hard.

'I wouldn't use that one,' Sal said.

Sawney looked into the mug and wrinkled his nose. He put the mug down, raised the bottle to his lips, took a swig, then handed it to Sal. 'Clean your mouth out, girl.'

She was swilling the grog around her gums when Maggett came back in, looking confused. Having accompanied Sawney outside, and then been told to stay put for five minutes, he'd been kicking his heels on the landing, wondering what the hell Sawney was playing at. Now he knew. The big man glanced down at the verger's corpse. His face betrayed no emotion. If Sawney had thought it necessary to kill the verger, then it would take a braver man than Maggett to question the decision. He sniffed. 'Aw, Jesus!'

Sal poured some grog into a mug and passed it to Maggett. 'There you go, Maggsie. This'll take your mind off the smell.'

As Maggett took the mug and raised it to his mouth, Sal glanced at Sawney and stifled a grin.

Sawney's eyes flicked to the mug and, as Maggett swallowed, he let go a snort of laughter.

Maggett lowered the mug and frowned. 'What's the joke?'

'Not a thing, Maggsie.' Sawney smiled benignly at his lieutenant. 'Not a bleedin' thing.'

Maggett drained the mug and nodded towards the chair. He missed Sal turning her head away as the giggles took hold. 'What'll we do with his 'Oliness? You want to hang on to him? Or should we feed 'im to Reilly's hogs?'

Behind him, Sal's shoulders were shaking.

Sawney clamped his mouth shut and shook his head. He tried not to look at Sal. He could feel himself starting to go.

Reilly was a slaughterman with a yard off Hosier Lane. He'd dispose of anything for a price; he wasn't particular. Neither were his hogs. He kept three of them in a pen in his yard; huge, vicious brutes, with a reputation for devouring whatever was put in front of them. The word was that Reilly kept them hungry on purpose, starving them periodically in case their services might be required. Keeping them hungry made them less likely to question their menu. Sometimes Reilly let people watch – for a fee, of course; always the businessman.

'We'll stow 'im with the others for the time being,' Sawney said, managing to control himself. 'I'll ask around. One of the schools might like him. Don't see why we should bring that bogtrotter into it when we can do it ourselves an' make money from it.'

'You want me to take 'im downstairs, Rufus?' Maggett asked, though he didn't look overjoyed at the prospect. The smell was getting worse with each passing minute.

Sawney nodded. 'We can swab 'im down later.'

'What about the bastard outside?' Sal asked. She had recovered from her giggling fit. Her face

155

was instantly serious.

'I'll take a look,' Sawney said, and moved to the wall.

Attaching his right eye to the peephole, Sawney surveyed the taproom. The Runner, if that's what he was, was still at his table, but as Sawney watched he pushed his chair back and rose to his feet. Suddenly, he paused and turned. For a moment, it seemed as though he was staring directly into Sawney's eyes. Sawney's breath caught in his throat. He knew there was no way he could be seen, but it had been a heart-stopping moment, nonetheless.

Sawney let go his breath as the tall, unsmiling man strode off through the tables, heading for the door to the street. He followed the black-coated figure's progress, noting how calmly and easily the man moved through the crowded taproom. As he disappeared, Sawney stepped away from the wall and repositioned the light bracket.

'He's on his way.' Sawney relit the candle and looked down at the body in the chair. 'Stupid sod, thinkin' I'd let the likes of him tell me what I should do!'

Sal and Maggett said nothing. When Sawney was off on one of his rants, it didn't pay to interrupt.

But it seemed that was all Sawney had to say, on the subject of insubordination, at any rate. He turned to Maggett. 'You had that word with Hanratty, right?'

Maggett nodded. 'All done.'

Sawney nodded. 'We'd best get busy then. I'll go and get the cart. You take care of that–' Sawney

156

nodded towards the chair. 'Check 'is pockets first. You never know, he might 'ave some spare cash. We can use it to give 'im a send-off. Let the bugger pay for 'is own bloody wake.'

A chill rain was falling as Hawkwood left the Dog. There were no street lamps. The insipid candle glow seeping from the pub's small, square, smoke-blackened windows cast a leathery sheen across the saturated cobbles. Further down the street faint pinpricks of light the size of fireflies were all that could be seen through chinks in the rough wooden shutters of the adjacent tenements. The rest of the alley was as dark as a catacomb.

The heavy drizzle had driven most people indoors, though there were still a few hardy souls around. Through the murk he could make out vague, waterlogged shapes darting under the overhanging eaves in an attempt to stay dry. Heads bowed, their cast-down faces were little more than pale blurs in the shadows.

Hawkwood turned up the collar of his coat. The rain, cold and hard against his face, matched his mood.

A series of ear-splitting feline howls pierced the night. The din was followed by the sound of an object being thrown and a high-pitched shriek that ebbed away into an uneasy silence. The rain continued to fall.

A sickly smell was drifting along the alleyway. The city was full of such odours, but Hawkwood recognized the stench. It was the Fleet. After two nights of heavy rain, the river had burst its banks. Not that anyone referred to the Fleet as a river.

157

Most people called it the Ditch. Though even that was a euphemism for a trough of filth that was no more than an open sewer. The Fleet didn't flow so much as ooze. That was if it bothered to move at all. It was said the rats didn't need to swim across the Fleet, they sauntered.

Some stretches ran below ground, but where the Fleet saw the light of day, such as the section that ran behind Field Lane, it was used as a dumping ground for every type of effluent matter, solid and liquid, that humans and animals could excrete, as well as discarded waste from the nearby meat markets. The smell hung over the confined streets and alleyways like a blanket. On some days, depending on the weather, the stink would carry for miles. Even for a city renowned for its foul odours, the Fleet was in a class of its own.

The smell did at least give Hawkwood his bearings. He was skirting the southern boundary of the district known as Jack Ketch's Warren, in memory of the city's former hangman. Most locals referred to it simply as the Warren. A labyrinthine web of narrow lanes and passages, the slum was aptly named.

Hawkwood hunched into his coat and tried to ignore the water dribbling uncomfortably down the inside of his collar. Holborn Bridge lay around the next corner. Once there, he would be back on the main thoroughfare and out of the midden. He looked up. A small uneven gap had appeared in the clouds. Framed in the opening, a round moon hung like a pearl-grey teardrop. Caught by the ghostly radiance, rooftops and chimney pots rose in stark silhouettes against the night sky. The rain pricked like tiny arrows against his skin while above him overspill from the gutters ran down the slatted walls of the tenement houses in bright ribbons of quicksilver.

The sound of a heavy tread to his right drew his attention; a boot heel striking the cobbles, someone else hurrying to escape the wet. Hawkwood was aware of an indistinct shape moving at the edge of his vision; a vague shadow tucking itself into the side of the alleyway, blurred behind the drifting curtain of rain.

Then, as the slit in the clouds widened, he saw a dark form detach itself from the shelter of a low archway. He caught, too, the dull gleam of metal as moonlight glanced off an object in the figure's hand: some sort of hooked implement, held low and partially concealed.

He sensed rather than saw the second shadow materialize from the entrance to a dark passageway to his left, close to the end of the bridge's low wooden railing, and knew immediately that this was more than two bedraggled pedestrians seeking shelter from the inclement weather. His suspicions were confirmed when he saw that the second man was also armed with a broad, oblong blade, some kind of cleaver.

Hawkwood was already turning, his left hand pulling aside the hem of his coat, allowing his right hand access to the ebony tipstaff. He pulled the baton free.

It was hard to make out specific features in the shadows. Both men wore cloth caps, pulled low, and short jackets, collars turned up, with neckerchiefs round the lower halves of their faces. The one to Hawkwood's right was the closer of the two. Hawkwood had an impression of muscle and agility. It occurred to him that he should identify himself as a police officer, but in the darkness and the downpour and with the hook scything towards him, his first thought was purely of self-preservation.

Hawkwood turned aside, his right hand slamming the tipstaff against the side of the attacker's wrist. The crack of ebony on bone seemed unnaturally loud even with the noise of the rain coming down. It was accompanied by a sharp exclamation of pain. He swung the baton again, a reverse strike against the attacker's elbow, his full weight in the blow. There was another yell, followed by a ringing clatter as the metal hook struck the cobblestones and skidded across the alley floor. Without pause, Hawkwood pivoted on his left heel, his open coat swirling around him. Keeping his arm rigid, he drove the side of the tipstaff up against the base of his attacker's nose. He felt the cartilage give way as the strike followed through, crushing the nasal bones, driving the splinters up and into the brain. It had been meant as a killing blow and the effect was devastating. It was as if the attacker had run into a brick wall. He simply stopped all forward momentum, fell to his knees and collapsed face down on to the cobbles.

Without pausing even to draw breath, Hawkwood spun. The second man had come closer but there was a noticeable hesitation in his step. Clearly, the speed of Hawkwood's retaliation and the brutal force of his counter-attack had given this one pause for thought. He stared down at the figure sprawled motionless on the cobblestones.

'Don't be a fool,' Hawkwood warned. 'I'm a police officer.'

The attacker's head lifted. Above the scarf, his eyes widened.

'Not what you expected, was it, cully?' Hawkwood said. Without diverting his gaze from the masked figure, Hawkwood tossed the tipstaff into his left hand. The attacker's eyes followed the flight of the baton. Then his attention flicked back to Hawkwood. Rain dripped from the peak of his cap and ran down the blade held low in his fist. The moonlight reflected the doubt in his eyes.

'Your choice, cully,' Hawkwood said calmly, and waited.

And then he saw the subtle shift in stance, the transference of weight from one foot to the other, and with it the unmistakable tightening across the knuckles of the hand that gripped the cleaver. He saw the white crescents in the attacker's eyes shrivel and darken, and thought wearily, *Oh, Christ.*

But the attack, when it came, was clumsy. The new man was not as light on his feet as his companion and not as limber and in order to deliver a blow he first had to draw back the cleaver.

In that second of indecision, Hawkwood, unlike his opponent, did not hesitate. He feinted the baton towards the hand holding the blade. Instinctively the attacker lifted his arm to ward off the threat, realizing his mistake as soon as he had done so. Hawkwood saw his opening and launched his boot towards the exposed belly. His

161

kick drove the air from the attacker's lungs, slamming the man backwards.

In the drenching darkness, Hawkwood's attacker had failed to see how close he was to the waist-high wooden fence at the edge of the bridge. Had it not been for the rain it was possible he might have recovered his footing, but in places the uneven cobblestones had become as slippery as winter ice.

Almost lifted off his feet by the force of Hawkwood's kick, the attacker staggered back against the wooden slats, heels scrabbling for traction. Arms flailing, he made a desperate attempt to stay upright. Gravity, however, had the upper hand. The rotten staves splintered under his weight and the blade wielder toppled over the side of the bridge, the cry of terror rising from his throat as he tumbled into the void.

Hawkwood approached the shattered railing. Returning the tipstaff to the pocket of his coat, he peered cautiously over the edge. The smell that rose to meet him was foul beyond belief. He drew back sharply, fighting the urge to retch. Forcing himself to take a deep breath – a difficult feat given that the appalling stench seemed to be devouring the air around him – he peered once more into the abyss. Even in the shadows cast by the surrounding hovels, he could tell that the water in the Ditch, swollen by the rain, had risen considerably. It was only a few feet below the curved underside of the bridge and was almost solid with filth. It was like looking down into a trough of black treacle. He could hear the rain striking the surface. It sounded like musket balls tearing into flesh.

162

There was no sign of his attacker. A bundle of what looked like matted fur close to the opposite bank drew his attention; the carcass of some long-dead animal, a dog, he guessed. Within the grey tangle he could make out a pale curve of bone, part of a ribcage. He caught a glimpse of a small, sleek black pelt scampering along a piece of driftwood, followed by the ripple of a long hairless tail, but it was gone in an instant.

He heard it then, a faint snuffling grunt, the sort a pig might make grubbing for roots. He realized it was coming from directly below him, close in to the bridge's brick supports. Mindful of the precarious state of the rail and trying not to inhale too deeply, he leaned over and searched for the source of the sound.

He spotted movement down in the filth; a pale, spider-like shape clawing desperately for purchase against the worn brickwork. It took Hawkwood a second to realize he was looking at a human hand and that the area of shadow surrounding it was the partially submerged body of his attacker.

As Hawkwood watched, the attacker made another vain grab for freedom. The oily black crust broke apart, releasing the man's upper arm, enabling him to turn his head. But the release was temporary. His neckerchief had become dislodged, but the attacker's face was unrecognizable beneath the mask of shit and mud. Only his eyes, white and wide with fear, were visible. His mouth was open but no sound emerged. Then, as quickly as it had relaxed its hold, the sticky effluence began to drag him under. In the blink of an eye he was gone, drawn into the black maw beneath the bridge as if the ground had opened and swallowed him whole.

Hawkwood straightened. He turned and walked over to where the first attacker was lying on the ground. Heedless of the wet, he gazed down at the dead man without sympathy. He looked around. There were no signs of life; no flicker of candlelight to indicate a curtain had been pulled aside, no cries of alarm, no running footsteps that might have suggested witnesses running to summon help. Nothing moved other than the rain, which continued its relentless fusillade against windowpane and tile. Ignoring the widening puddles, Hawkwood knelt and turned the body over. The lifeless eyes were dull and staring. The thin scarf that had concealed the attacker's lower features had slipped. It was soaked with rain and stained black with blood. The face was not one that Hawkwood recognized. He switched his attention to the dead man's clothing, moving through the pockets. No help there either; they were empty. He rose to his feet, his eyes quartering the cobblestones. His gaze caught the gleam of steel. He walked over to the wall and picked up the hook, turning it in his hands, pondering its significance.

It was weighty and there was a simple beauty in its smooth curves. The handle ended in a T-shape, allowing the holder to grip the bar of the T in his palm so that the shaft of the hook emerged from the gap between his middle fingers. It was a remarkably effective tool as well as a fearsome weapon, and one he'd seen many times in the markets and slaughter yards of Smithfield, used by butchers and meat porters to drag animal car-

164

casses on and off cutting slabs.

Hawkwood considered the implications. That there was a connection between his attackers and his visit to the Dog seemed glaringly obvious.

It was possible, he supposed, that they'd been no more than a couple of opportunists who'd spotted him in the taproom, seen him pay for his drink rather than receive it on credit, viewed him as an easy mark and, acting on impulse, followed him into the alley.

An alternative explanation was that they'd been villains he'd come up against before; men out for revenge. But that seemed doubtful, given that he hadn't recognized either of them, certainly not the one lying at his feet. The one that had fallen prey to the Fleet's uncharitable grip, he couldn't be sure of, but he guessed it unlikely they'd met previously, a theory more or less confirmed by the shock in the man's eyes when Hawkwood had identified himself as a police officer.

He looked down at the hook and remembered the cleaver. The choice of weapons was intriguing. They were tools of the meat trade. Poke a stick down a rat hole, he thought, and you were never sure what was going to come crawling out. Maybe his enquiries about Doyle had touched a raw nerve. He looked again at the body.

In the normal course of events, at odds of two to one and given the weapons they had brandished, it would have been their victim lying face down on the cobbles. Unluckily for them, they hadn't expected to be confronted by a former officer in the Rifles who'd spent the last six months of his army career living rough in the Spanish moun-

165

tains slaughtering Frenchmen. They'd paid for their mistake with their lives. Not that Hawkwood intended to lose any sleep over it. His attackers had dealt the hand. Unhappily for them, it had been Hawkwood holding the trump cards.

He closed his eyes. There were too many damned ifs and buts floating around in the broth.

And it had been a long day – two grisly murders, one suicide and a visit to a madhouse; not exactly commonplace, even by a Bow Street officer's standards. It was late, he was soaked through and bone-tired. A good night's sleep wouldn't come amiss. That way he'd be refreshed and ready to resume the investigation in the morning.

His decision made, Hawkwood tossed the hook over the rail into the Ditch and continued on his way; a dark figure disappearing into a darker night.

8

Sawney was at his usual booth, counting the night's earnings. A jug of porter and a wooden platter of bread and cheese stood by his elbow, but they remained untouched while he did his sums. His sallow face was drawn in concentration. His lips moved in soundless calculation.

It was a little after eight o'clock and the Dog was almost empty, save for a trio of brawny, blood-stained Smithfield porters who'd stopped in for breakfast, while over by the hearth a couple of exhausted whores, dresses askew, were sleeping off the exertions of the night before. A fire had been newly lit and the taproom stank of smoke and grease, sawdust, stale sweat and beer.

They'd offloaded three of the five corpses from the cellar, the two males and the boy. The males had gone to Guy's. The boy's cadaver had been delivered to a private anatomy school over on Little Windmill Street. They'd received a fair price for the two males – nine guineas for the pair – but it had been the child's corpse that had seen the best return. Smalls – children – sold according to height; six shillings for the first foot and ninepence an inch for the rest. The boy had been tall for his age, added to which he'd suffered from a deformed foot. Anatomists paid extra for abnormalities, so Sawney had made eight guineas from the child alone. He'd even found a buyer for the teeth he'd extracted from that bugger, Doyle. A dentist over on Dean Street had taken them off his hands. There had been some minor haggling, but the final price had been acceptable to both parties.

All things considered, they'd turned a tidy profit.

Sawney's thoughts turned to the female cadavers. They had been promised to an anatomist over on Chapel Street, but Sawney had decided to hold off in the hope of driving the price up further. It was a pity they hadn't been pregnant.

Pregnant females were at a premium. The only legitimate source for bodies was still the gallows, but the law drew the line at hanging pregnant women. As a result, condemned female prisoners would often try to get themselves knocked up by fellow inmates in the hope of cheating the hangman.

Sawney reckoned he had maybe another twenty-four hours before the smell down in the cellar got too strong to bear. The Dog reeked bad enough as it was but rotting corpses had an aroma that was unmistakable. He was reminded of St Clement Dane's church, where the crypt had held so many rotting bodies the congregation couldn't hear the hymns for the buzzing of the flies and people had fainted in the aisles from the smell.

On second thoughts, Sawney decided, maybe he'd take the Chapel Street offer after all, move them that night, cash value notwithstanding. Get them out of the way. Of course, if he did hang on and the bodies went off in the meantime, they could always render them down. There was more than one way of skinning a cat. Ha ha.

Sensing a brooding figure behind his shoulder, he looked up. Taking this as an invitation, Hanratty slid on to the opposite bench, a concerned look on his rough-hewn face.

Sawney frowned. 'What?'

'They've found Jem Tate's body. It was stuffed down an alley off Thieving Lane. He was missing his boots, shoes and breeches.'

Sawney was silent. The evening's takings were temporarily forgotten.

'How'd he die?'

'His face was stove in. Wrist was broke, too.'

Sawney absorbed the information. 'What about Murphy?'

Hanratty shook his head. 'Ain't no sign of 'im.'

Sawney gnawed the inside of his cheek.

Hanratty leaned close. Shadows played across the crown of his head. His face was seamed and coarse, his jowls were shaded with stubble. 'Chris'sake, Rufus, I told you it was a mistake sending them after a Runner. I bloody *told* you!'

Sawney stopped chewing. His eyes hardened. 'And I recall you tellin' me that Tate and Murphy were good men.'

Hanratty sat back. 'So they were.'

'Not bleedin' good enough, though,' Sawney grated. 'Were they?'

Hanratty coloured. 'Maybe Murphy got him.'

'Maybe,' Sawney said. 'So why hasn't he reported back?'

It was Hanratty's turn to chew his lip. 'P'raps 'e's hurt, gone to ground somewhere.'

'All right, so if they took care of 'im, where's the bastard's corpse?'

'I told 'em to toss 'im into the Ditch. The rats'd pick his bones clean in a couple of days. His own mother wouldn't recognize him. Maybe they got 'im.'

'Maybe,' Sawney said cautiously.

Dumping a body in the Fleet was a tried-and-tested and very efficient means of disposal. If you didn't want to risk doing it in the open, there were plenty of access points throughout the Warren; hidden trapdoors and flagstones that could be lifted to allow unwanted items to be consigned into the black mire. The Fleet was London's equivalent to the River Styx, except there was no Charon to ferry the shades of the dead to the afterlife, just the rats.

'What'll we do?' Hanratty fixed Sawney with an anxious gaze.

Sawney thought about it. 'Nothing.'

Hanratty blinked. A nerve flickered at his throat. It looked as though a worm had burrowed under his flesh and was trying to escape through his skin.

'Tate's dead,' Sawney said. 'And Murphy's absent without leave. Neither of 'em is talkin'. Far as you an' me is concerned, if any other Charleys come callin', we know nothing. None of my lot'll talk. Tate and Murphy were working for themselves. There's nothing to link 'em to us.'

'Their names are in my ledger,' Hanratty said.

'So cross 'em *off*.' Sawney's voice was a snarl. 'They always were troublemakers, weren't they? The Dog's a legitimate labour exchange, ain't it?

No room for either of 'em in an honest, up-standin' establishment.'

Hanratty thought about it, eyes narrowed. Sawney waited. He could have sworn he heard wheels turning. Finally the publican nodded. 'That might do it.'

'Course it will,' Sawney said. 'We got a good arrangement here, you an' me. I ain't about to see it swept downriver by some nosey lawman.'

'What about Tate and Murphy?'

'What about 'em? We know Tate's no threat, not now he's been stripped bare.'

Sawney spoke the truth. Unless there had been witnesses who could prove otherwise, as far as anyone else was concerned, Tate could have been the victim of an unexpected assault himself. There'd been any number of luckless souls who'd been murdered for their boots, shirt and breeches on the banks of the Fleet. Could be, someone had seen Tate coming out of the Dog on payday and thought he'd still have money in his pocket.

'And Murphy?'

'If the useless bugger does show 'is face, your boys can deal with him. In fact, it might be worth our while them makin' a few enquiries to see if he 'as turned up somewhere – discreetly like.'

Hanratty nodded, his mind clearly more at ease. 'Aye, they can do that.'

'And while they're at it, see what they can find out about this bleedin' Runner, just in case he's still around. What did Symes say he was called? Hawkwood, was it?'

'Consider it done.'

'Good. In that case, I'll get back to my

'counting,' Sawney said. He separated out a pile of coin and passed it across the beer-stained table. 'This week's storage fee.'

Hanratty scooped the money into his palm and closed his fist. His fingers were stubby and the skin over his knuckles was crisscrossed with scars. His nails were ingrained with dirt and bitten to the quick.

Sawney looked up. 'Chances are, Tate and Murphy did their job, otherwise there'd be a mob of Charleys outside, 'ammering on the door. There ain't, so it looks like we're still in business, right?'

'Right.' Hanratty pocketed his cut and nodded.

Sawney watched him go. Perhaps it had been a mistake, going after the Runner. There again, Sawney reminded himself, he had a livelihood to protect. He had responsibilities – and they didn't come cheap. Maggett and the Ragg brothers didn't work for him out of the goodness of their hearts.

And there was Sal, of course. Had to keep her happy. Though Sawney had had the feeling for some time that Sal wasn't in it for the money. She was in it for the excitement, the thrill. At times it was almost as if she craved it.

Sawney recalled more than one occasion when, after a night's successful retrieval, Sal's excitement had manifested itself in a way that had left both of them bathed in sweat and hotter than a farrier's furnace. When Sal got excited, she got inventive; and Sawney had to admit that an inventive Sal was almost as enjoyable as cash in hand. She had stamina, too; there had been times when Sawney had found himself hard pressed to keep up with her.

Sawney accepted that Sal went with other men. In fact, he found her independent streak a relief after some of his other liaisons. Sal needed sex like some people needed alcohol. She thrived on it. She was a whore; it was her nature. Sal would laugh and say that she needed the exercise. Besides, she said, it helped keep her supple, and she knew that Sawney liked her supple. Supple like an eel.

But Sawney drew the line at police officers. Sal had told him she'd been joking when she'd hinted that she fancied the Runner, but for a second there he hadn't been so sure. There had been a light in her eye that suggested she might have been half serious. Sawney's threat, on the other hand, had been real. He'd rather she entertained Maggett than a bloody Runner. Having seen the way Maggett looked at her sometimes when he thought no one was watching, Sawney wondered if the two of them hadn't been at it behind his back anyway. He wouldn't have put it past them.

They'd met a year or so back, when Sawney had picked her up in Covent Garden one night. He'd just sold a brace of cadavers to an anatomist over on Webb Street, south of the river, and was feeling flush and looking for company; right place at the right time, as far as he was concerned. Sal had been on the game for a while by then, working out of a three-storey brothel on Henrietta Street. The place had catered for clients who liked them young, and Sal's looks, smooth skin and firm body had meant she'd rarely been without com-

173

pany, although she wasn't as young as she led her customers to believe. Even now, Sawney wasn't sure of Sal's true age. He wondered whether she knew it herself. Twenty or thereabouts, he reckoned, though she had an old head on her. She told him she'd lost track of the number of times she'd been passed off as a sweet virgin looking to be deflowered by a kind gentleman. It was amazing the rewards that could be enjoyed by concealing a tiny balloon of sheep's gut filled with pig's blood in the palm of the hand and puncturing it with the sharp edge of a ring at just the right moment.

In reality, she'd lost her virginity at the age of thirteen, to one of her father's drinking pals, a labouring man over in Shoreditch. Her father's mate had told her not to tell anyone, that it would be their special secret. So Sal had never told a soul, until she told Sawney. She went on to reveal how she'd slit her abuser's throat with her father's razor before emptying his pockets and heading for the bright lights. Sawney wasn't entirely convinced that she'd been telling the truth; you couldn't always be sure with Sal. She had a temper on her, no doubting that. He'd witnessed it often enough, usually at the expense of some luckless moll who'd made a play for one of Sal's regulars.

The first time she'd gone with Sawney she'd asked him about the set of teeth he'd been folding into a handkerchief as he got dressed. So beguiling was her expression that Sawney told her.

After their third time together, she asked if he'd take her with him on the gang's next job.

174

'I could be your lookout,' she'd told him. 'No one'll suspect a girl.' Then she had grinned and taken him in her mouth. Sawney, breathing heavily, had decided it might not be a bad idea.

Convincing the others had been the challenge. Unsurprisingly, the initial reaction of Maggett and the Ragg boys had been somewhat less than positive, but the more they went at it, the more the idea seemed to grow, because no one *would* suspect a girl. A female loitering on her own was more likely to be suspected of touting for custom than acting as a sentinel for a crew of resurrection men. Right from the start her looks had proved a positive bonus. Like the time she'd been surprised by a night watchman outside St Sepulchre's burying ground. While a quick-thinking Sal entertained the watchman up against the front wall of the graveyard, Sawney and his boys were able to haul three stiffs over the back wall. Everyone had profited from that night's efforts, including the watchman, who'd been so overwhelmed that it was a good five minutes after resuming his patrol that he remembered he'd left his lantern on top of the wall. That same evening, Sal's inventiveness had taken Sawney to places he'd only visited in fevered dreams.

Since then, they had never looked back. Sal had proved her worth. In any case, she was Sawney's woman and Sawney was top dog and his word was law. That was all anyone needed to know.

Sawney finished his counting. The others would be along shortly to divide the spoils and plan their next sortie. With the anatomy schools well into the stride of the new term, the demand for bodies was bound to increase. Sawney felt a warm tingle of satisfaction at the thought and treated himself to a sip of porter to celebrate his good fortune and the promise of profits to come.

'You are Rufus Sawney.' It was a statement, not a question.

Sawney started in his seat. He had not heard anyone approach. He turned.

The figure behind his right shoulder was standing straight and eerily still. One hand grasped a walking cane, the other hung by his side. The face was colourless, the skin drawn so tightly over the cheekbones and jaw, it appeared almost translucent in texture. And yet it was not the outline of the face that caught Sawney's attention but the colour of the man's eyes. In contrast to the pale flesh that encased them, they were the deepest set, darkest eyes Sawney had ever seen. So dark it was difficult to determine where the pupils ended and the irises began. Their raptor-like gaze was made even more pronounced by a triangle of hair that was combed back from the high forehead like a sharp, pointed beak.

It occurred to Sawney that the stranger must have been seated in the adjacent booth, concealed behind the dividing wall. How long he might have been there, Sawney didn't know. He wasn't sure why, but he found that thought, rather like the alluring quality of the stranger's voice, vaguely unsettling. He took a quick look round for reinforcements, but Hanratty was nowhere to be seen.

Sawney found his voice. 'Who's askin'?'

'My name is Dodd.'

176

Sawney didn't like being blindsided, especially in what he considered to be the heart of his personal domain. What was that stupid sod, Hanratty, doing, letting a stranger get so close without so much as a by your leave?

'You *are* Sawney?'

For a moment, Sawney was tempted to deny it, but if the stranger had been in the next booth he'd have overheard his conversation with Hanratty and would therefore have been well aware of his identity before initiating the enquiry.

'What's it to you?' Sawney asked truculently.

'I wish to hire your services.'

'Is that right?' Sawney's eyes narrowed in suspicion. 'And what would that be for?'

'Procurement.'

Sawney blinked.

'That is your forte, is it not?'

'My what?'

'Your area of expertise.'

'Nah,' Sawney said quickly, shaking his head. 'Sorry to disappoint you, squire. You've got the wrong man. Not sure I know what you're talkin' about.'

'Really?' Dodd looked genuinely surprised. 'I had it on very good authority that you *were* the man to ask for.' Without waiting for an invitation, and ignoring Sawney's glare at his temerity, the newcomer lowered himself on to the opposite bench and rested the handle of the cane against his knee.

'That so?' Sawney's eyes narrowed warily. 'An' who might that 'ave been then?'

'Thomas Butler.'

Sawney tried to keep his face neutral.

He knew he hadn't succeeded from the half smile that played along the lips of the man seated opposite, who continued: 'A gentleman who is currently employed as head porter at the dissecting rooms at St Thomas's Hospital.' The smile faded. 'But then, you knew that; after all, Butler is your middleman, is he not?'

Sawney stiffened. It was as if the dark eyes were boring into his soul. Over on the bench by the hearth the two whores had begun to stir, perking the interest of the Smithfield boys on the next table who were nudging one another at the prospect of some early-morning exercise. The women's faces were pink from the heat of the burning logs.

Dodd's voice broke into Sawney's thoughts.

'I see my words have unnerved you. Forgive me. Though, were I in your shoes, I suspect I would be just as circumspect. Indeed, your friend Butler suspected this might be your response. It was his suggestion that I furnish you with a snippet of information only the two of you would know, to prove that I have his trust. Can I assume such a gesture would vouchsafe my character?'

Sawney said nothing. He picked up his mug of porter. It kept his hands occupied and, more importantly, it provided him with several vital seconds in which to think.

The newcomer did not seem at all intimidated either by Sawney or the nature of the surroundings. In fact, it was Sawney who was experiencing disquiet. Somehow, this Dodd, as he called himself, seemed to have gained the upper hand. As if to emphasize the subtle shift in authority, the man

178

leant close. Sawney felt himself trapped in the dark gaze. 'He told me to tell you that he would have paid another five guineas for the Chinaman.'

Sawney took a sip of porter and slowly lowered his mug to the table.

'He also suggested, should you be in further doubt, that I address you as...' Dodd paused and his voice dropped '...*Private* Sawney.'

Sawney's fingers tightened around the handle of his mug. The silence stretched for what seemed like minutes. A sudden crackle of laughter from the two whores eventually broke the tension.

'Nobody calls me that,' Sawney breathed softly. 'Not now, not any more.'

Dodd held his gaze for several seconds before sitting back and nodding in brisk acquiescence. 'Quite so, quite so. A man's history is his own affair. It does not behove a person to dwell on the past. Let us say no more about it.' He placed his hands palm down on the table. 'So, now that the tiresome introductions are over, do I pass muster?'

Sawney's pulse began to slow. He frowned; not at the question, nor the lingering tone of condescension, but at the interesting use of words. *Muster?* Not a term you generally heard away from the parade ground. Was Dodd making fun of him? He stared at the man across the table, but if there was another, deeper message in those dark eyes it remained resolutely out of view. Sawney thought he saw a slight movement at the corner of Dodd's thin mouth, the ghost of another smile perhaps, but it did not linger. He looked down at the man's hands. The fingers were long and

179

tapering, matching their owner's stature. Moving his eyes along, Sawney couldn't help noticing that the man's wrists, though slender, were tight with sinew.

'All right,' Sawney conceded, 'so you've proved it was Butler who sent you. What's it you want from me?'

Dodd hesitated, as if formulating his reply. Finally he said, 'I wish you to procure a certain item for me.'

There was an expectant pause. 'You mean a thing?' Sawney said.

'A thing?' Dodd frowned at the term, then nodded in understanding. 'Ah, yes, of course, that's what you call them, isn't it? How original. I suppose that's one way of distancing yourselves from the nature of the merchandise. Yes, I do indeed wish you to procure a *thing* for me.'

Perhaps it had been the note of sarcasm, Sawney could not put his finger on it, but Dodd's knowing manner was beginning to grate.

'Retrievin' don't run cheap.'

'I did not suppose otherwise.' The corner of Dodd's mouth twitched. 'Which is why I'm pre-pared to offer generous remuneration.'

Sawney frowned. 'Come again?'

'You will be well paid.'

Too bleedin' right, Sawney thought.

'And just so we understand one another,' Dodd continued, 'you may address me as *Doctor...*' The words, again softly spoken, sounded almost like a warning. 'I should also inform you that, subject to your performing this initial endeavour to my

180

satisfaction, it is probable I will have further work for you.'

Sawney's ears pricked up. 'What sort of work?'

'I will require you to provide me with several ... specimens ... *things.*'

Sawney did not respond. He could tell from the doctor's tone that there was more to come.

'I have but three stipulations...' Dodd paused, and then said, 'They must be fresh, female, and young.'

'Young?' Sawney asked.

'Not mature. Ideally less than twenty-five years of age.'

Sawney considered the brief. He had no qualms about fulfilling the order. The doctor wasn't asking for anything out of the ordinary. Over the months he'd been in business, Sawney had had far stranger requests. But it didn't do to let the customer know that.

'Stealin' to order'll cost you,' Sawney said.

Dodd's expression did not alter. 'It would also be on the understanding that our agreement is mutually exclusive.'

'Eh?'

'You are to work solely for me.'

Sawney raised his eyebrows and shook his head. 'Sorry, squire – er, Doctor. That ain't possible. I got other commitments.'

'It would be for a limited period.'

'Don't make no difference,' Sawney said. 'I got my regular customers.'

Dodd nodded gravely as if sympathizing with Sawney's dilemma. 'Loyalty to one's clientele is an admirable quality, and I commend you on it.

181

But perhaps I could persuade you to reconsider...?'

He reached into his pocket. When he opened his hand and laid the cross on the table between them, Sawney stared at it.

The doctor spread his arms in a gesture of apology. 'I regret that I am unable to access my main accounts at the moment. However, I trust this will suffice, at least for the time being.' Dodd laid his hands open, as though presenting an offering. 'It is not without sentimental value to me. However, I'm sure a man of your talents should be able to realize its monetary worth in some form or another. Perhaps you'd allow me to offer it as a token of – how shall I put it? – my good *faith*.'

Sawney looked up sharply, searching for a glimmer of humour in Dodd's face, but despite the obvious play on words, none was apparent.

The cross wasn't very big, no more than three or four inches in length, but the silver hallmark was clearly visible. Sawney picked it up and ran the grubby ball of his thumb over the tiny indentations. Despite its size, it was probably worth four or five retrievals. Not a bad return for a few days' work. And just because he might agree to work on an exclusive basis didn't mean it had to be so. There were bound to be opportunities to earn a little extra on the side; stood to reason.

It was then that another thought leapt out at him: the prospect of killing two birds with one stone. He placed the cross back on the table and fixed the doctor with a speculative gaze. 'Suppose

I was to agree, how many ... things would you be wantin'?'

Dodd shrugged. 'I am not certain at this time. Two or three, possibly more. It would depend on the quality.'

Sawney sucked in his cheeks as it he was giving the proposition some serious consideration. Finally, after what he thought might be an appropriate interval, he nodded.

'All right, Doctor. Don't see why not. As it 'appens, you could be in luck. I've got a couple of items in stock at the moment that'll be right up your alley, er ... given your particular requirements, that is. Already wrapped, too.'

A flicker of interest flared in the doctor's eyes. 'Really? And what might that be?'

Sawney told him.

'I see, and how fresh are they?'

'Day and a half,' Sawney said. He wasn't sure if that statement was entirely accurate, but it was close enough. He knew their ages were about right. One out of two was worth a try.

'You can deliver them tonight?'

'Signed and sealed,' Sawney said. 'You just tell me the time an' place.'

Once more Dodd reached inside his coat. This time his hand emerged clutching a small notepad and a stub of pencil. 'Do you know your letters?'

'You askin' if I can read and write? We ain't all 'eathens down 'ere, Doctor.'

'I am delighted and relieved to hear it.' Dodd tore a page out of the notebook and began to scribble. 'Here is the address. Can you read my hand?'

183

Sawney peered down at the information. He frowned.

'What is it?' Dodd asked, as he returned the pencil and notebook to his pocket. His expression was still.

Sawney shook his head. 'Thought I knew all the schools. Didn't know there was one there, that's all.' He folded up the page and tucked it into the pocket of his waistcoat. 'Right then.' He reached for the cross.

Sawney never saw the doctor's left hand move. The next thing he knew it was clamped round his wrist. Dodd's eyes were as hard as stone. When he spoke, his voice was couched low and as brittle as broken glass.

'Be aware of one thing, Sawney...' The doctor's gaze moved to the silver cross. 'Do not think of disappearing with your down-payment. If you run, I will find you. Be assured of that. I expect you to stand by our agreement. I expect my instructions to be carried out to the letter and with the utmost discretion. There is to be no deviation. Is that clear?'

Sawney tried to pull his arm away, but the strength in the doctor's grip was astonishing.

'Is that understood?' Dodd repeated.

Sawney winced as the doctor's grip tightened. 'Jesus, I said we'd do it, so we'll do it. And what do you take us for? You think we're going to stroll up and down the Strand postin' bleedin' bills?'

'Your word, Sawney. Do I have your word?'

Sawney found himself transfixed. There weren't many things that unnerved him, but the coldness in Dodd's eyes made his blood run cold. He

184

swallowed and nodded.

'Capital.' Dodd released the hand abruptly, picked up his cane, and got to his feet. Then, looking Sawney straight in the eye, as if nothing untoward had happened, he smiled. 'I look forward to our next meeting.'

The doctor turned away. At that moment Sawney sensed something dark skitter across the back of his brain, as if someone had opened a door on to a dim-lit room allowing him to see a glimpse of shadow pass behind a guttering candle flame, that disappeared as quickly as it had arrived and yet which left him with such an intense feeling of dread that the breath caught in his throat.

It was only as Dodd paused and turned that Sawney realized the sound of his exhalation must have carried. A chill moved through him.

The doctor's head was cocked as he looked back over his hunched shoulder. 'What's wrong, Sawney? You look as though you've seen a ghost.' In the low light, the doctor's eyes were still as black as coal, without warmth.

Sawney looked down and saw that the skin along his arms had become a patchwork of goose pimples. Each individual hair was standing to attention like a bristle. He shook his head quickly and nodded towards his plate. 'Bit of cheese went down the wrong way, that's all.'

The doctor held his gaze for what seemed like minutes. 'There is one more thing, Sawney. The bodies are to be delivered whole. Leave the teeth.' With the instructions hanging ominously in the air, Dodd turned and continued on his way out.

Sawney waited for the doctor to make his exit

before releasing his breath. He got up, pocketed the cross, and walked unsteadily to the counter, taking his mug with him. Hanratty kept a bottle of Spanish brandy beneath the boards. Sawney emptied the dregs from his mug into the slop bucket, lifted the brandy from its hiding place and poured himself a measure. He raised the drink to his lips, took a long, deep pull, and waited for his heart to slow down.

Then he asked himself what had just happened.

He wasn't sure what his mind had shown him – a flash of memory, perhaps, or an omen of what was to come. He didn't know. He tried to recall what it was he had seen, but his brain did not respond. Whatever it was, Sawney had the feeling that it was malevolent. If that same door was ever to stand ajar again, he wasn't sure he wanted to know what lay on the other side of it. He took another swig of brandy.

'Rufus?'

Sawney jumped; the second time in a day. The snarl erupted from his lips.

'Jesus! Don't ever bleedin' sneak up on me like that again, you stupid bastard!'

Maggett flinched and stared at the brandy. 'You all right, Rufus?'

Sawney didn't answer. Maggett frowned and nodded towards the taproom door. 'Who was that then?'

Sawney ignored the question. 'Where are the boys?'

Maggett jerked his thumb skywards. 'Upstairs with some moll. Surprised you can't hear 'em. Bleedin' animals.'

Sawney put down his mug. 'Go bring them down. Don't take any shit. I've a job for them. There'll be a run on tonight, too. I got a customer for their ladyships downstairs.'

Maggett looked pointedly at the mug in Sawney's hand and the half-empty bottle on the countertop and raised an eyebrow.

'Medicinal purposes,' Sawney snapped.

Maggett turned away. He had no idea what was irking Sawney. He suspected it might have to do with the man who'd just left. He hadn't seen Sawney looking that shaken for a long while. Trouble was, whenever Sawney got the hump, he had a tendency to take it out on everyone else. Maggett sighed. He hoped the mood was temporary. Otherwise it looked as if it was going to be a long day, not to mention a longer night. He just hoped the job was going to be worth it.

As Maggett turned and made his way to the back stairs, Sawney wiped a hand across his lips. He felt a little better. The brandy had done the business. He straightened. Probably nothing more than his nerves playing tricks. It wasn't unusual when a retrieval was in the offing to get a touch of the jitters.

Sawney felt the shape of the cross in his waistcoat pocket and pressed his hand against his chest. Taking his mug, he headed back to his booth, realizing, as he retraced his steps, that he'd left the bag containing the night's takings in full view. He cursed and shook his head at his forgetfulness, then looked towards the porters' table, but the trio were now too ensconced with the whores to have noticed anything else. The anticipation of a quick fumble with a willing participant tended to make a person oblivious to his or her surroundings. Sawney could probably have driven a coach and four through the taproom door and they wouldn't have been aware of anything except the wind from its passing.

Sawney sat down and took out the cross. He stared at it, turning it in his hand, and thought about the man who had given it to him. He was a strange one, this Dr Dodd. Curious, too, that he should have come in person rather than using Butler as an intermediary. Not that Sawney was going to complain. This way, he wouldn't have to give Butler a cut for brokering the job. Not that he'd have paid out willingly, anyway. Not with Butler having stiffed him over the Chinaman. He reminded himself to have words with the porter about that one, the fly bastard. Foreign corpses weren't dissimilar to cripples, pregnant women and children. They didn't come on the open market that often and you could make good money from them, if you knew what you were doing. It dented Sawney's pride to know that he could have earned a few extra guineas had he been more alert.

And while on the subject of money, a silver cross was a curious form of currency. Worth a fair bit, though. There'd be no problem getting a good price for it. Sawney wasn't too sure about the doctor's story, however; especially the bit about not having access to his accounts. What was all that about? He ran his finger over the hallmark once more. Sentimental value, my arse, he thought. Couldn't be that sentimentally attached if he was prepared to barter it for a

188

couple of day-old stiffs.

Sawney hawked up a mouthful of phlegm and spat it out on to the floor. Not that he was going to let it worry him. He wouldn't have lost any sleep had the doctor confessed to smothering his grandmother and hocking her pearls to raise the necessary. As far as he was concerned, if someone wanted to pay him, who cared where the bloody money came from? And Dr Dodd had hinted there'd be more if he played his cards right. Sawney liked the sound of that. Sawney took another swig of brandy and grinned to himself. Things were looking up.

9

'Sometimes,' Maddie Teague sighed, through a cascade of auburn hair, 'I think that's all I am to you: a seamstress and washerwoman.'

'And a grand cook,' Hawkwood said. 'Don't forget that.'

The reward for that comment was a withering look and a sharp dig in the ribs. Hawkwood winced.

Maddie's emerald-green eyes clouded with immediate concern. Raising herself on to one elbow, she ran her hand gently over the horizontal, four-inch ridge of scar tissue that marred the flesh two inches below Hawkwood's ribcage. 'It still hurts?'

'Only when I'm with company,' Hawkwood said, grinning. He braced himself for another dig, which was duly delivered, though with marginally less force than the first.

Before he could respond, Maddie lowered her head and placed her lips against another, smaller indentation high on his left shoulder.

'So many scars, Matthew,' she murmured softly.

She touched the scimitar-shaped cicatrice etched into the side of his chest below his left arm, then moved her hand to the uneven, crown-sized discoloration on his right shoulder. They were old wounds, like most of the scars on his body; the legacy of twenty years' soldiering.

Weapons of war had left their mark with varying degrees of severity, yet Hawkwood knew he was the fortunate one. He had survived. The bullet scar below his ribs and the knife wound on his left shoulder were the most recent; sustained during his time as a Runner. It was ironic, Hawkwood thought, despite having left soldiering behind, people were still intent on trying to kill him.

Maddie made no mention of the marks on his throat. She never had. Hawkwood recalled the first time they had lain together. Maddie had frowned and traced the bruising with her fingertips and Hawkwood had read the question in her eyes. Then, in a gesture that had astonished him, she had placed her finger against his lips to prevent him speaking, kissed his throat with great tenderness and, still without saying a word, lowered her head on to his chest. Since then, in the quiet moments, she had often enquired about the bullet wounds and the assorted nicks and cuts he carried, but at no time had she referred to the bruises on his neck. It was as if they had ceased to exist.

She kissed him again. 'It's getting late,' she whispered, nodding towards the window where the grey dawn light was trying to peer through a gap in the drapes. 'And some of us have a business to run.'

Maddie Teague's business was the Blackbird Inn. The tavern was situated in quiet seclusion close to the southern end of Water Lane, a short walk from Temple Gardens and King's Bench Walk. Maddie was a widow and had inherited the Blackbird from her late husband, who'd bought the inn with profits he'd made as captain with the East India Company. The captain's Will, however, had also included a number of debts. Hawkwood's need for accommodation on his return to England had solved Maddie's immediate money problems, reassured her creditors and provided breathing space for her to turn what had been a modest endeavour into a profitable one.

Like the marks on his neck, Maddie had not questioned the provenance of Hawkwood's financial contributions. She was not unaware that military campaigning often provided opportunity for financial gain. Seamen benefited from prize money gained through the capture of enemy ships, she knew that from her late husband. But soldiering? Maddie presumed that similar opportunities arose. She was not so naïve as to think army pay, even for an officer in the Rifles, was *that* generous. Presumably, during his two decades of service, cities had been sacked, forts plundered, baggage trains captured. But none of that mattered. Maddie Teague trusted Hawkwood. She'd trusted him from the day he'd walked through the door. She had accepted his offer of financial assistance – there had been no preset conditions other than an agreement giving Hawkwood use of two of the tavern's back rooms – and not once had she questioned his motives. Later she had also come to accept and value his friendship.

And she knew the feeling was mutual, even if he'd never told her so. He didn't have to.

Besides, it didn't hurt, having a peace officer living on the premises.

When Hawkwood arrived back at the Blackbird,

soaked, chilled and in severe need of a brandy, dry clothes and a warm bed, he had not been surprised to find that Maddie was still working. The Blackbird, like most of the city's drinking establishments, kept long hours. To its regular clientele – lawyers, for the most part, with a smattering of clergy thrown in for good measure – it was a comfortable haven away from the pressures of court and congregation. Maddie provided an excellent menu, while the girls who waited on the tables were efficient and friendly without being overly familiar. And waiting on tables was the only service they provided. Maddie had a strict rule, rigorously enforced: no soliciting or propositioning on the premises. You wanted that kind of thing, you took your business elsewhere, Covent Garden or Haymarket. No exceptions, no second chance. The Blackbird was a respectable house and Maddie Teague intended it to remain that way.

Maddie was in the kitchen, delegating chores, when Hawkwood made his presence known. Right hand on hip, she'd eyed his arrival and damp clothes with a raised eyebrow. 'I hope you scraped your boots before you came in. I don't want to go out there and find you've tracked mud all through my dining room.'

'And a good evening to you, too, Mistress Teague,' Hawkwood said, suspecting, guiltily, that mud might not have been the only thing he'd left in his wake. It was too late to retrace his steps. He started to remove his wet coat.

'Don't you dare, Matthew Hawkwood! You hang that up outside in the passage by the door.'

193

By the time she'd completed the sentence, Maddie had both hands on her hips, a sure sign that she meant business. It didn't make her look any less attractive. The kitchen was basking in warmth from the hearth and the cooking stoves. Maddie's scoop-necked blouse did little to conceal the soft swell of her breasts. Her pale Celtic skin was aglow with perspiration. 'And in case you hadn't noticed, it's gone midnight, so it's not evening, it's morning.'

Hawkwood grinned.

'And I suppose you'll be wanting a bite to eat?' Maddie enquired drily as Hawkwood turned away. She shook her head. 'I don't know why I even bother to ask.' She nodded to one of the girls by the hearth. 'Give the remains of that stew a stir, would you, Hettie, and make sure it's hot. Daisy, you go up to Officer Hawkwood's rooms and see the fire's lit, there's a good girl.'

Hawkwood returned from hanging up his coat to find a place had been set at the head of the table. Maddie indicated the empty chair. 'Sit. There's mutton stew. It'll warm you up.'

Maddie waited until he was seated, then announced, 'Right, I still have customers out there who have homes to go to. Hettie will look after you.' Then, before he could respond, she was gone.

She had still not put in an appearance when Hawkwood left the kitchen and made his way upstairs.

His accommodation on the top floor was modest but comfortable; two low-beamed rooms separated by an archway. The similarity to the late

Colonel Hyde's quarters had struck Hawkwood when he'd returned to his rooms after his visit to Bethlem. He'd found it both startling and not a little depressing when he realized that the comparison extended to the furnishings. Bed, table and chairs, nightstand and desk, and over against the wall his brass-bound campaign chest.

His few possessions didn't amount to much, but he'd been a soldier for almost all his adult life, fighting the King's enemies, and during that period he'd probably spent more time on foreign soil than he had at home. Then again, where was home? He had no estate, no family – other than the army, and that part of his life was now over – and few friends.

He thought of other former soldiers he'd come across. It wasn't hard to recognize them. They were the limbless cripples usually to be found in dark doorways, begging for alms from passers-by too contained within their own world to spare concern for any other unfortunates. They'd given their limbs for King and country only to find themselves abandoned and ignored by both.

Many had turned to petty crime. Sometimes it fell to Hawkwood to apprehend them. Where possible, he was inclined to turn a blind eye and let them go with a warning. Transportation or a spell in Newgate seemed poor reward for a man who, having been maimed in the service of his country, had been forced into stealing a loaf of bread or a half-side of bacon because he couldn't afford to put food on his family's table. More than once he had thought, *There but for the grace of God...*

Hawkwood had been fortunate. Thanks to character references and recommendation, albeit unconventional in nature, he had secured employment and a roof over his head, and for that he was thankful. Had that not been the case, it was more than likely, instead of sharing a warm bed with Maddie Teague, he would still have been shivering by a *guerrillero* campfire in some snow-bound cave in the Spanish mountains.

The fire in the grate was, therefore, a welcome sight and Hawkwood mouthed a silent prayer of thanks for Maddie's thoughtfulness. He could no longer hear the rain outside, though the steady drip of water from the gutter on to the windowsill was like the slow ticking of a mantelpiece clock.

He saw that the girl, Daisy, had even provided him with a jug of hot water to wash. It had been a kind gesture and he made a mental note to thank her. He was drying himself when a knock sounded at the door. Hawkwood slipped on his shirt, and went to investigate.

'Would the gentleman like his bed warming?' Maddie Teague asked. The light from the sconce-mounted candle in the hallway outside the door made her eyes dance.

'What with?' Hawkwood asked, eyeing the glasses and bottle of brandy balanced on the tray in Maddie's hands. He looked up at her face and waited.

Maddie smiled. She reached up with one hand, pinched out the candle flame between finger and thumb, and walked past him into the room.

'Me,' she said.

It had been afterwards, lying naked, the blanket

thrown over them to keep the chill at bay, that he had told her about his visit to the Dog and the attack on the bridge. His explanation had been prompted by Maddie's enquiry about the stains on his coat that, in the dark, had escaped his notice. There had been blood on the hem; probably from the man whose nose had been shattered by Hawkwood's tipstaff. So much for my powers of observation, Hawkwood had thought.

'If they weren't footpads,' Maddie said, 'who do you think might have sent them?'

'I don't know,' Hawkwood said.

'Will they send someone to try again, do you think?'

'Maybe.'

'What are you going to do?'

'I don't know that either,' Hawkwood said. 'Not until it happens.'

'But you'll deal with them?'

'Yes.'

'You sound so certain.'

'It's what I do,' Hawkwood said. 'It's what I'm good at.'

He looked at her. Maddie turned her face away quickly. 'I have to go,' she said. 'I've breakfasts to prepare. If I leave those girls alone for five minutes, Lord only knows what mischief they'll be up to.'

'Maddie...' Hawkwood said.

She shook her head and got up from the bed. Without turning, she said, 'Next time it might be someone better.'

'Then I'll be careful.'

Hawkwood watched her as she dressed. He wasn't sure what was the more alluring, Maddie removing her clothes or putting them back on. There was a natural grace to her movements that was a constant source of wonder to him, no matter what she happened to be doing at the time.

She sensed his eyes upon her, turned and wiped her cheek. 'What?'

Hawkwood said nothing. He looked at her and shook his head wordlessly.

Maddie walked back to the bed and sat down, her face serious.

'You said you thought the reason the second man attacked you after you'd told him you were a police officer was that he might not have believed you.'

'It's possible,' Hawkwood said, shrugging. 'I didn't think about it at the time. It was only when you and I were talking that it occurred to me.'

'Well, perhaps you should think again.'

Hawkwood looked at her. Maddie's emerald eyes gazed back at him, moving over his face.

'Did it ever occur to you that, if they weren't footpads and somebody did hire them to attack you, the reason he still tried to kill you after you'd identified yourself was that he was more fearful of the person who sent him than he was of you?'

With that, Maddie stood, secured her fiery mane in a clasp at the back of her neck and left the room without a backward glance.

But she did so gracefully.

The cellar lay in semi-darkness and was as cold

as a cavern. Formerly a church crypt, it was situated below an annexe of Christ's Hospital, in an alleyway off Newgate Street. Because of its proximity to both Christ's and St Bartholomew's and, more importantly, because its stout doors made it impregnable to the resurrection gangs, the authorities had been using it as a mortuary for a number of years.

The flagstone floor was uneven and covered with a grainy black residue. Hawkwood assumed most of the stains on the floor were congealed blood, accumulated over God knew how long. As for the rest, he tried not to think about it. He was more than familiar with the sweet, sickly odour of death, but in the enclosed space the smell of body fluids and decaying flesh was overpowering, somewhere between overripe fruit and rotting meat. Looking around at the cellar's contents, he decided he'd seen cleaner field hospitals.

With its low curved roof, rough brick walls and encircling ring of dark alcoves, the only difference between the crypt's previous function and its current one was the condition of the occupants.

The walls of the alcoves were lined with narrow ledges. In the past, they'd have held coffins. Now, they were the resting places for corpses awaiting either examination or burial. The crypt had become a waiting room for the deceased; a dead house.

The main central space was being used as the examination and dissection room. In the middle of the floor were four wooden tables. Upon each of them lay a body, covered by a coarse sheet.

The sheets were filthy and encrusted with gore, as was the apron of the surgeon, who, in response to Hawkwood's arrival, did not bother looking up from his task but instead gave a brusque instruction to close the door.

Hawkwood did as he was bid.

The man in the apron still did not look up, but continued probing the body in front of him. 'Good man. You are...?'

Hawkwood told him.

'Ah, yes, Hawkwood. Come away in! I'll be with you momentarily. Name's Quill, by the way. You're looking a bit doubtful. You were expecting someone else perhaps? I'm afraid my predecessor has the gout. You'll have to make do with me.' With that, the speaker finally raised his head.

Hawkwood found himself looking at a man whose stature suggested he might have been more at home running a boxing booth at a country fair than wielding a surgeon's knife. His head, which was bullet-shaped and completely shaved, gleamed with sweat, while the blood-smeared pinner he was wearing was more reminiscent of a Smithfield slaughter yard.

Hawkwood had indeed been expecting someone else. The usual surgeon, McGregor, a large, vain, overbearing man, did not like dealing with subordinates – a category which included Runners – so Hawkwood had not been looking forward to the meeting. Seeing this new face was like taking in a breath of fresh air, which, given the circumstances, was a commodity somewhat in short supply.

The surgeon put down his knife, stepped away

from the table, and wiped his hands on a cloth tucked into the apron strings. He crooked a finger at Hawkwood, beckoning him over.

'It appears you've been busy.'

Quill drew back the first sheet. It was the remains of the porter, Doyle. In the darkness of the crypt, the crow-ravaged eye sockets gave the grey-skinned features the hollowed appearance of a skull.

'This one died hard,' Quill said. The surgeon's breath hung in the air like a cloud of steam. He appeared impervious to the chill in the cellar and unaffected by the smell of the cadavers around him.

Hawkwood looked again at the body, remembering how he had first seen it. Time had done little to erase the memory. His eyes fastened on the face. There was something protruding from the corpse's open mouth, he saw. He stared. It looked like frog spawn, though he knew it wasn't.

Quill, following his gaze, frowned, and gave a dismissive grunt. 'Purge. It's caused by an expansion of gases in the body. You'll have seen it before, no? The gases put pressure on the stomach, forcing recent contents into the oesophagus and up into the mouth. It's not uncommon. If he were alive, he'd either be burping or farting. Another week or two and it won't be bile he'll be leaking, it'll be what's left of his brain.'

Hawkwood said nothing. He couldn't think of an appropriate response.

The surgeon pursed his lips. 'Cause of death was a broken neck leading to asphyxiation, though I dare say you'd assumed that already.' Quill did not look up but walked around the body, lifting and peering at each of the corpse's wrists in turn. 'Interesting.'

'What is?' Hawkwood asked.

Quill raised the arm he was holding. 'These stigmata. The nails were placed through his wrists and not the palms of his hands. Had that been done, the nails would not have supported the body's weight but would likely have been torn free. One wonders where the killers learned their trade. There's a lot of damage to the wrists, not consistent with the nailing, by the way.'

Hawkwood explained the efforts by the two gravediggers to get the dead man down from the tree.

'Could he have been alive when they nailed him up?' Hawkwood asked.

Quill did not respond immediately. He lowered the dead man's arm and then said, 'Probably done post mortem. I found traces of skin beneath his fingernails. They correspond to the scratch marks on his neck – d'you see there?' The surgeon pointed. 'That would be from clawing at the rope, which would indicate he was alive when he was raised up. I would surmise he was lifted, probably with someone holding on to his arms and legs. Once he was in position, his limbs were released, leaving him to hang, struggling for air. The weight of his body, pressure on the rope and gravity would have done the rest.'

'They took out his teeth and his tongue,' Hawkwood said.

The doctor grimaced. It was the first time he

had shown any emotion. 'Indeed they did. And the removal, as you saw, was crudely done.'

'They couldn't have done *that* while he was still alive,' Hawkwood said. 'Could they?'

'Unlikely. I doubt he'd have opened his mouth voluntarily.' Quill smiled grimly. 'And it is difficult to force someone's mouth open against their wishes. Most probably they waited until he was dead, then lowered him back to the ground, performed the deed, and raised him back into place, which is when they would have hammered home the nails to keep the body in position. Somewhat convoluted, I admit, but effective, nevertheless. As I said, he died hard.'

Hawkwood wondered how many it had taken. At least four, he thought: two to hold the arms while they secured the rope, another to hang on to the feet, the fourth to do the job. It didn't bear thinking about.

The surgeon draped the sheet back over the bloodless face and moved to the next table. The second sheet was lifted away.

'Remarkable,' Quill murmured, staring down.

Hawkwood wondered if it was his imagination or whether he had detected a note of admiration in the doctor's voice.

Quill looked up. 'A man of the cloth, I understand?'

'Reverend Tombs,' Hawkwood said.

'Interesting name for a God-botherer,' Quill observed.

Hawkwood wondered if the comment had been the doctor's attempt at humour. He didn't respond.

'No evidence of restraint here,' Quill murmured. 'There's no question the victim was dead before the mutilation was performed. I examined the chest; the lungs were healthy, but there was a slight engorgement of blood. I suspect laudanum could well have been swallowed, probably administered by means of a beverage. There was a faint smell around the mouth. As I perceive no other signs of injury, other than the obvious, I would deduce that the victim was smothered after the narcotic had done its work. The facial skin was removed once death was established. There was clearly a degree of expertise involved.' Quill looked up. 'Curious that asphyxiation should be the common denominator, though I doubt it was the same killer. I take it the crimes are *not* related?'

Hawkwood nodded. Quill's conclusions confirmed some of Apothecary Locke's suspicions. More damningly, they also indicated that the scalpel hadn't been the only thing the colonel had purloined from the apothecary's bag. Hawkwood recalled the empty bottle of cordial that had been on the table in Hyde's room. The colonel hadn't needed to hit his victim to subdue him. He'd used the laudanum, mixing it with the cordial. It probably wouldn't have taken too much to make the priest drowsy. Perhaps Hyde had then offered him use of his bed. Which was when the pillow would have been used.

Another nail in the apothecary's coffin, never mind the parson's.

Quill gazed down at the corpse. 'Remarkable,' he said again.

Hawkwood had been bracing himself for the third and fourth bodies. Even so, he could never have prepared himself totally. He'd seen the effects of fire on a corpse before. In war it was inevitable, but it didn't make this sight any more palatable.

Each body had been reduced to little more than a grossly deformed lump of charred flesh and blackened bone. There was a curious mantis-like look to the way the limbs had contracted in the heat, transforming the extremities into gnarled claws. The cadavers bore more resemblance to a species of grotesque insect than anything human.

Ashes to ashes, Hawkwood thought.

What appeared to be remnants of burnt cloth hung from the blistered bodies of both decedents, though he supposed it could just as easily have been strips of seared skin. Hawkwood felt the gorge rise to the back of his throat. He swallowed, determined that Quill should not see his reaction. He didn't want to give the doctor the satisfaction of knowing that Doyle's wasn't the only stomach in the room suffering side-effects.

He listened as Quill went through the results of his examinations. Two bodies, one male, one female, the male aged in his late forties, the female older, perhaps in her sixties. Each of them burnt beyond recognition.

'Not that they died from the fire, of course.' The surgeon regarded Hawkwood with a speculative expression. 'The female has a crushed larynx, probably caused by strangulation. The male has suffered a broken clavicle and splintered radius of the right arm, a cracked tibia of the right leg and fracture of the frontal bone of the skull. I would say those are injuries consistent with a high fall.'

A vision rose into Hawkwood's mind. He saw again the black-robed figure outlined against the open window of the bell tower, turning and pitching into the flames. It had been a long way to the ground.

The porter, Doyle, hadn't been the only one who had died hard, Hawkwood reflected. But that didn't mean he felt any sympathy. Hyde had killed a priest and an elderly woman. Hell, Hawkwood thought, was probably too good for the murdering bastard.

Hawkwood stared down at the bodies. Quill's examination and conclusions were confirmation that the investigation into the murder of the priest was at an end. In all respects, the outcome was final.

So, why am I suddenly not convinced? Hawkwood wondered.

Colonel Hyde, according to Apothecary Locke, had been an intelligent man. Despite the man's mental tribulations, Locke had even admitted to consulting with the colonel on medical matters on more than one occasion. As for the killing of the priest, all indications pointed to the colonel having plotted his escape from Bethlem with murderous efficiency. There had definitely been method in his madness, if such a thing were possible. And yet, no sooner had the colonel achieved his goal than he had brought his short-lived freedom to a spectacular end by killing himself out of a sense of guilt.

It didn't make any sense.

Chief Magistrate James Read regarded Hawkwood with what might have been sympathy.

'Sense, you say? I'm not sure that would apply in this particular instance. The colonel's mind was clearly unhinged. Do not trouble yourself looking for rhyme or reason. I doubt you'll find either. The man's dead, the coroner's surgeon has performed his duty. The coroner will reach his verdict. The case is therefore closed. It is time to move on. There are more pressing matters that demand our attention.'

They were in the Chief Magistrate's office at Bow Street. James Read had adopted his customary stance, facing the room with his back towards the open fire. Read's eyes flickered to the window. His brow furrowed. Hawkwood followed the magistrate's mournful gaze and saw that a thin sleet had begun to fall.

The magistrate turned away from the weather, a weary expression on his narrow face. 'How goes the Doyle investigation?'

Hawkwood grimaced. 'Not as well as I would have liked. No one's talking.'

There was a silence in the room, interrupted only by the slow, monotonous ticking of the clock in the corner and the crackle of burning wood in the hearth.

'What about the men who attacked you? Have you given any further thought as to whether they might have been working under orders rather than by their own volition? Perhaps you have informers who can make enquiries?'

He meant Jago, Hawkwood thought.

There was a sudden sharp report from the direction of the hearth. Read jumped in alarm. A stray spark, Hawkwood realized, must have struck the magistrate.

James Read sidestepped smartly and swatted the back of his right knee. 'Mr Twigg!'

The door opened so promptly that Hawkwood suspected the clerk had been hovering outside, awaiting such a summons.

'Yes, sir?' Twigg blinked behind his spectacles as the magistrate turned towards him.

'A guard for the hearth, Mr Twigg. Before the day is out, if you please. That's the second pair of breeches I've ruined in as many weeks.'

The clerk rewarded the Chief Magistrate with a weary *I told you so* look. 'Shouldn't stand so close then, your honour.'

The look Read gave his clerk was priceless. Hawkwood suspected that only Ezra Twigg could have got away with such a retort.

'Yes, well, thank you for your acute observation, Mr Twigg; straight to the nub as always. But you'll see to it? I believe there's a guard downstairs in the sitting magistrate's chambers – I'm sure he won't raise any objection.'

As if the poor bugger would have any choice in the matter, Hawkwood thought.

Twigg nodded. 'Right away, sir.'

The little clerk departed on his errand, closing the door behind him, but not before he had caught Hawkwood's gaze and rolled his eyes.

Hawkwood bit his tongue.

'You were about to say...?' Read said, frowning.

His sharp eyes had evidently caught the exchange. Hawkwood shook his head. 'Nothing, sir.'

'Very good. In that case,' Read said drily, 'don't let me detain you.' The magistrate moved to his desk, sat down and picked up his pen. 'But be sure to keep me appraised of your progress. That is all. You may go.'

10

'Christ on His cross, Maggsie, will you hold that bloody light steady? I can't see a bleedin' thing!'

Sawney threw the big man a glare, which was difficult, given that he was on his hands and knees, head pressed to the ground, arse in the air.

'Sorry, Rufus,' Maggett whispered, and held the lantern lower. Three of the lantern's four sides were blacked out, which made it possible to direct the candle beam in a specific direction. It also decreased the chances of the light being spotted by prying eyes.

Sawney shook his head at his companion's idiocy and resumed his inspection of the gravesite. The two men standing guard behind Maggett's broad shoulders looked on in nervous anticipation.

It was half an hour after midnight. Apart from the four men, the graveyard was deserted. Tendrils of mist drifted in spectral coils around the canted and fallen headstones, while on the ground a thin veneer of frost had already started to glisten.

Sal had done the legwork on this one. There were several tried-and-tested means of tracking down fresh corpses, but most of the gangs relied on informers – gravediggers, sextons, corrupt local officials and the like – to tell them about impending deaths or recent burials. On this occasion, the information had come courtesy of the undertaker. Sal had been cultivating the ninny for months, leading him on, letting him think he was God's gift. Never underestimate the power of a pretty girl and the information she could extract with the proffer of a quick feel. Sal's flirtatious grin and silken promises of carnal delights had paid dividends. The burial ground of St Anne's was one of a dozen sources, visited in rotation, which had proved profitable due to this particular moonstruck fool's loose tongue.

On this occasion, they'd been lucky. They needed the body in a hurry.

The two female corpses had proved unsatisfactory. Dodd had informed Sawney of that fact when he had taken delivery, viewing the remains in silence before finally shaking his head. 'Regrettably, they're not as fresh as you implied. The decomposition is too advanced for my purposes.' Dodd had looked up and fixed Sawney with a penetrating stare. 'Which makes me suspect they've been in circulation for some time and surplus to your requirements. Am I right?'

Sawney flushed. The attempt to palm the women's corpses off on to the doctor had been worth a try. It just hadn't worked, that was all. Sawney waited for the sky to fall, but to his immense relief Dodd appeared unexpectedly philosophical, accepting the condition of the cadavers with calm equanimity and what might have passed for a slight smile.

'Come now, Sawney, no need for the long face. The spontaneous nature of your offer showed initiative, not to mention a head for business,

211

even if the gesture was, shall we say, misguided? On this occasion I'm disposed to overlook the matter. I trust, however, you'll make restitution with your *next* delivery.'

Sawney wasn't too sure what that meant exactly, but he nodded nonetheless because he did not want to appear slowwitted. He presumed that Dodd felt he had not fulfilled his side of the bargain. The silver cross was still burning a hole in his pocket and so far Dodd had nothing to show for it, save two unwanted cadavers that were rapidly going off.

'You want me to take 'em off your hands?' Sawney had asked. Might as well show willing, he thought, and maybe make a bit on the side by selling them to someone who wasn't so fussy about their less-than-pristine condition.

Dodd, however, after contemplating the corpses at length, pursed his lips and said, 'That will not be necessary, at least for the time being. While there is, as I have said, a substantial amount of deterioration, further examination may reveal one or two organs that are still suitable for harvest.'

Sawney wasn't too sure what the doctor meant by 'harvest', so all he could do was look knowledgeable while confirming that he would honour the first part of their arrangement the following night. The next delivery, Sawney promised, would be far superior in quality. Dr Dodd could count on it.

'Oh, I'm sure I can,' Dodd said softly. 'I know it would not occur to you to make the same mistake *twice*.'

Sawney had known exactly what the doctor

meant that time. There was no mistaking the emphasis and, by its nature, the implication.

Which was why he was in the middle of a burial ground, freezing his rear end off, while trying to get his accomplice to keep the bloody light still.

Sawney stiffened. He'd almost missed it. Would have too, if Maggett hadn't stopped buggering about. But there it was, plain as day, caught at the edge of the lantern beam. The snare.

By themselves, the acorns wouldn't have looked out of place, three inconsequential little pods lying on top of the soil, no different to the thousands of others that lay scattered around the graveyard, as common as rabbit droppings. Except these ones were in a straight line, each of them two fingers' width apart, an arm's length from the small wooden cross that marked the head of the grave. Sawney knew it was two fingers and an arm's length because he measured it out. Nice try, he thought, but some people never learnt.

It needn't have been acorns; it could just as easily have been shells, a strategically placed stone, a couple of twigs, or perhaps a flower, placed on the grave in such a way as to detect if any interference had taken place. Many anxious relatives had adopted the practice of late.

An amateur might not have noticed, but Sawney, with his experience, had known what to look out for and he knew how to get around it.

Carefully, Sawney lifted the acorns from the soil with his fingertips, placed them in his pocket, and got to his feet. 'All right, let's do it. Sharply now, we ain't got all bleedin' night!'

Maggett set the lantern on the ground and

immediately the two men standing beside him stepped forward. Both carried short-handled wooden shovels, the oval blades bearing closer resemblance to a paddle than a digging tool. From a sack across his shoulder, Maggett drew out a roll of canvas and laid it alongside the grave, at the same time removing from its inner folds some loose sacking and two butcher's hooks.

Sawney, blowing on his hands in a vain attempt to generate warmth, took a look around. The burial ground was hemmed in on all sides; to the east by the church and to the north and south by the backs of houses. To the west was the rest of the graveyard, which was separated from the road beyond by a shoulder-high wall.

'Shift yourself, Maggsie,' Sawney hissed. 'Let the dogs see the bleedin' bone.'

Lemuel Ragg rested the shovel against his right knee and spat on his hands. His brother Samuel did the same. Then, trading knowing grins, they picked up their tools and began to transfer the soil from the grave to the canvas sheet.

The Ragg brothers were similar in looks and physique and had often been mistaken for twins, which they were not. Lemuel was the older by two years. Dark-haired and sallow-skinned, they were neither tall nor brawny, being both shorter and smaller in stature than Sawney, but what they lacked in height and breadth they made up for in raw cunning. Insult one Ragg boy and you insulted his brother by default; anyone foolish enough to do so risked dire, usually fatal, consequences.

The brothers worked fast. The undertaker had

214

advised that the coffin was buried deeper than normal, supposedly as a deterrent to disinterment, which meant that there was, potentially, a larger than average amount of soil to remove. The Raggs, however, took this as a personal challenge, with the result that the excavation became a contest between them.

The grave had only been filled that morning and, despite the rime-glazed surface, the earth immediately below the topsoil was still loose and not yet compacted, which made the removal of the soil relatively easy.

The Raggs dug like men possessed. Shovels dipped. Earth flew. The hole deepened and the mound of soil on top of the canvas grew steadily higher. Occasionally, the edge of a shovel would strike a stone, but the wooden blade ensured the sound was no louder than a dull thud. It was the reason body stealers favoured wooden shovels over metal ones. Sawney checked his pocket watch by the lantern light. They'd been on site for ten minutes. They were making good progress.

The sound of wood striking wood came suddenly, accompanied by an excited hiss from Samuel, his shovel having been the one that had made contact. The brothers moved back. Sawney lifted the lantern and held it over the excavation, grunting with satisfaction when he saw that the head of the coffin had been exposed. He signalled to the waiting Maggett. Grabbing the sacking and the hooks, the big man stepped into the grave.

And from the darkness beyond the edge of the light came the sound of a low cough.

215

The men froze, then ducked down. Quick as a flash, Sawney blew out the lantern flame.

The sound came again, closer this time. The hairs on the back of Sawney's neck prickled. He could feel his heart pounding like hoof beats inside his chest. He peered around him, but the mist had thickened into a solid layer a foot deep that hovered above the ground like cannon smoke, impenetrable to probing eyes.

Then, at the edge of Sawney's field of vision, a shape appeared. It was low down, approaching quickly. Sawney's hand eased towards the knife in his belt. Beside him, he sensed Lemuel Ragg reach inside his jacket, extract a six-inch length of tortoiseshell and, with practised ease, flick open the wafer-thin razor blade.

The fox padded past them with a vulpine look of disdain, silent as a wraith.

Sawney let out his breath. He relit the lantern using a tinderbox and a sulphur-dipped cord. 'Well, don't just sit there with your gob open, Maggsie,' he said. 'Tick-tock.'

Maggett draped the loose sacking over the head of the coffin exposed by the digging. The rest of the coffin was still covered and weighted down by soil. Standing on the tail end, Maggett inserted the point of each hook beneath the sacking and under either side of the coffin lid. Then, gripping the T-bar of each hook, he heaved upwards. With Maggett's bulk and the weight of the earth on the rest of the lid acting as a counter-weight, there could only be one outcome. The coffin lid snapped across. The sacking had been put down to deaden the sound of the breaking wood, but the noise still rang out like a distant pistol shot.

Sawney's crew, however, did not pause. They were now racing against the clock.

Tossing the hooks aside, Maggett reached down, pulled back the splintered lid and grasped the corpse under the shoulders. Unfortunately, it didn't want to come. Maggett's shoulder muscles bulged. He tried again. He felt a sharp tug inside the coffin. The burial shroud was snagged. Maggett swore, put his back into it and pulled hard. This time his efforts were rewarded, accompanied by the sound of cloth tearing. The corpse came out of the coffin like a pale grey moth emerging from a pupal sac, with the remains of the shroud clinging to it like folded wings.

Maggett laid the corpse on the ground and, without pausing, removed what was left of the torn cloth and tossed it back into the open coffin. The four men stared down at the body. It was female and shapely, with dark, matted hair, skin ghostly pale against the dirt and grass.

'Nice tits,' Lemuel murmured appreciatively, his head on one side. 'Wouldn't 'ave minded giving her one.'

Samuel giggled. 'Still time, Lemmy. You want us to wait?'

Lemuel grinned and cuffed his brother around the back of the head.

'Enough!' Sawney snapped. Gathering up the sacking from the top of the coffin, he tamped down the broken lid with his boots and climbed out of the grave. 'Fill 'er in.'

The brothers picked up their shovels. Sawney collected the two hooks and wrapped them in the sacking, leaving Maggett to attend to the body.

Maggett knelt down and removed from his pocket three rolls of dirty bandage, two short and one long. His broad face betrayed no emotion as he concentrated on using one of the shorter rolls to bind the corpse's ankles. He used the second short roll on the corpse's wrists.

Maggett prodded the corpse, testing the consistency of the dead flesh. The smell coming off the body was like wet leaves. Death – the result of a convulsive attack, according to the undertaker – had taken place only the day before; long enough, Maggett knew, for rigor to have worn off, though with some corpses that could vary. Sometimes it passed off within ten hours, other times it took as long as two days.

Maggett grunted with satisfaction. This one wasn't going to be a problem. He wouldn't have to break any joints. Pinioning the bound wrists between the corpse's knees, Maggett pressed the legs back towards the chest, trapping the arms. Taking the last strip of bandage, he tied it round the compressed legs and torso, cinching it tightly until the bound corpse resembled a plucked and trussed chicken. Then, after a quick check to make sure the knots were secure, he went and retrieved the sack. Stuffing the corpse inside it was easy.

Maggett finished tying off the sack at the same time as Lemuel Ragg shovelled the last heap of earth on to the top of the grave. Sawney removed the three acorns from his pocket and placed them in their original positions in the soil. Due to the digging, no frost remained on the top of the grave.

The absence was noticeable compared to the rest of the terrain, but Sawney knew it wouldn't take long for a new coating to form over the disturbed patch. Come the morning, it would all look the same. He gathered up the canvas sheet, mindful to shake the last granules of soil back on top of the grave. Then, placing the sacking containing the hooks within the canvas, he rolled the lot into a bundle and hoisted it on to his shoulder. He looked again at his watch. The removal had taken exactly sixteen minutes. He gave a satisfied grunt, looked at the others and nodded. 'Let's go.'

The four men left the gravesite and headed towards the church. Their footsteps made soft crunching sounds in the crisp frost.

They could hear the snoring from twenty paces away. There was a small, wooden hut nestling against the church's wall. The reverberations were coming from inside.

'Hope that's not Sal sleepin' on the job,' Lemuel Ragg whispered.

Samuel let go a snort of laughter, quickly suppressed by the warning look on Sawney's face.

'I heard that,' Sal said softly. She emerged from the open doorway, a shawl over her shoulders, and stuck out her tongue. 'Cheeky sod.'

Sawney said nothing but looked past her into the hut. There wasn't a great deal to see; a small, rough wooden table and an upturned keg for use as a chair. On the table sat a lantern, an earthenware jug and a grubby square of muslin, upon which rested a slab of sweaty cheese, a bruised apple and a hunk of dry bread. Seated on the keg, wedged against the wall, head tipped back, mouth open, was a beery-looking man with a pock-marked face, bushy side-whiskers and bad teeth. Sawney gazed down at the snoring man with contempt. The man's breeches were open, he noticed. His eyes moved to the side. Resting against the wall, butt to the floor, was a rusting musket. Next to it was a small cudgel and a rattle. *So much for the bloody watchman,* he thought. He turned to Sal. 'Give you any trouble?'

Sal shook her head. 'Good as gold. Didn't take long. The grog was enough. I didn't even 'ave to show my titties.'

'Showed you 'is gun though, did 'e, Sal?' Peering over Sawney's shoulder, Lemuel Ragg leered suggestively. ''Ave a big barrel, did it?'

'At least 'e's got a gun, Lemmy,' Sal said, and winked.

Lemuel's face flushed red. His jaw tightened. His brother sniggered.

Sawney looked at Sal and nodded towards the sleeping man's lap and the unbuttoned trouser flap. 'Been practising, 'ave we?'

'Don't need the practice.' Sal ran her tongue along her teeth. 'You should know. But I do like to keep my hand in.' She grinned wickedly.

Sawney felt his loins stir.

'Should I do 'im, Rufus?' Lemuel had the razor in his hand. His thumb played a silent tattoo along the side of the open blade.

Sawney shook his head. 'Not this time. Let the bugger dream. He'll wake up with 'is buttons open and he'll remember Sal and think he had a really good night. He doesn't know we've been here. No one does. Might as well keep it that way.'

'Spoilsport,' Ragg muttered, putting the blade away.

'Take this,' Sawney said, passing him the canvas roll. 'Maggsie and I'll deliver the goods. We'll see you back at the Dog. And you–' he turned to Sal '–keep your bleedin' 'ands to yourself.'

'Only 'til you get back,' Sal said, thrusting out her chest and pouting prettily.

Lemuel beckoned to his brother, who was taking a piss against the outside wall of the hut. Samuel shook himself dry, wiped his hands on his breeches and trotted over to join them. Sal blew Sawney a kiss and then headed off with the Raggs in the direction of Church Street and Seven Dials.

Sawney and Maggett watched them go. Maggett adjusted the sack on his shoulder, hawked up a gobbet of phlegm, and spat into the dirt. 'Dunno why you let 'er talk to you like that, Rufus. It ain't respectful.'

Sawney waited until Sal and the brothers had been swallowed up by the darkness then turned to Maggett and grinned. ''Cos she's got the face of an angel and an arse like a peach, Maggsie. Now stop moanin' like an old woman, we've still got an errand to run.' He nodded towards the sack. 'An' mind you don't go dropping the merchandise. Our man's paid good money for that, an' from what I know of 'im so far best not to keep him waiting.'

They didn't have far to go. Which was just as well because two men walking in the dead of night, one of them with an oddly bulging sack over his shoulder, might have attracted some unwelcome attention. True, there were not many people on the streets and those that were about were more than likely involved in dubious activities of their own, but the last thing Sawney needed was a run-in with an enthusiastic member of the Watch or a constable hoping to make his mark in the annals of criminal detection. So they stayed in the shadows and by using the maze of side passages and alleyways that crisscrossed their route, they were able to arrive at their destination without incident.

Crouched beneath an archway, the two men waited. Everything looked quiet. Somewhere, out of sight, a dog barked. Instinctively, they shrank back. The commotion passed and peace resumed.

With its plain front door and peeling façade, the four-storeyed house didn't look much different to the ones lining the rest of the grimy, rubbish-strewn street, save for one unusual feature. Maggett eased the sack off his shoulder and stared at the darkened building.

'Still don't look like no school, Rufus,' he murmured.

Maggett had expressed the same thought the previous night when they'd delivered the first two cadavers. Sawney was inclined to agree, but he saw nothing suspicious in a private anatomy school choosing not to advertise its purpose.

Although various alternatives had been tried, ranging from wax effigies to animals and papier-mâché models, there was no substitute for the dissection of real cadavers in the teaching of anatomy. Hospital schools could count on an almost constant supply, courtesy of former patients who'd died in their wards. Indeed, it was a widely held belief that most of the coffins consigned to the burial grounds of the capital's hospitals were empty, their occupants having been diverted to the anatomists' tables. The private schools, however, were forced to rely on the resurrection men to provide specimens for their dissection tables. And the last thing they wanted was for the neighbours to find out they were living next door to an establishment involved in the receipt, rendering and dismemberment of stolen corpses.

The drawbridge was interesting, though.

It was the one thing that set the house apart from the rest of the street. Suspended above a ramp to the right of the front door, it was slightly wider than a carriage width. Once lowered, it allowed access down the ramp to underground stabling. Raised, it denied entry, transforming the house into a small fortress. Cut into the drawbridge was a smaller door, through which pedestrians could gain entry to the subterranean coach house.

Sawney checked the building for signs of life. The wooden window shutters on the ground floor were all closed. He thought he'd seen a light earlier, through a gap in the curtains at one of the top-floor windows, but he couldn't be sure. There was only one way to find out. Casting a wary glance around him, he tapped Maggett on the shoulder. The big man hefted the sack once more and followed Sawney across the street at a lumbering jog. There was a bell-pull set in the

223

wall by the door. Sawney tugged it. Deep within the house, he heard a faint jangle.

Sawney had half-expected the drawbridge to be lowered, as it had been the night before when they'd had the cart, but it was the smaller, pedestrian door that opened. Dodd stood framed in the gap, a candle held high in his hand. He was dressed informally in an open-necked shirt with the sleeves rolled above the elbow. His lower half was concealed behind what had, presumably, been a once-white apron but which was now stained dark. His intimidating gaze moved between them, taking in Maggett and the sack he was carrying. His eyes moved briefly to the unlit street beyond, before he stepped back to allow them to enter. There were no formalities, no greetings exchanged, as the door closed behind them.

For a moment, Sawney wondered how Dodd had known who it was and then, as the door swung shut, he saw the tiny spyhole cut into the wood at eye level. He noticed too that the doctor's hands, like his apron, were heavily stained with dark, viscous matter.

Sawney nodded towards the sack. 'Second helpin', as promised.'

'Bring it,' Dodd said. He turned abruptly, candle flickering, leaving them to follow him down the ramp.

At the bottom of the ramp, lit by candles set in niches around the wall, the stabling arrangements were no different to those of a normal livery yard. There were enough wooden-sided stalls in the low-roofed chamber to house half a dozen horses, as well as space for two carriages, standing abreast. The floor was layered with straw.

Various items of tack hung from hooks around the sides, while against one wall there stood a workbench and a selection of tools. On the floor next to the bench was a large, square basket. From the moment they reached the base of the ramp Sawney had been aware of the sickly odour. It grew stronger the further they advanced. It wasn't coming from Maggett's load, Sawney knew. It was emanating from the square basket. It was a smell Sawney recognized.

Dodd pointed to the workbench.

Sawney nodded to Maggett, who lifted the sack on to the table. He did it without effort, as if the contents were weightless. Sawney took the knife from his belt and cut the ties around the neck of the sack. Maggett tipped the body out. Sawney used the knife to cut away the bandages. Maggett straightened out the legs and, in a curious, almost reverential gesture he crossed the dead woman's hands over her breasts.

'Picked fresh today,' Sawney said, throwing his companion an odd look. 'Ain't that right, Maggsie?'

Maggett said nothing, content to remain watchful, and silent.

Dodd bent over the corpse and examined it closely. He lifted and replaced each limb in turn, kneading the blue-grey flesh with thumb and palm. He manipulated the wrist, knee, ankle and finger joints. He pulled back the sunken eyelids and opened the corpse's lips to examine the teeth. Maggett was reminded of an ostler checking the health of a sick horse. Finally, he stepped

225

away and nodded.

'The quality appears to be acceptable.'

Sawney gave what he hoped was an equally nonchalant nod. Inwardly, he breathed a sigh of relief. 'You want us to give you an 'and takin' it inside?'

The offer was met with a dismissive shake of the head. 'That will not be necessary. I will see to it. You may, however, dispose of those–' Dodd nodded towards the basket. The smell was very strong now.

Bugger, Sawney thought. 'Not a problem. Maggsie?'

'Leave the basket,' Dodd instructed.

Sawney picked up the empty sack from the bench and stood by as Maggett lifted the basket lid.

The stench seemed to erupt out of the hamper. Sawney jerked his head away quickly. Beside him he heard what sounded like a gag reflex deep in Maggett's throat and saw the big man's eyes widen.

'Jesus!' Maggett breathed. He threw Sawney a look. 'We'll need another sack, Rufus.'

Sawney looked around. There were some empty straw sacks lying next to one of the stalls. He went and picked one up.

Dodd appeared to be taking no notice. He had turned away and was re-examining the newly delivered cadaver.

Maggett was standing with his lips clamped closed. It looked to Sawney as if the big man was trying to hold his breath. Quickly, Sawney placed the open end of the sack over the top of the basket. Then, tipping the basket on its side, the two men transferred the first part of the load. It was smoothly done, due to Maggett's strength and Sawney's ability to keep the head of the sack over the basket all the way through the switch. Sawney tied off the head of the sack and the two men repeated the process with the basket's remaining contents. Sawney caught Dodd's attention, nodded towards the workbench, and raised a questioning eyebrow.

Dodd nodded and watched as Sawney dragged the empty basket to the bench and tipped the newly arrived corpse into it. He had to bend the knees and press down on the top of the head to get the thing to fit before he was able to close the lid.

'All yours,' Sawney said, when the task was done. He wiped his hands on his jacket. 'You sure you can manage?'

'Quite sure, thank you.'

'Right,' Sawney said. 'We'll be off then.'

He nodded to Maggett, who swung one of the sacks on to his shoulder. Sawney hoisted the other one.

'You may let yourselves out, gentlemen,' Dodd said. 'I will be along directly to secure the door.'

Sawney paused.

'Was there anything else?' Dodd said. His head turned.

'I was thinking,' Sawney said. 'About the next one. When would you be wantin' to take delivery?'

'I'm not certain. I'll know after I've examined tonight's consignment. Return in twenty-four hours. I will advise you then.'

'Right you are.' Sawney tapped Maggett on the arm and the two of them headed up the ramp.

Back on the street, Maggett took a nervous look around. He nudged the sack over his shoulder. 'What the bleedin' 'ell are we goin' to do with these? I thought we'd got shot of them.' He stared anxiously at his companion. 'Rufus?'

'Chris'sakes, shut up and let me think!' Sawney snapped. He bit his lip. He should never have offered to take the bloody things back. If he hadn't made the offer, it was possible that Dodd would have hung on to them. It was his own fault for putting the idea into the man's head, giving the doctor the impression that the deal had been on a sale-or-return basis, which was a damned stupid way to conduct trade in dead bodies; so much for the doctor's comment about him showing shrewd business acumen. In reality, it had been a poor transaction, with the doctor taking the choicest morsels and leaving the rest for them to dispose of; like a chewy piece of gristle left on the side of the plate. Too late to do anything about it now. Alongside him, Maggett was shuffling his feet, anxious to be on the move.

'We can take them to Bartholomew's,' Sawney said eventually. 'It's on the way.'

'It's a fair bloody walk,' Maggett said doubtfully. 'You sure?'

'I know it's a fair bloody walk, Maggsie, but 'ave you got a better idea?'

'What about Chapel Street? It was them as made the first offer.'

'Yeah, but that was when they were in good nick. Don't think they'll be interested in seconds.'

'We could dump 'em,' Maggett suggested.

'I'm not bloody dumping them. Not when we might still make a bob or two. No, we'll try Bartholomew's. You never know. Now, you comin' or not?'

Maggett sighed and nodded. 'Whatever you say, Rufus.'

'Right then, that's what we'll do.'

Cursing under his breath, Sawney turned up his collar and, with the sack draped over his shoulder, he led his companion down the deserted street. This, he thought, was all he bloody needed.

Five minutes later it began to snow.

11

'Well, well.' Surgeon Quill looked up. 'Officer Hawkwood. Back so soon? This is indeed an honour.'

The surgeon was standing over one of the examination tables, scalpel in hand, paused in mid slice. Laid out before him was the body of a man. Quill had already begun his dissection. A Y-shaped incision had been carved into the corpse's chest from each shoulder to the base of the sternum and on down to the pubic bone. The skin had been peeled back to reveal the ribcage, muscles and soft tissue that lay beneath. Each of the surgeon's brawny forearms was streaked red to the elbow.

'You've got a couple of bodies,' Hawkwood said. He was in no mood for preamble. He tried not to look at the bloody mess on the table and suspected that Quill was probably grinning inwardly at his discomfort.

'I do indeed. In fact, I have several.' The surgeon extended an arm to encompass the examination room. The movement shook a gobbet of blood from the scalpel blade on to the floor. Quill appeared not to notice the splatter. He paused only to wipe the blade on his filthy apron and raise an eyebrow. 'I take it you have specific ones in mind?'

'They were delivered this morning?'

'Ah, yes, indeed.' The surgeon nodded.

'I'd like to see them,' Hawkwood said.

The surgeon showed his teeth. 'I thought you might. This way.'

Hawkwood followed the surgeon to a table in the centre of one of the vault's dimly lit alcoves. Retrieving a candle from a nearby niche, Quill held it aloft. A sheet covered the table and its contents. It was almost as filthy as the surgeon's apron. Quill drew it back.

'Behold,' he said.

Hawkwood sucked in his breath, and stared down. A chill moved through him that had nothing to do with the temperature in the vault.

The discovery had been made in the early hours, by two Night Patrol constables. The officers had been making their rounds, protecting the capital from rogues, vagabonds, creatures of the night and assorted mischief-makers, when the snow began to fall. Already cold and miserable, the pair had decided to seek temporary shelter inside the archway at the entrance of St Bartholomew's Hospital, with the intention of fortifying themselves for the rest of the patrol with a pipe of tobacco and a warming sip of grog from the small flask each of them carried.

It was as they were scurrying towards the hospital entrance that sharp-eyed Constable John Boggs alerted his companion, Constable Patrick Hilley, to the two figures skulking inside the hospital gates. Neither of the patrolmen was particularly inquisitive by nature, despite their office, and in the normal scheme of things would probably have hesitated before proceeding. But both men were aching from the cold and did not

231

relish seeking alternative shelter by venturing further than they had to in the snow flurries that were beginning to swirl around them. Also, the quick snifter of grog had served to imbue them with a sense of confidence they might not otherwise have enjoyed.

Somewhat inevitably, it was Boggs, the younger of the two, who broke into a trot first, holding his lantern aloft, announcing his identity and calling for the shadowy figures to show themselves.

The two figures appeared to be male. One was of average height, his companion was taller, a lot taller, and big with it. Each bore a load of some kind, but as the underside of the archway lay in deep shadow it was hard to make out details. Boggs saw the ease with which the bigger man moved with the object on his back, unlike his companion, who seemed to be struggling with his burden. Both had shown an impressive fleetness of foot, though with two constables in pursuit, it was hardly surprising.

It soon became clear to the constables that the fleeing men were now empty-handed. Whatever they'd been carrying had been left behind in the rush to evade the constables' clutches.

Arriving at the hospital entrance, Hilley and Boggs watched their quarry fade into the darkness beyond the falling snow, knowing it was pointless to follow. Not too dispirited at the thought, the constables returned to the archway to see what the disappearing duo had discarded.

Lanterns held high, they approached with some caution. A short way inside the entrance, arranged against the wall, were three large wicker hampers.

Hesitantly the constables lifted the lid of each hamper and peered inside. All three were empty. The two men looked at each other, mystified.

Then Hilley spotted the sacks. They were lying between the last hamper and the wall, and looked as if they'd been flung there in a hurry. While his companion raised both lanterns overhead to shed light, Hilley took out his clasp knife and, with shaking hands, cut through the binding of the nearest sack. He was already conscious of the awful smell.

Hilley was the first one to throw up. Boggs wasn't far behind him.

'Intriguing,' Quill said. 'Wouldn't you agree?'

God Almighty, Hawkwood thought. He stared down at the horror before him and nodded dully. He tried to close his nose against the smell, but it was impossible.

Quill used the scalpel as a pointer. 'As you can see, incisions have been made in both cadavers, allowing access to the internal organs, a number of which have been removed.'

'Organs?' Hawkwood said.

'Spleens, kidneys...' Quill began, then looked at him. 'You don't want the entire list?'

'No,' Hawkwood agreed.

'Curious that many of them are digestive in nature,' Quill mused.

'Is that important?' Hawkwood asked.

'I have no idea,' Quill said cheerfully, and then pointed. 'As you can see, sections of skin have also been excised from the forehead and cheeks, the upper arms and thighs, the calves and the

233

back.' The surgeon turned. 'You're going to ask me if it was the same person, aren't you?'

'Was it?'

The surgeon looked down at the bodies and frowned. 'Well, the similarity's striking; especially with regard to the facial excisions. Whoever wielded the knife on these poor women certainly did so with the same degree of skill as the person who removed the facial skin of the body I examined earlier.'

'You mean they had medical knowledge?' Hawkwood said.

'Almost certainly.'

'A surgeon?'

'Quite probably. If not, then it was definitely someone with an intricate understanding of anatomy. I can also tell you that the procedures were carried out not only post mortem but post burial. They were found outside St Bart's, I understand?'

Hawkwood nodded.

The surgeon pursed his lips. 'Not an unusual occurrence.'

Quill was not wrong. The three wicker hampers stowed inside the hospital entrance gates were proof of that. They had not been left there by a forgetful hospital porter. They had been placed there deliberately, for the convenience of the resurrection men. Most of the gangs were in league with hospital staff; porters or dissection-room assistants working on behalf of surgeons, and the baskets made it easier for the sack-em-up men to transport bodies, especially if they needed to deliver the merchandise to their customers in multiples.

The surgeon gazed at the remains and frowned. 'Though, I confess it's unusual for bodies to be in this condition *prior* to delivery. Interesting that all the teeth are still intact.' Quill inserted the blade of the scalpel between the nearest corpse's lips and levered open the mouth. 'See?'

'I'll take your word for it,' Hawkwood said.

'And the hospital has denied all knowledge?'

Hawkwood nodded. He suspected, however, that if the Night Patrol men had arrived ten minutes later, the bodies would have been in one of the hampers and probably on their way to the dissecting room. The hospital would have been unlikely to query the cadavers' condition. Hospitals were so hard up for specimens they'd probably have accepted the things, no questions asked. It had been the thieves' misfortune to be spotted before the bodies were picked up. They hadn't even had the chance to drop them in a hamper. Even so, the discovery might have gone unreported if the two constables had opted to forget what they'd seen and go find somewhere else to have a drink and a smoke. They probably would have done just that, if they hadn't leapt to the assumption that they were dealing with victims of cruel murder rather than medical malpractice. While Hilley had remained with the bodies, his partner had alerted Bow Street. It had been the two constables' reports and description of the awful wounds that had aroused Hawkwood's interest. He stared down at the dead grey flesh.

'You look perplexed, Officer Hawkwood,' Quill said.

'I am,' Hawkwood said. 'I'm wondering how

235

and why a dead man did all this.'

James Read's expression was one of incredulity.
'What exactly are you telling me, Hawkwood?
That you expect me to believe the individual who
violated the women's corpses and the person
who murdered and mutilated the Reverend
Tombs are one and the same?'

'Surgeon Quill seems to think so.'

'Is that what he said?'

Hawkwood hesitated. 'Not exactly, but he said it
was a possibility. Parts of the women's skins had
been removed, including around the face. He said
whoever had done it knew their anatomy.'

Read looked sceptical. 'The bodies were found
outside a hospital. They originated from there,
surely?'

'No. The constables saw them being delivered.
In any case, porters wouldn't have left bodies
either in sacks or in that condition. Hospitals
don't dump bodies, they take them in. They
certainly don't leave pieces of them lying around.
They're far too valuable for that. It was Hyde. I
know it was.'

The Chief Magistrate sighed. 'It seems to me
that we – you – don't know *anything* for certain.
And even if it was Hyde, why would he be cutting
up dead bodies?'

'He's a surgeon. It's what he does.'

James Read's expression continued to mirror
his doubt. 'You think he was one of the men who
left the bodies?'

'I don't know. Either way, I doubt he dug them
up. And he must have a roof over his head. He

236

needs a place to work. Which means *someone's* helping him.'

Read shook his head. 'No, I'm sorry, Hawkwood, I fail to see it. This is all pure speculation. Colonel Hyde's dead. He took his own life. You saw him die.'

'I saw him jump. I didn't see him die.'

The Chief Magistrate sat back in his chair and steepled his hands. 'So, what of the bodies recovered from the church? You visited Quill, you saw the remains – Or had the memory slipped your mind?'

Hawkwood shook his head. He knew the Chief Magistrate was right, of course. The idea was as insane as any of Bedlam's patients. And yet...

He felt a stirring at the back of his mind; a memory of his meeting with Apothecary Locke. He tried to recall the conversation; it had involved the Reverend Tombs. What was it? And then, suddenly, it came to him. It was the reason for the parson's visit being later than usual. The apothecary's words came back to him: ... *attending to parish matters. A burial, I believe it was.*

And a tiny thought began to grow.

The Chief Magistrate returned to his desk.

'I need you to arrange something for me,' Hawkwood said.

Read looked up. 'What is it?'

Hawkwood told him.

The Chief Magistrate looked sceptical. 'What you're asking is highly irregular. It might even be considered unethical. And what would be the purpose? I'm not certain it will prove anything.'

'It'll ease my mind,' Hawkwood said.

237

The Chief Magistrate pursed his lips. 'Your peace of mind is hardly sufficient grounds for carrying out such a serious procedure.' Read sighed. 'However, I can see by your face that you have the bit between your teeth. You are not going to let the matter rest, are you?' Read favoured Hawkwood with a shrewd look. 'No, somehow I didn't think so. Very well, I *will* make the necessary arrangements. Though I fail to see what good it will serve, other than to raise more questions. Was there anything else?'

'I might need a little help.'

'I was afraid of that, too.' There was a weary acceptance in the Chief Magistrate's tone. 'And did you have anyone particular in mind?'

'Hopkins. He struck me as a capable lad. And he's young and healthy.'

James Read raised an eyebrow. 'Is that relevant?'

Hawkwood grinned. '*Someone* has to do the digging.'

The fire had done its work.

The tower was still standing, as was the body of the church, but they had been gutted by the flames. The bruised and blackened stonework told the story. Glass splinters from the broken windows lay strewn over the ground like shattered eggshells. Inside the nave, two charred roof beams rested in disarray across the remnants of the altar and half a dozen scorched pews. All the decorative material items – tapestries, altar cloths, drapes and the like – had been reduced to strips of tattered rag. The snow that had fallen during the night, and which had helped dampen the fire, had melted away, leaving glistening streaks of moisture in its wake. The smell of burnt wood hung uneasily in the damp air.

Sexton Pegg stared at the ruins. His face was haggard. Judging from the devastation, Hawkwood doubted there was much left worth saving but he was reminded that the sexton had lost not only his livelihood but his wife as well.

He had assigned Hopkins to find the sexton and bring him to the church. The old man's first words on seeing Hawkwood had been, 'When am I going to get 'er back?'

It had taken a second for Hawkwood to realize that the sexton was referring to his late wife. He sensed Constable Hopkins throwing him a despairing look behind the old man's back.

'We're still making enquiries,' Hawkwood said tactfully. 'It might be some time.' *And you wouldn't want to see her anyway*, he thought. *Not the way she looks now.*

The old man accepted the news with a philosophical shrug. 'She could be a right cow, but she'll need buryin' all the same.'

There was an awkward pause.

'There *was* a burial...' Hawkwood said into the silence. 'A man, maybe middle-aged. Buried a few days ago; probably late afternoon or evening. It would have been Reverend Tombs' last funeral.'

The sexton looked up. His forehead creased at the change of subject. 'That's right. Name of Foley.' Then he frowned. 'Why you askin'?'

Hawkwood jerked a thumb towards Hopkins. 'Because he's going to dig him up.'

The sexton's jaw dropped. Even Hopkins looked taken aback, and he'd known what to expect. 'You ain't serious? I can't let you do that. It ain't...' the sexton searched for the right word '...legal. Is it?'

'I've a paper says it is,' Hawkwood said. 'Signed by a Bow Street magistrate.' Hawkwood wondered why Hopkins had not warned the old man beforehand, and then it occurred to him that the constable had opted to play it safe, absolving himself of the responsibility by leaving it to Hawkwood to break the news. At least it proved that Constable Hopkins had a mind of his own.

The sexton peered around him vaguely, at what had once been his place of employment. He looked like a man wading slowly out of his depth and knowing he was powerless to prevent it. When he spoke, his voice was a subdued murmur. 'Still don't seem right.' His narrow shoulders slumped in defeat.

'Why don't you show us the grave,' Hawkwood prompted. 'We'll need a shovel and a couple of lanterns.'

'Lanterns?' The sexton looked doubtful. 'It's broad daylight.'

'Just get them,' Hawkwood said.

The burial ground lay adjacent to the church. The grave was sited off to one side, close to a small hummock and the stump of what might have been a long-dead oak tree. There was no headstone, only a small wooden cross on which had been carved, in none too neat lettering, the name of the deceased.

'Cross was temporary,' Pegg explained. 'Mason's

240

still workin' on the inscription for the stone.'

The young constable looked first at the shovel, then at Hawkwood, and then at the task in hand. When Hawkwood had told him what his assignment was, Constable Hopkins had been curious, then strangely excited by the prospect. Now, faced with the imminent unearthing of a dead body, enthusiasm had rapidly given way to a growing feeling of unease.

'Look on the bright side, Constable,' Hawkwood said. 'It could be worse. It could be raining.'

Hopkins looked neither happy nor convinced.

'You do know what a shovel's for, Constable? You use the big end to shift the dirt from one place to another. It's easy, once you get the hang of it.'

The constable blushed.

'He'll 'ave 'is bleedin' work cut out,' Sexton Pegg said morosely. As if to emphasize the validity of his observation, the sexton followed his remark by clearing his throat and expectorating the resulting sac of mucus against the side of a nearby tomb marker. 'We buried this one deep.'

Hearing the sexton's words, the constable's heart sank further. But then he remembered that Hawkwood had asked for him by name, which at the very least meant that the stern-faced Runner did not consider him to be a total numbskull; unless, of course, no one else had been available. This could be the chance he'd been waiting for, the opportunity to show he was ready for advancement. What was it they said about mouths and gift horses?

Bolstered by a fresh surge of self-confidence, Constable Hopkins squared his shoulders and began to dig.

Fifteen minutes later, the constable paused in his digging. Despite the cold, it was proving warm work. The soil was hard on top while underneath it was damp and heavy and clung to the blade of the shovel like fresh dog turds. Rain might have been a blessing. At least it would have cooled him down. He removed his cap and jacket and hung them over the grave marker. Taking a gulp of air, he pulled a handkerchief from his waistcoat pocket and wiped his brow. The old man had been right, it was taking longer than he had expected. He stole a quick glance over his shoulder, half expecting to be met with a cold glare, but Hawkwood had his back to him. Wrapped in his riding coat, the Runner looked to be deep in thought, gazing out across the burial ground like a lookout atop a masthead. Hopkins wondered what was going through his mind.

'Not far to go now,' Sexton Pegg said, interrupting his thoughts. 'You're almost there.'

It took another ten minutes. By the time he had dug down to the coffin lid, Hopkins was already counting the blisters on his hands and the number of aching muscles in the small of his back. His russet hair was plastered to his scalp.

Under the sexton's gaze, the constable scraped away the last of the soil and waited for orders.

Hawkwood stared into the hole, at the all too familiar jagged crack that ran across the top end of the coffin lid.

'Open it up.'

242

Hopkins swallowed nervously.

'Don't worry,' Hawkswood said. 'It's empty.'

The sexton and the constable both turned and stared at him.

Hopkins jammed the blade of the shovel under the lid and bore down on the handle. Then, with a creeping sense of dread, he levered off the broken section of lid and propped it against the side of the grave.

'Well?' Hawkwood said.

Hopkins knelt down and peered into the open coffin, wrinkling his nostrils at the loamy smell that rose to meet him. He looked up. 'You were right. There's nothing there. How did you know?'

Hawkwood ignored the question. 'What was he wearing when they buried him, Mr Pegg?'

''Is Sunday best.'

'You said there's no body, Constable. Is there anything else? Clothing, maybe? Get down. Have a good look. Feel around.'

The constable did as he was instructed. *Feel around?* He was going to need a new uniform after this, he thought gloomily. He looked up and shook his head. 'There's nothing.'

'You're certain?'

'Yes, sir.' Why was Hawkwood so insistent? he wondered.

'All right, you can come up.' Hawkwood held out a hand. Hopkins grabbed it and hauled himself over the lip. 'And I've told you before; don't call me sir.'

The constable reddened.

'The bastards took him.' Pegg spat another mouthful of green phlegm into the earth.

243

'No,' Hawkwood said. 'They didn't.'

The sexton nodded down at the half-open coffin. 'Pissing thing's empty, ain't it? Course they got him!'

Hopkins ignored the outburst. 'How did you know it would be empty?' he asked again. The armpits of his shirt were stained dark with sweat from the digging. He rubbed his breeches to remove the worst of the mud and reached for his cap and jacket.

'I didn't; not for certain. It was a guess. I wanted confirmation.'

'It wasn't the Borough Boys?'

'Evil buggers!' the sexton hissed, to no one in particular.

Hawkwood shook his head. 'It wasn't the resurrection men.'

The sexton's head swivelled.

'Why do you say that?' Hopkins asked.

'Because whoever dug him up took the whole damned lot,' Hawkwood said.

Hopkins looked back down at the hole. 'I don't understand.'

'A corpse is fair game. Take a body, the law can't touch you. Steal the clothes, it's theft. You can be taken down for that. Whether he'd been dressed in a smock or a winding sheet, it'd make no difference. Two weeks in the hulks and a voyage to Botany Bay. But there's nothing down there except the coffin. Whoever did it took everything. If it *had* been the sack-'em-up men, they'd have thrown the clothes back.'

'If it wasn't them, who was it?' Hopkins asked, nonplussed.

Hawkwood did not reply. At the outset he'd outlined what they were going to do, but he had not told Hopkins the reason behind the exhumation; for the moment he was content that the latter should remain ignorant. In any case, Hawkwood had concluded, it was probably best if only he and the Chief Magistrate knew the full extent of his failure and embarrassment if his theory was proved wrong.

He stared at the church, at the tower and the walls that were left standing, and turned to the sexton. 'The man who was buried here. How did he die?'

'Crossin' the street. Got knocked down by a carriage. Driver lost control. The poor bugger was caught underneath the wheels an' dragged 'alfway down the road before they were able to stop it. Broke 'im up some. It weren't a pretty sight.'

The male corpse examined by Surgeon Quill had suffered, among other things, a broken leg, a broken arm and a fractured skull. Both the surgeon and Hawkwood had accepted the evidence at face value, consistent with injuries sustained by falling from a great height. They could equally have been caused by a collision with a carriage travelling at speed.

But if Hyde had dug up the body and substituted it for his own, there was still the matter of his escape from the fire. Hawkwood and scores of witnesses had seen him cast his body into the flames. And by that time the place had been engulfed. Hawkwood continued to gaze towards the tower, stark against the cold winter sky.

245

'Bring the lanterns,' Hawkwood said.

The constable and the sexton looked at each other. Neither said anything, but the unspoken question was there. Then, taking up a lantern each, they followed Hawkwood towards the church.

When they got there, Hawkwood looked up. It was a long way from the tower window to the ground. There had been no hesitation when Hyde had jumped into the flames. One second he was there, the next he was gone, his leap accompanied by the tolling of the bell. No one could have survived the drop, or the fire. There was a bird, Hawkwood knew, the Phoenix, which burned itself every five hundred years, only to rise rejuvenated from its own ashes. But that was a myth and this hadn't been a bird; it had been a man. Nothing arose from a pile of ashes, except perhaps the smell of them.

Hawkwood turned. The sexton was leaning against a section of wall, breathing hard.

'The church,' Hawkwood said, 'when was it built?'

The sexton blinked at this new enquiry.

'This isn't the original building,' Hawkwood said.

'Course it bloody ain't.'

'That's because the one before burnt down as well,' Hawkwood said. 'Didn't it?'

'Everyone knows that. They all went up in smoke, the whole bleedin' lot, and 'alf the city with 'em.'

One hundred and fifty years ago, it had been, or as near as made no difference, and there were parts of the capital that still hadn't recovered. It had started, so it was said, in a baker's, and the close-packed wooden houses had stood no chance against it. The Great Fire had raged across the city destroying all in its path, including all but a handful of parish churches, and the King had commissioned Wren to rebuild them. Over fifty had been completed. St Mary's had been one of them, built, like so many others, on the foundations of the old; a Phoenix made of brick, glass and stone.

Hawkwood grasped the sexton's arm. 'Is there a crypt?'

The sexton winced. 'Course there's a bloody crypt. It's a church, ain't it?'

'Where is it?'

The sexton tugged his arm free and pointed to the tumble of burnt and broken debris that looked as though it was the result of a bombardment from a battery of howitzers. 'Where do you think? It's under that lot.'

'Show me,' Hawkwood said.

The sexton muttered something unintelligible under his breath, as if fed up to the back teeth of being told what to do, but he crooked a finger and stomped off with Hawkwood and the constable following him into the ruined building.

Picking his way through the wreckage, the sexton led them towards what had been the head of the nave. The smell of charcoal hung in the air. The rain had turned the ash into a black sludge. Hawkwood could feel it sticking to the soles of his boots. Looking around, he was struck by the amount of damage the church had suffered.

Rafferty had said the fire started suddenly and intensified at a surprisingly quick rate. It was clear the colonel hadn't just lit a match and hoped for the best.

'The bugger used the lamp oil,' Pegg said. 'We'd just 'ad a fresh supply delivered to see us through winter. The barrels were stored in the vestry.'

That's how it had been done. Hyde had distributed the oil around the inside of the building, emptied it over the pews and the altar and up the stairs in the tower. And the wall hangings and the tapestries and the linen altar cloth, soaked in the oil, would have acted like wicks. It explained how the flames had been able to take such a strong hold.

The old man stopped suddenly and pointed through the two splintered and blackened beams to the crushed remains of the altar. 'Down there.'

Hawkwood assessed the extent of the damage. Beside him, the constable's face fell. Hawkwood straightened and took off his coat. He found a length of beam that was relatively dry and draped the coat across it. Then he turned to the constable. 'Jacket off, lad. There's more work to be done.'

The sexton joined them, though Hawkwood could see the multitude of questions in the old man's eyes. At first sight, the task seemed overwhelming, but Hawkwood had seen that much of the immediate wreckage, although considerable, was not immovable. With the three of them doing the work, it did not, in the end, take long. Mostly, it consisted of careful lifting and leverage, but by the time they had cleared the worst away their clothes and faces were caked in ash and grime.

Before them, at the base of the flame-blackened altar, lay what had once been some sort of floor covering. The flames and the melted snow had rendered it down to a misshapen strip of water-sodden, ash-singed matting. To one side, cut into the stone floor and clearly visible, was the outline of a trapdoor. Inset into a recess in the door was a large iron ring.

Hawkwood felt a quickening inside his chest. Lifting the ring, he bent his knees, braced himself, and pulled. The stone lifted with remarkably little resistance, almost taking him by surprise. Hawkwood slid the stone to one side. A waft of cold, moist air rose to meet him.

'Ain't much down there,' Pegg said, sniffing. ''Cepting a few bones.'

The constable paled. Hawkwood reached for his coat and held out his hand. Wordlessly, the sexton passed over one of the lanterns, then reached into his pocket and passed Hawkwood a small tinderbox.

Hopkins put on his jacket and picked up the second lantern. He had no idea why Hawkwood wanted to enter the crypt, any more than he'd understood why the Runner had wanted to examine the grave, but as he'd come this far, it didn't seem right to hang back now. Besides, he was becoming more and more intrigued by Hawkwood's bizarre behaviour. Something strange was going on. He didn't know what, but if he remained in Hawkwood's shadow there was a possibility he would find out.

Hawkwood lit the lantern and handed the tinderbox to the constable. Holding the lantern over the hole, he looked down. A set of grey stone steps came into view.

If Hyde had taken shelter in the crypt, how had he been planning to get out? There would have been no guarantee he'd be able to open the trap again. The two collapsed roof beams, which Hawkwood, Hopkins and the sexton had just moved, were proof of that.

'There's another entrance,' Hawkwood said. He turned to the sexton. 'Isn't there?'

The sexton's head came up. 'Aye, that's right.' His eyes narrowed. ''Ow come you know about that?'

'Where is it?'

The sexton nodded back the way they had come. 'There's a tunnel. Comes up in the corner o' the burial ground. Inside the old dead house.'

Hawkwood recalled seeing the small stone structure, shaped like a miniature castle keep, complete with crenellated battlements, while he'd been waiting for Hopkins to excavate the grave. Common to a few churchyards, they were used to store coffins. Increasingly, they were also used to store bodies, sometimes for weeks, in the hope that the resulting putrefaction would prevent grave robbery. Hawkwood wondered if Foley's body had been stored there. He didn't know enough about the deterioration rate of bodies after death to know if the cadaver he'd seen in the mortuary had begun to putrefy before it had been consigned to the flames. Quill hadn't said anything, but then even if it had been in storage, the extent of decay might not have been noticeable because of the fire damage. Not that it mattered now.

Hawkwood considered the distance between the nave and the dead house. It meant the tunnel had to be close to eighty or ninety paces in length.

The sexton read Hawkwood's expression. 'It's old. They reckon there was another tunnel, once, which came out nearer the river. They say it was used for carryin' the dead to the plague boats for shippin' downstream. Not there now though, if it ever was. Probably one o' them fairy tales told to scare the little 'uns.'

Hopkins, who had been listening to the exchange, took a step back.

'Don't worry, Constable,' Hawkwood said softly. 'It was a long time ago. It's probably safe enough.'

'You might need this,' Pegg said.

Hawkwood looked down. The sexton was holding out a key.

'What's this for?'

'Key to the dead-'ouse door. Didn't think you'd want to come all the way back again in the dark. You can let yourselves out and bring it back to me later.'

Of course the place was going to be locked, Hawkwood thought. They wouldn't store fully laden coffins in the place and then leave the bloody door open, would they? But then Hyde would have had to open the door to gain his freedom, and the sexton had just handed him the key. Which must mean...

'How many keys are there?' Hawkwood asked.

'Two. Vicar kept the other one.'

'In the house?'

'That's right.'

'Is it still there?'

''Ow the 'ell should I know?'

'Find out.'

'Eh?'

'I want to know if the other key's still there. Do you know where it was kept?'

'With the rest of 'em. They're all on hooks behind the scullery door.'

'Won't take you long to check, then, will it?'

'But the place is locked up,' the sexton said. 'On order of the bishop.'

'Break in, then,' Hawkwood said, putting his foot over the lip of the trapdoor.

Pegg stared at him, his mouth opening and closing like a fish as Hawkwood sank from view.

Hopkins was still thinking about Hawkwood's use of the words 'probably safe enough' in relation to the amount of risk involved in treading in the footsteps of plague victims. It was the 'probably' that worried him. *If I don't get a commendation after this,* he thought dolefully, *there's no such thing as justice.* Lighting his lantern, he returned the tinderbox to the sexton.

'Was 'e serious about breakin' in?' Pegg asked hesitantly. 'Not sure I should do that.'

'Put it this way, Mr Pegg,' Hopkins said, 'I wouldn't want to be in your shoes if he finds out you haven't done it.'

'But–'

'Do it, Mr Pegg. Don't think about it, just do it.'

'Right, well, just so you know, it ain't my responsibility, is all I'm sayin'.'

'Understood, Mr Pegg. Best not waste any time though, eh?' The constable smiled. Then, gritting his teeth and leaving a reluctant Sexton Pegg to investigate the vicarage, he pressed his cap firmly on to his head and followed Hawkwood down the stairway.

Hawkwood could see immediately that the chamber was very old. The walls, from what he could make out in the darkness, looked to be a mixture of ancient brick and crumbling stone. The roof was low and curved. It reminded him of Quill's mortuary, though a less well-lit, smaller and more claustrophobic version, and it undoubtedly predated the remains of the church above them, if not the one that had gone before, and, quite possibly, the one before that. He heard Hopkins' boots clumping down the steps behind him and moved aside to give the constable room.

Holding his lantern at shoulder height, Hopkins surveyed his surroundings. Shadows played across his pale face. 'What are we looking for, s–, Captain?'

Maybe I'll know it when I see it, Hawkwood thought. He left Hopkins' side without answering and moved away from the steps, following the line of the wall. The roof wasn't much more than a foot or so above his head. The urge to tuck his neck into his shoulders increased with every step he took. As his eyes became accustomed to the gloom he saw there were cavities along the walls. Some of them held stone coffins. There were carvings on them: skulls, leaves, crosses, Roman numerals. A few of the lids carried effigies, some in ecclesiastical dress, others in what appeared to be military garments. Like the crypt that housed them, they appeared ancient.

He heard footsteps behind him and saw that Hopkins had also begun to explore. At the bottom of the steps they'd had the advantage of daylight slanting through the open trap, but the further they moved away from the point of entry, the darker their surroundings became. The lanterns only served to illuminate a few yards on either side of them. Nevertheless, they cast enough of a glow to reveal that Hawkwood and the constable were not the only ones down there.

Hawkwood had spotted several rats out of the corner of his eye, their sleek fur rippling in the candlelight as they scampered for cover. He'd felt more than one brush past his feet. Judging from the expletives voiced by Hopkins, the constable had felt them too.

But he could not see any evidence of recent human occupation.

He heard a faint skittering sound close to the ground and felt the contact of tiny claws running across the toe of his boot. Instinctively, he kicked out and heard the high-pitched squeal as his foot made contact, accompanied by the brittle sound of glass striking stone.

He looked down. There was no sign of the rat. The rodent had survived to fight another day. What the lantern glow did pick up was a reflection. He squatted down, thinking it might have been a trick of the eye, but then he saw it, lying on its side at the base of one of the stone coffins: a long-necked bottle, lying on its side. A little further back in the alcove he saw a tin plate and a cup. He picked up the bottle and brought it closer to the lantern. It was corked and there was liquid inside it. Hawkwood put the lantern down and levered the cork from the bottle. Pouring a small measure of the contents into the mug, he took a sniff, then a tentative sip. Wine; still drinkable.

He straightened as he heard Hopkins emit a sharp intake of breath.

The constable was standing a few yards away with his back to him. He was motionless, staring at something ahead of them. Hawkwood put the mug and bottle down, picked up the lantern, and walked forward cautiously.

'Ceptin' a few bones, the sexton had told them.

Only there weren't a few. There were hundreds of them, perhaps thousands, rising out of the earthen floor; a wall of bones, as wide as a door and piled as high as a tall man, extending down the centre of the chamber as far as the light could reach, like the fortifications of some ancient underground citadel. There were more bones in the side alcoves. Every available space, recess and shelf was crammed with them. Skulls, large and small, so many that from a distance they would have looked like pebbles on a beach, the empty, eyeless sockets and hollow nasal cavities black with shadow in the lantern glow. And alongside them, thighbones, stacked from floor to roof, like stored winter logs.

The constable was rooted to the spot, as if he couldn't quite take in what he was seeing. Hawkwood moved past him. As he grew closer to the bone piles, he realized their sheer volume was reflecting the light, extending the radius of illumination. The chamber was more than a crypt. It was a charnel house.

The place must have been in use for centuries, Hawkwood realized. As the burial ground became clogged, the older remains would have been relocated by generations of gravediggers, transferring the bones direct via the tunnel from graveyard to crypt without the need to carry them through the church. The skulls and thighbones were the most prominent because superstition dictated they were necessary for the Resurrection. He looked to his right. The constable's hand was twitching.

'They're only bones,' Hawkwood said. 'They won't bite.'

'There was a charnel house beneath my father's church,' the constable said hoarsely. 'There were men working. One day the floor gave way and two of them fell through. They landed on a pile of skulls. It collapsed on top of them. They were down there in the darkness for hours. It was said that by the time they'd got them out, they'd both lost their minds. They wouldn't stop screaming.' The constable's voice faded away.

No wonder Hopkins had shown reluctance to accompany him, Hawkwood thought.

They moved on, following the bone wall. Occasionally there would be a crunch underfoot as a boot heel bore down on a stray shard of skull. The crypt was a lot bigger than Hawkwood had expected.

He estimated they had travelled about sixty or seventy paces from the entrance when the bone wall came to an abrupt end. He saw that the section of crypt that lay ahead had begun to narrow. There was a muttered oath from Hopkins as the top of his cap grazed the chamber roof. Hawkwood suspected they were probably about to enter the tunnel leading to the burial ground entrance. Both men were forced to lower their heads. Their shadows formed strange hump-backed silhouettes on the walls as the earth pressed in around them. Transporting the bones of the dead down the tunnel and into the charnel house must have been like working in a mine. But at least those involved in the grim work would have had some light to guide them. A series of eye-level niches had been hacked into the walls on either side of the shaft. Set into the base of each one was a short stub of unlit candle.

Hawkwood was reminded of the shafts he'd seen during his army days, dug by engineers to undermine enemy ramparts by means of well-placed explosive charges, where the men doing the excavating had been forced to crawl on hands and knees. Sometimes mistakes were made and charges had been detonated before all the sappers had made their withdrawal, burying the men alive. It had been a terrible way to die.

The tunnel floor began to slope upwards. A break appeared in the floor ahead. Hawkwood could see the base of another set of stone steps, rising towards a closed wooden door. They moved in that direction.

Hawkwood went first. The door was unsecured and opened outwards and he found himself emerging into the dark confines of the dead house. The relief at being able to stand upright once more was almost intoxicating. The lantern glow revealed a square, windowless storage space containing six wooden trestles. Four of them held cheap coffins, all with lids closed. There was a smell to the place that he couldn't identify, like sickly, sweet incense. He suspected that at least one of the coffins held a body that had started to putrefy. With the vicar dead, he wondered how long it would be before the bodies were consigned to the ground. And what would the smell be like then? He crossed the room quickly, inserted the key in the lock of the outer door, and hauled it open.

Inhaling the cold fresh air, Hawkwood felt a surge of excitement. The cup and plate and the half-finished bottle of wine were an indication that the crypt had been visited recently, although there was no proof they'd been placed there by Hyde. Still, it was a possibility, and it meant he at least had something to take back to the Chief Magistrate other than the dried mud and rat shit on his boots and the streaks of ash on his face and cuffs. But was it enough to convince James Read that the colonel might still be alive?

He heard a sigh of relief as Hopkins emerged into the room behind him. Followed by an exhalation of air as the constable's nose picked up the smell from the dead house's other occupants.

Hawkwood turned. As he did so, the corner of the nearest coffin lid, trapped by the light spilling through the open doorway, caught his eye. The lid was not lying flush, he saw, as if it hadn't been fastened down securely. He could also see there was something poking out between the coffin and the lid. Curious, Hawkwood moved closer. It looked like material of some kind. Lining perhaps, although the coffin didn't look to be of good enough quality to warrant a lining. Hawkwood reached out and rubbed the dark cloth between his fingers. It felt too coarse for a lining. It felt more like...

Placing the lantern on the top of an adjacent coffin, Hawkwood hooked his fingers under the lip and lifted the lid.

He heard the constable gasp in surprise.

The faded white dress showed that the body was female, as did the slender form beneath it. The crumpled black coat and matching breeches lying across the body and head as if they had been thrust there in a hurry, however, were undeniably male. By the light from the lantern, Hawkwood could see that they were heavily stained and speckled with what looked like white dust. He lifted the clothes from the coffin and stepped away, taking them towards the open door. They felt slightly damp to the touch. Hawkwood turned the coat over in his hands. There were more marks on the sleeves and on the coat tails. He held the coat up to his face. The smell was instantly recognizable. It was smoke. He knew then that the white marks hadn't been caused by dust. They were minute flakes of ash.

And then from what seemed a mile away, he heard Hopkins say in a small, very still voice, 'Officer Hawkwood, there's something here I think you should look at.'

Hawkwood turned. Hopkins was staring into

259

the open coffin. 'Sir?' the constable said again. There was a new urgency in his voice.

Hawkwood walked back. Hopkins was leaning over the coffin, his lantern held close to the body. He was peering at something. His eyes were narrowed, as if he couldn't quite make out what he was seeing. Suddenly he straightened. Sensing Hawkwood beside him, he turned. His face was transfixed, an immovable yellow mask. Then his lips parted. They continued to move in silence, his throat constricting, as though he was about to disgorge something recently swallowed. No words were uttered. It was the expression of horror in the constable's eyes that compelled Hawkwood to look down.

'Look at her face,' Hopkins whispered.

Hawkwood did so.

Affixed to the front of the corpse's skull, in perfect alignment with the eyes and nose, cheeks and jaw, was what appeared to be some kind of visor. It was the nature of the material the visor had been fashioned from that had caused the tremor in the constable's voice. The visor was not made of metal, neither was it cut from cloth or hide, though it did bear some semblance to seasoned leather. It also gave the impression the deceased had suffered from some terrible flesh-wasting disease. It was a mask of human skin.

12

'Very well, Hawkwood. You've convinced me.'

The Chief Magistrate pushed himself away from his desk and moved to the window, hands clasped behind his back. 'Even though you saw him fall. You and a hundred others.'

'No,' Hawkwood said. 'We didn't see him fall. We saw him jump. He didn't trip. He didn't over-balance. He bloody jumped. It was deliberate. He knew what he was doing and he fooled us all. That's why we heard the bell toll. He used the rope to lower himself to the ground. Then he climbed down into the crypt, closed the trap after him and made his way through the tunnel. Came up inside the dead house and made his escape. It would have been a close-run thing. It would have taken exceptional timing, but he did it. It was bloody clever.'

'And he is not a young man,' Read said.

'No, he's not, but Apothecary Locke told me he's an athletic man who kept himself in good physical shape by performing regular exercises.'

'In other words,' Read said flatly, 'he was preparing himself.'

Hawkwood nodded. 'He planned everything, even down to the theft of the scalpel and the laudanum. The apothecary said that Tombs was a regular visitor to the colonel's cell. Hyde used the visits to bleed Tombs for information. He'd have

261

found out about the church, the charnel house and the tunnel, even the spare bloody key. Tombs probably made him laugh with a story of some poor bugger getting locked in, which was why they had another key made. The sexton checked the house. The second key was missing. I'll wager the bastard even got the parson talking about recent burials during each of his visits and timed his escape to coincide with the burial of someone close to his own age and size. He knew if he could fake his own death and make us all believe he'd done away with himself, we'd give up the chase. So he waited until the right corpse came along and then made his move. Dug the poor sod up, maybe even dressed him in some of the parson's spare clothes – he'd have found them in the house – and placed the body in the church, then he lit his funeral pyre. It wouldn't surprise me if he'd been wearing Foley's burial suit when he made his escape. Probably stowed it in the crypt in preparation. The shine I saw on his clothing before he jumped would have been water. He'd doused himself as a precaution. That's why the jacket and breeches I found felt damp. They hadn't had time to dry.'

'And the sexton's wife got in his way,' Read said heavily.

'She probably disturbed him at the house, or maybe she saw him moving the body. Either way, he had to kill her; she was a witness. By God, the man was thorough, I'll grant him that; all that quoting from the scriptures and the Book of Titus. And he's an arrogant bastard. He couldn't resist that final joke, leaving the parson's face in

262

the woman's coffin. But his arrogance made him careless. He didn't close the bloody lid properly.'

Read looked thoughtful. 'How is the constable, by the way?'

'He might be due for a few sleepless nights, but he'll get over it. It's worth a commendation, though. He did well.'

'I'll see to it,' Read said. The Chief Magistrate moved to his desk. 'You still think Hyde is responsible for the mutilations?'

Hawkwood nodded.

Read stared at him for what seemed like a long time. Finally the Chief Magistrate sighed. 'What do you intend to do?'

'Catch the bastard. But to do that I'll need to know more about his background.'

'You intend to revisit Bethlem?'

'It's the logical place to start,' Hawkwood agreed.

Read looked pensive.

'What is it?'

'My sources tell me that the hospital governors are most anxious to avoid releasing information that might alarm the public.'

'What the hell does that mean?'

'They feel it would be best for all concerned if the full details of the colonel's escape were kept confidential.'

Hawkwood stiffened. 'You mean they want to cover it up?'

'Admitting that murderers can wilfully abscond from the country's foremost lunatic asylum in order to create mayhem is hardly conducive to the retention of public confidence. Bethlem is

263

not a country estate; it lies within a city, surrounded by a million people going about their business, most of them lawfully. Far better if they are able to sleep easy in their beds than worry about escaped murderers on the loose.'

'The bloody place is crawling with murderers on the loose,' Hawkwood said, unable to keep the exasperation from his voice. 'That's why you employ people like me.'

Read sighed. 'You know very well what I mean.'

'So, what are they going to do: swear everybody to silence? How are they going to explain the church going up in smoke? That's already in the newssheets.'

'A church burned down, a parson died. A tragedy occurred.'

Hawkwood stared at the Chief Magistrate. 'The parson didn't just die, he was murdered. So was the sexton's wife. And the murderer's still out there, *loose on the bloody streets!*'

'No, as far as the public is concerned, the murderer died in the fire,' Read said.

The significance of the magistrate's words struck home. 'So the poor bloody parson's going to take the blame?'

'A hundred witnesses heard his confession and saw him commit suicide. It suits our purpose if they continue to believe that.'

'But too many people know what really happened.'

'Not that many. Only two members of the hospital staff know the truth: the apothecary and the keeper, Leech. They have been persuaded to amend their story, in the interests of the hospital.

If anyone should make enquiries, it was the colonel who was killed, not his visitor; and if rumours of an alternative scenario should circulate, that's all they'd be: rumours. The only other people who know the correct version of events are in this room.'

'There's Hopkins.'

'Hopkins knows?'

'He does now. I thought it was only fair to tell him. Though I warned him, if he breathes a word, I'll hang him by his ears from Blackfriars Bridge. And he does have *very* prominent ears.'

'Let us hope they were in full working order when you made your threat.'

'Keeping the knowledge that Hyde is alive between ourselves could play to our advantage,' Hawkwood conceded. 'He probably thinks we're a bunch of clodhoppers and that he's outwitted us. And that may make him even more careless...' Hawkwood paused. 'If I'm going to run him down, I may have to step on a few toes.'

The Chief Magistrate nodded. The corner of his mouth twitched. 'I'd be very surprised if you didn't,' he said drily. 'You'll be discreet and keep me appraised, of course?'

'Don't I always, sir?' Hawkwood said.

The stench was just as bad as it had been before, but at least the rainwater was no longer flowing down the walls, which was some sort of progress, Hawkwood supposed, as he followed Attendant Leech up the main stairs. After the frantic activity that had greeted his last visit, the atmosphere in the building seemed strangely subdued. But the lull was temporary. As they reached the landing, a long-drawn-out scream broke the spell. As if it had been a signal, it was answered by a dozen more. Hawkwood was reminded of the wolf packs that roamed the Spanish mountains. The first time he had heard their howling, the hairs had risen up on the back of his neck. He felt the familiar prickle beneath his hairline and the memory came flooding back. Leech saw his reaction and grimaced. 'The Devil's chorus, we call it. Pretty, ain't it?'

The room was as he remembered it. The musty smell had not dissipated and there were still traces of moisture high along the covings and beneath the windowsills. The only difference was that a fire had been lit in the grate, as much to keep back the encroaching damp as to provide warmth and comfort, Hawkwood suspected. Apothecary Locke was at his desk. He looked just as apprehensive as he had the first time.

'Thank you, Mr Leech. I'll ring if I need you.'

The attendant hesitated and then left the room.

Locke spread his hands. 'So much paperwork. There are times when I swear I will drown under its weight.' The apothecary stared morosely through his spectacles at the sea of forms before him then stood up. 'A terrible business. The *Chronicle* stated that most of the church was destroyed. Is that true? I've not been to see for myself, and one never knows whether the reports in the newspapers are exaggerated. The governors asked for a full report, of course. It goes without saying that I shall be including details of my own ... lapses of judgement. I'm only hoping they will be magnanimous in their deliberations.'

Locke took off his spectacles and reached for the handkerchief in his sleeve. 'So, Officer Hawkwood, what can I do for you?' The apothecary smiled nervously.

Hawkwood wondered how much of that nervousness was due to the apothecary's discomfort with the governors' new confidentiality directive. Leech's manner hadn't seemed any different, but as a keeper in a madhouse he was probably used to being ordered around, even if he didn't like it. But then, Leech didn't look like the sort of man who had too many scruples, especially when his job was at stake. The apothecary, though, was different. Hawkwood sensed a streak of integrity in Locke and, if that observation held true, the apothecary's unhappiness at having to conform to the governors' desire for secrecy was understandable.

'You assume correctly, Doctor. I want to see the admission documents relating to Colonel Hyde's commitment to the hospital.'

Locke nodded. 'Your visit is most timely, for I recently retrieved them from Dr Monro's archive. I thought they would be useful for my summation. I've not yet read them, though I could tell they have not emerged unscathed from their hibernation. As you will have observed, we are not immune to the vicissitudes of Mother Nature. Over the years flooding has been a persistent enemy and the accumulative damage has been considerable. Fortunately, with regard to the colonel's records, not all has been lost. If you'll allow me a moment, I'll see if I can locate them. I put them down here somewhere.'

Without waiting for a reply, the apothecary began to rifle through his papers.

Finally, he held up a thin collection of yellowing documents secured in a black ribbon. 'Yes, here we are. As you will see, the elements have left their mark. The damage may not be too severe, however.' The apothecary glared at the tell-tale stains running down the walls. 'I shall be glad when we move to our new premises. The conditions here are becoming quite intolerable.'

Clearing a space on the desk, Locke untied the ribbon.

Hawkwood moved closer and looked over the apothecary's shoulder. Locke's collar was quite frayed, he noticed, and there were strands of hair and white flecks of dandruff on both it and the back of his jacket.

Carefully, the apothecary laid the ribbon to one side and began to flatten out the papers.

The documents had indeed been severely affected by the rain and damp. Dark water stains framed the top edges and extended in ugly brown blotches for two or three inches across the upper half of each page. Separating the first sheet, the apothecary tutted as his fingertips traced the unsightly marks.

'This is the Admittance Document. There are the particulars: patient's name, age, period of distraction, and so forth. As you can see, and as you may recall from our last discourse, Colonel Hyde was admitted to the hospital on the grounds of melancholy.'

Ignoring the rain damage and the smudges to the ink, Hawkwood ran his eye down the page. At the top of the document, in faint print and just discernible beneath the water stains, he could make out the words: *It is necessary the following Particulars should be made known for the Admission of Patients into Bethlem Hospital.*

The rest of the form was as Locke had described; a concise summary of the patient's personal circumstances. The period of distraction, Hawkwood noted, had been given as four months. Which didn't seem very long. Other than that, for all the rest of the densely worded text, there was precious little information on the state of the patient's mind, other than the one-word diagnosis. Interestingly, there was no space for the date of the admission, but in the margin, someone had written in an untidy hand: *23rd Oct 1809.*

His gaze moved down the page. His eye caught the word *Bond.*

'What's this?'

'The bond? It is purely a note of surety. The signatories agree to cover the cost of the patient's clothing, the cost of their removal if discharged, or their burial when dead. It's a set amount, as you see: one hundred pounds. I have the colonel's here.'

Locke produced another page from the sheets on the desk and muttered with annoyance. Of all the pages, the bond looked to have suffered the most discoloration. The ink had run and the top quarter of the page was completely illegible. Grimacing, Locke smoothed the page out as best he could with the palm of his hand. The rest of the document was readable, but only just.

Hawkwood's eyes moved to the two signatures

269

on the bottom right-hand side of the page.

The first signature was illegible. Had the top half of the document not been ruined, it would have been possible to read the official scribe's notation, with the names clearly rendered, but water damage had made that impossible. In any case, it was not the name of the first signatory that had drawn Locke's attention. It was the second, more legible signature over which his finger hovered.

Eden Carslow, FRCS.

Hawkwood read the name again. '*The* Eden Carslow?'

Locke nodded. A little cautiously, Hawkwood thought.

'You're sure?'

'I doubt there's another,' Locke murmured.

While there were many men whose names commanded instant respect, the number whose reputation bordered on the supernatural based solely on their profession could be counted on the fingers of one hand. If the Army had Wellington and the Royal Navy had Nelson, the world of medicine had Eden Carslow.

'They say he makes over fifteen thousand a year from private practice alone,' Locke said. There was a note of awe in his voice. 'And that his lectures to students command audiences of four hundred or more.'

'Which makes you wonder why he's bothering to stand as security on a £100 bond for a patient in a madhouse,' Hawkwood murmured.

Locke was silent. At first Hawkwood presumed it was because the apothecary was still over-

270

whelmed by the proximity of greatness. But it turned out it was because he was preoccupied with another of the pages. 'There's more,' Locke said quietly, passing over the page. 'Look.'

It was a letter, written in an elegant hand:

Whitehall, 27th October 1810

Gentlemen,
It is my recommendation that you continue to detain in your hospital as a fit and proper subject the patient, Titus Xavier Hyde, a lunatic, who is at present under your charge. It is also my recommendation that care shall be taken that the customary expense of clothing, etc, together with the expense of his funeral, in case he should die, shall be settled.
I have the honour to be your most obedient humble servant,
Ryder

Hawkwood read the words, his mind turning. Finally, he pushed himself away from the desk and took a deep breath. Someone had to say it.

'All right, Doctor, I've two questions for you. The first is: why would a man of Eden Carslow's standing put up a bond for a patient in your care? The second is: would you mind telling me exactly how many of your other patients have had their discharge from the hospital denied by a personal note from the Home Secretary?'

Sawney and Hanratty were in the Dog.

'Done some checkin', like you asked,' Hanratty said. 'On that Runner.'

271

'Oh, yes?' Sawney sucked on a tooth cavity and winced as a nerve twanged. 'An' what 'ave you found out?'

'He's a right bastard.' Hanratty slid into the booth.

'Jesus, *I* could've told *you* that,' Sawney said, shaking his head in disbelief. Ever mindful of earwiggers, he took a quick look around. The Dog was filling up. The floor was already awash with spilt beer, black sawdust and spit.

'What I mean is, he's a bigger bastard than most, and useful with it.'

'Probably why Tate and Murphy didn't make it then,' Sawney said scathingly. 'Serves 'em bleedin' right.'

'Rumour is, he used to be army.'

Sawney felt a vague ripple of interest. 'Is that right?'

'Makes two of you, don't it? Be funny if'n you'd met up before.'

'That ain't likely,' Sawney grated. 'I'd 'ave remembered. What else did you find out?'

'About what?'

'The price of apples. Christ! This bleedin' Hawkwood, of course.'

'I 'eard he was the one who shut down that old witch Gant and her brood a while back.'

'That the one with the idiot son?'

'That's her. Likely they're somewhere off the Malabar Coast by now, spewin' their guts over the side of a bloody transport.'

'Maybe we should be buyin' the bugger a drink then,' Sawney said sarcastically.

'How about I set *my* boys on him? They'd make

272

sure.' Hanratty grinned lopsidedly. "Sides, they could do with the exercise.'

Sawney shook his head. He'd already come to the conclusion that Hanratty had been right in the first place. Sending Tate and Murphy after Hawkwood had been a mistake. With both of them dead, or at least one dead and the other having disappeared or gone to ground, it was probably best if everyone calmed down.

'We'll take things easy for a bit,' Sawney said. 'But we'll keep our eyes open in case he comes sniffin' round again. Not that the bastard's got anything on us. Far as anyone here's concerned, Tate and Murphy were just two 'pads tryin' their luck. The verger ain't around any more, so that trail's gone cold.' Sawney gave a grin. 'In a manner of speakin'.'

Hanratty drew a blunt finger down his stubble. 'What about Sal?'

'What about her?' Sawney's eyes narrowed.

'People 'ere will 'ave seen her with Symes, seen that she *knew* him.'

'If you mean like in the scriptures,' Sawney said, 'that'd apply to 'alf your bleedin' customers, or all the ones who've ever 'ad money in their pocket, at any rate. Christ, that'd include anyone with a pulse between here and Limehouse Reach. Besides, who's goin' to say anything? Sal sure as hell ain't. It'll be all right. We'll take a breather, the fuss'll die down and that Runner'll get bored and move on. It's already been a couple of days.'

Hanratty shifted in his seat.

'What?' Sawney said.

273

'I heard he 'as a few eyes and ears over on our side of the street.'

'Meanin'?'

'There's word he's been seen with that bastard Jago.'

'Jago?'

'Jesus, Rufus, you should get out more. He's definitely one you don't want to cross. Runs the rackets over St Giles' way.'

'An' that's supposed to impress me, is it?'

'Bleedin' impresses me,' Hanratty said with feeling.

'Well, just as long as 'e keeps to 'is patch and stays upwind...' Sawney said.

'Let's hope so. I'll keep diggin', though. See if there's anything else I can find out. Never does any harm, keepin' an eye on the opposition.' Hanratty hawked and spat. 'Far as the rest of it's concerned, we sit tight then, right?'

'You can sit tight,' Sawney said. 'Some of us have work to do.'

Hanratty frowned and stroked his crown. 'Thought you said we should take things easy.'

'So I did, but that don't mean we should stop altogether. There's mouths to feed. We'll put an 'old on our regular stuff. I've got a client who's prepared to pay big money for special deliveries. That should tide us over for a bit.'

'You got a job on?' Hanratty asked.

'Could be. Won't know until I get the nod. I'm meetin' 'im later. You seen Maggsie or the Ragg boys, by the way?'

'Think Maggett's over in 'is yard. The Raggs took a couple of the girls upstairs a while back.

274

They like to do 'em together and swap 'alfway through. 'Ave to say, you wouldn't catch me putting my old man anywhere either of them 'as been.'

Sawney passed no comment. The appetite of the Ragg brothers had long since ceased to impress, repel, or even interest him. Provided they did their bit and followed orders, Sawney couldn't care less what they did with the rest of their time. They could have had a troupe of monkeys and a marching band upstairs, for all he cared, long as they kept the noise down, of course, and didn't attract the attention of the law.

But that didn't mean that Sawney couldn't indulge his own appetites. He had several hours to kill before he was due to pay the doctor a call. Sal was upstairs, and when he'd left her to nip down for a swift wet, the look in her eye had made it clear that, once his thirst had been slaked, it would be worth his while if he hurried back. As Hanratty left the table and returned to the counter, Sawney slid out from the booth and headed for the stairs. Be a shame to let the mood go to waste, he thought.

James Read frowned. 'Eden Carslow *and* the Home Secretary? And what was Apothecary Locke's response?'

'He had no answer to my question about Eden Carslow. As to the other, he said there was one other instance he knew of where the Home Secretary had denied release, and that was Matthews.'

'Matthews?' The Chief Magistrate's head came up.

275

'James Tilly Matthews. Apparently he was locked away fifteen years ago after he'd accused Lord Hawkesbury of treason. Reckoned Frog Revolutionaries were controlling his mind. Now, he *was* bloody mad. The odd thing is, it took only a year for the Home Secretary to deny Hyde his freedom, whereas in Matthews' case it took twelve years, by which time the man he'd accused of treason had become Home Secretary, so it's hardly surprising he wasn't about to approve his release.'

Read's face remained neutral. 'Matthews ... yes, I believe I do recall the occasion. He's still a patient, you say?'

Hawkwood nodded. 'They've thrown the key away on that one. I'll say one thing for our colonel, he's no stranger to the high and mighty.'

'So it would seem,' Read murmured.

'But I still don't know why,' Hawkwood said. 'In fact, I'm no wiser than I was before I went. Their damned records were about as much use as a one-legged mule – I hope ours are better, by the way. I'd be interested to know on whose authority he was admitted. He had no family, from what I could see. No wife. There was a daughter, Locke told me that on my first visit, but she died.'

Read frowned. 'What are you suggesting?'

'I don't know. The Admittance Document says he entered the hospital in October 1809, by which time he'd been in a state of melancholy for four months. So the first signs would have occurred in June. Where was he then?' Hawkwood sucked in his cheeks. 'Mind you, the only other choices, apart from melancholy, were "raving" and "mischievous". He wasn't either of those. Maybe the

276

records were vague on purpose.'

'Your point being...?'

'According to the hospital documents the only thing he was suffering from, until now, was melancholy. And yet twelve months after his admission, we have a note from Whitehall – the Home Secretary, no less – recommending they keep him locked up, which seems a bit bloody harsh. Now, it's my guess that if you get a recommendation from Whitehall, it's not really a recommendation, it's an order.'

'Forgive me, Hawkwood, but I fail to see–'

'I'm saying Locke didn't consider Hyde to be dangerous, certainly not murderous. None of them at the hospital did. But if, as we suspect, the colonel had been planning the killing and the escape for some time, then maybe he was murderous from the beginning and the fact was kept hidden, which would mean the only people who knew what he was really like were the ones who arranged his detention and who denied his release.'

'You're suggesting he was admitted under a false diagnosis? But why? For what possible reason?'

'Maybe that's what we should try to find out. I'd like to know what the connection is between Colonel Hyde and Eden Carslow, for a start. That certainly intrigues me.'

'You intend to question Carslow?' Read asked. There was a distinct note of caution in the magistrate's voice.

'I promise I'll be civil,' Hawkwood said, before he could stop himself.

'You will need to be. Carslow has powerful

friends. He has influence.'

'That sounds familiar. Isn't that what we said about Lord bloody Mandrake?'

'No, that was what we thought about William Lee. As far as we were aware, Lord Mandrake was just another of his highly placed friends.'

'Who turned out to be a traitorous bastard,' Hawkwood said.

Lee was an American adventurer who, with the support of Lord Mandrake, had been the leading agent in a French plot to assassinate the Prince Regent. Lee had died in the attempt; Mandrake had taken a boat from Liverpool and fled to safety across the Atlantic.

'Indeed. Carslow, on the other hand, is probably this country's finest surgeon. His contribution to medicine has been outstanding. You said earlier you might have to step on a few toes. Where Eden Carslow is concerned, you would be wise to tread carefully. I mean it, Hawkwood. While I place great store on your investigative instincts, there are others of a more – how shall I put it? – refined disposition who may interpret your direct approach as a recalcitrant attitude towards authority. I urge you to be circumspect.'

'Yes, sir. Understood. In that case, may I offer you the same advice in your dealings with the Home Secretary?'

Read blinked. 'I beg your pardon?'

'Well, it struck me that, while I question Carslow about his connection with Colonel Hyde, you could use your authority to find out why Home Secretary Ryder felt the need to add his name to the list of people who would have

278

preferred the colonel to remain in Bethlem.'

'You have the nerve of the devil, Hawkwood.'

'Yes, sir. Thank you, sir. May I take that as confirmation that you will speak to the Home Secretary? After all, you do meet regularly with him on matters of security. It would be a pity not to take advantage of that. Or am I being recalcitrant, sir?'

'You're bordering on insolent, which rather proves my point,' Read said.

'But you'll speak to him?'

Read sighed. 'One does not speak *to* the Home Secretary, Hawkwood. One speaks *with* him. I rather suspect the same principle will apply in your forthcoming conversation with Carslow.'

'I'll bear that in mind,' Hawkwood said.

'See that you do. Now, was there anything else? Public chastisement of the Prime Minister, perhaps?'

'Possibly,' Hawkwood said, striding towards the door. 'The day's not over yet.'

13

The lecture room was full to bursting; standing room only. The five horseshoe-shaped tiers rising from the floor of the theatre reminded Hawkwood of a steep-sided cockfighting pit. Even the atmosphere wasn't dissimilar; the closely packed spectators, the vibrant hum of conversation, the heightened sense of anticipation as the crowd waited for the spectacle to begin.

Hawkwood had presented himself at Guy's only to be met with a lofty refusal when he stated his wish to see the hospital's Chief Surgeon. Mr Carslow was about to perform surgery. Police business would have to wait. Knowing he had no option but to bide his time, curiosity had led Hawkwood to take his place with the rest of the gallery.

It was warm in the room due to the mass of people. Removing his coat, he draped it over the wooden rail in front of him. From his seat in the top tier, he looked down across a sea of eager young men who didn't appear to have seen more than fifteen or sixteen summers. But then some of the boys he'd commanded and fought alongside in the Peninsula hadn't been that much older.

He glanced up. The theatre was illuminated by a large skylight, supplemented by chandeliers suspended above the centre of the room by a system of pulleys. Directly below the skylight, occupying centre stage, was the operating table.

It was a robust piece of furniture with a hinged headboard at one end and an extension leaf at the other. On the sawdust-strewn floor beneath the extension leaf was a large oblong tray containing more sawdust. In the corner of the theatre was a large cupboard. The back wall held a rectangular blackboard. Below it stood two smaller tables and a small oak cabinet.

Several chairs had been set up on the floor, facing the foot of the operating table. The seating was for distinguished visitors, some of whom had already taken their places. The lowest tier of the horseshoe was reserved for members of the hospital's medical staff. The upper tiers accommodated the students.

A movement on the floor caught Hawkwood's eye and prompted a buzz of chatter, but it was short lived when the crowd realized it was only the dressers bringing in linen and towels and a pitcher of hot water. Nevertheless, the air of expectation remained as it was now apparent that the operation and lecture were only minutes away. The two dressers appeared unconcerned at the reaction their appearance had caused and went about their business calmly and unhurriedly, placing the linen on the centre table, and the towels and pitcher on the oak cabinet next to an enamel basin. Another small square table was positioned near the main operating table. On top of it sat a deep-sided wooden box and a small tin bowl. One of the dressers began to transfer a selection of surgical instruments from box to tabletop. When they had finished laying out all the equipment, they moved to the side of the room and stood in silence, hands behind their backs, waiting.

Suddenly the level of conversation dropped. Hawkwood felt the students on either side of him tense. Three men entered through a door in the corner of the theatre, their footsteps resonating on the wooden floor. Two of the men were dressed in dark tailcoats, and the younger one was holding the arm of a third man, who was wearing a white calf-length nightgown and slippers. The young man ushered the night-shirted individual to the table and invited him to sit, leaving his companion to take the floor.

So this was the great man, Hawkwood thought.

Carslow had presence, there was no denying it. Tall, well built, with a bearing that was almost military and a high forehead crowned by swept-back hair, his elegant stature and steady, unflinching gaze reminded Hawkwood of Arthur Wellesley.

A hush fell over the lecture room.

'Lithotomy, gentlemen. Cutting the stone. From the Greek: *lithos* – stone – and *thomos* – cut. The removal of one or more calculous form-ations that cannot exit through natural channels and must therefore be extracted by means of surgical incision.'

The speaker turned and indicated the man in the nightgown. 'The patient is a forty-three-year-old male and a merchant by trade. His symptoms – abdominal pain and acute discomfort while urinating – indicate the presence of a stone in the bladder. This afternoon I will be operating to remove the offending object.'

The spectators turned their heads towards the patient seated on the table. His brow was bright with sweat. Dark stains were visible under his armpits. There was a noticeable tremor in his right leg. The man looked terrified.

'The operation to remove a stone or stones is one of the most important a surgeon can perform. It requires not only a detailed understanding of anatomy, but also a mind that never wavers and a hand that never shakes.' Carslow paused in his address and ran a stern eye over the faces of the onlookers.

Then the surgeon turned to the waiting dressers and removed his coat. 'Let us begin.'

A dresser stepped forward to take the surgeon's coat, exchanging it for an apron that had been hanging on a hook next to the door.

Carslow addressed the room once more. 'There are only two safe routes to enter the bladder; the first is from directly above, through the lower abdomen. This is referred to as the high operation. The second is by way of the perineum, known as the lateral operation. It is the latter that I shall be performing today. However, before I begin the procedure, I shall require the services of two more assistants.'

Carslow placed a forefinger to his lips. His eyes swept the encircling tiers. Hawkwood, watching from above, had the impression this was a charade enacted before every operation. He could see students nudging each other and grinning as if it were a contest where the team captain got to pick his right-hand man.

The surgeon's gaze settled on the second tier

down, to the left of where Hawkwood was standing. He pointed. 'You, sir, and the young gentleman to your right; if you'd be so kind as to join us. Your names, please? Mr Liston and Mr Oliver, is it? Very well, if you would attend my colleague Mr Gibson, he will instruct you.' Carslow ushered the two students in the direction of his companion, who was still standing by the table, his hand placed reassuringly on the patient's shoulder.

'Now, gentlemen, if you'd kindly prepare the patient by placing him in the lithotomy position.'

The audience watched as the hinged headboard was raised to form a shallow angle and locked. A linen cloth was placed over the table. The patient was then laid on his back, hands by his sides, with the back of his head resting against the slanted board. His legs extended out beyond the end of the table, above the tray of sawdust.

The patient's nightshirt was lifted and rolled back over his chest. Beneath the gown, the man was naked. His skin was as pale as paper. On Carslow's instructions, a strap was secured around each of the patient's ankles. On a further nod from the surgeon, the patient's knees were drawn up and back towards his chest, and his legs were pulled apart until his genitalia and buttocks were fully exposed.

Carslow again addressed the onlookers. 'The patient must be restrained and kept absolutely still. The slightest deviation, a slip of the blade for example, could mean inadvertent damage to the patient's leg or rectum, or even the surgeon's finger, and we would not want that, now, would we?'

A polite ripple of laughter ran around the room. The look of alarm on the patient's face made it clear that at least one man present did not share the surgeon's sense of humour. His body was visibly quaking.

Carslow moved towards the foot of the operating table. His hands hovered over the row of instruments.

'Mr Liston and Mr Oliver, a wrist each, if you please. Mr Allerdyce and Mr Flynn, if I may direct you to take the patient's ankles and knees. A firm hold is required, gentlemen. Are you ready, Mr Ashby?'

It was the first time the patient's name had been used. But from the stricken expression on his face, Hawkwood suspected that the poor man had probably forgotten what his own name was. There wasn't even so much as a weak nod.

Carslow cocked an enquiring eye at the dressers, the two students and his colleague, Gibson. All five helpers nodded back imperceptibly. Hawkwood saw the muscles along their forearms stiffen as they took up the strain.

The surgeon's hand dropped to the table. It rose into view holding a straw's-breadth metal rod, curved at one end like a large un-barbed fishhook. The implement was held up for the audience to see. 'The bladder sound. Note the groove in the outer curve of the staff.'

Holding the rod in his right hand, Carslow leaned forward, took hold of the patient's flaccid manhood with his left hand, held it upright and, without pausing, placed the hooked end of the rod into the tip of the penis and pushed it down

285

inside the shaft.

Christ Jesus! Hawkwood clenched his fists at the unexpectedness of it.

A bellow of pain erupted from the patient's mouth and his body arched. The table became a mêlée of thrashing arms and legs.

'Hold him still, gentlemen! Hold him! Calm, Mr Ashby!

Calm!'

It was clear from the speed with which the two dressers hauled down on the straps that they were accustomed to grappling with patients. The two students, however, despite their hold, had plainly been taken by surprise at the ferocity of the resistance. It was only with the help of the surgeon's chief assistant, Gibson, who laid himself across the patient's chest, that they were finally able to renew their grip.

It took several seconds before the man on the table was held fast. Through it all his head continued to whip from side to side like a newly landed fish.

Hawkwood found that his palms were slick with sweat. It had been an extraordinarily unnerving scene. There couldn't have been a man watching who hadn't imagined himself in the patient's position as the probe went in.

Ignoring the patient's yells, Carslow continued where he had left off. Gripping the metal staff once more, he began to feed the rod down the inside of the penis. His voice remained measured though louder than when he had started, to counteract the noise from the man struggling on the table. 'We place the rod through the urethra and into the bladder, like so, and we listen...'

Hearing the surgeon's words, Hawkwood was suddenly aware of how still the rest of the room had become. It was as if everyone was holding his breath. Even the patient's cries subsided into a series of low mewling sounds, though the pain must have been excruciating. Then, to Hawkwood's astonishment, the surgeon bent and placed his ear to the base of the patient's cock.

'There!' Carslow announced. 'The villain is located.'

Hawkwood realized the surgeon had been listening for the click as the curved end of the rod knocked against the stone.

Swiftly, keeping a hold on the end of the rod, which was sticking out of the patient's penis like a stopper in a decanter, the surgeon reached for his scalpel.

Hawkwood's stomach twisted.

'Hold him fast, gentlemen, if you please.'

The dressers bore down on the patient, exerting pressure. The leather straps were pulled tight.

'Now for the first incision. I place the blade against the perineum, so. And remember, slowly and deliberately...'

Placing the point of the blade against the skin behind the patient's scrotum, he pressed in and drew it carefully down towards the patient's rectum. The flesh parted like grape skin. Blood welled. A bleating wail rose from between the patient's clenched teeth.

Hawkwood sucked in his breath.

The patient writhed as the surgeon continued. 'I divide the prostate gland and with the point of

287

my blade I press against the bladder wall, feeling for the groove in the bladder sound, while taking care to avoid damage to the surrounding tissue.'

Blood, Hawkwood could see, had started to drip from the incision.

A pig-like squeal rose from the head of the operating table.

'Heads!' The shouts came out of the blue, from the top tier away to Hawkwood's right. 'Heads!'

Jesus, now what? Hawkwood wondered. And then he realized the calls were coming from spectators who were unable to see the operation because the heads of the dressers were blocking their view.

Other students took up the chant. Obligingly, the dressers leaned away from the table, still maintaining their control of the patient's legs. As the cries ceased and the onlookers settled down, Hawkwood could see that the patient also seemed to be becalmed, as if he'd surrendered to the inevitable. Carslow's assistant, Gibson, was stroking the man's sweat-streaked head and whispering in his ear.

The wound had started to bleed profusely. A thin dark-red stream was seeping down the cleft of the patient's buttocks and dripping into the blood box beneath the table.

'Having located the groove, I cut through the wall of the bladder, using the groove in the sound as my guide.' The surgeon's voice rose from the foot of the operating table. 'I take my forceps, insert them through the perineum and on into the bladder, and remove the stone. Note that the insertion and extraction is gradual rather than sudden.'

With his left hand pressing down on the exposed end of the bladder sound, the surgeon insinuated the forceps into the incision. The look on his face was one of studied concentration.

The patient gave a piercing shriek.

Hawkwood took a surreptitious glance around. There was more than one student who was looking a bit unsteady; he presumed they were the ones attending their first operation.

Suddenly there was a grunt from the direction of the operating table and a collective gasp from the gallery.

Hawkwood turned quickly.

At the foot of the table, Carslow was holding the forceps aloft, a look of satisfaction on his face. Caught in the metal jaws was a round, dark object the size of a hen's egg. It was dripping blood.

With a flourish, the surgeon dropped the stone into the metal bowl and withdrew the bladder sound from the end of the penis. As if on cue, the onlookers burst into a round of applause.

Carslow held up his hand. The room fell silent.

The surgeon returned his attention to the patient, who was lying motionless, with the exception of his chest, which was moving up and down with the rapidity of a fiddler's elbow as he fought to recover from his exhausting ordeal.

'Bravely borne, Mr Ashby, the ordeal is over. My assistant, Mr Gibson, will attend to you. Mr Liston and Mr Oliver, you may return to your places.'

The patient gave no sign that he had heard.

The surgeon waited while his two recruits made

their way back to the gallery and the envious smiles of their friends, before addressing the audience: 'Remember, it is the surgeon's duty to tranquillize the temper, to beget cheerfulness, and to impart confidence of recovery.'

Behind Carslow's back, Gibson had turned the patient on to his side and was staunching the blood seepage with pads of soft lint.

The surgeon raised an eyebrow towards one of the medical staff standing on the lowest tier of the gallery. 'How long, Mr Dalziel?'

'One minute and forty-three seconds, Mr Carslow.'

A murmur went around the room. Hawkwood wondered if that meant it had taken longer or shorter than expected. To the patient stretched out on the table below, it had probably seemed like hours.

The surgeon accepted the time with a thoughtful nod. 'Thank you.' He looked up at the students. 'It is said that my illustrious predecessor, William Cheselden, could perform the operation you have just witnessed in under one minute. While swiftness is an admirable trait, never let the desire for speed dictate your actions. Let expediency be your guide. Cheselden was quick because he was a good surgeon and because he knew his anatomy. Anatomy is the cornerstone of surgery. Remember that, and you will not fail...' Carslow paused. 'It is also incumbent upon me to point out that Cheselden did not pioneer the operation, he merely refined it. It was, in fact, a man of humble origins, one Jacques Beaulieu, who developed the lateral perineal approach. As you may have gathered from

290

the name, he was a Frenchman. There are no frontiers in Science and Medicine, gentlemen. You would do well to remember that also.'

Cheselden. The name had been on some of the pamphlets in Colonel Hyde's cell, Hawkwood recalled.

As the students filed out of the lecture room, their faces animated by what they had seen, Carslow walked over to the pitcher, poured water into the enamel basin and began to wash his hands.

Hawkwood picked up his coat.

In the small waiting room behind the lecture theatre, Carslow finished drying his hands and passed the damp towel to his dresser. 'Please inform Mr Savage that rounds will begin on the hour.'

The dresser, with Carslow's soiled apron laid over his arm, nodded, handed the surgeon his coat and left the room, taking the towel with him. The surgeon watched him go, then turned with a frown.

'Now then, Officer... Hawkwood, was it? What is so important that you feel the need to disrupt my afternoon lectures?' Carslow slipped an arm into his coatsleeve.

There were dark stains running down the legs of the surgeon's trousers, Hawkwood saw. Many of them looked crusted over, as though they'd been there for some time. Others looked fresh. He remembered the blood that had run from the last patient's arse and assumed that it hadn't been the day's only operation. He suspected also that a lot of the stains weren't just blood but had

291

probably come from other body fluids. Some of them looked like dried pus.

'The sight of blood disturbs you, Officer Hawkwood?' The surgeon inclined his head.

'Only if it's mine,' Hawkwood said.

Carslow considered Hawkwood's response and allowed himself a taut smile. Close to, Hawkwood was struck by the ruddy hue in the surgeon's cheeks; it was a complexion that would not have been out of place on a gentleman farmer. He wondered about the surgeon's origins. In the lecture theatre, Carslow's voice, while not strident, had reached every corner of the room, and his delivery had been clear and concise. But despite the well-modulated tones, there was a detectable burr that hinted at an upbringing some distance from the capital. The occasional rolling consonants suggested somewhere to the east, Suffolk or Norfolk, perhaps.

'Now, sir, I do believe we were on the point of discussing the reason for your visit?' Carslow made a display of shooting his cuffs and moved to a small wall mirror, where he proceeded to adjust his collar and stock.

'Colonel Titus Hyde...' Hawkwood began. 'I'd like to know why his Admission Bond at Bedlam Hospital carries your signature.'

The hesitation was so slight that, if it hadn't been for the tightening of the material across the shoulders of the surgeon's coat, Hawkwood might well have missed it.

Carslow turned, his fingers playing with the knot of his cravat. 'I wondered whether someone might come.'

Hawkwood waited.

'The answer is simple. I signed my name to the bond because I felt it was my duty to do so.'

The surgeon paused, considering his words.

'Titus Hyde and I were students together. We were from different backgrounds, but similar in age. We attended the same lectures. We had the same teachers. Our mentor was John Hunter. You've heard of Hunter, of course?'

Only from the book spines in the colonel's rooms, Hawkwood thought. He shook his head.

Carslow looked surprised. 'Really? He was a great surgeon. A pioneer. He taught us so much: anatomy, respiration, the circulation of the blood... Hunter changed the way students were taught. Our lessons weren't just about medicine. They included chemistry, natural history, physiology, the function of living things; even philosophy. Hunter wanted to sweep away all the old superstitions. He wanted students to question, to think for themselves. He once said that hospitals were not just places where surgeons gained experience before trying their luck on the wealthy, but centres for educating the surgeons of the future. Titus and I worked as his dressers during several of his operations. We were like explorers, charting the oceans, discovering new worlds...'

Apothecary Locke had said much the same thing, Hawkwood remembered. It could have been an echo.

Carslow smiled. 'He would tell us not to make notes during our lessons because he was a student himself and his views were constantly changing. I recall someone – it may even have been Titus – challenging him on that, and Hunter said that by altering his views he hoped to grow wiser every year. I know there were some who judged his style too informal, and it was true that he had a tendency to meander but Titus and I found his methods wonderfully liberating.

'He used to call the body "the machine". He was the finest surgeon of his age, and yet he had a profound respect for the healing powers of nature. He was the one teacher who told us that surgery should only ever be considered as a last resort.' Carslow paused. 'He was an inspiration; an exceptional man.'

The surgeon fell silent. The colour in his cheeks deepened. He looked vaguely embarrassed. 'Forgive me, Officer Hawkwood; it would appear that I've inherited my mentor's gift for obliquity. You are here, after all, to ask me about Titus Hyde.'

Obliquity? Hawkwood thought.

The surgeon collected himself. 'After our studies in London were complete, we went our separate ways. I spent time in Paris. Titus travelled to Italy. Their anatomy schools enjoy a particularly fine reputation. When I returned, I entered private practice. Titus embarked on his military career. His father was in the army; his grandfather too. He saw it as carrying on the family tradition. He was fortunate in having the patronage of John Hunter to assist in his deployment. Mr Hunter had recently been appointed Surgeon-General. It was through Hunter's help and family connections that Titus was able to purchase his commission.'

Hawkwood had wondered about Hyde's rank. Army surgeons commonly held the rank of captain. Few, if any, held the rank of colonel. There was an old saying about rank having its privileges. In the army it was often the other way round.

'What was his regiment?'

'The 6th Regiment of Foot.' Carslow's face softened. 'It's a sad fact, Officer Hawkwood, that the battlefield provides great opportunities for the surgeon. It offers him the chance to investigate all manner of injury. I think it was Larrey who said that war carries surgery to the highest pitch of perfection. He's Bonaparte's chief surgeon, so I'm more than content to take his word for it. Ironically, the vast number of casualties returning from Spain has allowed civilian surgeons like myself the chance to hone *our* particular skills.'

Hawkwood thought back. From what he could remember of Hyde's regiment, they'd been in the thick of it from the beginning. The 6th had probably seen as much action as the Rifles. As a regimental surgeon, Hyde would have had his work cut out, that much was certain.

'Titus and I continued to exchange letters, though our correspondence became more infrequent as time went by. A few months would pass, sometimes a year, and then a letter would arrive telling me of his travels in some distant land. I would write back about my life in London, and then another year or two would elapse. Then, just when I thought I would never hear from him again, a letter would turn up out of the blue. And so it went on.'

The surgeon hesitated. There were two chairs in the room. Carslow took one and indicated that Hawkwood should take the other. 'It was in his letters from the Peninsula that I first began to notice the change. It had been a while since I'd received any correspondence from him, though he did send a brief note from Ireland – I remember he was not taken with the weather there. It rained so much, he thought he would rust. The next letter was from Spain. There'd been a battle, Rol... I forget the precise name. I–

'Rolica,' Hawkwood said.

'Yes, that was it.' There was a questioning look in the surgeon's eyes.

'I was there,' Hawkwood said, and wondered immediately why he'd felt the need to admit it.

The 95th had played a crucial role in the battle and the lead-up to it. Hawkwood had led raiding parties against the enemy's rearguard, employing hit-and-run tactics that had infuriated the French general, Delaborde. The weather had been blisteringly hot, Hawkwood remembered. Hyde would have found it vastly different from the rain-sodden Ireland.

Carslow stared at him. A shadow fell across the doorway. It was one of the dressers. 'Time for rounds, Mr Carslow.'

Carslow turned. 'Thank you, Mr Flynn, you may tell Mr Gibson to begin. I'll join him presently.'

The dresser frowned, threw Hawkwood a curious glance, then left.

Carslow leaned forward. 'So you were there?'

'I was a soldier,' said Hawkwood.

For a moment it looked as though the surgeon

296

was waiting for Hawkwood to expand on his statement, but the dark shadow in Hawkwood's eyes must have told Carslow that was not going to happen.

'Titus wrote that there were many wounded,' Carslow said.

Hawkwood nodded.

'His letter said that conditions in the aid posts were very bad.'

That was an understatement. Hawkwood glanced quickly at the surgeon's blood-smeared trousers. Conditions in the forward dressing stations and battalion field hospitals hadn't been bad, they'd been appalling.

'You said there was a change in him?' Hawkwood prompted.

The surgeon looked thoughtful. 'Not then, but later, over the following year, as his letters became more frequent. He wrote of other battles. Vimeiro was another one I remember.'

Carslow's expression grew solemn. 'That was the first time his letters had shown real anger. They were very descriptive, too. He wrote of the men he worked with, the soldiers he tended, the type of wounds he had to treat; the lack of proper equipment, the dreadful food, and the filth. The list of diseases was endless: dysentery, typhus, pneumonia, cholera – you name it. More men were dying of infection than from their wounds. He described how the wounded were left on the field of battle, often for days, before they were retrieved. How local villagers would descend like wolves to steal personal belongings from the dead and dying. You could see in his words that he was becoming disillusioned by the knowledge that he could not save them all.'

Hawkwood listened to the litany without interruption. He'd seen it for himself. He didn't need any embellishment. He'd known the treatment stations and the tents where patients lay two to a bed, where the overwhelmed staff had to light fir-log fires to try and conceal the stench of so many men packed together. He'd stood by the burial pits, too, and watched the orderlies torching the bodies to prevent contagion. The reality of war was never far from the minds of the men who had served and, more importantly, survived.

Carslow pursed his lips. 'Titus felt that surgeons were too quick to intervene. He believed that meddling with wounds often resulted in a worse outcome than if the wounds were left to heal on their own. He'd learned that from Hunter. He worked among the French prisoners, sometimes with captured French surgeons. He said their methods were just as bad, that they preferred to amputate rather than let nature's balm take its course. Though he and his French counterparts were in agreement that evacuation of the wounded from the battlefield should be much quicker. Were you at Corunna, Officer Hawkwood?'

Hawkwood nodded. *We all were,* he thought.

The winter retreat from Sahagun to the sea had taken nearly three weeks, over some of the most inhospitable terrain Hawkwood had ever encountered. There had been no mobile hospital facilities. The severely ill and injured had been left by the side of the road. Of the survivors who'd made it back to England on the transport ships, nearly a quarter had still required treatment.

Carslow's mouth tightened. 'When the troops arrived home, the government closed the hospitals in Gosport and Plymouth. There were not enough beds. They had to use barracks, storehouses, hospital ships, anything they could find. Some of the casualties were even placed in hulks. There weren't enough surgeons, either. Local medical students offered their services and military surgeons were sent down from London. According to Titus, the conditions were bestial. That was the word he used: bestial.'

Hyde had returned to the Peninsula the following April with the rest of the army to begin the advance into Spain. Conditions hadn't improved; still not enough transport or food. The commissariat hadn't been able to cope. Many of the soldiers, fresh from English barracks and newcomers to the climate, fell victim to the heat and the hard marches. The vast bulk of the army had been on half-rations, some troops on even less. Hyde's work had begun the moment he'd disembarked from the transport ship. It must have seemed as though he'd never been away.

Listening to Carslow's account, Hawkwood had no trouble picturing the scene. He was also aware from the Bethlem hospital documents that it must have been around this time that Hyde's 'distraction' had begun to manifest itself.

'Titus's next letter to me was written shortly after his arrival in Portugal. It was sent on a packet from Lisbon. Mostly it concerned details of the voyage and the conditions on board ship.

That was the last letter I received. It was not until I was approached to cover his bond that I learned what had happened to him.'

The way Carslow described it, the colonel's continuous remonstrations over the inadequacies of the medical facilities and what he had perceived to be gross dereliction on the part of the general staff, had begun to irk both his fellow surgeons and his superiors. According to the latter, the colonel's manner had started to become increasingly erratic. In the end, he had been relieved of duty, examined, and admitted to one of the base hospitals. From there he was taken back to the coast and transported home.

'A part of him must have remained lucid for him to have mentioned our friendship. I was asked if I would co-sign his bond. How could I refuse?'

'Who was the other signatory?'

'James McGrigor.'

There was a pause. For one awful moment Hawkwood thought Carslow was referring to the coroner's irascible surgeon. Then he realized, from the Christian name and the subtle difference in pronunciation, that it was someone else entirely, and yet a person with whom he was familiar.

'The Surgeon-General?'

Carslow nodded. 'He knew Titus. They'd met when they were out in the West Indies. He worked with him again after the evacuation of Corunna. And it was McGrigor who commandeered make-shift hospitals in Portsmouth for the returning troops. He supported a number of Titus's ideas, such as better transport for the wounded and training for the surgeon's mates. He knew when Titus was brought home the army had lost one of its most experienced surgeons. He was as saddened as I was.'

'Did you ever visit Colonel Hyde in Bethlem?'

'To my shame, I did not.'

'Why was that?'

'The pressure of my work here had much to do with it. Also – and this might sound selfish – I wanted to remember Titus as he used to be. Fortunately, I am not unknown to the hospital governors. So, although I was not able to see him, the governors were kind enough to keep me apprised of his progress.'

'You didn't call on your oldest friend?' Hawkwood said.

The surgeon stiffened. It was the first time Carslow had looked annoyed. 'Allow me to describe my day, Officer Hawkwood, then perhaps you will understand. I rise at five, sometimes at four. I conduct experiments in my dissection room until breakfast, after which I give free consultations until lunchtime. I then come here, where I attend rounds, present lectures and perform operations. Afterwards I visit my private patients, who sometimes require operations which I carry out in their homes. I return to my house for a brief supper, usually around seven, after which I'm out visiting more patients or lecturing. I'm rarely in my bed before midnight. Now, does that answer your question?'

James Read would probably have called that a recalcitrant moment, Hawkwood thought to himself. But Carslow's reaction had been interesting.

The surgeon definitely looked more than a little uncomfortable. Hawkwood wondered whether Carslow had also stayed away from Bethlem because of the stigma that was attached to madhouse residents. The surgeon was a man with a reputation to maintain. It was possible that he wouldn't want his association with a lunatic to become public knowledge, fearing that it would drive away his more prestigious patients.

'When I arrived, you said you'd wondered whether someone might come. Why was that?'

A flash of irritation showed in Carslow's eyes. 'When the governors informed me of Titus's death and the violence involved, I thought it possible that my connection with him would prompt a visit from the authorities. I understand, however, that his murderer was chased down and that he took his own life? Is that correct?'

'Yes.' How easily the lie came.

'And that he was a priest? That cannot be true, surely?'

'I understand the colonel had a child, a daughter?' Hawkwood said, sidestepping the question.

The surgeon hesitated and frowned. 'Yes, that is so.'

'The child died?'

'Sadly, yes.'

'And his wife?'

The surgeon's eyes darkened. 'He did not marry. There was a brief ... liaison. It was a long time ago. I'm not in possession of the full details, though I know the lady was ... well ... there was another man ... and Titus's regiment was sent to the West Indies. He did not know she had been with child until some years later.'

Carslow dropped his gaze and then stood up, smoothing his coat. 'You must forgive me, Officer Hawkwood, but I'm beginning to find this quite distressing. You've awakened memories that I would rather have left dormant. If you have no objection, I would like to continue my rounds.' The surgeon took out his watch. 'My students will be growing restless. If there's nothing further...?'

Hawkwood rose to his feet. 'Not at this time. Though I may need to talk with you again.'

The surgeon slipped the watch back into his pocket. 'Tell me, Officer Hawkwood, if the murderer is dead, why are you here, raking over the ashes?'

Hawkwood raised an eyebrow. 'Now there's an interesting choice of words.'

'What?' The surgeon seemed taken aback by Hawkwood's brusqueness. Then a faint blush rose in his face. 'Ah, yes, dashed poor taste. A slip of the tongue. I meant nothing by it.'

'And I just wanted to get my measure of the man, Mr Carslow. That's all.'

The surgeon held Hawkwood's gaze for several seconds before giving a faint nod. 'Then I trust I have been some help to you. I'll summon one of my dressers to see you out. The hospital can be a maze to those who do not know their way around.'

'Thank you. I'll make my own way.'

'As you wish.' The surgeon hesitated. 'Titus Hyde was an exceptional surgeon, Officer Hawkwood. He was not afraid to try new procedures. One could say he was ahead of his time. From what I understand, he was highly thought of by his patients and the men under his command. There were many who hoped that his distraction might only be temporary and that he would be able to resume his duties. Sadly, that was not to be. He died a deeply troubled man, Officer Hawkwood, in terrible circumstances. Those of us who cared for him and who valued his friendship pray that the peace of mind he searched for in life will at least be visited upon him in death. He deserves that much.'

'Don't we all,' Hawkwood said.

Deep down, Sawney knew it could only be his imagination, but there was a feel to the house that made him distinctly uneasy. And that, Sawney had to admit, was strange, for he was not a man who was often discomforted. In his line of work, discomfort was a punishment he usually visited upon others.

The place had a dark, brooding presence, as if it was lying in wait for someone. There were other anatomy schools that he did business with during twilight hours – the ones on Great Windmill Street and Webb Street to name but a couple – but even allowing for the grim aspect of his trade, none of them seemed to exude the same degree of menace as this particular location, especially with the shutters closed.

Sawney didn't consider himself a religious man, so he felt a little self-conscious reaching into his pocket for the silver cross. He turned it over in his hand. You couldn't help but admire the beauty of it. Sawney recognized good craftsmanship when he saw it. He'd been intending to sell it on at the earliest opportunity, but somehow he hadn't yet got round to it. Curious that. What was also strange, though Sawney wouldn't have confessed to it in a month of Sundays, was that holding it between his fingers with the night all around him felt oddly comforting.

Suddenly aware of what he was doing, Sawney swore softly and returned the cross to his waistcoat. I'll be singing hymns in the bloody chapel next, he thought. Good thing Maggett and the Ragg boys hadn't witnessed his moment of piety.

Sawney rang the bell, waited for admittance, and winced.

He'd been suffering minor toothache for a couple of days, ever since he'd bitten down hard on a mutton shank. He'd tried to ignore it, and in the general run of things had gotten used to the dull throb, but every now and then the nerve would send a reminder that relief was purely transitory.

And it was bloody freezing; a sure sign that more snow was on the way. Not that he should be complaining. Winter was a good time for the schools and the stealers. The cold preserved bodies longer, keeping decay and putrefaction at bay. Huddled in the lee of the drawbridge, Sawney decided it was about time he got himself a decent bloody coat. Not that he intended shelling out good money for one. Stealing one would give him far more satisfaction.

The rattle of a turning key sounded behind him and the front door swung open. It would be the first time Sawney had been admitted to the house. The other times, he'd only got as far as the underground stable.

As before, Dodd stood half concealed behind the door, his face in shadow, as if wary of being seen by passers-by. Sawney stepped inside.

Dodd closed the door. 'Your lieutenant has the night off?'

He meant Maggett. Sawney nodded. 'He 'ad other business.'

Maggett was back in his slaughter yard, sharpening knives and hooks and doing whatever else he had to do to prepare for tomorrow morning's meat market. It was probably just as well. Things had been a bit tense after their narrow escape from the law. When they'd got back to the Dog, words had been exchanged. Maggett had told Sawney they should have dumped the bodies at the first opportunity instead of lugging them halfway across the bloody city. All they'd ended up with were stiff backs and sore feet. Maggett had also skinned a knee slipping on a patch of snow at the corner of Long Lane. He'd limped off in a mood, leaving Sawney to reflect in solitude upon the night's fiasco. They hadn't even had the chance to remove the teeth, Sawney reflected glumly. They'd lost out on all counts.

Dodd nodded. 'Good. We can discuss our business in private.'

Sawney followed Dodd down the hallway, past two closed doors, into a small, square vestibule from where a flight of stairs climbed steeply towards the upper floors.

Taking a furtive look around, Sawney could see

that there was a fine layer of dust on every flat surface. It looked as though the house hadn't been lived in for a while, which seemed odd. He wondered how many students attended Dodd's anatomy classes. Maybe the doctor hadn't started taking in pupils yet, which would explain why the rooms looked unused. But then why would he have wanted Sawney to retrieve bodies, if not for lessons? Dodd was probably still in the process of assembling the specimens he would be using in his lectures, Sawney decided. He sensed eyes upon him. When he looked up, Dodd was studying him intently.

'This way,' Dodd said. The doctor led Sawney behind the stairs into a cramped room containing a table and chairs.

There wasn't so much dust here, Sawney noticed. There were several newspapers on the table, along with a plate that held the remnants of a meal along with a half-full bottle of Madeira and an empty glass. Sawney's gaze moved over the newssheets, taking in some of the headlines. A newly formed regiment was heading for Spain, a church had burnt down near the river, and the Prince Regent was to attend a pageant at Drury Lane. Dodd stepped forward and turned the pages over.

Sawney eyed the bottle. He was still feeling the cold. A snifter would help to warm him up. But he suspected Dodd was not about to offer him a glass.

The doctor was wearing his apron again. It seemed to have gathered a few more stains since Sawney's previous visit. The front was black and shiny. It looked as if it had been daubed with paint. A piece of cloth was tucked in the apron's waistband. Dodd lifted it out and began to wipe his forearms and hands, working it in between his fingers.

'You told me I was to come back,' Sawney said, 'see if you wanted any more ... things.' As he spoke, he bit down inadvertently on his injured tooth and let out a grunt.

Dodd's eyes narrowed. 'Are you well, Sawney? You sound as though you're in pain.'

Sawney shook his head quickly. 'It ain't nothing. Just a bleedin' tooth giving me gyp is all.'

Dodd stepped forward, tucking the cloth behind his apron strings. 'Let me see.'

Sawney took an involuntary step back. The pain was bad enough as it was. He didn't want some bloody quack doctor rooting around there as well. God only knew what manner of hurt would ensue. The only thing was, in his haste, he hadn't realized one of the chairs was directly behind him. Before he knew what was happening, Sawney was sitting down and the doctor was bending over him holding the candle up to his face.

Sawney made to get up but found that Dodd was standing too close to the chair, trapping his legs. The doctor put a hand on Sawney's shoulder and pressed him down in his seat.

'I told you,' Sawney said, trying to get up again, 'it's nothin'.' The doctor's grip was surprisingly strong. Sawney tried to disguise a rising sense of panic.

'Open your mouth,' Dodd said softly.

The last thing on earth Sawney wanted to do at that moment was open his mouth, especially having been invited to do so in the dead of night by a man holding his upper arm in one hand, a candle in the other, and wearing a blood-smeared apron. At least, Sawney assumed it was blood. He wondered what else it could be and, more to the point, what Dodd might have been trying to remove from his hands with the cloth. The doctor's long fingers didn't look any cleaner than they had before he'd wiped them. His fingernails looked as though they were encrusted with shit. And the meaty smell coming off the apron wasn't anything to write home about, either. It looked like the type of thing Maggett might wear in his slaughter yard while quartering a carcass.

Dodd moved the candle closer to Sawney's face.

Sawney shrank back.

Dodd's face was eight inches away from his own. 'If you don't let me look, I won't be able to help you. I *can* help you, Sawney.'

Sawney realized that Dodd's hand was stroking his shoulder. The movement was gentle, almost a caress.

'Tell me where the pain is,' Dodd said.

Instinctively, Sawney moved his tongue to the injured tooth.

Dodd nodded. 'On the left? Place your head back.'

Sawney blinked. Then he realized that Dodd had traced the location by the slight bulge of his tongue against the side of his jaw.

'Open,' Dodd said. It came out more like an order than a request.

Sawney hesitated.

'I can take away your pain, Sawney. You'd like me to do that, wouldn't you?'

Sawney stared at him, his jaw pulsing. He nodded wordlessly.

'Well, then,' Dodd said.

Against his better judgement, Sawney eased his mouth open. It wasn't a pretty sight.

Dodd leaned forward and peered into the open maw. There was a pause. Sawney, fists clenched in anticipation of further twinges, held his breath and wondered what was taking so long. He had rarely felt so vulnerable.

Then Dodd said calmly, 'You've lost part of a molar. The tooth will need to be extracted.'

Sawney felt the sweat spurt from the underside of his arms and down the crease of his back. He clamped his teeth shut, jarring the nerve in the process.

'But not at this moment,' Dodd said, straightening. 'However, I will give you a salve for the pain.'

Turning away from the look of relief that flooded across Sawney's face, Dodd moved to a wooden chest on the floor behind him. On it rested a black bag. Dodd rummaged in the bag and brought out a small glass phial. From another pocket inside the bag he took a thin glass pipette. He brought them to the table. Removing the phial's stopper, he dipped the pipette into the phial and placed his finger over the opposite end to create a vacuum. His movements were unhurried. Removing his finger, he drew a small amount of the phial's contents into the slender pipe. Resealing the end of the pipette with his fingertip, he instructed Sawney to open his mouth once more.

Apprehensively, Sawney did as he was told.

Dodd inserted the end of the pipette inside Sawney's mouth and released the contents on to the broken tooth and the exposed nerve.

The effect was almost instantaneous. Sawney couldn't help but let out a low moan of relief as the pain melted away. Tentatively, he lifted a hand to his jaw.

'Oil of cloves,' Dodd said. 'Some say it's as valuable as gold.' He smiled thinly. 'Tell me, Private Sawney, did you ever consider, while you were removing the teeth from the bodies of your fallen comrades, that you might one day require some of them for yourself?'

Sawney froze.

Dodd placed the stopper back in the phial and put it back in the bag along with the pipette. 'Ironic, wouldn't you say?'

Sawney stared at Dodd. His tooth no longer ached, but now the back of his throat felt strange, as if he'd just swallowed several large cobwebs. Deep in his stomach, the spiders responsible for spinning the webs began to stir.

'You look surprised,' Dodd said. 'What? Did you think I knew nothing about you, about your service in Spain, as a driver with the Royal Wagon Train? Very convenient for your extracurricular activities.'

Sawney regarded Dodd with awe.

Dodd said nothing. He merely returned the stare.

Suddenly, Sawney's eyes widened. 'Jesus!' he said.

'Ah,' Dodd said. 'I wondered how long it might take you. Not that we ever met face to face, of course.'

Sawney's face continued to mirror his shock.

'Normally, I'd suggest a libation to steady your nerves,' Dodd said. 'But that might not be such a good idea. We wouldn't want that tooth to flare up again.'

'You were the surgeon Butler worked for in the hospitals.'

'Well done, Sawney. Butler thought you would catch on eventually. That was one of the reasons he recommended you; because of our previous association, indirect though it was. If you cannot trust your former comrades-in-arms, who else is there? After all, that's why you and Butler went into partnership together, was it not?'

'You ain't in uniform now,' Sawney said.

'No. Those days are long past.'

'Don't recall Butler mentionin' any surgeon called Dodd neither.'

'No, you wouldn't have,' Titus Hyde said.

'It ain't your name. Why'd you change it?'

'Oh, reasons. The nature of our work, both yours and mine, dictates that we must conduct our business beyond the view of prying eyes. People are afraid of that which they do not understand. There are many who look upon our work as sorcery, branding us as heretics. They'd burn us at the stake if they could, even if *they* still cling to the old ways, the superstition and the spells. Butler vouched for your integrity, but I had to be certain for myself.'

Sawney said nothing.

'You can see that, can't you?'

There was a silence. 'S'pose so,' Sawney admitted grudgingly.

'I still require your assistance, Sawney.'

'Is that right?'

'A revolution is coming, Sawney; in medicine, in science, in so many things. It began with Harvey and Cheselden and John Hunter; men who weren't afraid to turn away from the old traditions and step towards the light; brave men who were prepared to risk their reputations to explore beyond the existing boundaries of knowledge. The only thing that limits us, Sawney, is the breadth of our imagination. There's a new way of thinking we call natural philosophy, and it's going to change the world.'

'An' you openin' this new school 'as to do with it?'

'School?' The question was accompanied by a frown.

'This place,' Sawney said, indicating the room and, by inference, the house.

'Ah, yes, I see. Indeed it has. More than you will know.'

'So you'll be wanting us to bring you another one, then?'

'Correct.'

Sawney considered the answer, and nodded. 'All right, I can do that.'

Just so long as I don't have to salute you, Sawney thought.

'There is one thing, however,' Hyde said. He moved to the table and sat down. 'While the last specimen you supplied far exceeded the quality of the first two, I do have a more ... specific ... requirement.'

'There was something wrong with it?' Sawney frowned.

'Wrong? No. Butler's faith in you is well founded. As I said, the previous specimen was most satisfactory. I've made excellent use of it.' Hyde leaned across the table. 'No, my only concern is that it was – how shall I put it? – still not as fresh as I would have liked.'

Sawney's brow creased. 'Fresh? You ain't going to get them any fresher. Jesus, any fresher, and they'd be walkin' and talkin'. Christ, they'd be knockin' on your bleedin' door, askin' to be let in.' Sawney grinned, shook his head in amusement and let go a coarse chuckle. Then he saw that Hyde wasn't sharing the joke. In fact, there was no humour whatsoever in the doctor's gaze. What there was looked more like ... expectancy. A little bird began to trill and flutter its wings deep inside Sawney's chest.

Hyde remained silent. His gaze was unwavering, and unnerving. Time seemed to slow down.

Then, suddenly, Sawney understood. He sat up. 'You serious?'

At first, Hyde said nothing. He was as still as a statue.

Then he said, 'Can you do it?'

'Well, it ain't like pullin' a rabbit out of a

314

bleedin' hat,' Sawney said. 'It'll cost you extra, and it won't be pennies.'

Hyde nodded. 'I understand. I'll pay you twenty-five guineas, and no questions will be asked. It will be at your discretion.'

Twenty-five guineas. Three months' earnings for the average working man; the equivalent of six or seven retrievals – not counting pregnant women, children, and cripples, of course.

Sawney stared at the doctor, at the sharp widow's peak and the dark, raptor's eyes. The seconds ticked away; one, two, three...

'Thirty,' Sawney said, and waited.

Hyde reached into his apron strings and took out the cloth. He began to wipe his hands as he had done before. 'Half the payment now, half on delivery.'

Sawney let out a slow breath, and nodded.

'I'm relying on you, Sawney. It's important that I complete my work. An early delivery would be appreciated.'

'I'll see what I can do,' Sawney said, thinking that maybe he should have asked for more. He noticed the doctor's hands were turning raw from the chafing of the rag. 'What about the last one? You goin' to 'ang on to the remains, or do you want 'em taken away?'

'My space is limited. I'd like it removed.'

Knew I shouldn't have asked, Sawney thought, and wondered why he had.

'I'll send someone round.'

'There is one other thing,' Hyde said.

'What's that?'

'I mentioned before that there are those who

315

would view seekers of the truth, such as myself, as dabblers in necromancy. It's come to my attention that they may have enlisted the services of a base member of the constabulary. While I'm sure a man in your line of work is adept at avoiding the attention of the authorities, I would urge you to be extra vigilant, especially given the terms of our intended transaction. Though, as someone who managed to evade the clutches of the army provosts for so long, I'm sure you'll have no difficulty maintaining your anonymity.'

Sawney had no idea what necromancy was – probably another word for trading in the dead, he guessed – so he just nodded. 'Don't you worry, I won't have no problems giving the Charleys the slip. They couldn't find their own arses in the dark if they used both hands. Do you know the bugger's name?'

'Hawkwood.'

Sawney didn't say anything. He didn't have to. He knew the shock was written across his face.

Hyde's fingers stilled. 'You know him?'

Deny everything, was Sawney's immediate instinct, but it was too late for that. 'Yeah, I know 'im, sort of. But he ain't no Charley. He's a Runner.'

'Indeed.' Hyde's eyes darkened. 'You've had dealings with him?'

'Indirectly,' Sawney said cautiously. 'He crossed paths with some business associates.'

'Recently?'

'Recent enough.' Better not to mention Tate or Murphy, Sawney thought.

'How much of a nuisance is he likely to be?'

316

Sawney hesitated and then said, 'Word is he's former military, and a bastard.'

'Really?' Hyde fell silent. His expression was noncommittal.

'How come you know about him?' Sawney said.

'What?' Hyde snapped out of his reverie. 'Oh, just some information that happened to come my way.' Hyde tucked the cloth back into his apron and rose to his feet. 'Wait here.' He left the room.

Sawney got up and moved quickly to Hyde's black bag, opened it and peered inside. Three seconds later the phial containing the clove oil was in his pocket. He closed the bag and sat down.

Hyde returned carrying a small cloth pouch. There was a dull chink as he placed it in Sawney's palm.

'I assumed you'd prefer coin of the realm.'

'That'll do nicely,' Sawney said, getting to his feet. He opened the bag's drawstring and tipped the money into his palm. It was a fair weight, and immensely reassuring. Coinage was always best. Easier to divide up, easier to spend. Notes could be a bugger. Besides, you started flashing paper money around and you were asking for trouble. Especially given Sawney's haunts.

Sawney poured the money back into the bag. 'So how come you picked the name Dodd?'

'Why not?' Hyde said, unsmilingly. 'It's as useful a name as any.'

Sawney absorbed the reply. 'S'pose so.' There didn't seem anything else to add. He slipped the bag of coin into his pocket. There was an awkward silence. 'Right then. Time to go to work.'

Sawney paused when the doctor laid a hand on his arm. A fresh light shone in Hyde's eyes.

'No need to leave just yet. This Hawkwood fellow – tell me what you know about him. He sounds most intriguing.'

14

It was early morning when Hawkwood climbed the front steps of number 4 Bow Street and made his way up to the Chief Magistrate's office on the first floor.

Twigg was at his desk in the ante-room, head bowed and scribbling, when Hawkwood entered. He looked up, peered through his spectacles, and frowned in mild annoyance. 'Could've wiped your feet.'

Hawkwood glanced down at his boots. They were wet with slush from the melted snow that had fallen during the night. Looking behind him, he saw the tracks he'd left across the wooden floor.

'You'd have made someone a grand wife, Ezra,' Hawkwood said. He grinned at the clerk's pained expression. 'How about if next time I take them off and carry them upstairs with me?'

The corners of Twigg's mouth drooped. 'Oh, very droll, Mr Hawkwood. You ought to be on the stage.'

Hawkwood started to remove his coat, but Twigg shook his head. 'He's not here.'

Hawkwood raised his eyebrows in enquiry.

Twigg sighed and passed Hawkwood the note. 'He left a message. You're to attend him directly. Caleb's waiting with his carriage downstairs.'

Hawkwood pulled his coat back on and the

clerk muttered under his breath as yet more meltwater dribbled from the coat's hem on to the floor beneath.

'Sorry, Ezra – I didn't catch that.'

Twigg nodded towards Hawkwood's feet. 'If I were you, I'd clean my boots. Where you're going, they won't take kindly to mud on their carpet.'

Twigg wasn't wrong, thought Hawkwood, as he was shown into the grand, high-ceilinged room. The expression on the face of at least one of the men facing him hinted that his presence was an imposition. Nothing new there, then, he thought, not without an element of satisfaction.

'Ah, Hawkwood.' James Read stepped forward. There was no welcoming smile, just the vocal acknowledgement of his arrival.

Two other men occupied the room. One was standing by the window, the other was seated in a chair by the fireplace. They turned towards him. It had been the man by the window who had cast a dour look at the marks Hawkwood's boots had left on the rug.

During all parliamentary sittings, a Runner was required to be on duty in the lobby of the House of Commons. The task was rotated among the squad; some considered it to be light, if un-exciting, work, and were content to be away from the streets, but it wasn't a job Hawkwood enjoyed. He found the proximity of so much hot air excruciating and was more than happy to trade places. As a consequence of being so close to the chamber, however, he had become familiar with many of its occupants, including the Home Secretary, Richard Ryder, although the two of them had never been formally introduced.

'Home Secretary,' Read said. 'Allow me to present Officer Hawkwood.'

Ryder nodded, his face solemn. He was a relatively young man, only a few years older than Hawkwood, with thinning hair and watchful eyes. 'Officer Hawkwood. Yes, I recognize you from the House.'

Hawkwood wondered if that was true or whether Ryder was just being icily polite.

Read turned back and indicated the man by the fireplace.

'This is Surgeon-General McGrigor.'

The Surgeon-General was perhaps four or five years younger and slightly leaner in the face than the Home Secretary, though both men had the same air of authority about them. Ryder, Hawkwood knew, was from an aristocratic family. McGrigor came from merchant stock.

McGrigor stood up and held out his hand. 'Grand to meet you, Hawkwood.'

'You, too, sir,' Hawkwood said. He could see the Home Secretary was puzzled by the Surgeon-General's enthusiasm.

'We've not met, though I know of Captain Hawkwood from my brother-in-law's letters,' McGrigor explained in a soft Highland lilt. 'They fought together in Spain.'

Ryder looked momentarily nonplussed until McGrigor took pity on him. 'Captain Colquhoun Grant.'

'Ah, yes, of course,' Ryder said. He threw

Hawkwood a look, obviously as intrigued by the reference to Hawkwood's rank as he was by his indirect relationship with the Surgeon-General.

'How is the captain?' Hawkwood asked.

McGrigor smiled. 'Still giving the Frogs a good run for their money, you'll be pleased to hear.'

Hawkwood hadn't seen Grant for over two years, not since leaving Spain. Grant was Wellington's chief intelligence officer, operating behind enemy lines, providing Wellington with details on the disposition of French troops and equipment. He worked closely with the Spanish *guerrilleros.*

It had been Grant who'd persuaded Wellington to employ Hawkwood as a liaison between the resistance fighters and British intelligence units. Hawkwood's fluency in French and Spanish had proved invaluable. He'd fought alongside the *guerrilleros,* deep in the mountains, passing additional information to Grant whenever he could. When Hawkwood returned to England, it had been Grant, through his contacts in Horse Guards and Whitehall, who'd provided the rifleman with the necessary references, enabling him to take up his role as a Bow Street officer.

'So, gentlemen,' James Read said, 'to the matter in hand.'

The Surgeon-General made a gesture of apology for the diversion and sat down again. Ryder remained by the window. Hawkwood was left standing, as was Read, who went and joined McGrigor by the fire. There was a guard in place, Hawkwood noted with inner amusement.

Read addressed Hawkwood. 'I've advised

Home Secretary Ryder and the Surgeon-General of our interest in Colonel Hyde's background. That is why they have agreed to meet with us.'

Looking at the three men, Hawkwood wondered about the authority wielded by the Chief Magistrate that he could, with remarkable ease, interpose himself between a member of the cabinet and Wellington's chief medical officer in a government office deep in the heart of Whitehall. He decided there were still aspects of James Read's sphere of influence that would remain for ever a mystery and that it was probably unwise to broach too many questions on the subject.

Hawkwood saw that both Ryder and McGrigor were looking at him expectantly. So that was the way it was going to be, he thought. They weren't going to volunteer information; he would have to delve for it. He'd warned Read he might have to step on some toes. Well, there was no time like the present.

'Why was Colonel Hyde held in Bethlem Asylum? It wasn't because he was melancholic, was it?'

Both men, Ryder in particular, looked taken aback by the bluntness of Hawkwood's question. It was McGrigor who recovered first. With a sideways glance towards the Home Secretary, he sat forward. 'I take it you have some knowledge of the colonel's medical background and his army career?'

'Not as much as we'd like,' Hawkwood said.

'Colonel Hyde ran field hospitals in the Peninsula. Guthrie reckons he was probably the

323

bravest surgeon he'd ever met. Hyde was considerably older, of course, much more experienced. Guthrie said he watched Hyde treat wounds that would have made other surgeons hold up their hands in horror. The man's knowledge of anatomy was astonishing.'

Hawkwood knew Guthrie. He'd met him once. For his age, the young Irishman was rated as one of the army's best surgeons. He'd begun his military career as a hospital mate in Canada. He had the ear of Wellington.

The Surgeon-General's face clouded. 'You know Colonel Hyde and I served together in the West Indies?'

Hawkwood nodded.

'We met again after the troops returned from Corunna. I was Deputy Inspector of Hospitals for the southwest. It was my job to procure beds for the wounded. I saw the changes in him then. There were times when he appeared more than a little distracted. I put it down to the work. We'd talk about the war; the effect it had on men's lives. We'd discuss medicine and surgery, of course, and how things were changing, and what the future held. It's true to say that I found some of his views rather fanciful.'

'In what way?'

McGrigor pursed his lips. 'He saw the human body as a form of machine, and believed that it could be mended by taking working parts from other machines. We're already doing it with teeth, he'd say, why not skin or blood and bone? Why not the liver or the bladder, or even the heart?'

With a shake of his head, McGrigor went on:

'When I suggested that such a thing would go against the laws of God, he said that when a wounded soldier's lying on a hospital table, God has nothing to do with it. It's the surgeon who's wielding the knife.' The Surgeon-General paused. 'I thought it was nothing more than random musings. But when he was in Oporto, there was some talk.'

'Talk?'

'Murmurs really, nothing more, that some of the colonel's operating procedures were becoming a little ... unconventional. There was no basis, at least as far as we could tell. Certainly, there were no reports of mistreatment from either the British or French casualties.'

No one queried the Surgeon-General's statement. Treating wounded enemy combatants was a fact of war and not uncommon. Mostly it occurred in the wake of a withdrawal. It could take a long time to evacuate a field hospital and, in such a situation, speed was of the essence. The walking wounded were usually no bother, provided they could keep up with the retreat. The seriously injured, however, were often left at the mercy of the enemy, with a skeleton medical staff remaining behind to act as overseers. In the case of the British, that duty tended to fall to an assistant medical officer or a surgeon's mate, who would be exchanged for their French counterparts at a later date.

Hawkwood remembered Oporto. The French commander, Soult, had left so fast that he hadn't just left his stores, guns, bullion and his sick and wounded, he'd also left his still-warm dinner.

There had been a lot of French casualties, he recalled.

'Anyway,' McGrigor continued, 'it was put down to contention in the ranks. If the colonel had an obvious flaw it was that he was too intolerant of the conditions and some of the procedures carried out by less able surgeons. We were in a hospital in Portsmouth when I saw him berate one of his colleagues for continuously bleeding a man. Yelled at him that if he took any more blood the only things left on the bed would be boots and bones. The colonel was a brilliant surgeon and he knew it. But he tended towards arrogance, and the others resented him for it.'

'So there was no truth to these "murmurs"?' Hawkwood said.

There was a long pause. 'None that we knew of ... at least, not then.' McGrigor brushed a speck of dust from his knee. 'But it had become plain that his attitude, his insinuations and his contemptuous manner had won him no friends among the other medical officers. On duty, they tolerated him. Off duty they excluded him. He began to spend his free time alone, and in doing so became increasingly isolated and withdrawn. It was at Talavera that we finally learned the truth.'

A nerve flickered along the Surgeon-General's cheek. Hawkwood suspected that McGrigor expected mention of Talavera to cause him unease. He wondered if Ryder was aware of that part of his history. Nothing in the Home Secretary's demeanour indicated that he knew. It was probably better if it remained that way.

'Go on,' Hawkwood said.

'Field hospitals were set up in preparation – commandeered farms, schools, churches and so forth. *You* know how these things work. Colonel Hyde's hospital was located in the monastery of San Miguel. It was on the outskirts of a village about four miles from the battlefield. It took a lot of the injured.'

Talavera had been a great victory though it had been far from clean cut. French losses had exceeded those of the British, yet Wellington's forces had been reduced by a quarter.

'They hadn't been there long when they had to begin the withdrawal.' McGrigor scowled.

Shortly after the battle, Wellington's scouts advised him that Marshal Soult, the man who'd fled from Oporto, had reorganized his troops and descended on the British line of communications at Plasencia. With his Spanish allies unwilling to commit, his army reduced and supplies for an extended campaign dwindling, Wellington had been forced to retreat towards the Portuguese border. He'd set up camp at Badajoz.

'A lot of the wounded were left behind,' McGrigor said. 'It was hoped the French would honour their side of the bargain. They damned nearly didn't.'

James Read frowned. 'What happened?'

'When the French moved up they took the hospitals, including the monastery...' McGrigor paused, collecting his thoughts. 'There were several outhouses. When the French began their inventory they discovered that one of the more isolated buildings was a winery. Most of it had

327

been destroyed by fire, but the reconnaissance patrol thought there might be a few bottles still intact, so they decided to explore. When they broke into the cellars, they discovered a room full of dead French soldiers. All the bodies, according to witnesses, showed signs of severe disfigure-ment...' Again McGrigor paused. 'And it wasn't from their battle wounds.'

Hawkwood glanced towards the Chief Magistrate. Read looked back at him, his expression still.

McGrigor continued: 'They also found an assortment of preparations.'

'Preparations?' Hawkwood said.

'Specimens.'

Hawkwood wasn't sure he wanted to know the answer, but he knew he had to ask the question. 'Of what?'

'Body parts, bones, tissue, teeth – that sort of thing. Most of them were wet.'

'The place was flooded?'

McGrigor shook his head. 'It's a term anatom-ists use. Preparations are either wet or dry. Wet ones are preserved in solution – spirit of wine, usually; alcohol at any rate. It was a winery. There was a ready supply. Dry refers to muscles and organs that have been air-dried, usually by hanging. As I said, there weren't as many of those.'

'Like curing game, what?' Ryder murmured to no one in particular. He had the grace to look shamefaced as soon as he'd said it.

'No,' McGrigor said coldly. 'Not like that, at all.'

328

Ryder's cheeks coloured.

'How do you know all this?' Read asked.

'Captain Grant's agents intercepted French dispatches, including a report from a French surgeon who was called to examine the scene. From the state of the bodies, he concluded that someone had been trying to perform restorative surgery. One example was a cadaver with a severe sabre wound in its skull. A portion of bone from another skull had been fashioned to size and inserted into the wound. There was one soldier who'd suffered a serious wound to the face, including the loss of an ear. An attempt had been made to rebuild the face, using the skin and ear from another man's corpse. Two of the bodies had burns to the legs...' The Surgeon-General glanced towards Hawkwood. 'You recall the fires on the battlefield?'

Hawkwood nodded. It was the smell he remembered the most, like pork on a spit.

'The burnt sections of their skin had been removed and replaced with skin taken from other bodies. Some of the adjacent corpses were missing corresponding areas of skin. According to French military surgeons' reports, it looked as though they'd been flayed.'

McGrigor shifted in his seat. 'A number of graves were also discovered. They'd not been filled in properly. Most likely they'd been dug in haste. Upon examination, it was found that some of the interred bodies had been interfered with: organs removed, flesh excised, limbs severed... A lot of the missing organs matched the ones found in the preparation room in the cellar.'

There was a pause, and then McGrigor continued: 'They also found ... animal parts.'

'What?'

'One of the corpses had a bowel wound. Someone had tried to join the two segments of the bowel together using a section of windpipe from a goat.'

For a moment, Hawkwood thought he must have misheard. 'Did you say a goat?'

'The goat's trachea had been inserted into both ends of the bowel, which had then been drawn together over it. I've heard about it, but never seen it performed. They also found that a section of the goat's intestines had been removed. The French surgeon's report stated that it was most likely intended as some sort of a conduit and that Hyde had been attempting a transfusion of blood.'

'From a goat to a man?' Hawkwood stared at the Surgeon-General in disbelief.

'Good God, no!' McGrigor shook his head, but then, to Hawkwood's astonishment, he said, 'Although Denys and Lower carried out similar procedures using lamb's blood.'

Hawkwood looked over towards the Chief Magistrate. James Read's face was pale, as was the Home Secretary's; though presumably the latter wasn't hearing anything he didn't already know.

McGrigor frowned. 'I read the French surgeon's report – fellow by the name of Lavalle. He said the corpses in the cellar were not the remains of men. They were monsters. He referred to the cellar as *l'abattoir*.'

The word hung in the air. No translation was necessary.

'You're telling us,' Hawkwood said, 'that Colonel Hyde carried out surgery on prisoners of war using body parts taken from the corpses of French soldiers, and animals?'

'That is what I am saying, yes. The report suggested that he had been trying to mend them, using flesh, bone and blood from their dead comrades.'

'And when he couldn't mend them and he received his orders to withdraw, he left them to their fate,' Read said, staring balefully at Mc-Grigor. 'The fire and the graves were clearly a deliberate attempt to conceal the evidence of his activities.'

'At least we know where he got the notion to burn down the church,' Hawkwood said heavily. Then he caught the look on the Surgeon-General's face. 'What? You mean there's more?'

McGrigor hesitated. He looked uncomfortable. 'Lavalle's report also hinted that some of the casualties' wounds would not have been considered terminal.' McGrigor paused again to let his words sink in.

'You mean their deaths were induced in order to provide the body parts?'

McGrigor nodded.

'When you caught up with him, did he have anything to say for himself?'

McGrigor shrugged. 'He was remarkably calm, philosophical almost; as if he'd been expecting it. He told us we'd never understand. He said there could be no barriers in science and medicine and that our minds were closed, and if surgery was ever to advance we should open ourselves to the endless possibilities that lay before us. He even had the nerve to quote Hunter at us. I remember it distinctly. He said it wasn't enough for a surgeon to know the different parts of an animal, he should know their uses in the machine, and in what manner they act to produce their effect. You'll note his use of the word "machine".

'To add to our woes, we'd received a direct communication from the French Commander, Victor. He sent a courier under flag of truce. Threatened that if we didn't hand over the man responsible, we couldn't expect French surgeons to show any mercy to British casualties. Needless to say, the medical officers we'd left behind at Talavera had already been given a rough ride, though they'd sworn blind they had no idea it had been going on. It seemed that Hyde had managed to keep his experimentation secret. Don't ask me how.

'We presumed he'd had some assistance, probably from the lower ranks. But with all the troop movements and with so many men spread over such a large area, it was impossible to pin anyone down. We knew all about the teeth being taken from the dead, but this was different, far worse.'

'Obviously you didn't hand Hyde over,' Hawkwood said. 'How did you answer the French demand?'

McGrigor made a face. 'We knew we couldn't dismiss it. Especially since one of the letters carried by the courier was a personal request from my opposite number, a fellow called Percy.

'It was clear that Colonel Hyde had become severely distracted, but we certainly weren't prepared to surrender him. That was out of the question. Equally, it would have been impossible for him to remain. You know what the army's like. If word got out that our surgeons were experimenting on the wounded, there'd be panic in the ranks. We couldn't let that happen. Our only solution was to relieve Colonel Hyde of his duties and ship him back to England. Lord Wellington advised Percy that he had taken charge of the matter personally, and that the colonel was being transported home with all dispatch. He would be dealt with, and he would not return.'

'And the French accepted that?' Hawkwood said. He was unable to conceal his scepticism.

'Victor and Percy are, for the most part, honourable men. They understood that, if Lord Wellington gave his word, the British would not go back on it.'

'So he was brought back and admitted into Bedlam? Why not a military hospital?'

'We learned that the colonel had been corresponding with an old friend, Mr Eden Carslow, who had influence with the Bethlem board of governors. I, too, am acquainted with Mr Carslow. It seemed fitting, given his influence and our personal knowledge of Colonel Hyde, that Bethlem would be more suitable. So we arranged for his admission and guaranteed his bond.'

'On the Admittance Document you stated he was melancholic. He was a lot more than that, wasn't he? He was as mad as a bloody mule.'

McGrigor spread his hands. 'To be admitted to the hospital, a patient is diagnosed as either raving, mischievous, or melancholic. We did not consider Colonel Hyde to be raving. It was clear he was suffering from a severe form of distraction, an aberration, but he was certainly not violent. As for mischievous; you and I may view the colonel's actions as horrific and by our own standards wholly unacceptable, but from my conversations with him, I think he believed, bizarrely, that he was engaged in legitimate surgery. Once he was removed from that world, there was no reason to suppose he'd be a risk, either to the staff or his fellow patients. He was calm and coherent at all times. We didn't think him a threat to anyone.

'Also, we were rather anxious to keep the full details of the colonel's activities in the shadows. The trust between the public and the medical establishment is uneasy at the best of times. The line between enlightenment and ethical considerations is a thin one. In many respects, the colonel was right when he said that people do not understand. Sometimes, and I speak bluntly, it pays to keep them in the dark.'

Hawkwood looked at Ryder. 'If you didn't think he was a threat, why did you write a personal letter to the governors, stating that he was to remain detained?'

Ryder stiffened. 'We made an agreement with the French that the colonel would remain incarcerated for an indefinite period. The intention was to observe his condition on a regular basis. It was possible we could look forward to his eventual discharge and convalescence. The war was unlikely to last for ever, once we had Bonaparte on the run.'

'Pity the Reverend Tombs happened along then, wasn't it?' Hawkwood said grimly. 'Not to mention the sexton's wife.'

'Indeed,' Ryder nodded, missing the irony. 'A most regrettable situation. Had we any idea at the time, of course–'

'You should have handed the bastard over to the French,' Hawkwood growled. 'If you had, we wouldn't be in this bloody mess. And *I* wouldn't have to clean it up.'

McGrigor's eyes widened.

Ryder's face went rigid.

McGrigor, sensing a possible explosion, hastily rearranged his expression into one of curiosity. 'These latest mutilations – the women's bodies – what makes you think that the colonel is responsible?'

'The way the skins were removed. Surgeon Quill told me the mutilations and removal of the organs were almost certainly performed by someone with medical knowledge. It struck me as too much of a coincidence when I saw that parts of the women's faces had been taken.'

'I see...' McGrigor looked thoughtful.

'But do you want to know what really convinced me?' Hawkwood said.

McGrigor tilted his head.

'It was you. It was everything you've just told us about him. There's an old military saying: "Once is misfortune. Twice is coincidence. But three times? That's enemy action." And that's what Hyde is – the enemy.'

The room went quiet.

'Thank you, Hawkwood,' James Read said quickly into the tense silence. 'That will be all. Perhaps you should wait outside.' The Chief

Magistrate's warning look made it clear this was not a suggestion.

The Home Secretary waited until Hawkwood had left the room before casting his glare at the Chief Magistrate. 'You'd do well to keep your man muzzled, Read. I don't care whose damned ear you're close to, I'll not have anyone talk to me that way, especially a constable. I'm a minister of the Crown, for God's sake!'

McGrigor coughed. 'Perhaps Hawkwood is right. Perhaps we should have handed Hyde to the French when we had the chance.'

Ryder swung around. 'Well, I rather think the consequences of *that* decision rest on your shoulders, McGrigor, not mine.'

'I'll not disagree with you, Home Secretary,' Mc-Grigor said calmly, the lilt in his voice sounding even more pronounced. 'Though it's a decision we'll *all* have to live with. I'd say we share a collective responsibility, wouldn't you?'

Ryder stared at the Surgeon-General for several seconds before giving a noncommittal grunt and shifting his gaze to James Read. 'Can your man hunt him down?'

'I believe so. He's very resourceful. Though from what we have seen so far, Colonel Hyde may prove to be an elusive quarry.'

'Then we must pray that he picks up Hyde's scent soon, eh? You'll keep me informed on his progress?'

Read nodded. 'Of course.'

Ryder moved away from the window, towards the door. It was a clear signal that he considered the meeting to be drawing to a close.

336

'You expect him to kill again, don't you?' McGrigor said from his chair.

Ryder frowned at the interjection.

Read hesitated. 'Officer Hawkwood is of the opinion that Colonel Hyde has some sort of agenda. It's possible he could kill again if he feels that agenda to be either threatened or stymied. Our difficulty lies in not knowing the nature of the agenda.' Read looked at McGrigor. 'You have greater knowledge of the man. Do you have *any* thoughts that could assist us? Why he might be obtaining bodies. Why he's doing what he's doing?'

McGrigor lowered his eyes and shook his head. 'I wish I did. I'm truly sorry, I've told you all I know.'

'Then perhaps an educated guess?' Read said.

McGrigor pursed his lips and looked thoughtful. 'It is possible, if it *is* Colonel Hyde, that he's doing it because he believes his work is incomplete.'

Read frowned. 'How so?'

'The colonel was removed from his surgical duties against what he thinks of as his better judgement. It could be that he believes there are still lives to be saved, bodies to be mended.'

'You mean he's obtaining body parts in order to use them?' Read looked taken aback. 'On whom?'

'There you have me. I've no idea. You asked for an educated guess. It's the only one I can come up with.' McGrigor gave a helpless shrug. 'Frankly, any guess *you* made would be as valid as anything I might propose. I'm not a mad-doctor, Read. Whatever's going on in Colonel Hyde's brain is outside my sphere of knowledge. That's why we

337

signed him over to the Bethlem authorities.'

And look what good that did, Read thought.

'Dear God, the man's insane! One might as well try and fly to the moon on a broomstick as attempt to make sense of anything he does.' Ryder stared at them both.

Read suspected the Home Secretary's outburst derived from concern for his own office rather than the colonel's state of mind or the danger the latter might present to an unknowing populace. The last thing Ryder would want was for his deal with the French and the machinations behind the colonel's incarceration in Bedlam – and by association the control his department was exercising over the country's system of asylums – to be brought before the public gaze.

Ryder glared. 'Forget the whys and wherefores, Read. That isn't your function. Your job isn't to come up with a cure, it's to catch him! Set your dogs loose and catch him!'

Read looked at McGrigor, who said nothing but lifted an eyebrow in silent communication of a common understanding.

Read allowed himself to look thoughtful, then nodded. 'In that case, Home Secretary, I will take my leave. Your servant, Surgeon McGrigor. Thank you for your time. Good day to you both.'

'My secretary will see you out,' Ryder said stiffly, moving towards the bell-pull.

'There's no need,' Read said, picking up his hat and cane. 'I know the way.'

James Read winced as the carriage lurched over a pothole. From above them came the crack of a whip and a sharp curse from the coachman, Caleb, as they turned into the Strand. They were heading back to Bow Street.

'So our colonel's a bloody maniac,' Hawkwood said. 'No wonder they wanted it hushed up. They even kept Eden Carslow in the dark.'

'McGrigor thinks Colonel Hyde may be obtaining the bodies in order to carry out surgical procedures,' Read said.

Hawkwood closed his eyes. 'God's teeth.'

'He was unable to expand on his theory. He simply said it was a possibility.'

'What about Home Secretary Ryder? Did he have anything else to say?'

'I'm afraid the Home Secretary doesn't like you, Hawkwood. He told me I was to keep you muzzled. He also wants you to hunt the colonel down.' Read gazed out of the carriage window. 'One wonders how you can do one if you're constrained by the other.'

'The man's an idiot,' Hawkwood said.

'A harsh judgement.'

'Not really,' Hawkwood said. 'From what I've seen of them, most politicians are idiots. It's a known fact. All the trouble in the world is started by politicians. And when they realize they can't get themselves out of trouble, they expect people like you and me to step in to protect their arses.'

'And how do you propose to protect the Home Secretary's ... er ... arse?' Read asked.

'Maybe I should be looking for the men who are working for Hyde,' Hawkwood said. 'If I can find them, it's possible they'll lead me to the colonel.'

'You're talking about the men who left the bodies outside Bart's?'

'You still think I'm clutching at straws?'

Read stared out of the window. Finally he turned back. 'Have you thought how you are going to find them?'

'By doing something I should have done a while ago.'

'Talking to your former comrade-in-arms, perhaps?'

'*With*,' Hawkwood said. 'Not *to*.'

A nerve trembled at the corner of the magistrate's mouth.

'If anyone can get me information on them, it's Nathaniel. Though it's been a while since we talked.'

Read raised an eyebrow.

'I think he might have been insulted when I offered him Henry Warlock's job.'

'You're surprised he turned the position down?'

'Not really. I can't see him as a Runner. Besides, he told me he couldn't afford the drop in salary.'

There was a definite twitch along the Chief Magistrate's jawline that time.

The carriage slowed, clattered towards the kerb, and stopped. Hawkwood got out and held the door open. The coachman tipped his hat and waited until the two men had entered the building before driving off.

'There's a message for you,' Twigg said, when they entered the ante-room. 'He said his name was Leech.' The clerk held out the folded paper.

Hawkwood broke the seal.

340

I have information that may be pertinent to your investigation. Locke

If she dropped her price any lower, Molly Finn thought dejectedly, she'd be giving it away. Business had been depressingly slow so far and it didn't look as though it was going to get any better any time soon.

Molly put it down to the weather. It couldn't seem to make up its mind. One moment, rain; the next sleet and snow. What she was offering had been known to warm up a body and bring a rosy glow to the cheeks – both sets – but if your pig of a landlord kept an eye out for you bringing men back to your room, leaving you with only a cold, damp alleyway in which to conduct your trade, one drop of rain or a snowflake down the back of the neck might be all it took to cool the ardour, then the only thing you'd be left sucking would be your own thumb. And that didn't pay the rent or put food on the table.

The market's fruit and vegetable stalls were already enjoying a steady trade, so it wasn't as though prospective customers were few and far between. The trouble was, even at this early hour, she wasn't the only moll on show. With its taverns and coffee houses, the competition was starting to build up. Still, the spot she'd secured under the archway at the end of the Piazza was at least dry. Molly undid a couple more buttons of her bodice. A girl had to use what God had given her. In Molly's case, the good Lord had been very generous. She was a pretty girl, with blonde

341

ringlets, a shapely figure and a pout that would have tempted an archbishop.

Should have, too, but with archbishops thin on the ground, Molly had been forced to flaunt her charms to a less pious clientele; so far, without appreciable success. She was beginning to think that the Haymarket might be a better bet, though it was probably too early for that.

An army officer came striding down the colonnade, handsome in his scarlet uniform and shako cap. It was too good an opportunity to miss. Hands on hips, Molly stepped out, struck a pose, ran her tongue across her lips and favoured him with her trademark smile.

'Hello, Colonel! Lookin' for some company?'

The colonel, if he was a colonel – flattery never did any harm – walked on without stopping. Molly sighed and watched him disappear into the crowd. Pity, she thought. He hadn't been bad looking. She eased back against the wall, lifted her shawl over her shoulders, and looked for her next target.

'Makes you wonder if they 'aven't all turned queer, don't it?'

Molly turned. The speaker was leaning against the next pillar, arms folded across her breasts. She had elfin features and blue eyes, framed by a cascade of raven hair. An impish grin split her face.

Molly nodded. Rivalry among the working girls could be fierce, but it didn't mean they didn't chat in between punters.

'Thought I might try the Haymarket,' Molly said, drawing her shawl about her. 'Might get a bite there.'

The dark-haired girl shook her head. Her curls bounced around her cheeks. 'Wouldn't bother. I was there not long back. It was as dead as old Jack. Bloody nippy, too.'

Molly was surprised the girl hadn't agreed that a change of venue might be worth exploring. With Molly off on a wild-goose chase, it would have increased the other girl's chances of nabbing a customer.

Molly accepted the information with a rueful smile. The girl put her head on one side and eyed Molly speculatively. 'Don't suppose...?' The girl made a face. 'Nah, p'raps not, lass like you.'

'What?' Molly asked.

The girl held Molly's gaze for several seconds, as if turning a thought over in her mind. Finally, she said, 'It's just that I've 'ad an offer from one of my regular gentlemen for a two-up; him an' a pair of ladies. Nice-lookin' toff. Likes 'is early-mornin' exercise. Asked me to pop out and see if I could find somebody.' The girl lifted a suggestive eyebrow. 'What d'you think? You interested? Probably wouldn't take much more than an hour. 'E pays 'andsomely, too. Wouldn't have to spend the rest of the day freezing our tits off.'

Molly thought about it. 'How much is he offering?'

'A guinea for the two.'

Molly's eyebrows went up.

'Told you he was generous.' The girl grinned. 'Not bad, eh?'

Molly usually charged her customers two shillings. Half a guinea for an hour was good money.

343

'An' you said he was a toff?'

'Proper spoken. He's a good laugh, too. Better than standin' around 'ere. You up for it?'

Molly thought about it for all of two heartbeats. 'All right, why not?'

The girl laughed and clapped her hands.

'How far is it?' Molly asked.

'Just round the corner. He's got this room 'e rents, for entertaining, if you know what I mean.' The girl tapped the side of her nose and winked. 'Told me when I found someone we were to go right round.' The girl took Molly's hand. 'So why don't you an' me go and pay him a little visit and warm ourselves up?'

The two girls left the shelter of the colonnade. Weaving between the stalls and taking care to avoid the puddles and the rats, they made their way across the Piazza.

'What's your name, sweet'eart?' The girl squeezed Molly's hand.

'Molly.'

'Mine's Sally. Pleased to make your acquaintance, Molly.'

Molly grinned in return. Cutting down Southampton Street, the girls turned into Maiden Lane.

The entrance lay between two Roman columns, next to Half-Moon Alley. Above the door were two signs. One proclaimed the place to be the Cider Cellars. The other sign, in the shape of a lantern, advertised *Beds*.

'Says 'e likes to keep a room 'ere, so it's nice and 'andy.' Sally giggled. 'Just like me!' She tugged Molly down the stairs. The place was packed, traders mostly, enjoying a quick breakfast warmer. The reek of rough liquor, sweat and tobacco was overwhelming.

Sally led the way towards a set of stairs at the far end of the room. Her language was coarse as she slapped away the roving hands. Molly took hold of the hem of Sally's dress and hung on. They tripped up the stairs and down a passage towards the rear of the building.

'Here we are,' Sally said brightly, stopping outside a door. She smoothed her dress, tugged her bodice down and pinched her cheeks. Reaching out, she pushed up Molly's breasts and winked. 'Might as well let 'im see the goods, eh?'

Sally took Molly's hand and knocked on the door. There was the sound of approaching foot-steps and the door opened.

Sally pulled Molly inside. 'Look what I've brought,' she called brightly.

There were two people in the room, Molly realized. The one who had opened the door and the one seated on the bed. The man on the bed stared at Molly and ran his eye up and down her body. As the door closed he leered suggestively over her shoulder.

Molly turned.

'Hello, darlin',' Lemuel Ragg said.

15

Apothecary Locke turned away from his window. 'You know, I've never considered myself a foolish man.'

Hawkwood looked at him. 'I don't recall saying you were, Doctor.'

The apothecary dipped his head and peered at Hawkwood over the rim of his spectacles. 'Then perhaps you should confide in me. I may be able to help you.'

'I'm not sure I understand you, Doctor.'

'Tell me what you're doing here,' Locke said.

'You sent for me,' Hawkwood said. 'Shouldn't I be the one asking the questions?'

Locke raised his head. The youthfulness that Hawkwood had seen at the time of their first encounter had disappeared. There was weariness there now. The apothecary ran a hand along the edge of his desk.

'Forgive me, but on your previous visit I asked why you'd come. After all, with Colonel Hyde dead, surely the investigation was closed. You replied – somewhat curtly, as I recall – that it was for your report.' Locke smiled, almost shyly. 'A logical reason, given that our first meeting was interrupted by the arrival of the constable summoning you away. You requested access to Colonel Hyde's admission documents, and I was able to grant that. And yet, evidently, that was still not the end of it, for here we are again. I send you a message, a vague offer of information, and you arrive at my door within the hour.'

The apothecary lifted his hand and stared at the dust on the ends of his fingers, as if seeing it for the first time. Then he looked up. 'I find that most curious. It leads me to believe that your investigation continues, despite Colonel Hyde's demise. I'm wondering why that should be. I can think of only one explanation.' Leaning back against his desk, the apothecary took off his spectacles and misted the lenses with his breath. 'You think Colonel Hyde is still alive, don't you?'

The room was still. Locke reached into his sleeve and took out his handkerchief. He began to polish his spectacles vigorously.

'I don't *think* Hyde's still alive,' Hawkwood said. 'I bloody *know* he is!' The words were out before he could stop them.

He'd expected an immediate gasp of astonishment from Locke, some show of surprise, but the apothecary's expression remained curiously impassive. '*How* do you know?'

'The body in the church wasn't Hyde's. He made another substitution – dug up the body of a recently deceased man of similar age and build, and left it to burn in his place.'

'So the colonel must have known about the burial before he made his escape.' Locke spoke matter-of-factly.

Hawkwood nodded. 'Reverend Tombs would have told him. Reverend Tombs would have told the colonel a lot of things, especially if the

347

colonel asked the right questions.'

Which is what I should have been doing, Hawkwood thought.

Locke returned the handkerchief to his sleeve, placed his hands behind his back and began to pace the room. 'So your subsequent visits here have been part of your effort to track him down?'

'Yes.'

'And what have you discovered?'

'I know he's obtaining and dissecting dead bodies.'

Locke stopped pacing.

'Two cadavers were left outside Bart's Hospital. Some of their insides had been removed. Parts of their skins had also been taken, including their faces.'

A nerve quivered in the apothecary's cheek. He put his hands together as if about to pray and rested the tips of his fingers against his chin. Then he started pacing again. 'Go on.'

'I know that all Colonel Hyde's actions have had a purpose. His cultivation of the priest, the theft of the scalpel and the laudanum' – at this, Locke coloured – 'the murder of Reverend Tombs, the escape, the digging up of the substitute corpse, the burning of the church to divert us from his scent, and now the mutilation of the women... I know it's all part of some grand scheme. I just don't know what that is.'

Locke said nothing. The silence stretched for several long seconds. Finally the apothecary moved to his desk. 'Let me explain why I summoned you. I was in the colonel's quarters and I discovered these–'

They were papers, Hawkwood saw, folded in two.

'I was gathering up the colonel's effects,' Locke said, lifting one of the sheets and opening it out.

At first glance, it looked similar to the etchings Hawkwood had seen on the walls of the colonel's room; a series of anatomical studies of the lower half of the torso and limbs, displayed in lifelike detail. And yet they were not the same. Hawkwood stared at the sketches. He knew his brain was telling him there was a difference but for the life of him, he couldn't see what it was.

And then it came to him.

It was the legs. They were completely out of proportion. The thigh and calf muscles and the bones beneath the skin were clearly defined, but the limbs were too slender and elongated and it was the way they were displayed, with the thighs spread wide and the knees bent. It didn't look natural. It looked bizarrely like the sort of pose a fencer would assume before executing a riposte, or a tumbler about to attempt a somersault. And then there was the torso, or at least what Hawkwood assumed was the torso, for it didn't resemble anything that he'd ever seen before. In fact, it looked more like a sac of eggs. His eyes moved down. The anklebones looked too fragile to be able to bear even a modest weight and as for the feet, well, they were the oddest feature of all, each one impossibly long with the toes limp and obscenely splayed. In fact, if he didn't know any better, they looked more like–

'Frogs,' Locke said.

'Frogs?' Hawkwood echoed, feeling immediately stupid. *Of course, they were bloody frogs. What else could they have been?* 'Why frogs?'

'Many surgeons practise their early anatomy on the corpses of animals. Even schoolboys dissect frogs in school. Galen used to cut open apes. Eden Carslow once dissected an elephant.'

Why has he got me looking at bloody frogs? Hawkwood wondered. He stared again at the illustration. 'What are these?'

The apothecary followed his finger.

Running from the muscles at the ends of the severed limbs were a series of wavy lines. The end of one of the lines was attached to whatever it was that looked like an egg sac. The other end was connected to some kind of wheel, complete with a winding handle.

'Fascinating, isn't it?' The apothecary's voice was a whisper.

'It might be if I knew what the devil it was,' Hawkwood said, though he had to admit the drawing was intriguing.

'I believe it to be an illustration of one of Galvani's experiments. He was an Italian physician who believed that all animals possess a special electrical fluid that is generated in the brain and which passes through the nerves into the muscles. In order to prove his theory, he conducted a number of experiments with amphibians.' Locke tapped the etching with the end of his finger. 'I believe that is what's represented here.'

The apothecary indicated the lines. 'I suspect these are the wires through which his fluid passes.' Locke shook his head in wonder before sliding the illustration to one side. 'And then

350

there are these.'

The second sheet contained a drawing of what looked like twelve sealed, jar-shaped containers, arranged in three rows of four. A thin tube protruded from the lid of each jar. The top of each tube was linked to the next one in line in each direction so that the jars appeared to be covered by a squared grille. The top half of each jar was transparent. The bottom half was either opaque or else the containers held some kind of liquid.

Hawkwood didn't know why, but the illustration rang a faint bell.

'What's this?'

'An electrical machine. Look, see, there's more.' With excitement in his voice, Locke reached over and unfolded the third sheet. Smoothing it out, he laid it across the desk.

As soon as Locke mentioned the word 'electrical', Hawkwood knew why the drawing of the jars looked familiar. Electrical demonstrations had been a popular form of entertainment in some of the London theatres. Hawkwood had been in the audience at Astley's when a black-cloaked master of ceremonies had exhorted several dozen giggling volunteers to form a circle and hold hands; he had then proceeded to send them into convulsions by the touch of a wire and several glass bottles. Hawkwood recalled that women had been more susceptible to electrification than the men. He had no idea why. It hadn't seemed to matter very much at the time. It had been an amusement, nothing more.

The third sheet made no sense at all. It showed what appeared to be a column of discs stacked one on top of the other, enclosed within four vertical retaining rods. At the base of the column was a basin-shaped container. The bottom disc was attached to the basin by what looked like a thin flow of liquid. The discs were arranged in pairs, each pair separated from the pair below by a smaller, darker-coloured disc. There were sixteen of the larger discs, making eight pairs in all. Each disc was marked by a letter; the upper disc in each pair carried the identification letter Z, the bottom disc the letter A.

'And this?' Hawkwood asked.

'The same, though I believe it represents a more advanced device.'

Hawkwood pointed to the column of discs. 'All right, so what are *these*?'

Locke adjusted his glasses. Behind the lenses his face was quite animated. 'See, there's a key at the bottom of the page. The A represents silver; the Z is zinc. I believe it's also possible to use copper discs instead of silver.'

'All right, Doctor, I'll admit this is all very fascinating, but what would Colonel Hyde want with electrical machines?'

'Perhaps we should ask the man who drew them.'

'I'm sorry?'

'Look at them closely. Regard the style of the illustrations and the attendant lettering. Would you say they look familiar?'

Hawkwood looked. He shook his head. 'You've lost me, Doctor.'

Locke lifted the papers and placed them to one side. 'Perhaps I can refresh your memory.'

352

Locke moved around the desk, opened a drawer, and took out another sheet of paper. He opened it out. 'Do you remember this?'

Hawkwood recognized it. It was the drawing that Locke had shown him on his first visit: the Air Loom.

'Compare the style of the illustrations and the lettering,' Locke said. He moved aside.

Hawkwood stared at the drawings, his gaze moving from one to another, and back again. The similarity between the two was striking.

'Note the lettering in particular,' Locke said. 'The bottom curlicue in the letter A, for example.'

Hawkwood followed the apothecary's fingertip. It was undeniably the same small, neat hand.

'Matthews?' Hawkwood said. 'They *knew* each other? But they had their own rooms. I thought you kept patients like them separated?'

Locke shrugged. 'By their nature, hospitals are enclosed communities. Bethlem's no different. Despite the popular assertion that we are England's Bastille, we are not a prison. We do allow some patients a certain amount of fraternization. Indeed, where we feel the experience will be of benefit to the patients, we actively encourage it. We have common rooms where they can meet – under supervision, of course. James Tilly Matthews is one of our best-known residents. I remember the colonel expressing great interest in Matthews' designs for the new hospital, and I recall seeing them in conversation on a number of occasions.'

Hawkwood looked down at the papers. He'd

353

assumed that Hyde had spent all his time in isolation in his rooms, his only contact being the keepers and the medical staff and, latterly, the late Reverend Tombs. He hadn't expected this.

'I want to see Matthews. Now.'

Locke nodded and picked up the drawings. 'Come with me.'

The apothecary led the way along the first-floor corridor. Most of the cell doors were open. Patients were mingling freely with the blue-coated attendants.

They stopped outside a closed door and Locke murmured softly, 'He does not have a very high opinion of the judiciary. It would be best, therefore, if you do not tell him you are a police officer.'

Before Hawkwood could respond, Locke knocked twice on the door and pushed it open. 'James, my dear fellow,' he announced amiably. 'How are we today? May we come in?'

The room was considerably smaller than the colonel's quarters; probably no more than twelve feet by nine. There were the same basic items of furniture, however: bed, chair, small table, and a chest. There was a sluice pipe in the corner for waste. To add to the claustrophobia, there were several shelves full of books and the walls were covered in drawings. They were all architectural plans. Hawkwood recognized a copy of the design for the new hospital. It was less detailed than the one Locke had shown him and he assumed it was an early draft. Nevertheless, the attention to detail was exceptional.

A short, compact, dark-haired man was leaning

over the table. He had a pencil in one hand and a rule in the other. He did not look up, but continued to fuss over the drawing laid out before him. His pale face was fused in rapt concentration as he tapped the pencil against his right leg.

'James?' Locke said again.

The man started and turned around. 'Dr Locke! Come in! Come in!'

'James, allow me to present a colleague of mine, Mr Hawkwood.'

Hawkwood found himself perused from head to toe by a pair of eyes that were as bright as buttons. 'A pleasure, Mr Hawkwood!'

Locke approached the table. 'James has taken up engraving. He's working on some new architectural illustrations. Come and see.'

Hawkwood walked forward.

The drawing was of a town house; a rather grand one, with steps and a portico and an honour guard of tall trees. A ground-floor plan of the house was laid alongside. As with the sketches on the wall, the quality was exceptional.

Locke patted the patient on the shoulder. 'James has plans for a magazine of architectural illustrations. What's it to be called again? I'm afraid it's slipped my mind. Do tell Mr Hawkwood.'

Matthews' face lit up. 'I will indeed! It's to be called *Useful Architecture*. It will explain the basics of architecture for the common man. It is also my intention to provide designs, so that each reader can make use of them for his own purpose,' he added grandly.

'Doesn't that sound like a splendid idea?' Locke said, blinking behind his spectacles.

'Splendid,' Hawkwood agreed warily.

'There'll be hothouses for cabbages,' Matthews said suddenly. He took Hawkwood's arm. 'You do know the efficacious benefit of a good hothouse, don't you, Mr Hawkwood? I explained it to the French but the damned fools took not a jot of notice. And look what's happened to them,' he added darkly.

Hawkwood looked blankly at Locke, who shook his head imperceptibly, but Matthews hadn't finished. Hanging on to Hawkwood's arm, he drew himself up. 'Each home will have its own hothouse. I shall then petition the government to commandeer the great army of the unemployed to gather up all the filth in the city. This will be transported by cart and barrow and barge to every hothouse, where it will be used as fertilizer upon the cabbages, which will grow in abundance, thus providing a nourishing supply of vegetables for the nation. Now,' he concluded triumphantly, hand on hip, 'what do you think of that, sir?'

Hawkwood wondered whether the patient was waiting for applause. He rescued his sleeve. He could see that Locke was sending him warning signs across the table. Behind his spectacles, the apothecary's eyebrows were going up and down like signal flags.

Hawkwood nodded. 'That's the thing about the French. They wouldn't recognize a good idea if it bit them on the arse.'

There was a pause. He saw Locke's eyebrows lift almost to his hairline. Then, beside him, James Matthews jabbed the air with his pencil. 'Ha! Exactly, sir! Exactly! I couldn't have put it better myself!' He looked down at his drawing and began to take measurements with the rule. His movements were brisk and precise.

Locke stepped forward quickly. 'Well, James, we mustn't keep you from your work. We'll leave you to get on.'

Matthews nodded distractedly. 'So much to prepare, and so little time.' He glanced up, a determined expression on his face. 'One must stay busy, what?'

'Oh, absolutely, James! Indeed one must.' Locke nodded enthusiastically and then paused. 'Though, before we go, I wonder if we might ask your advice. Mr Hawkwood and I are not, alas, of a technical persuasion and we were hoping you could assist us with an explanation of these—' Locke held up the papers he'd taken from the colonel's cell. 'They are quite beyond our comprehension, I'm afraid. I thought a draughtsman with your expertise could shed some light... What say you?'

Hawkwood was wondering if Locke wasn't laying it on a bit thick, but then he saw the patient's eyes flicker towards the papers and he remembered Locke saying that some patients thrived on companionship. On flattery and curiosity, too, it seemed. Locke was playing his patient well, like a fish on a line.

'But of course, Doctor. It would be my pleasure. What do you have there?'

Locke spread the drawings across the table.

Matthews smiled broadly when he saw the top sheet. He reached for it. 'Ah, yes! Galvani!'

'Is that so?' Locke said, without a hint of guile.

357

'It's his frog experiment. He dissected a frog and placed one of its legs on an iron plate. When he touched the nerve with a metal scalpel, the leg twitched violently. He reasoned, therefore, that there must be electricity in the frog. Fascinating conclusion. He was quite wrong, of course. Volta proved that.'

Another bloody name I don't know, Hawkwood thought.

Locke lifted the paper to reveal the second drawing.

Matthews gave an exclamation of amusement. 'Why, it's one of mine!'

'We thought it might be,' Locke said, with a sideways glance towards Hawkwood. 'We were wondering what it was.'

Matthews smiled indulgently. 'I'm surprised you don't recognize them, Doctor. It's a battery of Leyden jars. They're for storing an electrical charge. One can either fill them with water or line them with metal foil. The rods you see are made of brass. The more jars there are in the battery, the greater the charge. An electrical discharge can only be performed once, however, after which the storage process must begin again and a new charge built up. Crude, but remarkably effective,' he added breathlessly.

'How is the charge created in the first place?' Hawkwood asked, remembering the theatre audience tumbling like ninepins.

'Friction machines. The charge is collected by rubbing together different materials, such as glass globes and leather.' Matthews held up a finger. 'Wait, I do believe I have an illustration.'

358

He left the table and looked along his book-shelves. 'Now then,' he muttered to himself. 'Adams, Adams, Ad – ah, yes.' He took a book down, opened the cover, wet his finger and began to flick through the pages. His finger stopped moving. 'Yes, here we are.' He held the page open for them to see.

'There, a child is being attended by a doctor, possibly for pain or paralysis of the forearm. The friction machine is on the table next to them.'

It was a peculiar-looking contraption, comp-osed of a winding handle, a pulley, and several cylindrical objects with curious, curved attach-ments.

'You see, the cylinder generator is to the right. That would be made of glass. The main receptor, or terminal as it is sometimes called, is that object in the centre. You see the Leyden jar hanging from the rod at the end of the metal globe? A metal loop goes from the jar to a treatment fork – which, as you see, is touching the child's forearm. When the handle is turned, the glass generator revolves, building up the charge, which is transferred to the receptor where it is stored. When a sufficient amount of charge is accumulated, the doctor dis-charges the electricity down the wire to the treat-ment fork. The result would be a sudden jolt, a stimulation of the senses, activating the nerves and muscles in the child's arm. It can be most bene-ficial, I'm told. You know, Cavendish used a battery of Leyden jars to replicate the properties of the torpedo fish.'

Hawkwood realized the shock must have shown on his face, because both Matthews and Locke

359

were throwing him odd looks.

'You've heard of the torpedo fish, Mr Hawkwood?' Matthews asked hesitantly.

Hawkwood found he was massaging his left shoulder. Self-consciously, he lowered his hand. 'Oh, yes, I know all about bloody torpedoes.'

Matthews' eyebrows lifted. 'Do you now? How interesting. Most people don't, you know. Poor Cavendish. They accused him of sacrilege for suggesting that a man-made machine could perform in the same way as a creature created by God. The fellow was right about the principle, though.'

Despite the illustration in the book and Matthews' enthusiastic commentary, Hawkwood wasn't sure he understood the principle any more than he had before. He wondered if Matthews' explanation of the last drawing would be any easier to keep up with.

'Another of your illustrations, I believe, James,' Locke said affably, revealing the last sheet.

'So it is!' Matthews exclaimed excitedly. 'Ah, now, this is the most sophisticated device of them all. You recall I mentioned Volta when we were looking at the first illustration of Galvani's frog experiments? It was Volta who concluded there was no such thing as animal electricity, that it was, in fact, the interaction between the two dissimilar metals of the scalpel and tabletop and the salt water in the frog that created the electrical charge. He proved it by constructing what he called his pile. We call it a battery now, as it performs the same function as the friction machines and the jars. The difference with this,

360

however, is that one does not have to store up the electricity in order to discharge it. With this, the electricity remains constant, like the current flowing in a river. There's no need for winding handles or glass cylinders or jars. It's all down to a chemical reaction.'

The apothecary tapped the paper. 'Using zinc and silver?'

'Yes, well done! Though zinc and copper work equally well. The smaller discs separating the pairs are the equivalent of the frog. Card paper dipped in brine. If you then run one wire from the top disc and one from the bottom disc and close the circuit, the electrical current begins to flow. It's so simple!'

'And the more discs there are, the greater the charge?' Hawkwood said.

'That's it!' Matthews frowned and indicated the illustrations. 'But how did you come by these?'

'They were left by Colonel Hyde.' Locke dropped his voice. 'You know Colonel Hyde is no longer with us, James? Well, Mr Hawkwood and I were putting his things in order and we came across these among his belongings and thought you might like to have them back.'

'Why, Doctor, that's most thoughtful of you. Thank you.'

'So, did you know Colonel Hyde well, Mr Matthews?' Hawkwood asked.

'Oh, yes. We became good friends. He promised that in exchange for my drawings he would do all he could to pursue my case with the Home Secretary. I expect to hear from him any day now.'

'I'm sure you will,' Hawkwood said. He saw

Locke was looking at him. 'So the colonel asked you to draw these for him, did he? And did he say why he was interested in the machines?'

'Colonel Hyde believed electricity had the power to change the world. He said one day it would be able to move mountains.'

'Did he now? And how did he think it was going to do that?'

Matthews screwed up his face and had a think, but then shook his head. 'He didn't say.'

Hawkwood stared down at the drawings. So far, everything Hyde had done, he'd done for a reason. So why had he asked Matthews to draw him these? And then Matthews said, 'Do you have the other one?'

'Other one?' Locke asked blankly.

'There were three.'

'You gave the colonel three drawings?'

'Yes. Where's the last one I did for him? He said it was the most important one of all.'

'What was it?'

'He wanted me to design a larger battery.'

'More jars?' Hawkwood said.

'Oh, no, it was the Volta battery he was referring to. He asked me if it was possible to design a more powerful device, using the same principles. I told him it was and showed him how it was done.'

'Did he say why he wanted it?'

'Yes, though I did not understand his meaning.'

Hawkwood waited.

Matthews glanced over to Locke, as if seeking permission for what he was about to say.

'What did he tell you, James?' the apothecary asked.

'He said it would bring him closer to God.'

'All right, Doctor. Suppose you tell me what's going on here. What do you know that I don't?'

They were back in Locke's office. The apothecary was looking pensive.

'How much do you know about the colonel's background, his education, his medical studies, for example?'

'I spoke with Eden Carslow. They were students together, went to the same lectures. They'd remained friends. That's why he signed the bond. When he left London, Hyde went to study anatomy in Italy. His studies complete, he joined the army, working in field hospitals in the West Indies, South America, Ireland and Spain. That's where it started.'

'It?' Locke frowned. 'You mean his melancholy?'

'He might have been melancholic by the time he got here, but that wasn't why they shipped him home, whatever it may say on your admission sheet.'

The apothecary paused in mid stride. 'I don't follow.'

'Colonel Hyde wasn't returned to England because he was melancholic. It was because he was murdering French prisoners of war and using them for butchery practice. He was placed here because he was a friend of Carslow's, and Carslow has influence with the governors.'

'What do you mean by "butchery practice"?'

'He was trying to rebuild them.'

'Rebuild?'

'Mend them. Or at least that's what McGrigor, the Surgeon-General, thinks. His is the second signature on the bond. The one we couldn't read. He said Hyde had grand ideas about the future of surgery and how one day it would be possible to mend the wounded by taking working parts from dead men's bodies.'

Locke closed his eyes. 'He got that from John Hunter.'

'He was Hyde's anatomy teacher, his mentor. Wait – you knew of the connection?'

'I knew a little of his medical studies. He would talk about them sometimes. He was one of the few students who were fortunate to have lived under Hunter's roof at his school in Castle Street.'

'It was Hunter who helped get Hyde his commission. Twenty years ago, it was Hunter who was Surgeon-General.'

Locke said nothing.

'That's it, Doctor. You now know as much as I do.' Hawkwood walked to the window and looked out over Moor Fields. 'Somewhere out there is a lunatic who thinks he's God and who's taken to cutting up the bodies of dead women, and who's persuaded another lunatic to draw him pictures of electrical machines. I tell you now, Apothecary, I need all the help I can get, and I'm open to suggestions.'

Hawkwood turned round, and found that Locke was staring at him.

'What?'

'Hunter...'

'What about him?'

'How much do you know about John Hunter,

364

Officer Hawkwood?'

'Other than his connection with Hyde and the fact that he's held in high regard, not a damned thing. Why?'

The apothecary hesitated, as if deciding whether or not to continue. Then he said, 'There was a story, many years ago. It appeared in the *Gentleman's Magazine*. It concerned a forger who was imprisoned in Newgate and sentenced to the noose. Despite a petition to the King requesting a pardon, he was taken to Tyburn and hanged. It was said that, following the hanging, the forger's body was carried by hearse to an undertaker's parlour in Goodge Street. There, it was delivered into the hands of several members of the Royal Society, Hunter among them. The story goes that, under Hunter's guidance, they rubbed the flesh and placed the body close to the fire to warm it, and used bellows to try and inflate his lungs. When that didn't work, they employed electric shocks from Leyden jars to activate the heart muscle and restore the forger to life.'

Locke fell silent.

Hawkwood said nothing. In a moment of dark recall, he felt the familiar tightening round his own throat, heard again the scrabbling of heels on planking, and the echo of coarse laughter.

'Officer Hawkwood?'

Hawkwood looked up. The memories retreated back into their lair.

The apothecary pushed himself away from his desk. 'I know what you're thinking, Officer Hawkwood. I told you a short time ago that I was not a foolish man and yet, here I am, telling you what sounds like a fairy story. Well, I have another tale for you. Eight years ago, a convicted murderer was hanged at Newgate. His name was George Forster. After one hour, his corpse was taken down and delivered to a professor of physics. The professor then performed a demonstration. He connected the corpse to a battery. When he activated the battery – or, as James Matthews would put it, he closed the circuit – Forster's eye opened. As the electrical current continued to flow, Forster raised a fist into the air. His back arched and his legs began to kick. The witnesses to the demonstration were convinced that, for a brief period, George Forster was brought back to life. The professor's name was Giovanni Aldini. He was visiting this country from Italy. He was Luigi Galvani's nephew.'

It's me who's going mad, Hawkwood thought.

But Locke hadn't finished. 'Have you heard of the Humane Society? It was founded by an apothecary, William Hawes, and a physician, Thomas Cogan; for the sole purpose of rescuing victims of drowning. The Society offered rewards of up to four guineas to anyone who succeeded in restoring life to any person taken out of the water for dead, within thirty miles of London. As you can imagine, quack medics for miles around came up with suggestions for how resuscitation could be achieved. Everything from bloodletting and purging to enemas and the ingesting of tobacco vapours. Eventually Hawes approached Hunter for advice. Hunter suggested using electricity. He said it was probably the only method there was for stimulating the heart.'

366

'Are you telling me it has actually *worked?*' Hawkwood couldn't believe he was even asking the question.

'I've not seen it done, but there have been reports of successful recoveries, yes.'

'The criminal, Forster?'

'No, Forster was not resuscitated. Aldini's demonstration proved to be an interesting experiment, no more than that.'

'What about the other one? The forger?'

'There were differing stories. Some say that Hunter failed and the forger was buried. Others say that he survived. One newspaper claimed that he was living in Glasgow, while another reported that he had dined with an Irishman in Dunkirk. I was trying to recall the fellow's name. It has just come to me. It was Dodd – Reverend William Dodd.'

Jesus, Hawkwood thought. Not another bloody parson.

He turned and looked out of the window. Most of the snow had melted away, though across Moor Fields a few small patches of slush were clinging doggedly to the edges of the ponds and between the exposed roots around the bases of the trees. From a distance they looked like smears of grey marzipan.

'It was seeing the drawings and remembering my conversations with the colonel that reminded me of Hunter's experiments,' Locke said behind him. 'You remember when I told you that I found some of Colonel Hyde's ideas innovative? It sounded fantastical, but now, hearing the true reason for the colonel's admittance to the

367

hospital and your belief that he's responsible for the mutilation of the two corpses found at St Bart's makes me fearful of the colonel's intentions. Even thinking about it, I cannot bring myself to believe that anyone would contemplate such a thing.'

Hawkwood turned back.

'I know how this must sound, but you said it yourself: everything Colonel Hyde has done, he's done for a reason. You remember I likened a distracted patient's mind to a maelstrom, and that sometimes out of that swirling mass a single thought can arise, a moment of epiphany, which sets events in motion and influences every subsequent decision the patient makes? Those decisions form the framework for the patient's existence, his reason for being. Perhaps it was seeing the Galvani drawing that planted the first seed. Colonel Hyde was a student of John Hunter. It's likely that Hunter would have talked about his experiments on electrical resuscitation with his students, certainly the more able ones. Hyde's conversations with James Matthews – who, despite his obsessions is possessed of genuine technical knowledge – could have acted as a catalyst, perhaps the final trigger that launched him on his grand design.'

'Grand design?'

The two men looked at each other. Hawkwood's brain was spinning. It couldn't be true. The idea was absurd, preposterous, the stuff of nightmares. He closed his eyes. 'It's madness!'

'Yes.' Locke nodded. 'I agree. That's precisely what it is. Tell me, Officer Hawkwood, do you know your Shakespeare?'

'It's been a while since I attended the theatre, Doctor.'

'There's a quotation, from *Hamlet:* "There are more things in Heaven and Earth, Horatio, than are dreamt of in your Philosophy."'

'Meaning?'

'Meaning, anything is possible.'

Both men fell silent. Neither wanted to be the one to voice what both of them were thinking.

Hawkwood broke first. 'McGrigor thought the colonel might be taking the body parts in order to carry out some kind of surgical procedure. You think he's going to try and raise the dead. I think you're both right. That's his grand design. That's why he's been obtaining corpses and removing internal organs. That's why he got Matthews to design his electrical machine. He's going to use the spare parts to repair a dead body, then he's going to try and bring it back to life.'

'That's not possible,' Locke whispered.

Hawkwood looked at him. 'A moment ago, you told me *anything* is possible.'

'Not that,' Locke said.

'The colonel seems to think it is. My question is, who's he planning to resurrect?'

He saw that the apothecary was staring at him, a stricken look on his face.

'Doctor?'

'I think I know,' Locke said softly.

'Who is it?'

'His daughter.'

16

Nathaniel Jago rose from the bed and padded naked to the window. He ran a hand across his close-cropped grey hair and looked out at the early-afternoon scene below. He did so without a trace of conceit or self-consciousness, totally at ease with himself. He was not a young man. His face was square and hard edged and carried the lines of someone who'd experienced the harsher side of life and all the adventures it had to offer, and met them head on. His stocky frame and broad shoulders gave him the look of a wrestler or a pugilist. Indeed, his body carried more than its fair share of wear and tear, but a keen-sighted and knowledgeable observer would have recognized the majority of his scars as having been made not by fist or elbow but by blade and bullet.

Jago was not a Londoner by birth. His childhood had been spent on the Kent marshes, a world away from the hustle and bustle that filled the city street below. He stared down at the clogged thoroughfare, at the horse-drawn carriages clattering over the cobbles, the hunched shoulders and bowed heads of the pedestrians, and wondered, not for the first time, why he felt so at home here. It was strange how things turned out.

'Penny for them,' a husky voice said behind him.

Jago turned. The crow's feet at the corners of his dark eyes crinkled. 'Just admirin' the view.'

'Me, too,' the voice said. The comment was followed by a throaty chuckle.

'You're a brazen hussy, Connie Fletcher,' Jago laughed. 'Have you no shame?'

The woman in the bed was laid on her side. She, too, was naked. Her head was propped on her right hand. A pair of warm blue eyes, framed by a tousled mane of blonde hair, regarded Jago with a mixture of humour and affection.

'Shame? You're a fine one to talk, standing by the window with your arse hangin' out.' Her eyes dropped. 'Mind you, it's quite a nice arse. Not too saggy. In fact, not bad for an old 'un.'

'Watch who you're callin' old,' Jago said, feigning insult. 'I'll 'ave you know, I've been told I've got the body of a twenty-year-old.'

'That so? Well, it's high time you gave it him back, then. Now why don't you come here and give Connie a squeeze?'

'You could always start without me,' Jago said, lifting a suggestive eyebrow.

'True, but it's not half as much fun.'

Jago looked up at the ceiling and rolled his eyes. 'The things I do for England.'

Connie Fletcher pulled back the corners of the quilt and grinned. 'God save the King!'

Jago returned to the bed and Connie moved over, taking the edge of the bedcovers with her.

'You in?'

'I'm in,' Jago said.

Connie drew the quilt over them both. Resting her head against his chest, she nestled in close.

'Snug as two bugs,' she said.

They lay in easy silence. Connie's breath was soft against his skin. After a minute or two, though, he felt her stir. She lifted her head.

'I didn't mean it about you being old,' she said. 'You're not.'

'I ain't exactly in my first flush,' Jago said.

'Who is?' Connie raised herself up. 'I've stockings older than some of the girls I've got working here.'

Jago looked down at her. 'You're a fine-looking woman, Connie Fletcher. And don't you let anyone tell you otherwise.'

Connie patted his stomach. 'And you're a smooth-talking flatterer, Nathaniel Jago,' she said. 'But I thank you for it, all the same.'

'Wouldn't say it if I didn't think it was so. And you've got the brains, and there's not many I'd say that to, neither.'

'Well, it's nice to know I'm appreciated for a bit more than these–' Connie dropped her gaze and cupped her left breast. 'Not that they haven't given me a good living, mind.'

With Connie's head against his chest and her leg across his thigh, Jago felt satisfyingly at ease. Which wasn't to say that his guard was totally relaxed. It was another legacy of his days in the army: the ability to rest and conserve energy while still keeping one eye open, just in case.

A peal of girlish laughter sounded beyond the room.

'That'll be Esther,' Connie chuckled. 'She's got his lordship with her. Don't know how he manages it at his age. He's a game old devil, I'll give him that. Esther says he likes to chase her round the bed. He reckons it's the only exercise he gets now that he's given up hunting. Will you chase me round the bed when you're old and grey?'

'I'm already old and grey,' Jago said. 'You want to run round the bed, be my guest.'

'And they say romance is dead,' Connie murmured.

The laughter along the landing faded away.

The room fell silent. The sound of the street could be heard faintly beyond the window.

'I need a favour, Nathaniel,' Connie said hesitantly.

'Wondered how long it would take.'

She turned her head and looked at him. 'What do you mean?'

'You've been fidgeting for the last five minutes. Come on, out with it.'

Connie sat up. Her breasts swayed enticingly. 'It's Chloe. A friend of hers has gone missing.'

Chloe was one of Connie's girls, a petite redhead with alabaster skin.

'Why the interest?'

'Because Chloe's worried and she came to me for advice.'

It was a good enough reason, Jago acknowledged. Connie was like a mother hen with her girls. She recruited them, taught them how to dress and how to conduct themselves in proper company. She looked after their welfare, too, arranging medical examinations with a local doctor who made regular visits to the house. To Connie, a clean house was an orderly house and an orderly house brought in the business. And with business came profit.

'This friend, she's a working girl, too?'

Connie nodded.

'Independent, I'm assumin'?'

Connie nodded again. 'Works the Garden and the Haymarket. Met her once. Chloe and I ran into her outside Drury Lane. Bonny-looking girl; just the sort to fit in here, with the right training. In fact, I had thought of getting Chloe to ask her if she'd be interested. Sadie told me the other morning she's expecting a proposal from young Freddie Hamilton, Lord Brockmere's son. He's been visiting her for the past six months. They say he has an income of five thousand a year. If he does ask, she'll be off, which would leave me with an opening.'

Jago refrained from comment, though several were on the tip of his tongue. The list of aristocratic offspring who'd become infatuated with working girls and actresses over the years would have stretched the length of the Strand and back. It wasn't unknown for regular dalliances to lead to a proposal of marriage, though usually the girl would be paid to break off the liaison by a senior member of whichever family the smitten youth happened to belong to. Jago was willing to lay odds that, if Sadie did take up with the Hamilton boy, it would all be over in a matter of months and she'd be knocking on Connie's door, asking to be taken back into the fold.

'How long's she been missin'?'

Connie hesitated. 'Since early morning.'

'God love us, you're not serious? Is that all?'

'I know,' Connie said. 'But Chloe's worried.

They've been friends a long time; almost like sisters, Chloe says. They used to look out for each other when Chloe worked the streets. Chloe's always insisted they meet up regular as clockwork. It's Chloe's time off. She's been out. Molly hasn't turned up at any of their usual places.'

Jago looked sceptical.

'It's true.'

'Ain't sayin' it's not. Maybe this time, the girl doesn't want to be found.'

Connie shook her head. 'Chloe tells me that's not likely.'

Jago shook his head and sighed. 'I take it there's no man around?'

'There was. He was a private in an infantry regiment. Got killed in Portugal. She couldn't make ends meet, so she went on the game.'

It wasn't anything Jago hadn't heard a hundred times before. There wasn't a town in the land that wasn't home to an ever-increasing number of war widows left to fend for themselves while the bodies of their menfolk lay bleaching under some foreign sun. For those with a child or children to support it was even worse, particularly for the widows of rank-and-file soldiers. Scores of women had been forced to take to the streets in search of crumbs and coin.

'So, you want me to put the word out?' Jago asked doubtfully.

'You know people,' Connie said.

'You insinuatin' that I'm acquainted with people of a nefarious disposition?'

'Well, probably not *all* of them,' Connie said. 'Maybe a few. But I've a better chance asking you for help than the constables. We both know what their response would be if I told them I was worried about a missing moll. They'd laugh themselves silly.'

'Aye, you're not wrong there. All right, as it's you who's askin', I'll see what I can do. But you'd best tell Chloe not to get her hopes up. It ain't likely I'll turn up anything and, if I do, it might take a while. Girls like that, with nothing to their name... Hell, you know what it's like. You've been there. It's why the law wouldn't give you the time of day.' Jago looked towards the window, and the shadowy shape of the city's rooftops. 'It ain't no land of milk and honey, that's for sure. What's the girl's name?'

'Molly, Molly Finn.'

'What's she look like?'

'Me, if you knock off twenty years.'

Connie's request suddenly began to make a kind of sense. Jago looked at her and raised his eyebrows. 'That another reason why you wanted the favour?'

'Maybe. Though maybe it's because it's not the only thing the two of us have in common.'

'Meaning?'

Connie smiled sadly and lowered her head on to his chest. 'We both fell for a soldier.'

Sawney, hemmed in by darkness, descended the stairway. He knew he should have brought a light with him, but for some reason the requirement had slipped his mind. He was navigating by touch alone; feeling his way down the cold stone wall with all the caution of a blind man in a mine shaft.

As if the lack of illumination wasn't bad enough, he'd become increasingly aware of the curious smell. He wasn't sure what it was. Can't have been damp – the walls were quite dry – but whatever it was, it hung in the air, an odd metallic kind of smell, so pungent that it seemed to catch at the back of his throat. Sawney generated saliva and swallowed in an attempt to erase the coppery taste, but the ruse had little effect. If anything, it only made it worse.

He could hear noises, too; distant and muffled. In the darkness it was hard to pinpoint where they were coming from. There were faint mewling sounds, like an animal was in pain, soft murmurings, and now and then a wheezing sigh, like air rattling in someone's throat.

Suddenly, the stairs ended. Sawney felt flagstones beneath his feet. He looked down. His eyes caught a dull yellow gleam several paces ahead of him and he saw it was candlelight leaking through the gap at the bottom of a closed door. Sawney stepped forward quietly. As he did so, a low whisper sounded on the other side of the wall. The hairs on his neck lifted like stalks. He placed his ear against the door. The whisper came again, but it was impossible to make out the words.

Sawney hesitated. The last thing he wanted to do was open the door, but he didn't want to be trapped in the darkness either. He was still considering his options when the latch clicked up as if by its own accord and the door swung open.

The cellar was long with a low, arched ceiling. Gloomily lit, it seemed to stretch away into the darkness like a tunnel. Pallet beds were arranged around the walls, feet facing outwards. Each was shrouded in shadow save for a pale areola cast by a stub of flickering candle set on a small wooden chest at the side of each mattress. The pallets, Sawney could just make out, were all occupied, but by whom it was difficult to tell. He could see vague shapes, some partially covered by a rough blanket, but individual features were indiscernible in the half-light.

A long moan rose from one of the beds. The sound was full of pain. Hairs rose along Sawney's forearms. He heard the whispers again, as indistinguishable as before. He tried to locate the source, but it was impossible. It was like listening to leaves rustling in the wind.

Sawney found himself moving cautiously towards the nearest bed. The shallow breathing grew in volume as he edged closer. He paused by the end of the pallet. He could see the pale blur of a face, but the form beneath the blanket looked odd and stunted, not fully grown. He realized then that the person lying on the pallet had no legs. He moved towards the bedhead. The patient's eyes were wide open and staring up at the ceiling. There was a familiar look to the man's face, which Sawney found curiously unsettling. At first, he wasn't sure why that was, and then realization dawned. As the shock hit him, the patient's head turned. The mouth opened but no sound emerged. When he saw why, Sawney backed away, stifling a scream.

He turned quickly and moved to the adjoining pallet. Here, the patient's arm had been severed at the shoulder. The bandage that covered the stump was black with blood, as was the blanket and the edge of the mattress and the floor beneath. Sawney's eyes lifted to the patient's face. As it looked back at him, the breath caught in Sawney's throat for the second time and he recoiled in horror.

Shaking, Sawney crossed to the next bed. In this one, the lower half of the patient's cheek and jaw had been shattered. For one awful moment, Sawney thought the man was grinning at him. But then he saw by the light of the flickering candle that only the patient's upper row of teeth remained. They were poking out of the gums like splintered yellow pegs.

Sawney spun away with a rising sense of panic. He looked around him. It was the same in every pallet, as far as he could see: wounded, disfigured men, the casualties of a terrible battle. Some still wore the vestiges of a uniform; a blood-smeared jacket or a pair of tattered, muddy breeches. Their injuries were horrific. Many were missing limbs. Others had terrible, gaping chest wounds. They were the ones making the wheezing sounds Sawney had heard earlier, their breathing ragged as bellows as they fought to drag air into their tortured lungs. There were men with half their faces shot away, some with deep gashes in their skulls, whether caused by sabre or shot, it was impossible to tell in the darkness.

A movement further down the cellar caught Sawney's eye. A figure was standing by one of the beds, dressed in a stained white shirt and dark breeches. He had his back to Sawney and was bending over the pallet, busy with some task.

Sawney moved forward warily. He tried not to look at the broken bodies or the faces of the men in the beds, though he knew their eyes were following him as he made his way down the cellar to where the man in the shadows was waiting.

The whispers began again, soft and insistent. He now knew where they came from. They were the voices of the men around him. It was the same word, repeated over and over again: *Sawney, Sawney, Sawney...*

Sawney was less than ten paces away from the figure when his ears were assaulted by a scream of such intensity it seemed to vibrate through every bone in his body. The sound hung in the air for so long, Sawney thought his eardrums would burst. He cupped his hands over his ears. As he did so, the figure standing by the bed turned. Sawney gasped. It was not the gore-soaked apron the figure was wearing that caused Sawney's breath to catch, nor the arms that were black to the elbows or the outstretched hand wielding the blood-stained knife. It was the creature's eyes. They were the darkest, coldest, most cruel eyes Sawney had ever seen. Sawney tore his gaze away, towards the other beds further down the room. More bodies, more patients, but somehow these looked different. It was only a fleeting impression, but to Sawney's eyes they didn't look real. They looked ... deformed ... freakish ... like the poor wretches exhibited in travelling shows. The thought that speared its way into Sawney's brain was that they did not look like men. They looked like monsters.

As Sawney stepped back he came up against

the side of the next pallet. Instinctively, Sawney flinched but he was too slow. The hand that reached out from beneath the blanket was too quick for him. Strong fingers clamped themselves around his wrist and began to squeeze. Caught in an immovable grip, Sawney began to struggle. As the scream dropped away, the whispers rose again out of the darkness.

'*Rufus ... Rufus...*'

'Rufus.'

Sawney came out of the dream, fists clenched, forehead beaded with sweat, to find Maggett looming over him, his simian brow furrowed with concern. For one awful moment Sawney thought he was still in the cellar. He shrank away from his lieutenant's touch.

Maggett reached out a meaty hand. 'Rufus? It's me, Maggsie.'

At the mention of the name, Sawney blinked. He looked around. No dark cellar, no pallets, no blood. Although it hadn't been the darkness or the blood that had disturbed Sawney so much as the faces. In each case, the face he had looked down upon had been his own. It had been like looking in a mirror.

'Maggsie?' Sawney said, trying to keep the relief out of his voice. He wiped a hand across his face, took it away and saw the bright sheen of moisture on his palm. He closed the hand quickly and sat up. 'What the bleedin' 'ell is it?'

The big man stepped away. His lieutenant's eyes, Sawney saw, were bright with excitement.

'Jesus, Maggsie, what?'

'It's Sal,' Maggett said. 'She's got one.'

The girl lay bound on the bed. Her clothing was in disarray. Her skirt and petticoat, which were riding high on her thighs, were torn and stained, as were her once-white stockings. Her bodice had been pulled apart, leaving her breasts exposed. There were bruises on her face and a smear of blood on her chin, and a look of abject fear in her eyes as she stared mutely at the four men standing at the foot of the bed and the woman seated next to her, who was gently stroking her arm and smiling.

'There, there, darlin', quiet now. Don't you fret none; Sal's here.'

The girl cringed at the touch. Tears coated her cheeks.

'Daft girl,' Sal murmured soothingly, tracing a tearstain with the tip of her finger. 'None of this would've happened if you 'adn't kicked up such a fuss. I don't know, I really don't. Shame on you, Molly. That's all I can say.'

Maggett eyed the girl's breasts. 'What do you reckon, Rufus? Think she'll do?'

'Oh, she'll do, all right.' Lemuel Ragg's thin features split into a weasel grin. 'In fact, she'll do better than all right. Ain't that so, Sammy?'

Samuel Ragg sniggered. 'You ain't wrong there, Lemmy. Sweet as sugar, she was. You did real good, Sal. Didn't she, Rufus?'

Sawney said nothing. He stared down at the girl, remembering the colonel's stipulations. The first, Sawney recalled, had applied to the dead women. The colonel had wanted their teeth left intact. Hopefully the ruling didn't apply to this one's virginity, he thought, although given the girl's vocation, it was doubtless too late for that. He wondered idly if there would ever come a time when the Raggs would be capable of keeping their cocks in their breeches for longer than it took to drain a mug of grog. As far as the colonel's other requirements were concerned, however, the woman on the bed fit precisely: she was young and she was alive.

'Cover her bleedin' tits,' Sawney said.

Sal tugged together the two halves of the girl's bodice and patted her on the arm. 'There you go, darlin'.' Sal jerked her head in the direction of the brothers. 'Don't want to give them two any more fancy ideas, do we?'

The girl's eyes widened with panic at the possibility. A low moan broke from her lips. It reminded Sawney of the sounds he'd heard in his dream. He turned away from the girl's despairing gaze.

'She'll do,' he said.

It was late afternoon. As he turned on to Water Lane and the path that would lead him to the Blackbird Inn, Hawkwood's thoughts were not of the warm, welcoming hearth only a few narrow streets away, but the words of Apothecary Robert Locke.

His daughter.

The chill Hawkwood felt had nothing to do with the cold wind seeping down the alleyway behind him.

Both Locke and Eden Carslow had referred to Hyde's daughter, though neither had been expansive on the subject. Hawkwood had therefore assumed she must have died years earlier, in

383

childhood. He'd been wrong on both counts.

She'd fallen victim to a fever, Locke had informed him, and had passed away only three months ago, at the age of eighteen. Hawkwood recalled his conversation with Eden Carslow. The surgeon had spoken of Hyde's involvement with the mother as a brief liaison, intimating that Hyde had not learned of the child's existence until after her death. Obviously, that could not have been the case. Which prompted the question: when and by what means had the colonel been informed of his daughter's existence and death?

'Find out,' Hawkwood had told the apothecary.

Whether the information would prove significant remained to be seen, but, given the revelations concerning the colonel's history, Hawkwood knew it was imperative that every avenue be explored.

Hawkwood had returned to Bow Street and directed Ezra Twigg to find out where Hyde's daughter was buried. Once the clerk had located the grave, it would be opened. But what then? What if the exhumation did reveal another missing body? The colonel didn't seriously believe he could raise the dead, did he? The question had been eating away at Hawkwood like a worm in an apple since leaving the hospital. It was beyond possibility, surely? Nothing more than his imagination getting the better of him, brought on by wild speculation following his conversation with an equally imaginative Robert Locke. That's all it was. It had to be.

He had begun to wonder if the itch between his shoulder blades might be his imagination too.

He'd had it since leaving the Public Office; not continuously, but every now and then. It wasn't anything he'd have been able to explain and it wasn't as if the sensation was anything new. As an agent operating behind enemy lines, and as a Runner walking a thin line between light and shadow in and around London's reeking slums, it was a condition he'd come to accept, a reminder to be always on his guard.

Suddenly, he heard a scraping sound; metal against stone.

He unbuttoned his coat.

'Captain Hawkwood.'

Hawkwood turned.

The dark, solitary figure was standing behind him, several paces away, but remained motionless in the shelter of the wall.

It was difficult to make out features. Hawkwood could see that the person was tall and lean, and there was a nonchalance in his stance that suggested an easy confidence.

'It's a cold end to the day, Captain.'

'I've known colder,' Hawkwood said, instinctively placing the wall of the alleyway at his back.

'Indeed. The Spanish air can be deceptively chilly, especially in the mountains.'

Hawkwood threw a quick glance to both right and left. There was no one else in sight. It was as if he and the speaker in the shadows had the alley to themselves. 'Do I know you, cully?'

'You know *of* me, though we've not been formally introduced. I thought it time we were.'

The speaker stepped away from the wall. His footsteps were light and almost silent. The small patch of fading daylight into which he stepped revealed his face. The dark hair was drawn back from the forehead, accentuating the sharply angled cheekbones and jawline, while the pale skin served to make the dark eyes even darker.

And Hawkwood knew then, even before the words were spoken.

'My name is Hyde. Colonel Titus Hyde.'

Instinctively, Hawkwood searched the colonel's hands for a weapon. There was nothing overt; no pistol, no knife or cudgel, nothing that posed a serious threat, though he saw immediately what had made the scraping sound he'd heard. He exhaled slowly. The colonel was leaning on a brass-tipped walking cane.

'Come to save me the bother, have you, Colonel?'

'Bother?'

'I assume you're here to surrender yourself?'

'Ah now, wouldn't that be convenient?' A smile formed a thin gash in the pale face. Hawkwood's hand slipped inside his coat.

'No, Captain. Still, if you please.'

In one fast and fluid flick of the wrist, the colonel pulled the two halves of the cane apart to expose the sliver of edged steel concealed within.

God, the man was quick!

Hawkwood looked down. The point of the blade hovered an inch from his heart.

Keeping the blade against Hawkwood's chest, Hyde lifted the empty scabbard and tapped Hawkwood's raised arm. 'Hand away from your coat, Captain, if you please.'

Hawkwood did as he was told.

'Excellent. Still responding well to orders. Once a soldier, eh?'

'Only when a lunatic's pointing his sword at me,' Hawkwood said. 'You do *know* you're a lunatic, don't you, Colonel? Apothecary Locke wasn't certain.'

A shadow moved across the sharp-etched features. 'Ah, Apothecary Locke. How is he? Capable fellow, in his own way, though a trifle slow on the uptake sometimes. He's recovered from the shock, I trust?'

Hawkwood said nothing.

'I've heard you're considered a capable man, too, Captain. It's why I wanted to take a good look at you. I confess when I heard a police officer was on my trail, I didn't expect to encounter someone quite so ... energetic. I thought I'd covered my tracks remarkably well. It would appear I was wrong.'

'Don't be too downhearted, Colonel. In the scheme of things, you didn't do too badly. If you made an error, it was in trying a little too hard.'

'You're referring to the fire? You could be right. It was a mite theatrical. The groundlings do like a good show, though.' The tip of the sword traced a small circle on Hawkwood's breast. 'But what do we do now? That's the question, isn't it?'

'Give yourself up, Colonel. It's your only choice. You'll probably end up back in Bedlam. You might even get away with the murders and escape the hangman. You're insane. They've got the papers to prove it. They'll most likely give you your old rooms back. It'll be as if you never went away.'

'My work's not finished. There's still too much

to do.'

'Your daughter's dead, Colonel. You can't bring her back.'

Hyde stiffened. It was only the second time his face had betrayed emotion. 'You won't be able to stop me trying, Captain.'

Hawkwood was already pivoting as Hyde drew the blade back for the killing thrust, but he knew he'd left it far too late and felt the fibres part as the tip of the blade pierced the lining of his coat. And then, incredibly, the blade was turning away. Hawkwood heard Hyde grunt with surprise as the sword tip met resistance. As the blade was withdrawn for a second attempt, Hawkwood thrust himself aside, hauled open his coat and reached for his baton. It was the only weapon he carried, apart from the knife in his boot, and he went for it because it was the closest to hand.

As he clawed the tipstaff free, his spine slammed into the wall of the alleyway. He grunted with pain, saw the blade coming at him again, and scythed the tipstaff to intercept the sword point. For the second time, the baton saved him. But he had forgotten the scabbard held in Hyde's other hand. Locke had told him about the colonel's reputation as a swordsman. He had only himself to blame. The edge of the scabbard cracked against his wrist. Pain seared through the joint, numbing nerve endings. The tipstaff fell from his grip and clattered on to the cobblestones. Hawkwood swore and threw himself backwards. The tip of the sword slashed towards his face and he felt his flesh open as the point of the blade pared across his exposed cheek, missing his eye by a hair's breadth before gouging a groove in the brickwork behind him.

As Hawkwood's body careered off the wall and went down, the colonel was on the attack once more. The man's sense of balance was astonishing. It was as if he was using the sword and scabbard as counterweights to keep him upright. As he hit the ground, Hawkwood was rolling, but the heavy coat which had provided protection only seconds earlier had now become a hindrance, hampering his movements. He saw Hyde coming in, recognized the determination on the gaunt face, and he knew that without the baton he was defenceless. He groped for the knife in his boot, knowing it was futile. As his fingers brushed the top of his calf, the colonel lunged towards him, sword raised.

'You there!' The shout sprang out of nowhere.

Hyde turned towards the sound. Out of the corner of his eye, Hawkwood saw a figure break from the shadows fifty paces away. He looked up, saw Hyde's expression change from one of shock at discovery into a mask of cold anger, and knew it was over. As the sword point skewered towards his heart, Hawkwood abandoned his attempt to grab the knife hilt and turned his left arm desperately into the path of the sword.

The steel blade seared through the sleeve of his coat. As the rapier point tore into the flesh of his upper arm, Hawkwood twisted his body against the sword's blade. He felt the tension in the steel as the blade bent, but the sensation was eclipsed as the pain from the sword thrust tore through him.

The pounding footsteps were approaching fast. Another shout rent the air. Hawkwood groaned as the sword blade was tugged free. He tried to lift his arm to ward off the next attack, but it never came. He was aware of the figure above him pausing, then it was moving past his field of vision towards the passageway from whence it had come. By the time he had raised himself on to his good arm, the figure was gone.

The running footsteps halted. A pair of boots clattered into view. A body crouched down by his side and he heard a voice that was remarkably familiar enquire breathlessly, 'Sir, sir, are you all right, sir?'

Hawkwood felt the warmth flowing down the inside of his coat sleeve. He could also taste the blood that had traced its way down from the gash on his cheek to his lips. He gazed up at the anxious face and sighed. 'I thought I told you not to call me sir.'

Hopkins put an arm under Hawkwood's shoulder. 'Sorry, s–, Captain. I forgot.' The constable stared at Hawkwood, taking in the blood on his face and the dark drips pooling on the cobblestones from the end of the coat sleeve. 'You're wounded!'

'I know,' Hawkwood said wearily. 'And it bloody hurts.' Hawkwood leant back against the wall. 'What brings you here?'

'You're bleeding, Captain. You need a physician.'

'I've had enough of bloody physicians,' Hawkwood snapped. 'I'm up to my arse in bloody physicians. Did you see where the bastard went?'

Hopkins shook his head. 'He's disappeared. Who was it?'

'Colonel Titus bloody Xavier bloody Hyde,' Hawkwood said, and winced as the pain streaked along his arm and up into his shoulder.

The constable's eyes grew wide. He stared in dismay towards the alley that had swallowed Hawkwood's attacker. 'I should have gone after him.'

'No you bloody shouldn't,' Hawkwood said. 'We'll find him. I asked what you were doing here.'

'I came to fetch you, Captain. Orders from the Chief Magistrate.' The constable paused. 'They've found another body.'

17

The corpse was wedged in the angle between two trusses spanning the Fleet. The thick timber beams had become a necessary feature of the Ditch. Held in place by wide metal brackets affixed to the brickwork on the opposing shores, they prevented the walls of the slums that lined the riverbanks from collapsing into the mud-black water.

Hawkwood knew the body would not have been left on the beam intentionally. More than likely it had been heaved from the bank in the hope that the river would take it into its stinking embrace, sucking it into the honeycomb of sewers, rat-runs and underground waterways that flowed beneath the city's streets. The ebb tide and the cessation of the rain had resulted in a considerable lowering of the water level, leaving the cross beams and their grisly decoration exposed for all to see.

They were growing careless, Hawkwood thought.

He watched in silence as the body was dragged up to the top of the bank. It had not been a job for the faint hearted. The constable who had lowered himself on to the beam in order to get a rope round the corpse had, more than once, come close to losing his footing and pitching into the effluence flowing turgidly beneath him. The

392

condition of the corpse had not helped. Even from where he was standing, and in the rapidly disappearing light, Hawkwood could see the gaping wound in the dead woman's belly and the places along her arms and legs where the flesh had been removed. The constable had lost the contents of his stomach within seconds of sitting astride the beam. He was ashen faced as he followed the corpse up to solid ground and the look he gave Hawkwood, who had directed him to retrieve the remains, left no one in any doubt what he thought.

There were a few onlookers, though not enough to constitute a crowd. Gawpers were a fact of life when a dead body was involved, even though corpses were not an uncommon sight. In this instance, a carved-up female cadaver had been enough to set tongues wagging more than usual; so much so that some upstanding citizen – a rare creature in this neck of the woods – had gone looking for a constable rather than abandoning the thing to its fate in the vague belief that the river would rise once more and drag it back down into its stinking depths.

Hawkwood flexed his left arm and winced as pain flared. There had been no time to get the wound seen to. Fortunately, the bleeding had stopped. The gash along his cheek was still weeping thin, watery tears of blood, but was not as serious as it felt or looked. It would heal quickly and, like the sword wound, would join the legion of other scars that crisscrossed his war-torn body. Hawkwood knew he'd been lucky. A heavier blade would have gone much deeper and probably taken his eye out. Though that wasn't to say that the cut didn't sting like a bastard.

He thought about the wound in his arm and wondered what had possessed him to attempt such a gamble. Then he decided not to think about it. He was still alive, that was what mattered. He looked down at his coat. It had saved him, but it was looking the worse for wear. He thought about Hyde; the arrogance, the swordsmanship and the speed at which the man had fought. This was definitely no imbecile, but a man who, until the final seconds when Hopkins had appeared on the scene, had displayed calmness and a clear sense of purpose. This was a killer who was determined and, as Hawkwood had nearly found out to his cost, very dangerous.

I wanted to take a good look at you, Hyde had informed him. It wasn't the words that worried Hawkwood so much as the knowledge that Hyde knew who he was. How? And how had the colonel tracked him down?

A shout from the riverbank interrupted his thoughts. It was Hopkins, indicating that the corpse was viewable. Hawkwood walked over to take a look. There was no question it had been subjected to the same form of mutilation as the others, as Surgeon Quill would doubtless verify. He stared down at the grey, splayed limbs.

'Small world,' a voice said behind him.

Hawkwood turned and stared at the tough, broad-shouldered man who had spoken, taking in the powerful frame, the short, gunmetal-grey hair and the hard, craggy features.

'Jesus!' Nathaniel Jago said, staring at Hawkwood's face. 'Looks like you've been in the bloody wars.'

'I've been trying to reach you,' Hawkwood said. 'I've sent messages.'

'Have you now? I've been away.'

Hawkwood raised an eyebrow.

'Takin' care of some business. Only got back this morning.'

Hawkwood's eyebrow remained raised.

'You don't want to know,' Jago said, and grinned.

Hawkwood knew Jago's commercial interests were many and varied; the majority of them bordering, if not crossing, the frontiers of illegality. Probably best if he didn't delve too deep, he thought.

Jago indicated the body and grimaced. 'That ain't a pretty sight.'

'No,' Hawkwood agreed. He looked at the big man. 'I didn't take you for a lollygagger.'

Jago shook his head, his face at once serious. 'I'm not. Thought it might be someone I'm looking for; a friend of a friend.'

Hawkwood waited.

'There's a lady I've been seeing. A workin' girl of her acquaintance's gone missing and I put the word out. I was told a body had turned up, female. Thought I should take a look, just in case.'

'It's not the one you're after?' Hawkwood said.

'Not even close. This one's been dead a while.' Jago frowned. 'What's your interest?'

'It's not the first,' Hawkwood said.

Jago looked at him.

'It's why I've been trying to get word to you. I

was hoping you might be able to help me with some information. I need help, Nathaniel.'

This time, it was Jago's turn to lift an eyebrow.

'What do you know about the sack-'em-up brigade?'

'Ah shite,' Jago said.

They were in Newton's Gin Shop, facing each other across a dirty table at the back of the room.

Hawkwood had left Hopkins in charge of the corpse, which would be delivered to Quill's cellar. Two other constables were engaged in tracking down witnesses. Hawkwood knew it would be a miracle if they came up with anything. The locals may have objected to a nude and mutilated corpse appearing on their doorstep, but no one in their right minds would have considered pointing the finger, even if the cadaver had been heaved into the river to the accompaniment of a twenty-one-gun salute.

Newton's had all the ambience of a night-soil barge, but it was the closest refuge where they could talk without fear of being overheard. It wasn't that the place was empty – it wasn't – but it attracted the sort of clientele who were certain to be far too drunk to listen to, or even care about, anyone else's conversation. Besides, Jago knew the owner, who had cleared a table for them and awarded two full mugs, on the house. Both men viewed the mugs' contents with suspicion and immediately pushed the drinks to one side.

'What do you want with those bastards?' Jago asked.

Hawkwood told him.

When he'd finished, Jago announced, 'Reckon I'll have a drink after all.' He turned and summoned the proprietor. 'You can take that swill away—' Jago nodded towards the untouched mugs. 'Bring us the good stuff. Leave the bottle.'

When the drink arrived, Jago did the honours. Taking a swallow, he drew the back of his hand across his mouth. 'So you think they're providing your lunatic doctor with stolen bodies? Catch them and you might catch up with him.'

Hawkwood nodded. 'That's about the size of it.'

'Maybe if you wait long enough, he'll have another go,' Jago said drily. He shook his head like a disappointed parent. 'Jesus, I can't leave you alone for a minute, can I?'

Hawkwood smiled grimly, and flinched as the muscles in his jaw tugged at the nerves running along the line of his injured cheek. 'So, do you know anybody?'

'Maybe,' Jago said warily. 'The buggers don't exactly advertise. It's all done on the nod. You got any kind of description?' The big man paused and stared over Hawkwood's shoulder, towards the door. His eyes narrowed and he nodded imperceptibly.

Hawkwood turned. A man was pushing through the room towards them. Hawkwood recognized him as one of Jago's cohorts; he went by the name Micah. He stopped by the table, gave Hawkwood the once-over and leaned down to Jago's ear. 'There's a moll outside.'

'Be surprised if there weren't,' Jago said, 'state of this neighbourhood.'

The messenger ignored the comment. 'She says it's to do with the information you were lookin' for.'

Jago considered the implications, then looked towards the door and nodded. 'All right, bring her in.' He addressed Hawkwood. 'Won't take long.'

Jago watched his lieutenant retreat, then sighed. 'Like as not, it'll be another waste of time. That's the trouble. Offer a bit of a reward and every drunk and 'is flea-bitten hound comes staggerin' out o' the woodwork.'

But Jago was wrong. It wasn't a drunkard or his dog, it was exactly as Jago's man had described, a moll – and not just any moll.

'Bloody hell,' Hawkwood said.

'What?'

'I know her.'

Jago stared at the woman being escorted towards the table. He looked back at Hawkwood in awe.

'No,' Hawkwood said wearily. 'I meant I've seen her before.'

'Thank Christ for that. For a moment, you had me worried. You want to bugger off before she gets here?'

'No need.'

It was too late anyway.

Having accompanied the woman to the table, Jago's man departed.

She was clearly apprehensive. Her face was flushed. Her hands were shaking. Jago looked up, his face neutral. 'What's your name, sweetheart?'

'Lizzie ... Lizzie Tyler.' As she spoke, the

woman's gaze moved to Hawkwood. For a second she showed no sign of recognition and then her eyes widened. She looked around quickly.

'So, Lizzie,' Jago said, ignoring the startled expression. 'I hear you might have some information for me. That right?'

The moll turned back and her gaze moved inevitably to Hawkwood's face. Hawkwood read the questions in the woman's eyes. There was no small measure of fear there too. It was the fear of an informer being seen by the informed upon. It was unmistakable, and he knew his freshly scarred cheek wasn't helping matters.

'It's all right, Lizzie,' Jago said. 'Don't mind him.' Jago pushed back the spare chair and nodded towards Hawkwood. 'He might look like 'e'd slit a nun's throat for a ha'penny, but he's harmless. Anything you say to me, you can say to him and it won't get past these four walls.'

The woman paused, clearly having second thoughts and yet knowing it was too late to back out. Finally, after taking another furtive survey of the room, she sat down, her bosom wobbling. The chair gave a sharp creak of protest.

'You want a drink, Lizzie? You look as though you could do with one.' Jago pushed his own mug across the table. 'There you go; get that inside you.'

The big woman stared at the mug before reaching out a hesitant hand and raising the drink to her lips. She took a deep swallow. Then, looking faintly embarrassed by her actions, she lowered the mug to the table.

'So?' Jago prompted.

399

Lizzie took a deep breath. 'I heard you was lookin' for Molly Finn?'

'That's right. You know her?'

Lizzie nodded.

'And you've seen her? Recently?'

A moment of hesitation, followed by another quick nod.

'Where?'

'The Garden. She was lookin' for business.'

'When was this?'

'This mornin'. Early.'

Hawkwood was astonished. Jago's intelligence network was even more impressive than he'd realized. The word could only have been on the streets a matter of hours and information on the girl's whereabouts had already filtered back. He wished his own cadre of informers were as swift to respond, though he suspected that Jago's methods of inducing people to heed the call were probably more persuasive than his own.

'Anyone with her?' Jago asked.

A significantly long pause was followed by a sideways glance in Hawkwood's direction.

'Sal Bridger, the little cow.'

'Who's Sal Bridger?'

Hawkwood sat up in his chair.

'What?' Jago said, catching the movement. 'Wait, don't tell me – her too?'

Hawkwood looked at Lizzie. 'Young? Black hair, blue eyes?'

Lizzie said nothing. The expression on her fleshy face was enough.

Hawkwood nodded. 'We've met.'

Jago looked at Lizzie. 'She a workin' girl, too?'

'That's right.'

Jago stared at Hawkwood askance. 'I can see we need to have a serious talk about the company you're keepin'.'

Lizzie frowned. 'Ain't nothin' wrong with a girl tryin' to make a livin'.'

'Never said there was, Lizzie. So, what is she? Independent?'

Lizzie nodded again.

'And you saw her with Molly?'

'It was underneath the arches, by the edge of the square. Molly was by herself. Didn't seem to be 'avin' much luck. Then I saw Sal turn up, and the next thing the two of them are skippin' off together. Arm in arm, they were, twitterin' like lovebirds.'

'You didn't see where they went, or if they met anyone?'

'No.'

Jago looked thoughtful. 'Tell me about this Sal Bridger.'

'She's a vicious little tyke.'

'Is that so?'

'Reckons she owns the world, don't she? Always has to 'ave her own way.' Lizzie nodded her head at Hawkwood. 'She 'ad you in 'er sights. That's why I 'ad to back off. Rules the roost, does Sal, especially in the Dog. She'll go for anything if she thinks someone else is interested. No offence,' Lizzie added hurriedly.

'None taken,' Hawkwood said.

'Don't matter if it's a porter or the boy who empties the piss-pots; if it's got a cock, she'll go for it. Not that she ain't had her share of swells, mind.

There's always one or two that come around looking for a bit of rough. I remember there was a lawyer once, and a vicar. From over Cripplegate way, he was.' Lizzie screwed up her face. 'No 'ang on, he weren't a vicar, I'm forgettin' myself. He was a verger. In fact, she's still seein' to him, I reckon, 'cos he was in there the night you came around. I remember 'e was coming through the door as I was goin' out. Not that he saw me. Probably wouldn't 'ave remembered me anyway, despite us 'avin done it a few times. Mind you, that was when I wasn't carryin' as much meat as I am now. He likes 'em slim. Him and me used to have some good times a while back, until Lady Muck turned up. Sal's got the looks, I can't deny that...' Lizzie paused in her monologue, caught by the look on Hawkwood's face. 'What?'

Hawkwood kept his voice calm. 'This verger, what's his name?'

'Dunno 'is last name. He used to like me to call 'im Lucy. In our intimate moments, that was.'

'Lucy?' Jago looked confused. 'What sort of man calls himself Lucy?'

'It's short for Lucius,' Hawkwood said.

'Now, how the hell would you know that?'

'Tell us about the Dog,' Hawkwood said, ignoring Jago's expression.

Lizzie sniffed disdainfully. 'It's Sal's main feedin' ground. Like I said, she thinks she's queen of the bleedin' May. Mind you, she's Sawney's woman. That helps. Ain't no one going to go up against Sawney and his crew.'

'Sawney?' Jago said. He caught Hawkwood's eye. 'You know him?'

'I've heard the name mentioned. He's a mate of Hanratty's.'

Hawkwood sensed there was more. 'And?'

'You asked me if I knew any resurrectionist scum?'

Hawkwood didn't reply. He knew Jago was going to tell him anyway.

'They say this Sawney's new to the game and he ain't too particular 'ow he earns a livin', if you know what I mean. Rumour is, he digs 'em up and Hanratty stores 'em prior to delivery. Rumour is all it is, though...' Jago paused. 'Other thing I seem to remember is that he was in the army; a driver with the Royal Wagon Train. Did a runner back in '09.'

Hawkwood sat back. *Jesus!* he thought wildly. A frisson of excitement moved through him. He tried to sound calm. 'This crew of his, what about them?'

'Princes, each and every one,' Jago smiled grimly.

'The Raggs ain't no princes,' Lizzie muttered. 'Bleedin' animals, they are. They like it rough. Some of the girls do too, but most don't – and they're the ones they go for. I've seen some of the girls after Lemmy and Sammy Ragg've been with 'em. It weren't a pretty sight. They like doin' it together. They take turns, if you know what I mean. Don't know about Maggett. He ain't so loud.'

'Maggett?' Hawkwood threw another questioning glance towards Jago, but the former sergeant seemed content to let Lizzie retain the honours.

Lizzie grimaced. 'He's Sawney's right-hand

man. His brain's smaller than most, but the rest of him makes up for it. I saw him break a man's arm once, just because the poor sod knocked 'is drink. Did it as easy as snapping a twig.'

'He's big?' Hawkwood asked.

Lizzie nodded.

'How big?'

'Big,' Lizzie said firmly.

'And what's this Sawney look like?'

'A shifty-eyed streak of piss.'

'I was thinking more about his size,' Hawkwood said. 'And his colouring.'

Lizzie grimaced. 'Well, he ain't nowhere as big as Maggett. Mind you, there's not many who are. He's about the same height as your man who brought me in here, only a bit more round shouldered. Got dark hair, goin' a bit thin on top. An' he's got bad teeth.'

'Sounds like God's gift,' Jago said. 'You wonder what this Sal sees in 'im.'

'There's no accountin' for taste,' Lizzie agreed. 'Though I did 'ear a rumour he's built like a horse, if you know what I mean.' She paused. 'But that still don't mean he's not a shifty-eyed streak of piss. Got a temper to go with it, too. He's not a man to cross.'

Hawkwood closed his eyes. His mind went back to the description of the two men who'd been seen leaving the corpses at Bart's. One had been of average height. The other had been a big man, who'd hefted the dead body he'd been carrying with ease, according to the constables who'd chased them. He was reminded also of the signs he'd found at the scene of the Doyle murder.

They had indicated that four people could have been involved in the hanging and crucifixion, with one of them having the strength to raise the body into position by the hangman's rope.

'Bloody Symes,' Hawkwood said, shaking his head. 'I should have guessed.'

Though he knew he probably wouldn't have, unless the bastard had been carrying some sort of sign above his head.

'Symes? Who's Symes?' Jago said.

'He's Lizzie's verger. And he's in it up to his neck.' Hawkwood clenched his fist. 'We need to talk, Nathaniel.'

Jago stared hard at the expression on Hawkwood's face, then nodded. He turned to Lizzie. 'You're a good girl, Lizzie. You see Micah on the way out. Tell him I said he was to settle up with you. He'll see you right.' For a second, the big moll looked uncertain, and then she realized the audience was over. She got to her feet, gave both men a cautious nod and an uncertain smile, then gathered up her skirts.

Hawkwood leaned forward. 'Know anyone called Doyle, Lizzie? Edward Doyle?'

Lizzie's brow wrinkled. 'Don't ring no bells, though I think there might've been an Eddie who used to do a bit of porterin' for Maggett. Maggett's a slaughterman. He's got a yard over near Three Fox Court.'

It was a common enough name but there might be something in it, Hawkwood thought. Perhaps Doyle hadn't been a member of a rival gang, after all. The murdered man could well have been part of Sawney's crew, and there'd been a falling out among thieves.

The information imparted, Lizzie continued towards the door. Then she paused. 'No one'll know you got all this from me, will they? Only Molly's a sweet girl. I wouldn't like to think anything had happened to her. She always 'ad time for a chat. Not like that other sly bitch.'

She was referring to Sal, Hawkwood presumed.

'Be our secret, Lizzie,' Jago said. 'Mind how you go, now.' Adding, when Lizzie was out of earshot, 'That's a turn-up. Didn't expect to hear anything so soon.'

'You probably wouldn't have,' Hawkwood said, 'if she hadn't been nursing a grudge against Sal Bridger.'

'Don't like her much, does she?' Jago agreed. He turned to find that Hawkwood was regarding him with a bemused expression. 'Look, I never carry small change, all right? So, what do you think?'

'I think we should have had this conversation a good deal earlier.'

Jago sucked in his cheeks. 'Might not 'ave done either of us much good. Molly Finn wouldn't have been missin' then, and Lizzie wouldn't have been feelin' the need to do her civic duty. We'd probably have been none the wiser. Likely, we'd have been sittin' here with our thumbs up our arses.'

Hawkwood sighed.

'I take it those questions you were lookin' to ask me have been answered?' Jago said.

'I'd say so. Most of them, anyway. One thing's clear. All roads lead back to the Dog.'

'For you and me both.' Jago frowned. 'You reckon that's where your mad colonel's been hiding himself?'

'It's possible, though I've no definite proof linking him to Sawney. It's just a gut feeling.'

'I've been with you when you've had *them* before. You weren't often wrong.'

'It also strikes me he'd consider himself a cut above Hanratty's usual clientele.' Hawkwood pursed his lips. 'Either way, I'm going to have to go back there to find out.'

'Funny you should say that. I was considerin' payin' the place a visit myself.'

'You're thinking that's where Sal Bridger might have taken Molly Finn?'

Molly Finn and Hyde? Even as Hawkwood posed the question, it didn't seem likely the two of them would be under the same roof.

'Right now it's all I 'ave to go on. I'd say neither of us has much of a choice.'

'I'm wondering what Sal Bridger would want with Molly Finn. It's not as though the Dog lacks molls,' Hawkwood said. 'And the last time I saw Sal, she was going out of her way to remove the competition.'

'You know what they say,' Jago replied, 'about dogs shitting on their own doorstep. Maybe they had something special in mind that they couldn't do with someone closer to home.'

'I don't like the sound of that.'

'Me neither.'

'It'll be two against seven, you know. Hanratty and his boys will side with Sawney; bound to.'

'So we get ourselves a little help. Even the

odds,' Jago said. He grinned wolfishly.

'You do realize I'm a peace officer. It's my duty to act within the boundary of the law.'

'Course it is,' Jago said, his tone serious. 'So how many do you think we'll need?'

'Another two at least, maybe three,' Hawkwood said. He could see that Jago was concerned about something. 'What?'

'They'll have to be bloody good. The Hanrattys are hard bastards and this crew of Sawney's sounds useful.'

Hawkwood knew what Jago was implying. This wasn't a job for the average constable, and use of fellow Runners meant the involvement of official-dom and that was going to take time, which both of them knew they didn't have.

'You got anyone you can call on?' Jago asked.

'Other than you, you mean?'

'Hell, you've always got me,' Jago said. 'Fact of life. Same as I've always got you.'

Hawkwood allowed himself a smile but the question made him think. With the exception of Jago, the list of suitable candidates with the necessary expertise was depressingly small.

'I've got one,' Hawkwood said. 'Maybe.' But there was no guarantee the person he had in mind would want to be involved.

'Up to me then,' Jago said. 'You got a problem using some of my boys?'

'Not if they're good.'

'Oh, they're good,' Jago said. 'Wouldn't be with me otherwise.'

'All right,' Hawkwood said. 'Let's do it.'

'Best get goin' then.' Jago got up from the table

and quartered the room. His gaze alighted on a table by the door where Micah was sitting patiently, a mug in his hand. Jago gave a silent indication that he and Hawkwood were leaving. Acknowledging the gesture, Micah drained his mug, stood up and waited until they had joined him.

The three men walked to the door to find that evening was upon them. The drop in temperature as they emerged from the warmth of Newton's was enough to make them wince. Jago looked up at the night sky. 'Likely there'll be snow by morning.'

Micah didn't answer and Hawkwood saw no reason to argue. He turned up his collar.

'Captain?'

Hawkwood felt Jago stiffen. Micah moved closer to Jago's side, Hawkwood turned and stared at the hovering constable.

'I thought you were escorting the body to the surgeon. Why are you still here?'

Hopkins hesitated, made unsure by Hawkwood's tone. 'Waiting for orders, Captain. Wasn't sure if you'd need me again. I sent the body off with Constable Tredworth. Thought I'd better wait for you.' The constable's eyes darted sideways towards Jago and his lieutenant.

Jago gazed back at Hopkins with an amused expression on his face. Micah maintained an impassive silence. If anything, he looked vaguely bored.

'Did you now?' Hawkwood stared at the constable, taking in the slim frame, the less than flattering uniform, the ears and the mop of hair

409

jutting from beneath the ridiculous hat. In the few days he'd worked with Hopkins, Hawkwood had found himself quietly impressed by the young officer's attitude. George Hopkins might not have had the chance to grow into his uniform, but Hawkwood sensed he'd matured in other ways. There was certainly a new awareness in his expression that had not been there before. Perhaps the events he'd been witness to had given the constable a sudden understanding of his own mortality.

Hawkwood could see that Jago was looking at him questioningly. He knew Jago well enough to know exactly what his former sergeant was thinking. He wondered if he would come to regret his next decision.

'Meet back here?' Jago said, as if it was already a foregone conclusion.

Hawkwood thought about it a bit more. Finally he nodded. He looked at Hopkins. 'You're to arm yourself, and you tell no one. You understand?'

'Yes, s–, Captain.'

'It'd be best if we use the back entrance,' Jago said, 'so's not to alarm the citizenry. What time?'

Hawkwood made a calculation.

'Don't be late,' Jago said to both of them, and winked.

Hawkwood entered the taproom of the Four Swans in Bishopsgate and paused to let his eyes grow accustomed both to the dim lighting and the pall of tobacco smoke that hung over the tables like a heavy sea fog. The place was busy, as usual. The clientele was a mixture of regular

410

drinkers who considered the inn their home from home, and those who were passing through. Most of the latter were travellers who were either recent arrivals from the early-evening coach or those who were awaiting its departure on its onward journey. The inn provided a very good supper and empty seats were generally hard to come by. Standing on the threshold, Hawkwood looked towards the booth in the far, dark corner, where he knew, almost certainly, one chair would be vacant.

The candle on the table was worn down almost to a stub. The man occupying the corner of the booth, his right side tucked in against the wall, was seated in shadow. He was eating his way through a bowl of thick stew. At his elbow rested a half-full pewter tankard.

'How's the mutton?' Hawkwood asked.

The man turned his head slowly and looked up. 'Wouldn't know. I chose the beef.'

Hawkwood slid into the booth and extended his left hand. 'How are you, Major?'

Major Gabriel Lomax put down his fork and extended his own left hand to meet Hawkwood's. 'I'm well, Captain. Yourself? Still hunting vermin?'

'It's a full-time job.'

'Isn't that the God's honest truth?' Gabriel Lomax said, and grinned. Or rather he gave an approximation of a grin. Lomax was a former cavalry officer. Like Hawkwood, he was a veteran of Talavera, but though he'd survived the battle, he had not escaped injury. Trapped under the weight of his dead horse, the former dragoon had

411

fallen prey to the fires that had ravaged the battlefield in the aftermath of the fighting. He'd been rescued from beneath his roasting mount by a French officer who'd seen his plight, but not before the flames had taken their dreadful toll. The right side of Lomax's face, from eyeline to throat, looked as if it had been scourged with nails. The black patch he had taken to wearing did little to conceal the ruin that lay beneath it, a fissured crater crisscrossed with scar tissue. When Lomax attempted a grin only the left side of his face showed any animation. The effect was that of a grotesque, lopsided mask. The fires had also transformed Lomax's right hand into a twisted claw. It was rare, therefore, that Gabriel Lomax didn't end up spending the evening in a corner seat at a table by himself. Invalided from the army, the cavalryman had put his experience to good use. These days, he commanded armed horse patrols, protecting travellers and coaches on the King's highways in and around London.

'Good God!' Lomax said when he saw the livid scar on Hawkwood's cheek. 'I know I have the devil's own job shaving, but at least I've a bloody excuse!' He peered closer, recognizing immediately the cause of the gash. 'Ah, my apologies. I trust, in that case, the other fellow came off worse?'

'Not yet,' Hawkwood said. 'But he will.'

Lomax drew back, his good eye glinting perceptively. 'Of that, I have no doubt. So, tell me, what brings you to my table on a cold night like this? Wait, you'll have a glass to ward off the chill? A brandy, perhaps? French, not Spanish,' he added conspiratorially.

'I wouldn't say no.'

'Good man.' Lomax looked for the nearest serving girl and raised his hand in a summons. 'Brandy for the gentleman, if you would. Make sure it's from the special reserve, Beth. This one's a friend of mine.'

The girl smiled and nodded, then she saw Hawkwood's face. The smile faltered but only for a fraction before she turned and went off with a sway of her hips.

'Typical,' Lomax said. 'I've just gotten them used to me, then you turn up. Probably thinks we're related. Mind if I finish my stew? I've been out all bloody day riding down bridle culls. Nothing like the thrill of the chase to give a man an appetite.'

'Catch anything?'

'Small fry. Two boyos tried to hold up a coach at the top of Mile End Road. Not the brightest of the bunch. Only got down off their horses to do the job! We happened by and their mounts bolted. Left the silly sods running around like chickens with their heads chopped off. Thought I'd die laughing.'

Lomax finished his stew, took a draught from his tankard and wiped his mouth on his sleeve. Hawkwood's drink arrived. Lomax waited until the girl left and Hawkwood had taken a swallow. 'So?' he said. 'I was about to ask again what brings you here, but I see you have that look about you. My guess is it involves a proposition. Would I be right?'

Hawkwood hesitated.

'Best come straight out with it, Captain.'

'I'm hunting tonight,' Hawkwood said. 'I need a good man at my back.'

'And you thought of me? I'm flattered. Is it dangerous?'

Hawkwood thought of Doyle's crucified body nailed to the tree. 'Probably.'

'Splendid! I'm your man. Will I need my horse?'

Hawkwood laughed. He couldn't help it. 'No, Major. We'll be going by shanks' pony.'

Lomax looked back at him in disbelief. 'You're asking a one-eyed, one-armed cavalryman to help you, on foot. You must be bloody desperate.'

'We'll have help.'

'I'm relieved to hear it. You're sure it's me you want?'

'Can you fire a pistol?'

'Aye.'

'Can you wield a blade?'

'Not at the same time.'

'There's not many who can,' Hawkwood said. 'But you know *how* to use them, and that's what I'm looking for. One after the other's good enough for me.'

'This sounds suspiciously as if it might be a private skirmish.'

'Not entirely, but I need someone who won't get squeamish if it does turn rough. We'll be looking for a man and a girl. It's likely the girl wants to be found. The man will not. There'll be people who'll want to stop us.'

'People?'

'Hard men with hard reputations. It's unlikely

414

quarter will be given.'

'How many?'

'Seven possibly.'

'You said we'd have help?'

'Friends of mine. Few in number, but they won't shy away.'

'Sounds intriguing. Do I get time to think it over and make my decision?'

'You'll have as long as it takes me to finish my drink.'

Lomax sat back. 'God Almighty. You've got a bloody nerve!'

'One other thing,' Hawkwood said, nodding at Lomax's blue coat and scarlet waistcoat. 'You won't need the uniform.'

There was a long silence. Finally Lomax leaned over and cast his good eye into Hawkwood's glass.

'Best drink up, then,' he said.

18

Sawney, nursing a mug of grog, was re-living his black dream. He was in the Dog, on his own, seated in his usual booth. The pub was moderately full, but Sawney was oblivious to the activity going on around him. He was in the dark cellar again and in his mind's eye he could see the figures in their beds and he could smell the stench of them and see the fear in their eyes, which, in his dream, had been his own eyes staring back at him. The image faded. He looked down and found that his hand was clenched tightly around the waist of the mug. Beneath the skin, his knuckles gleamed white in the candlelight.

It had been in the Peninsula, close to a village, the name of which escaped him; a sad, dusty little hamlet, hardly deserving of the description. A field hospital had been established in a local monastery. Sawney, as a wagon driver, had been tasked to transport the wounded from the battlefield to the surgeon's operating table. Thomas Butler, his co-conspirator in the resurrection trade, had been working as an orderly, tending to the wounded and preparing them for the ordeal of surgery. It had been Butler who, with contacts back in England, had secured buyers for the teeth and trinkets that Sawney and others prised from the bodies of the dead and dying that lay strewn across the bloodied terrain like discarded pieces of offal.

Sawney had been better at it than anyone and because of that it had been Sawney whom Butler had approached with a proposition that went beyond the scavenging of canines and molars. Butler wanted more than teeth recovered, he wanted the bodies of French soldiers; wounded ones, not dead. Sawney was to ask no questions. That way, if anyone were to intervene, Sawney could legitimately say they were being transported to the surgeon for treatment; in the same spirit that French army surgeons tended to British wounded.

Only Sawney hadn't delivered the bodies to the main hospital wards. Under Butler's direction, he'd taken them to one of the distant out-buildings, the monastery's winery.

Sawney wasn't sure how many French casualties he'd delivered into Butler's hands. Perhaps a couple of dozen, all told, roughly half of whom had been in a very bad way, with a slim chance of survival.

He had never set foot in the outbuilding; never had reason to. All he did was transport the bodies. That was as far as his responsibilities went. Until the day his curiosity got the better of him.

The heat had been oppressive and the brackish water in Sawney's canteen had failed to alleviate the dryness in his parched throat. Racking his brain for ways to quench his thirst, it occurred to Sawney that the answer was staring him in the face. The winery.

It stood to reason there'd be booze around somewhere; be it wine or brandy. Probably cellars full of the stuff, wall-to-wall barrels, just waiting to be liberated. Bloody officers had probably been helping themselves already, but the buggers couldn't have drunk it all. Hell, Sawney thought, even the dregs at the bottom of those barrels would be more palatable than the stuff in his canteen. So he had stepped down from his wagon to explore.

Avoiding the main entrance, he had approached the rear of the building. There, he had found what looked to be a long-disused doorway. At the base of an adjacent wall, there had been a set of wooden trapdoors embedded in a stone surround. They'd reminded Sawney of the kind found outside pubs back home, through which the delivery of ale and spirits were made. Old, bleached by the sun and half-hidden beneath overhanging weeds, they hadn't looked very promising – indeed, the buildings themselves didn't look as if they'd been in use for a while – but Sawney, sly and greedy and drawn by the possible proximity of a hidden trove, had pressed on. When he came across the stone stairway his excitement had soared.

He'd chanced upon a stub of candle and the light had given him added confidence. It had taken him a while and it had involved a lot of stumbling around, but Sawney's suspicions had eventually been proved correct. The winery did have cellars, though what with all the winding passages, dead-ends and stairways the place had seemed more reminiscent of an underground maze than a bodega.

It had been through accident rather than design

418

that he'd finally found himself in the main cellar, after what seemed like hours of wandering in the dark. Drawn down a side passage by a faintly flickering light, he'd emerged from the gloom, thinking he'd struck gold at last, only to discover the place was stocked with neither casks nor corks. In fact, there hadn't been a barrel in sight, only makeshift beds. And they had all been occupied.

Sawney had become inured to death and corpses and the wounded. Or so he had thought. He'd certainly grown used to the scenes outside the surgeons' tents, where it wasn't unknown for men to wait in line for days to receive treatment. That view never altered: blood-spattered uniforms, listless faces, sunken eyes and bloated limbs, all marinated in the sweet, sickly smell of gangrene that hung as heavy as a blanket in the fetid air around them. He remembered the surgeons, stripped down to shirt and breeches, arms and clothing caked with gore as they worked on the laid-out bodies, on tables that were no more than wooden doors supported by wine casks.

He remembered sounds too; the continuous creaking of the wagon wheels, the whimpering of the men as they were transported over terrain that would have tested the agility of a goat, and the constant drone of the flies feasting upon the open sores in swarms as black as coal.

This time it had been different. In that underground room, it hadn't been the sight of the beds' occupants, the blood or the nature of their wounds that had unnerved him, or even the low moans of discomfort. At least, not at first. It had been the scream.

It had not been uttered by a man. No human throat could have produced that sound or anything like it. It had been more like the screech of an animal, a fox caught in a snare or some kind of ape. Sawney had seen apes and monkeys in his travels. He'd heard the animals shrieking and clamouring, usually in tussles over food, and the noise in the cellar had been remarkably similar in tone and volume. But even as his mind tried to grapple with that unlikely possibility, he had known deep down that he was fooling himself and that even the most vociferous ape could not have made the ghastly cry.

He had never seen the face of the person holding the knife. All he had seen had been the shape of him, the curve of his shoulder, but the image and that piercing scream, allied to the things he had seen, or thought he had seen, in the other pallets further down the cellar had been enough to make him turn tail and run from the cellar as if the hounds of Hell had been snapping at his heels. Sawney had never referred to the incident, not even to Butler. He'd never returned to that hospital. He'd been assigned other duties, transporting equipment on the long journey to Badajoz. It was only after Hyde had revealed his true identity the previous evening that Sawney realized who the man in the cellar must have been and why he'd had that flashback when Hyde had introduced himself as Dodd. Only in the dream had the figure's face been revealed. Now he'd seen it for real. Sawney's life had come full circle.

Sawney raised the mug to his lips and took a sip. It tasted like gunpowder on his tongue. He looked about him. Maggett and the Raggs were around somewhere. Sal, too, plying her trade, he supposed. Thinking about the Raggs made Sawney tighten his grip on his mug.

He'd given them a simple job. All they'd had to do was retrieve the woman's corpse from Hyde's underground stable and dispose of it. After the last balls-up, there had been no thought in Sawney's mind to sell it on to any of his usual customers, so he'd given strict instructions to the brothers to make sure the thing disappeared, permanently, and not too close to home. The Raggs had assured him that had been done and, like a fool, Sawney had believed them. Then news came that a woman's naked corpse had been found high and relatively dry on a beam over the Fleet not much more than a hop and a skip away, which meant they'd transported the thing halfway across London to drop it virtually on their own doorstep. Sawney had let rip; told them they were useless bastards and as much use as a pair of one-armed fiddlers, which had left Sawney drinking on his own, his crew subdued and scattered around the pub. Sawney knew the bad feeling wouldn't last for long. It never did. Not when there was a lucrative living to be made by sticking together. They made a good team, the five of them; but that wasn't to say there weren't times when he would have swung for them, cheerfully.

Sawney's gaze moved to the couple over at the next table. The man had his hand on the woman's knee. Sawney watched as the hand disappeared under the dress. There was no squeal of protest, just a giggle as the woman repaid the favour by stuffing her hand down the front of the man's breeches. Sawney felt himself stiffen. He looked for Sal, spotted her over in the far corner, talking to one of the Hanratty boys. Bastard's probably thinking about getting his hand down her blouse, Sawney thought. Well, bugger that. If anyone was going to get his hand down Sal's blouse tonight, it was going to be him. He drained his mug and stood up. As he did so, he caught Sal's eye. When he jerked his head towards the door at the back of the room, Sal winked and stuck her tongue into the inside of her cheek to make it bulge. Sawney knew that meant she was in the mood too. He felt himself grow harder. Nothing like an inventive whore to get the blood flowing.

They met at the door.

'You want me to bring one of the other girls?' Sal asked. 'Make it a threesome? Rosie's feelin' a bit frisky.'

Sawney shook his head. 'Not tonight. One'll be enough.'

Sal looked at him and grinned. 'More than enough,' she said, and taking his hand she led him through the doorway and up the stairs.

'God's teeth,' Lomax muttered. 'When you said we'd be on foot, this wasn't at all what I had in mind.'

'Silence at the back. No talkin' in the ranks.' The instruction was followed by a rasping chuckle. The sound carried eerily in the semi-darkness.

'You're enjoying this, Sergeant. I can tell.' As the light from Jago's lantern played across Lomax's ravaged face, his left eye gleamed demonically.

'Away with you, Major. A drop o' water never hurt anyone.'

'Water, my arse,' Lomax said.

Jago grinned.

They were at least twenty feet below street level and they were wading through shit. Literally.

Odd how natural the short exchange had sounded, Hawkwood thought, as he listened to Jago and Lomax address each other by rank. It had been interesting, and not a little amusing, seeing the two meet for the first time, watching the way they had sized one another up. From their immediate rapport, it was clear that each of them had recognized in the other a man you'd want on your side, no questions asked. He was reminded of Hyde's comment back in the alleyway: *Once a soldier…*

'You think young Hopkins'll be all right?' Lomax asked.

'Micah's watching his back,' Jago said. 'He'll be fine.'

'Doesn't talk much, does he?' Lomax said.

'Who?'

'Micah.'

'Doesn't have to,' Jago said.

And that was the end of *that* conversation.

Another lantern wavered twenty paces ahead of them, casting an eerie molten glow across the walls and roof of the tunnel.

'How are we doing, Billy?' Jago called softly.

The reply came towards them in a broad Ulster

brogue. 'Not far now. 'Bout quarter of a mile.'

'Christ,' Lomax said. He gazed down with disgust at the slow-moving tide of filth running alongside them and cursed again as his boot squelched into the soft and yielding morass.

They had gained access to the tunnel through the cellar beneath Newton's Gin Shop. It had been at Jago's suggestion, prompted by Hawkwood asking if there was any way of approaching the Dog without being seen.

There was, the sergeant had told him, but it wouldn't be what you might call fragrant.

Jago had certainly got that right, Hawkwood reflected. The smell coming off the river had been bad enough topside. Down below, it went way past grim. It was unspeakable, almost beyond description.

Like Lomax, they were wearing neck cloths tied around their lower faces, but the protection this provided against the foul stench was marginal, which was to say non-existent. And, as they had soon discovered, the smell wasn't the only horror that lay in wait for them. The body that had been discovered earlier and which was now with Surgeon Quill had already provided ample proof that the Fleet's reputation as a communal midden was well deserved. In the dark, dank and dripping tunnels the evidence was even more explicit.

The glutinous stains that ran along both sides of the tunnel extended well above waist height. It was an indication of how high the water level could rise after a heavy rain or if there was a blockage further downstream, hindering the flow.

All around them, the brickwork was black with effluence that had been marooned by the retreating tide. It hung in globules, as thick as pitch, and oozed down the walls leaving slug-like trails in its wake.

Their path, which was not much more than a narrow ledge, was swirling with overflow. Each man had lost his footing at least once and had only been saved from sliding over the edge into the noxious soup by the prompt action of one of his companions, who'd been able to reach out a steadying hand.

Upstream, the underground channels were a lot narrower, Jago told them; during times of flooding the water would fill the tunnels in the upper reaches almost to the roof. The former sergeant had grinned. 'It'd be like tryin' to crawl up a cow's arse.'

A colourful turn of phrase, but it hadn't been hard to picture the image.

'Christ,' Lomax said again. 'I was over in St Pancras barely two months back and there were lads bathing. You wouldn't think it was the same bloody river.' He stopped suddenly and peered ahead. 'Jesus, is that what I think it is?'

Hawkwood raised his lantern and followed Lomax's gaze. The tunnel had widened, as had the ledge upon which they were walking. Blocks of heavy stone lay scattered around them in the mud and shit. They were obviously very old and circular in shape, probably the ruins of a roof column. Lying next to one of them, half covered by a moraine of black sludge, was what appeared to be part of a ribcage and a partially submerged human skull.

'One way to get rid of the old man,' Jago said, without breaking stride. 'A knock on the head when he's drunk, open the trapdoor and Bob's your uncle. Guarantee that ain't the first poor bugger that's been tossed down the well. God knows what else has been thrown down here over the years.'

Hawkwood thought about the two men who'd waylaid him by Holborn Bridge, the spider hand clutching for purchase and the black mud closing relentlessly over the pale-skinned face of his attacker. The body would be down here somewhere. It might even be close to where they were now walking. There was a possibility, Hawkwood supposed, that it would find its way eventually to the Thames, but he doubted it. Most likely it would get caught against some obstruction, and there it would remain until it had been stripped of flesh and reduced to spikes of bone, entombed in darkness until the end of time.

It occurred to him, given his new-found knowledge, that it had probably been either Sawney or the Dog's landlord, Hanratty, who'd set the duo on to him. Maybe Lucius Symes had spotted him and slipped them the word. The verger was going to be doing some serious talking once he caught up with him.

They moved on without speaking. The only sound was the splashing of their boots as they made their way along the tunnel. A few yards ahead, Billy's lantern drew them further into the sewer.

Billy Haig looked about seventeen, though

426

Hawkwood suspected he was probably around the same age as Hopkins. His fair hair and blue eyes no doubt stood him in good stead with the girls. The ready smile would help, too; though the shrewd look he'd exhibited when the introductions had been made had also hinted at a maturity his boyish appearance belied. Hawkwood had wondered about his inclusion – Micah's stoic presence had not been open to question – but when Jago announced that Billy had once been a runner for Hanratty and knew the layout of the Dog, the reason for the youth's selection became clear. Though that hadn't been the only reason why Jago had enlisted Billy's help. The lad, it transpired, had also enjoyed the favours of Molly Finn and would therefore be able to identify her.

The lantern suddenly came to a halt. Mindful of the slipperiness underfoot, the three men moved forward cautiously.

Billy was pointing to one side. Set into the tunnel wall was a dark, rectangular recess. There were stone steps, Hawkwood could see, rising into the blackness.

'This is it,' Billy said softly. Holding the lantern up, he inclined his head towards a faint mark scratched into the brickwork by the side of the opening. It was in the shape of a diagonal cross. It looked as if it had been made some time ago. Without the aid of the lantern it was doubtful they would have spotted it, but Billy had known what to look for. Beneath the lower legs of the cross were scored, equally roughly, two letters: BD.

Most of the access points had signs, Billy told them. It was one of the few ways people were able to find their way around the subterranean passages.

'What's up there?' Jago asked, nodding towards the steps.

Billy lowered his neck cloth, grimacing at the smell. 'Trapdoor.'

'How the devil do we get in?' Lomax asked. 'The damned thing's bound to be bolted.'

Billy shook his head. 'Levers, both sides. But you've to know where to look.' He grinned and tapped the side of his nose.

'See?' Jago said, clapping Billy on the shoulder. 'Told you he wasn't just a pretty face.'

''Tain't the only trap, neither,' Billy said. He jerked his thumb towards the tar-black ooze. 'There's another one further up. Opens directly over the water. Hanratty uses it to get rid of unwanted merchandise.' The corner of Billy's mouth twitched. 'If yous know what I mean. Saw him drop a fellow called Danny McGrew through it once. Can't recall what the poor sod had done to deserve it, but the last anyone saw of Danny was the back of his arse as he went to meet his maker.' Billy looked suddenly pensive. 'Not a quick way to go, I'm thinking.'

While Billy pondered the circumstances of Danny McGrew's undignified exit, Hawkwood lowered his mask and looked around. He wasn't expecting witnesses, but it paid to be sure. 'Check your weapons.'

Placing his lantern on the ground, Hawkwood drew the pistol from the holster on his belt and by the guttering light checked the flint, frizzen and powder. He pulled back the hammer to half-cock and released it gently back to the uncocked position. Replacing the gun in the holster he did the same with his second pistol. As well as the firearms, he also had the knife in his boot and his tipstaff.

The others followed suit. Jago, who had supplied the guns, was similarly armed, save for a stout blackthorn cudgel. The sound of hammers being drawn and reset filled the enclosed space, sharp and precise in the darkness.

Lomax had just the one pistol, tucked into a chest holster for ease of access. His other weapon was a short-bladed sword, secured in a scabbard against his right hip. Hawkwood was curious to see how Lomax was able to check the pistol one-handed, but it was clear from the way that Lomax tucked the barrel of the gun under his right armpit and removed the oiled leather cow's knee from around the lock with his good hand, that the former cavalry officer was in no need of assistance. Lomax, sensing he was being observed, looked up and chuckled. 'What? You afraid I'll drop the bloody thing?'

'Wouldn't have asked you along if I'd thought that,' Hawkwood said. He eyed the cow's knee as Lomax tucked it into his pocket.

Lomax looked sheepish, or at least as sheepish as a one-eyed man could. 'Thought it might rain.'

Hawkwood grinned.

Lomax grinned back, his face contorting, then his good eye flicked sideways and he said, 'My saints, lad, what are you planning to shoot? Elephants?'

He was staring at the weapon in Billy's hands.

Until then, it had been strung from a shoulder strap concealed beneath the youth's coat. It was a severe-looking piece; compact, not much more than twenty inches in length, with a walnut stock and a brass barrel. The muzzle of the gun was slightly flared.

'Yous want to swap?' Billy asked.

Lomax stared at the gun, clearly giving the offer serious thought, but then he shook his head. 'You probably need two sound hands. Am I right?'

Billy nodded. 'She's got a kick like a bloody mule, so she has, but anything you hit stays down.'

'I believe you,' Lomax said. He sounded almost wistful.

As well as the blunderbuss, Hawkwood saw that Billy, too, had a pistol tucked into his belt.

They were well armed, Hawkwood thought, but would it be enough? It would have to be, he decided. He retrieved his lantern and nodded towards the stairs. 'All right, Billy. Take us up.'

Jago gripped the blackthorn cudgel, caught Hawkwood's eye and grinned. 'Just like old times,' he said softly.

'So long as the rest of it doesn't turn to shit,' Hawkwood said, scraping the sole of his boot against the edge of the first step.

They ascended in silence and had climbed no more than a dozen steps before the lanterns picked up the outline of the trapdoor above them. The hinges, Hawkwood saw, appeared to be in good order and well oiled.

Billy paused and placed a finger to his lips. Then he reached out his hand to the side. It

430

looked as if he was stroking the wall, until Hawkwood realized he was counting along the line of bricks. Suddenly, his hand stopped moving. He turned and nodded.

Hawkwood and Lomax drew their pistols and slowly eased the hammers back. Then they listened.

The seconds ticked by. Hawkwood wondered whether the chill on the stairs was real or if the anticipation of what might lie ahead was fuelling his imagination.

Then Jago tapped Billy gently on the arm. Billy pressed his fingers against the corner of one of the bricks. The brick shifted, allowing Billy to remove it. Placing the brick on the step beside him, Billy inserted his hand into the exposed cavity. He waited and watched as Jago reached up, braced himself, and placed his palm against the underside of the trapdoor. They listened again.

'Do it,' Jago said.

The sound of cogs slipping into place came from above. Hawkwood tensed. The noise sounded horrifically loud in the confined space. Billy withdrew his hand from the wall and Jago pushed hard against the trap. As it swung open, Hawkwood raised the light and he and Lomax thrust their way past, pistols at the ready, sweeping the cellar. Jago and Billy were less than a heartbeat behind. With the shadows retreating before the advancing lanterns, the first thing they saw was the pale face staring back at them from the darkness.

In the alleyway outside the Black Dog, Constable George Hopkins placed the watch back in his coat pocket and turned to the man standing beside him. He tried to ignore the dryness that had gathered at the back of his throat. 'It's time,' he whispered.

Micah nodded, buttoned his jacket to conceal the pistols in his belt, and pushed open the door. 'Stay close,' he instructed.

Hopkins fastened his coat, turned his collar up, swallowed nervously and, cap in hand, followed Micah into the pub.

Their entry into the dingy, smoke-filled interior attracted little reaction. A few heads turned, but in the main they belonged to customers seated close to the door. The interest that was shown suggested irritation at the sudden cold draught, rather than suspicion at a stranger's presence.

Not for the first time, Hopkins was struck by his companion's composure. During their short acquaintance, he'd learned that Micah was a man of few words. It wasn't that Jago's lieutenant was surly, more that he saw no need for idle chitchat. So be it, Hopkins thought. What was important was that Jago trusted him and Captain Hawkwood trusted Jago. That was good enough for him; more than enough.

Which wasn't to say that he hadn't wondered about the relationship between the captain and Nathaniel Jago. Hopkins' mind went back to the stories he'd heard about the Runner and his network of informers. From what he had seen, it was obvious that Hawkwood and Jago's friendship was well established, and that Jago was far more than a petty eavesdropper whose loyalty was dependent on financial remuneration. As to the origins of the relationship, however Hopkins could only speculate. He assumed the two men had been comrades-in-arms during the war – theirs seemed to be a bond that had been forged in shared adversity – but, as to the specifics, he remained ignorant. He wondered if there'd ever come a time when he had someone with whom to stand shoulder to shoulder, secure in the knowledge that his back was protected.

Micah led the way to a table in the corner of the taproom not far from the door and the two of them sat down. Hopkins placed his hat on his lap. He noted how Micah arranged his chair so that his back was to the wall, providing him with an uninterrupted view over the rest of the room.

'What now?' the constable asked.

Micah looked around, caught the eye of one of the serving girls, and beckoned.

'We wait,' he said.

'You can lower your pistol, Major,' Hawkwood said.

Judging from the expression on Lucius Symes' face, death had come as a terrible surprise. The verger's body was propped against the base of the wall, the head canted at an unnatural angle. His lower jaw hung open so that it appeared as if he was drooling, while his glazed eyes were fixed on some unidentifiable point in the far corner of the cellar. A grimy sheet covered his waist and lower limbs.

Hawkwood squatted down, braced himself against the stink coming off the corpse, and studied the dark weal that encircled the verger's wattled neck.

'You know him?' Jago gazed down at the corpse.

The recognition must have shown on his face, Hawkwood realized. He stood up. 'It's Lizzie Tyler's verger.'

'Hell of a place to end up,' Jago said.

They looked about them. The chamber bore a closer resemblance to a dungeon than the stock cellar in a public house. Benches ran along two of the walls while against another sat two large metal vats. The vats were raised off the cellar floor. Each one rested on a metal brazier. They reminded Hawkwood of the large cooking pots used in regimental kitchens. Affixed to the ceiling above each vat was a block and tackle, from which were slung a chain and hook.

Hawkwood approached the nearest bench. An assortment of bladed tools lay scattered across it: knives of varying lengths, saws and cleavers. There were more hanging from pegs along the wall. These weren't carpenter's paraphernalia, Hawkwood knew. He was looking at a butcher's block.

The tools looked well used. The knife blades were heavily stained while the gaps between each saw tooth were encrusted with matter. Some of the blades showed tiny specks of rust.

Jago cursed. He had put his lantern down and placed his palm on the bench-top without looking. He lifted his hand away with another exclamation of disgust and wiped it on his breeches. Then, frowning, he rubbed his fingers and thumb together and held them up to his nose.

'Feels like tallow. Bloody odd smell to it, though.'

434

Whatever the substance was, the surface of the bench was coated with it. It gleamed like varnish in the lantern light.

Hawkwood looked down. Beneath the bench, a shallow drainage channel had been cut into the stone flags. He followed its line to the point where it disappeared into a recess in the corner of the cellar floor. The flags around the edges of the channel were black with residue. A cold feeling began to work its way through his bones.

'Oh, dear Lord,' Lomax said hoarsely.

Hawkwood turned. Lomax had picked up Jago's light and was peering into one of the vats. Suddenly he straightened, turned away quickly and, without warning, vomited against the cellar wall.

Billy, who'd been examining the contents of the other bench, looked up and stared. Hawkwood and Jago exchanged glances. They approached the vat. At first sight the vessel appeared to be empty save for a thick layer of congealed fat which had accumulated at the bottom and around the sides of the vat's interior. Both men recoiled at the smell. Small wonder Lomax had thrown up, Hawkwood thought. He could feel himself beginning to gag. Then he saw it. At the bottom; an object caught in the grease. He lowered the lantern and heard Jago suck in his breath.

It was the bottom segment of a human jawbone.

'Mother of God,' Jago breathed. 'What is this place?' He turned. 'Billy, get your arse over here. When you ran for Hanratty, did you know about this?'

But Billy wasn't listening. His attention was focused on the contents of the second worktop.

'Billy?' Jago said again. Then he looked over Billy's shoulder and went quiet.

Billy was backing slowly away from the bench.

Curious, Hawkwood followed the youth's transfixed stare.

Candles. Dozens of them; some loose and scattered in disarray, others tied together in bundles. Alongside them were coils of candle thread and a stack of rough wooden moulds. Further along the bench was what looked like a pile of small wax tablets.

Hawkwood knew the look in Jago's eyes would haunt him for a long time to come. Cautiously, he moved to the second vat. Bracing himself, he peered over the rim. From what he could see it contained only dirty water. A thin oily scum floated on the surface of the liquid, like lather in a laundry tub. Hawkwood examined the vat's exterior. Its base was blackened and pitted by heat, like that of its twin. Remnants of ash coated the floor of the brazier beneath it.

'Tell me you didn't know about this, Billy,' Jago said.

Over by the wall, Lomax wiped his mouth on his sleeve and stared around him in disbelief.

Billy shook his head. His face was white. 'I didn't. Swear to God. It was only a cellar. Hanratty used it for his kegs and contraband. It was one of my jobs – stacking the booze. There was none of ... this.'

Jago nodded towards the verger's body. 'You think that's what they planned to do with *him?*

Render the poor bugger down to soap and candles, and sell him on street corners? Sweet Mary, what have we gotten ourselves into?'

No one answered. They were too consumed by the horror they were seeing.

Hawkwood found his voice. 'If you were wondering what sort of men we were going to be up against, Major; now you know.'

At first, Lomax just looked back at him, saying nothing. Then he gave a brief nod of understanding. Both of them knew there was nothing more to be said.

Hawkwood turned to Jago and Billy. 'We've work to do.'

The way out was via a door at the top of a flight of wooden stairs. Without any expectations, Hawkwood tried the latch and wasn't surprised when it didn't open. Whoever had turned the room into a slaughterhouse wouldn't want to be disturbed or see their handiwork discovered.

Jago took the set of lock picks from his jacket. 'What's on the other side, Billy?'

'Passageway. There's another cellar leading off it. Then there's stairs leading up to the next floor. I did hear there are more passages towards the back; and tunnels joining all the other houses in the street. Dunno if that's true. There are places I never got to see. I can get you inside, but after that it's up to yous all.' He stole a glance at the dungeon behind them, crossed himself and shuddered.

There was a dull clunk from inside the lock. Jago gave a grunt of satisfaction. Returning the lock pick to his waistcoat, he retrieved his lantern from Lomax and reached for the latch.

The passage was unlit and empty. The stone floor indicated they were still some way beneath the pub. It also suggested the foundations were very old and constructed long before the Dog had been built.

Jago caught Hawkwood's eye. His expression was grim. Hawkwood knew what Jago was thinking. If Molly Finn was here, what were the chances of finding her alive? The girl's only hope was if they'd taken her for recreational purposes and weren't finished with her yet. Otherwise they'd probably dispose of her the way they had Lucius Symes.

They checked the second cellar anyway, just in case. This time there were no surprises, though Hawkwood suspected that the markings on some of the casks might well have sparked interest from the Revenue men. Other than the trapdoor through which the unfortunate McGrew had been dispatched, there was nothing else of interest.

Leaving the cellar behind, they proceeded along the passageway and paused at the foot of the stairs.

'Watch your backs,' Hawkwood said, thinking, even as he uttered the words, that it was unnecessary advice.

They began to climb.

19

Declan Hanratty had just released himself from his breeches when the interruption occurred. The moll, whose name was Sadie, was bent forward, head down, gripping the edge of the table, her skirt up over her rump, when she felt Hanratty's weight shift.

For what we are about to receive, she thought wearily and, hearing the grunt behind her, braced herself. When nothing happened, her second thought was that he was taking his bloody time, which wasn't like the Declan she knew and despised. It took a second for her to realize that Declan's hands were no longer around her waist. She looked back across her shoulder, fully expecting to see him hunched over, about to change grip, only to discover that wasn't the case at all.

Declan was still there, but from the expression on his face it was obvious sex was no longer uppermost in his mind. The new focus of his attention was the pistol pressed against his forehead, and the man holding it. The man was tall. He was dressed in a long, dark coat. It was his face that made Sadie catch her breath. Two scars marred his left cheek. One was small and ragged and looked old. The other was fresh and raw and weeping blood. A second man, with a hard face and pewter-coloured hair, was alongside, a finger on his lips. His pistol was pointing at Sadie's chest. He took his finger away. 'No screamin'. Understand?'

Sadie nodded mutely, her heart beating fast.

'Good girl. Now pull your skirt down. I think young Declan's lost his appetite.'

Sadie did as she was told, hands shaking. She noticed that the pantry door – which had been propped open, Declan having been in too much of a hurry to close it – was now pulled shut.

The grey-haired man took hold of her arm. When he spoke, his voice was calm; almost reassuring. 'What's your name, sweetheart?'

Sadie told him.

'All right, Sadie, you stand there and be quiet. We just want a few words with young Declan here.' The speaker turned to his companion. 'He's all yours.'

The dark-haired man's face grew hard. The smaller scar on his cheek whitened. 'I'm looking for Sawney and Sal Bridger,' he said, grasping Declan by the collar and placing the muzzle of the pistol squarely against Declan's brow.

Declan screwed up his face. 'What?'

'You heard.'

'Don't know 'im. Ain't no Sawney here.'

The man raised the pistol barrel and smashed it across the bridge of Declan's nose. There was a crack. Blood spurted. Declan yelped and raised his hands.

Sadie opened her mouth to scream, only to find herself stifled by the grey-haired man's callused palm. 'Remember what I said. Quiet now.'

'Wrong answer,' the scarred man said. 'And I'm

440

not in the mood. I'll ask you again: where's Sawney?'

'You're a dead man,' Declan spluttered. His eyes were watering copiously. Blood and mucus bubbled from his nose and dribbled down the cleft in his chin.

'Last time,' the man said. 'Maybe I should shoot your balls off instead. What's it to be?'

Declan squirmed at the possibility. 'Don't know if they're bleedin' here. Didn't see 'em. I've been out. Got back late. Honest,' he added nasally, and spat a mouthful of blood and phlegm on to the floor. He dabbed his upper lip with the back of his hand in a vain attempt to staunch the flow and stared at the dark crimson smear across his knuckles.

Sadie made a moaning sound, trying to free her mouth from the hand clamped over it.

'Think she might be trying to tell us something?' the older man asked.

'Ask her,' said the scarred man.

The hand was removed.

Sadie threw Declan a look that was part venom, part triumph, and part fear. 'They're upstairs; all of them – Sawney and the rest. Top two landings. They've been up there a while.'

'You stupid cow,' Declan spat. He made to lunge forward.

Sadie flinched, but the grey-haired man had already pulled her out of Declan's reach.

The scarred man jerked Declan upright, then, as Declan's head came up, he slammed the pistol barrel into the exposed throat. A look of pain and astonishment flooded the sallow, blood-smeared face. The scarred man released his grip and Declan went down gasping for air. By the time he hit the floor, it was too late. He was already drowning in his own blood.

Sadie felt as though she was going to faint.

'All right, lass.' The older man gripped her shoulder. 'No one's going to harm *you*. We're looking for a girl; blonde, pretty, name of Molly Finn. Sal might have brought her.'

Sadie stared nervously at the scarred man's face. 'The Raggs've got a girl with them. Didn't see who it was, though, poor little bitch.' She took in the body on the floorboards. She wasn't sure whether to grieve or gloat.

'Where are the other girls?'

She dragged her eyes away. 'Workin'. Hanratty don't like us skivin' off if there's customers out front. Not that there's many in tonight. I only came in 'ere for a slice of bread an' cheese. Ain't 'ad a bite all bleedin' day. Then that sod decided he wanted a free feel.' Sadie looked again at the dead man at her feet and shivered. Her face suddenly crumpled. 'Hanratty's goin' to kill me.'

'No, he's not,' the older man said. 'Because you didn't see anything.' He jerked his head towards a door in the corner of the room. 'Larder?'

'What?' Sadie followed his gaze, then nodded dubiously.

The older man ushered her across the floor and opened the door. 'Get inside and stay there. Don't come out. No matter what you hear. You got that?' He didn't wait for an answer but pushed her in before she had a chance to protest, then closed the door behind her.

Jago looked down at Declan's body without pity. 'If you hadn't, I would've. There's no way he didn't know what's been going on.'

Hawkwood said nothing. He paused, opened the door and Jago followed him out. Lomax and Billy materialized from the shadows beneath the stairwell. They had forsaken the lanterns and were reliant on the candles along the walls. It left their hands free to carry weapons.

'We need to move now,' Hawkwood said. 'We've been lucky to make it this far. Everyone's out front. Nathaniel, you're with Billy. He knows Molly, so the Raggs are yours. Gabriel and I will take care of Sawney. I want him for the murder of Doyle. He's also my link to Hyde. You ready, Major?'

'I'd say we're wasting time,' Lomax said, in a voice as hard as stone.

Lemuel Ragg pushed himself away from the girl's bruised and inert body, half covered by the grubby sheet, and glanced across at his brother, who was sprawled across the opposite end of the bed, legs akimbo. Samuel was clutching a half-full bottle of grog to his chest, as if protecting it against pilferers. He looked at Lemuel and grinned.

'Give us a snort,' Lemuel said, and held out his hand.

Samuel looked down at the bottle as if seeing it for the first time, and raised it to his lips. Taking a swallow, he tossed it the length of the bed. Some of the drink sprayed out and landed across the girl's naked breasts. She did not react.

Lemuel took a swig. Then he dribbled some of the contents into his cupped palm and rubbed it around his penis. 'Stops you gettin' the pox,' he said.

'Bit late for that,' Samuel said, and then thought about it. 'Give it 'ere, then.'

Lemuel passed the bottle, reached out a foot and nudged the girl's thigh with his toe. He was rewarded with a low whimper.

'Still with us. Thought she might have pegged it. We'll let her get her breath, eh?'

'Jesus,' Samuel said, wincing, his hand in his lap. 'Bleedin' smarts a bit.'

'Means it's workin',' Lemuel said. He lay back against the pillow and closed his eyes.

The door crashed back on its hinges.

Lemuel's eyes snapped open. He tried to raise himself but in his haste only succeeded in entangling his feet in the bedclothes. Samuel, also slow to react, found himself caught with one hand on the grog bottle, the other round his cock. Snatching his hand away from his crotch he fumbled for a corner of the sheet to cover his nakedness.

'You'll be the Ragg boys,' Jago said, stepping over the threshold. He had a pistol in one hand and his cudgel in the other. 'Pleased to make your acquaintance.' His eyes dropped to the tumble of bedclothes and the unmoving form beneath and his face turned to stone. 'On your feet, you bastards. Don't bother with your breeches. We ain't strong on formality. Billy! Get in here!'

Billy Haig sidestepped through the door, his

444

hands gripping the blunderbuss. His eyes darkened when he saw the small, blonde figure curled foetally on the bed. He stepped forward quickly and turned the girl's face gently towards him. He stared up at Jago and shook his head. 'It's not her.'

Shite, Jago thought. He turned to Lemuel, who had managed to extricate his feet and was trying to sit up. 'Molly Finn. Where is she?'

Lemuel blinked. 'Who the 'ell's Molly Finn?' He looked towards his brother for guidance, only to see Samuel's confusion mirroring his own.

It suddenly occurred to Jago that the Raggs might not know. He had no proof the brothers were involved in the girl's disappearance. He had assumed they were complicit by virtue of their association with the Bridger woman. Maybe their professed ignorance was genuine.

'She's the girl Sal Bridger picked up this morning. Don't bloody tell me you don't know what's happened to her.'

And then he saw it; at the mention of Sal's name, a flash of understanding in Samuel Ragg's eyes that disappeared so fast he could have been forgiven for thinking it had been a trick of the light. But it had been enough.

At that moment, the girl on the bed groaned and opened her eyes. She did it slowly, as if every movement was an effort of will.

'All right, darlin',' Billy said and looked back at Jago with a mixture of anger and pity.

Which was when Lemuel brought his left hand from beneath the pillow and slashed the open razor across the side of Billy Haig's throat. As

445

blood from Billy's severed artery fountained across the bedclothes, Samuel threw the corner of the sheet aside and clawed for the pistol that lay on the nightstand by the side of the bed.

Jago saw Billy go down and slammed the cudgel towards Lemuel's wrist. But he had been caught off guard and the swing failed to connect. As Lemuel twisted out of reach, Jago shot Samuel through his right eye. The ball exited from the back of Samuel's skull sending a cascade of blood and brain across the wall behind him.

As the sound of the gunshot echoed around the room, Lemuel came off the bed with a howl of rage and scythed the razor towards Jago's face. Jago jerked his head back. The razor missed him by a hair's breadth. Such was the force of Lemuel's attack that he almost overbalanced, which gave Jago his opening, enabling him to regain the initiative and smash the cudgel against the outside of Lemuel's forearm. Lemuel shrieked as the bone snapped. The impetus of Lemuel's forward motion, allied to Jago's counter-attack, drove Lemuel to his knees. The razor fell from his fist. Wielding the expended pistol like a second club, Jago, with massive force, drove the butt hard against the back of Lemuel's skull. There was a sound like eggshells splintering. With no change of expression, Jago followed through with the blackthorn and watched dispassionately as Lemuel Ragg's nude corpse collapsed across the floorboards.

Jago stuck the pistol in his belt and moved quickly to the bed, knowing he was far too late. 'Jesus, Billy,' he breathed. Billy Haig's eyes were still open. There was a look of bafflement on his face. His lips moved soundlessly as he tried to speak. His body arched and his hands scrabbled helplessly at the wound in his neck. Blood was pouring between his fingers. Suddenly, he shuddered. His body sank back on to the bed and his hands grew still.

There was a moan and for a second Jago thought it was Billy and the hairs rose at the back of his neck, until he realized it was the girl. He drew back the edge of the blood-drenched sheet. A pair of green eyes looked beseechingly back at him. Jago reached out, saw the instinctive self-defensive withdrawal as the girl cringed away from his touch.

Moving Billy's body aside, Jago lifted the girl from the bed. The quilt was on the floor. Hastily, he wrapped the compliant girl in its folds and carried her over to one of the room's two chairs. 'Don't know if you can hear me, girl, but they ain't going to harm you any more. You've Nathaniel's word on that. Rest here. I'll be back for you, I promise.'

Jago patted the girl on the shoulder. Then, with a last despairing glance at Billy's blood-splattered body, he retrieved the cudgel, grabbed Samuel Ragg's pistol from the nightstand, and ran from the room, leaving the smell of death behind him.

Hanratty was behind the taproom counter with his son, Lorchan, when he heard the gunshot. The sound of a door slamming had preceded it, but Hanratty hadn't deemed the noise significant. Slamming doors weren't an uncommon occurrence in the Dog and he put it down to the usual reason: a drunken argument. But a pistol shot was different.

'Christ!' Hanratty spat. 'Bloody Raggs feudin' again. I'll have their guts.' Instructing Lorchan to hold the fort, he reached under the counter, where he kept his own pistol primed and loaded.

'Leave it,' a voice said. The order was accompanied by a sound Hanratty recognized as a pistol hammer being cocked. He straightened and turned slowly.

Micah was standing less than five paces away. He was holding a pistol in each hand. One was pointed at Hanratty's chest; the other covered the taproom. Standing next to him was another, younger man with unruly hair and a pistol aimed at Lorchan's heart.

'Hands on the counter,' Micah said. 'Either of you moves, you die.'

Micah surveyed the room out of the corner of his eye. At this hour, the pub wasn't full. It wasn't pay night, so there was no line of sullen men queuing for wages. The cold winter weather had kept many of the Dog's regulars at home. There were maybe a couple of dozen people in the taproom all told, and that included the molls and the serving girls. Several drinkers, having seen the brandished weapons, were already pushing their chairs back.

'On your way, gentlemen.' Micah's voice, while not loud, penetrated all corners of the taproom.

'Who says?' a slurred voice enquired belligerently.

'*He* does.' Micah nodded towards Hopkins.

Heads swivelled. With his free hand, Hopkins placed his police hat on his head and unfastened the remaining buttons on his jacket to reveal his other immediately recognizable badge of office, his bright scarlet waistcoat. Raising the pistol, he took a deep breath. 'By the order of the Chief Magistrate, everyone is to vacate the premises.' The constable prayed no one could hear the quaver in his voice.

There were several sharp intakes of breath and a muted chorus of derogatory remarks.

'Now,' Micah warned, and fired one of his pistols into the ceiling.

One of the serving girls let out a scream.

The explosion and the scream had the desired effect. So much for the authority of the uniform, Hopkins thought, as he watched several chairs tip over in the scramble for the exit. I could have been togged up like a bloody general, and it would still be the guns that gave the orders.

The three house molls and the two serving girls remained. Sensing there'd be safety in numbers, they were huddled by the fire.

'What's your game, cully?' Hanratty lifted his hand from the countertop. His eyes, while reflecting anger, also carried a calculating gleam.

'Did I say you could move?' Micah levelled his pistol at the bridge of Hanratty's nose. He caught Hopkins' eye and motioned towards the door.

Hopkins went to the door and locked it.

'Now you can move,' Micah said. 'You can join the ladies by the hearth. That way I don't have to worry about what you're up to behind my back. Leave the pistol.'

'If you're after the takings, you'll be bleedin' lucky.' Hanratty eyed Hopkins' uniform, his brow furrowing. 'Besides, I already paid this month's dues to you bastards.' He had the sudden thought that their presence might well be connected with the gunshot upstairs, but for the moment he couldn't think how.

'It's not your takings we're after,' Micah said.

Hanratty frowned. 'What then? We just sit here?'

'That's right,' Micah said, moving to the counter and exchanging his spent pistol for the one the publican had been reaching for. 'And if either of you opens his mouth again, I'll blow both your heads off.'

It occurred to Hopkins that for a man who up until then had shown little sign of eloquence, Micah, when the mood took him, certainly had a way with words.

Maggett stumbled out of the privy, buttoning himself up. He was all fingers and thumbs. He'd heard the pistol shot while he was pissing in the back alleyway and recognized it for what it was and where above his head it had come from. The almost simultaneous screech of anger and the muffled thump that followed had been enough to send a warning to Maggett's brain that danger might be imminent and evasive action was a priority.

The second shot came from a lot closer and it stopped Maggett in his tracks. Advancing slowly, he peered round the edge of the taproom door. The sight of the pistols being trained on the

Hanrattys was enough to draw him back into the shadows, but it was the police uniform that removed all doubt the danger was real. He had to find Sawney.

Maggett retreated at speed down the passage. Passing the kitchen, he paused only to lift one of the heavy meat cleavers from the wall before setting off at a lumbering run towards the back stairs.

When the first shot rang out Lomax swore and muttered darkly, 'There goes our element of surprise.'

Hawkwood said nothing. They were on the top floor. Unlike the floors beneath, there were no candles along the walls to show the way, but a skylight was set in the roof, allowing moonlight to filter down on to the landing.

A splintering crash rose from below as a door gave way. Hawkwood knew it was Jago starting to go through the rooms. Lomax was correct. They had lost the advantage and speed was now the overwhelming factor.

Hawkwood tried the first door. It was locked.

A second pistol shot sounded from downstairs. Micah and Hopkins keeping the rest of the Hanrattys at bay, or so Hawkwood hoped.

Hawkwood drove his boot against the door lock. It took two kicks for the door to give way. The room was empty. Hawkwood backed out, just in time to hear the click of a latch and see a slim silhouette emerge from a doorway at the other end of the landing. He had a brief glimpse of a halo of dark hair framing a small, pale face and an arm coming up from behind the angle of a petticoat.

He heard Lomax yell, then there was a gleam of moonlight on metal and even as he brought his own pistol up and squeezed the trigger and saw the figure flung backwards against the side of the door by the force of the impact, there was a simultaneous flash of powder and a dull crack and he heard Lomax grunt and spin away.

As Sal started to go down, a second figure, which Hawkwood knew had to be Sawney, reached out, grasped her about the waist and, using her body as a shield, raised a pistol and fired. Hawkwood felt the wind from the ball as it ploughed past his ear and struck the wall behind his head.

A muttered curse came from below and to his left and a pistol roared. Hawkwood saw Sal's body slump and then he was bringing the second pistol up. The gun jerked in his hand as the explosion filled the landing, then Sal's body dropped to the floor and the figure sheltering behind her fell away, feet slithering.

At that moment, Hawkwood knew they'd failed. They had needed Sal Bridger and Sawney alive. Just one of them would have done. He cursed his stupidity. Sawney had only the one pistol. There had been no opportunity for him to reload and therefore there had been no need for Hawkwood to shoot a second time. He hadn't thought it through. Everything had happened too fast.

Hawkwood looked down. Lomax was half sitting, half lying against the wall, holding his shoulder. He rewarded Hawkwood with one of his macabre grins and then his attention shifted to the end of the landing and Hawkwood saw him stiffen. Following Lomax's gaze, Hawkwood saw movement close to the floor. One of the bodies was twitching.

Gripping the spent pistols, he walked forward. As he did so, a monstrous shadow arose from a second stairwell at the end of the landing.

Maggett erupted out of the darkness, the cleaver high in his fist. Hawkwood had a fleeting impression of a vast form filling his vision and then the massive hand was reaching for him and there was a flash of steel above his head and the blade was curving towards him with appalling speed.

And then there was a second shadow, which seemed to come from nowhere, and the world exploded with a roar as Jago slammed the muzzle of the blunderbuss against Maggett's jaw and pulled the trigger.

Maggett's face disintegrated as his corpse was blown sideways by the blast. The cleaver thudded on to the floor as the sound of the gun reverberated along the landing like the voice of God.

Jago stared down at the weapon, an expression of awe on his face. 'Good thing I went back for it. Jesus! She *does* kick like a mule.' Jago nodded down at Maggett's corpse. 'Lizzie wasn't wrong. He *was* a big bastard.'

Sawney groaned.

Hawkwood, ears ringing, looked down. Sawney was clutching his chest. The pistol ball had struck him an inch below the ribcage. The blood that was welling over his shirt and waistcoat looked black in the moonlight.

He stared up at Hawkwood. 'Bastard,' he whispered hoarsely. 'Knew we should have killed you.'

Hawkwood squatted down. 'Where's Hyde?'

'And Molly Finn,' Jago said.

'Sal?' Sawney tried moving his head to see.

'She's dead,' Hawkwood said. 'Same as you. You've been gut shot, Sawney. All the surgeons in the world can't save you from dying. Not even Colonel Hyde. Where is he? And where's Molly Finn?'

Sawney's chest rose and fell. His brow puckered. 'Molly Finn? The little cow Sal picked up? You came here lookin' for her?' Sawney tried to laugh and then coughed suddenly. Blood bubbled from between his gritted teeth.

'Where is she?' Jago grated.

'That's what's funny. She was never here, you stupid sods. We delivered her to 'im.'

'Who?'

'Colonel bleedin' Hyde. Who'd you think?'

'What?' Hawkwood said, not understanding.

'You deaf? He wanted a live one, so we gave her to 'im.' Sawney coughed again. Blood burst out of his mouth. His hands began to flutter across his chest, fingers tapping against his waistcoat. His eyes rolled in his head.

'Jesus!' Jago spat. He reached down and grabbed Sawney's collar. 'Where are they, you bastard?'

For a moment, Sawney seemed to recover from his convulsions. His eyes regained their focus and he frowned. 'You Jago? Hanratty told me about you. Said you were king o' the castle? That right? That's bleedin' funny. That's a riot.' Another spasm took him and he coughed once more.

'Christ,' Jago said. 'For once in your miserable life, do something right, you piece of shit!'

Sawney's eyes widened. He stared at Jago and then at Hawkwood. He moved his hand across his belly. His fingers began to play with the pocket on his waistcoat. Then they lay still and his lips parted.

'Why the bleedin' 'ell should I?' he hissed, and died.

'God Almighty!' Jago released his grip and stared down at the corpse in disbelief. 'God All bloody Mighty!'

A shadow blocked the moonlight coming through the skylight above them; Lomax stood with his neck cloth, dark with blood, pressed against his right shoulder. 'Is it over?'

'It is for that bastard,' Jago said. 'God damn him to Hell!'

Lomax gazed down at Sal Bridger's corpse. There was a hole in the middle of her forehead and blood on the front of her petticoat. 'She'd have been a pretty little thing once,' he murmured to no one in particular.

Hawkwood wasn't listening. He was still crouched over Sawney, wondering where they went from here. They were no nearer to finding Hyde or Molly Finn. The night's enterprise had turned into a bloody mess. Literally.

His eyes travelled down from the lifeless eyes to the bloodstained clothing. He noted how Sawney's left hand was clamped over the wound, while the right looked as if it was still reaching into the waistcoat pocket. In fact there *was* a slight bulge there, he saw. Half curious and yet not really knowing why, he moved Sawney's hand and reached inside.

Hawkwood tugged the object free. It was a silver cross. A strange thing for Sawney to own, Hawkwood thought. As he eased it out, a piece of paper came with it; a folded page from a notebook. Hawkwood opened it out. There was writing, he saw, in a small but neat hand. It was almost too dark to read clearly, but a word caught his eye. Hawkwood held the page up to the moonlight.

'Jesus Christ,' he said.

In the taproom, the women were still clustered together, while Micah and Hopkins stood guard over a glowering Hanratty and his son, who were seated back to back, hands on their heads, legs crossed, on the floor in front of the fire.

'You!' Hanratty said, as Hawkwood entered. His eyes opened wider when he saw Jago and Lomax follow behind. His attention settled on Jago. 'I know your face, too, cully.'

Jago ignored him. 'Micah?'

'We're good,' Micah said.

'There's a girl upstairs. The Raggs were usin' her.' Jago turned to the women. 'I don't know her name.'

'Callie,' one of them said.

Jago nodded towards Hopkins. 'Take the constable up to her and bring her down here. Go now.'

Hopkins looked to Hawkwood for guidance. Hawkwood nodded. 'Take my pistols. Give me yours.'

The constable frowned.

'Yours is still loaded,' Hawkwood said.

They swapped firearms and Hopkins and the moll who had spoken left the room.

'A word, Major.'

Lomax walked over.

Hawkwood tucked the pistol into his belt. 'Nathaniel and I are leaving. You're in charge here. How's the shoulder?'

'I'll live.'

'When they bring the girl down, see she's taken to a physician. Nathaniel tells me she's been sorely treated. There's another one, name of Sadie, hiding in the larder. Make sure she gets out as well. Get all the girls out. Hopkins can see to it.'

Lomax saw the darkness in Hawkwood's eyes. 'What about them?' he nodded towards the Hanrattys.

'Micah will take care of them.'

Hawkwood looked towards Jago, who was standing next to his lieutenant. Jago gave a small, unobtrusive nod.

'You have a problem with that, Major?' Hawkwood asked.

Lomax held Hawkwood's gaze for maybe two or three seconds. 'No,' he said. 'What about this place?'

'As far as I'm concerned, you can burn it.'

There was another pause.

'I might enjoy that,' Lomax said.

Hawkwood nodded. He turned to Jago. 'Ready?'

'Waitin' on you, Cap'n.'

'Bring a light,' Hawkwood said.

20

Jago looked up at the front of the house. 'Why here?'

'The address was on that piece of paper I found in Sawney's waistcoat: number 13 Castle Street. I think it's the home of Hyde's old mentor and hero: John Hunter. Apothecary Locke told me Hyde lived here when he was a student. Hunter used to give anatomy lectures here, so Hyde would have had everything he needed for his butchery. Sawney must have delivered Molly Finn here; that's why he laughed when he called you king of the castle.'

'No lights,' Jago observed. His eyes took in the shuttered windows and the raised drawbridge. 'What would he want with Molly Finn?'

'I don't know,' Hawkwood said. 'That's what worries me.'

Jago took the lock picks from his pocket and gave Hawkwood a wry look. 'Murder, arson *and* burglary. Anyone ever tell you, you've a strange way of upholding the law? Here, hold this.'

'Just open the bloody door,' Hawkwood said. He took the lantern from Jago and drew Hopkins' pistol from his belt.

Molly Finn came awake slowly. Her eyelids felt heavy and unresponsive. She tried to raise her head. That proved almost as difficult and when she tried moving her arms and legs, it was as if a great weight was pressing down upon them. Every movement was a huge effort. She opened her mouth to speak, but all she could manage was a weak swallow, and there was a strange taste at the back of her throat that she could not identify.

The room was candlelit, she saw, but everything was blurred. It was like looking up at the stars through a black lace curtain. She had the feeling that the room was large and her first thought was that she must be in a church or a chapel. She tried to recall how she might have got there, but her mind became a jumble of vague, confusing thoughts. She tried to concentrate, but that only made things worse. The candle flames around her began to dance and shimmer. Suddenly the whole room was spinning. It was much better if she kept her eyes closed, she decided, but when she did that, she could feel herself slipping away. The more she tried to fight the sensation, the more tired she became. In the end, it was easier just to succumb. And in truth, sleep, when it eventually came, was a relief.

'Looks like we got it wrong,' Jago said. There was anger in his voice as he stared around him. Samuel Ragg's pistol was held loosely in his hand.

They had checked the two doors leading off the entrance hall. The rooms beyond were dark, cold, and empty. The tiny arrows of desultory moonlight slanting down through thin gaps and holes in the window shutters had revealed no signs of recent habitation. The air smelled of dry dust and abandonment.

Hawkwood said nothing. He had been so sure the answer would be here. Yet there was no sense that anyone was present, other than the two of them. He stood at the foot of the stairway and looked up towards the next landing. All he could see was a well of darkness. He held out his hand. 'Give me the light.'

They were halfway up the stairs when Jago paused. 'Smell that?'

Hawkwood had already noticed it. It was the same odour as had been leaking from the vats and the benches in the cellar of the Black Dog. He suddenly felt an overwhelming sense of dread. It was as though the house was starting to close in around them.

The first floor was also empty. Most of it was taken up by one large room containing rows of empty shelves. There was an ancient wooden packing chest resting against one wall; inside were some paper boxes and a collection of empty glass jars.

The smell grew stronger the higher they climbed. Jago was the first to use his neck cloth to cover his nose. By the time they arrived at the second floor it was reaching in to the back of their throats. They stopped outside a closed door. The smell coming from inside the room was intense.

Hawkwood turned the handle and pushed.

'God in Heaven,' Jago said.

When Molly opened her eyes for the second time, little appeared to have changed. She still felt as if she could fall asleep for a hundred years, and the odd taste at the back of her throat refused to go away.

The mattress was as hard as a board. She was cold, too. She could still make out the glow of candles, scores of them, arranged around the room. Her eyes tried to penetrate the darkness beyond. The walls, she noticed, had a curious, curved shape to them; so much so that they seemed to be spiralling away from her towards the ceiling. It was a most peculiar sensation.

She went to push the sheet away, only to find that she was still unable to move her arms and legs. Her first reaction was to call out, but all she could manage this time was a dry croak. She strained to raise herself up but the harder she tried, the more difficult it became. Her efforts grew progressively weaker. Finally, exhausted, feeling as helpless as a kitten, Molly sank back and closed her eyes.

There was a noise. Molly started. The candles were still burning. She could see them, flickering dimly, and she could smell the tallow. Had she been asleep? she wondered. Perhaps she'd fainted. If so, for how long? It was very cold now, and growing colder by the minute. She shivered and tried to raise her hands to lift the sheet higher, but the simple task eluded her. The walls were behaving very oddly, too, the way they were revolving around her, like a child's top.

The noise came again, instantly familiar, even in her confused state: footsteps on a wooden floor. As she tried to locate the source of the sound, a dark shape detached itself from the edge of the shadows beyond the reach of the candle glow, and moved slowly towards her.

Hawkwood stared at the skull. It was some kind of monkey. The skull was in a jar on a shelf. The monkey's eyes looked as if they were on the point of opening, giving the impression that the animal had been sleeping when its head had been removed. The face, although heavily wrinkled, looked strangely young. It was framed by an incongruous cap of wispy reddish hair.

The jar was one of several score that filled the shelves along the right-hand wall. They came in all shapes and sizes, each one labelled. Every single jar was full of cloudy liquid. Suspended in the liquid, like insects trapped in amber, Hawkwood saw a bewildering assortment of objects. There were lizards with two tails and baby crocodiles emerging from eggs. According to the labels, others held brains of deer, of goats and dogs, the eyes of a leopard, the testes of a ram, the foetus of a pig, kittens, mice, snakes, baby sharks, two-headed chickens... All manner of oddities and abnormalities were displayed.

But it wasn't the freakish animal parts that drew Hawkwood's eye. He was no anatomist, but during his time as a soldier he'd seen surgeons at work and had been both the victim and beneficiary of their administrations. Similarly, as a Runner he had paid court to coroner's surgeons like McGregor and Quill and was thus familiar with some of the more gruesome aspects of their work. So he knew what he was looking at. They were human body parts.

Most of the specimens appeared to be internal

organs, at least according to the labels: hearts, livers, lungs, bowels, kidneys ... the list was extensive. Some of the contents were easily identifiable, like the coils of gut, which bore a strange similarity to empty sausage skins; others he could only guess at. The patina of dust on top of the jars and the faded ink on the labels indicated that they had been on the shelves for some time. The sealant on several of the jars had rotted away, allowing air to intrude and the liquid inside to evaporate. Whatever had been contained within them had long since disintegrated and so bore no resemblance to its original state. Beneath the shelves, a dozen or so jars lay broken, the contents having spilled out across the floor. It was hard to distinguish the remnants of their desiccated contents from the lumps of calcified rodent droppings that littered the floorboards.

'What the hell are these?' Jago whispered.

'Preparations,' Hawkwood said. His eyes moved around the room. In the darkness, he had not seen how large the room was. It occurred to him that an internal wall had probably been removed to create the space, as on the floor beneath. There were more shelves on the opposite wall. They supported another collection of jars. The middle of the room was occupied by an oblong table. He moved towards it. On top were what looked like a butcher's cutting board and an assortment of basins, both deep and shallow. There were some familiar items lying on top of the butcher's board. Hand tools. Not the butcher's tools of the Dog's cellar, however; these were much more refined. But he'd seen their like before, in the hands of

Surgeon Quill. These were medical instruments.

His eyes moved across the tabletop. It took him a moment to notice the difference between the table and the specimen shelves behind him. There was no dust.

The touch on her arm came from nowhere. Molly flinched.

'It's wearing off,' a voice said. 'She's waking up.'

When she heard the words and realized there were two people in the room with her, the memory of her ordeal at the hands of the Ragg brothers came flooding back. And with the memory came the panic. She saw again the Raggs' leering faces, felt the wiry strength of them, smelled their rank unwashed bodies, as sour as vomit, as they took turns with her. She remembered, too, the shame she had felt in allowing herself to submit to the degradation in the vain hope that they would spare her further hurt, knowing all the while that these were men without pity, men who derived pleasure from the humiliation of others. Now, when she felt the hands upon her, Molly knew she was about to be subjected to more of the same.

But this time she was not going to give herself to them without a fight.

When she tried to lash out, though, her arms and legs refused to obey. It was as if they belonged to someone else. She felt the sheet being lifted from her body. She looked down and understood immediately why she felt so cold. She was naked.

That was the moment true fear took hold. She tried to cry out, but what emerged was still no more than a feeble croak. Strong hands gripped

464

her shoulders, forcing her down.

'Hold her,' the voice said.

She felt her legs pinioned; then her arms. They were wrapping some kind of binding around her wrists and ankles. Her head snapped to one side and she saw the thick leather straps – and they were being drawn tight.

Molly realized then it wasn't a bed they were tying her to. It was a table. She continued to struggle, but the more she fought, the tighter the straps were pulled. Held fast, unable to move, she saw for the first time the rest of the room and realized with a jolt of terror that it was neither church nor chapel.

The true nature of her situation struck Molly like an arrow to the heart. She stared around her in horror. From what seemed like a thousand miles away, she heard a voice she recognized dimly as her own, whispering falteringly, 'Am I going to die?'

The reply, when it came, was soft spoken and reassuringly calm, almost affectionate.

'No, my dear. *You* are going to live for ever.'

Molly Finn's screams were already filling the room as Titus Hyde placed the point of the scalpel in the valley between her pale breasts and, using the minimum of pressure, drew the blade down the length of her sternum.

Hawkwood heard Jago mutter a curse under his breath. He turned and followed the upturned, awe-struck gaze.

Bones; too many to count, suspended from an array of ceiling hooks, like withered bats in a dark

465

cave. Femurs, fibulas, ribs, pelvic bones, bones from the feet and bones from the forearm, many with hand, toe and finger bones still connected, all blackened with age and candle soot, hung alongside clavicles and spinal columns; many of them with remnants of muscle and what might have been ragged strips of long-dead flesh still attached.

Hawkwood dragged his gaze away. The second, closer collection of jars also looked to be free of dust. The liquid inside them was a lot cleaner than in the containers on the opposite side of the room. He remembered what McGrigor had told him, that the favoured preservative was spirit of wine. Hawkwood wasn't about to take a sip to test it. The transparency of the liquid gave him a clear view of the contents. He tried to recall which items had been removed from the Bart's cadavers and the corpse found suspended over the Fleet. From their colouring and the consistency of the solution, there was little doubt the organs contained within these jars were much more recent additions to the collection.

'I've had enough of this,' Jago said, his face ghostly pale. 'And we ain't any nearer finding Molly Finn, or your damned sawbones.'

'No, but the bastard's been here.' Hawkwood turned, and found he was talking to himself. He left the room and its grisly contents and discovered Jago standing in one of the two doorways on the other side of the cramped landing.

At first glance the room was no different to the others they had looked in: peeling plaster, bare floorboards, boarded-up windows. There was, however, a mattress. On top of the mattress was a heap of soiled bed linen. Next to the mattress was a small table, on which sat a candle-holder and some sulphur sticks. A larger table was set against the wall. On top of it was a chipped basin and jug. Caught by the lantern light, several small beads of moisture glistened at the bottom of the basin. He glanced towards the fireplace. There was grey ash in the hearth.

Hawkwood reached down towards the pile of linen. He straightened. In his hand was a petticoat.

A woman's scream pierced the night.

'Sweet Mary!' Jago spun round.

The scream sounded as if it had come from below them. It was followed by a second of equal intensity and another after that, both in quick succession. By which time, Hawkwood had thrown the petticoat down and was running for the stairs with Jago in close pursuit.

They were halfway down the stairwell when the screams ended abruptly. Hawkwood wasn't sure what was the more disturbing, the screams or the uncanny silence that followed.

Jago stared about him wildly. 'Where the hell did that come from? We looked, damn it! There's no one here!'

Jago was right. They *had* looked.

And then, the moment they hit the ground floor, Hawkwood saw it. 'There!'

Jago swore. There was another doorway, tucked deep in the shadows beneath the stairs, almost hidden from view. They'd both missed it the first time around.

Another room, small and airless, but with signs of recent occupation: on the table stood an empty Madeira bottle and some mugs. Several news-sheets lay scattered across the tabletop. Beyond the table was an opening that led off towards the rear of the property. The house, Hawkwood was starting to realize, was like a rabbit warren. They ducked through the aperture and found themselves in yet another cramped room. A row of coat hooks ran along one wall. The only notable item of furniture was an old wooden desk.

They both saw it at the same time: a pale ribbon of light at the base of the far wall.

With a nod of agreement from Jago, Hawkwood stepped forward and hauled the door open.

It was smaller in scale than the operating room at Guy's, but the design was almost identical: a series of wooden benches rising in semi-circular tiers towards the ceiling. In the well of the amphitheatre, framed within the light of a hundred candles, two men dressed in shirtsleeves and bloodstained aprons were bent over an oval table. Between them lay the naked body of a young woman.

At the sound of footsteps, the two men turned, faces frozen in shock.

'It's over, Colonel,' Hawkwood said. 'Put the knife down. Move away.'

Titus Hyde stood perfectly still.

Hawkwood looked at Hyde's companion. 'That goes for you, too, Surgeon Carslow.' Hawkwood raised the pistol. 'And that's an order, not a request.'

Slowly the two men stepped away. Jago gave a

468

sharp intake of breath as the body on the table came into view.

A sheet covered the lower half of the woman's torso. If it had been placed there to preserve the victim's modesty, it had been a gesture too late. In a scene almost indistinguishable from the autopsy in Surgeon Quill's dead house, Hawkwood saw that the woman's chest had been cut open. The flesh on either side of the incision was on the point of being peeled back. Had her screams not told him already, Hawkwood did not need to be informed that Molly Finn was beyond help. In death, her young face, framed by her mane of blonde hair, looked remarkably serene; an expression undoubtedly in sharp contrast to the fear and terror she must have felt in the moments before Hyde cut into her with his scalpel. Wordlessly, Hawkwood pulled the sheet over the rest of her.

His eyes moved to the second table and the object that rested upon it. There was a covering sheet here, too. Cautiously, Hawkwood lifted it away and found himself looking down into a shallow metal trough. The trough was filled with a honey-coloured liquid. Immersed in the liquid was another body.

'Beautiful, isn't she?' Hyde said. There was a note of pride in his voice.

The corpse might have been beautiful once, Hawkwood supposed; perhaps in the full bloom of life. It had arms and legs and breasts and was undoubtedly female, but beautiful wasn't a word he would have used to describe what he was looking at now. The flesh had the appearance of melted wax. A patchwork of stitching, clearly visible along the arms, thighs, hips and hairline, indicated where the sections of skin excised from the Bart's cadavers had been transplanted. An incision had been made in the chest wall and the skin had been folded away, following the same procedure Hyde had been in the midst of performing on Molly Finn. But whereas Molly Finn's face still retained its colour and the freshness of youth, the face on this body looked about a thousand years old. It reminded Hawkwood of the monkey head he'd seen in one of the jars upstairs.

On the floor of the operating room, adjacent to the second table, was a cluster of cylindrical objects, about a dozen in all, each approximately half the height of a man. They were columns of metal discs. The top of each stack was connected to its immediate neighbour by a strand of copper wire. Hawkwood did not need to be told what he was looking at. It was an electrical battery.

Hawkwood swallowed bile. He turned. 'You really believe you can perform miracles, Colonel?'

Hyde held up his blood-stained hands. 'With these, yes.'

'You're not God, Colonel.'

'No, I'm a surgeon.'

'And that gives you the right to commit murder? I thought physicians took some kind of oath.'

'She's my daughter. She was taken from me. I have the power to restore her. I can make her whole again. I can turn back time.'

'Daughter? She's not your daughter, Colonel.

470

She never will be. I'm not even sure you could even call that *thing* a she. That's what the sack-'em-up men call them, by the way: things. All that thing is now is skin and bone and whatever fluid she's embalmed in. You think she's beautiful? God help you. Molly Finn was beautiful, before you butchered her. What in God's name were you after, Hyde? What had this poor girl ever done to you? Good Christ, you've killed three people – and for what? A bag of bones in a bathtub? You really are insane.'

Hawkwood turned his gaze on Hyde's companion. 'I wonder what that makes you, Surgeon Carslow?'

'You don't understand,' Carslow said.

'Don't I? Well, maybe you could enlighten me. I knew someone had to be helping him. It had to be someone with the money; and you, Carslow, you've got more money than God. And this is how you choose to spend it?'

Hawkwood turned back to Hyde. 'Your friend here told me he never visited Bethlem, but that didn't stop the two of you corresponding, did it? What did you do, Colonel? Write out a shopping list? What did you send him first, I wonder? The drawing you got from James Matthews? All this equipment doesn't come cheap. You'd need to have had it specially made. And he'd have told you about this place being empty, of course: your old school. You must have jumped at the chance. It's even got its own operating room. How's that for convenience? I did wonder how you knew who *I* was, too, but then I realized it had to have been Carslow here who gave you my name and description. It must have been damned cold, hanging around Bow Street, waiting for me to turn up. Oh, and it was Sawney who gave *you* up, Colonel, in case you were wondering how we got here. He's dead, by the way. They all are. It's been a busy night.'

Hawkwood smiled. 'Still, look on the bright side: we saved Jack Ketch a job. That way, he can concentrate on the two of you.' Hawkwood turned to Eden Carslow. 'What? You think keeping silent won't incriminate you? It's too bloody late for that.'

Carslow blanched, recovered quickly, and drew himself up. 'You know nothing. You think science stands still? Tell that to Leonardo and Galileo, and John Hunter. It's surgeons like John Hunter and Titus Hyde, men who are prepared to take that first step beyond the frontiers of knowledge, who light the way for others. You've been in the wars, Hawkwood, you've seen men like Colonel Hyde work, you've seen the miracles they *can* perform. I suspect you've even had occasion to thank men like Titus Hyde for sewing you back together after some bloody encounter. How do you think he acquired that sort of skill? It was because the men before him dared to explore beyond *their* boundaries.'

'You can save the lecture, Carslow. I'm not one of your damned students. I'm not impressed. You'll go down as his accomplice. Hell of an end to an illustrious career, don't you think? Swinging from a gibbet. I wonder what your students will think of that? You never know, you being a condemned murderer, they could end up with *your* body to dissect. Now that *would* impress me.'

Carslow went pale.

You don't look so hale and hearty now, Hawkwood thought. *Do you?*

Hyde's thin lips split for the first time. 'My dear Captain, you don't seriously think that's what's going to happen? You can't be that naïve. They don't hang surgeons, Hawkwood. We're at war. Who do you think is going to put all those wounded warriors back together again?'

Hawkwood said nothing. He could see that the look on Jago's face was murderous.

Hyde gave a contemptuous snort. 'Who was it you spoke with? McGrigor? That sanctimonious Scot! Calls himself the Surgeon-General? He might have succeeded him, but he's not fit to clean John Hunter's shoes. The man's more concerned about offending God than serving the cause of science. What did he tell you? That they refused to hand me over because we don't take orders from the French? You think that was the sole reason? You've been a soldier, Captain. You've seen inside the tents. You know what it's like: the hopelessness, the futility. Think of the potential, if we can learn to harvest the dead to heal the living. If we can accomplish that, the possibilities are endless. Good God, man, you think I'd have been removed from duty if the Frogs hadn't found that damned cellar? The reason they didn't hand me over was because they need surgeons like *me* to heal *British* soldiers.

'You said it yourself: the worst they'll do is put me back in Bedlam. The war won't last for ever.

473

When it's over and the Frogs are back in their pond, I'll be supping brandy in the officers' mess. In the meantime, I'll be able to renew my acquaintance with Dr Locke. As I said, not the brightest of fellows, but in a place like Bethlem one has to be grateful for what one can get. I'll be needing a new chess opponent, though. Still, mustn't grumble. The parson served his purpose. Interesting, the two of us meeting again. Strange coincidence, him visiting the hospital, don't you think?

'You *did* know Tombs was an army chaplain? That we were colleagues back in Spain? Ah, perhaps not, from the look on your face. Why, he was a regular visitor to the hospital tents. The scars on his face – he got those courtesy of a French mortar round. I was the one who stitched him back together afterwards. Ironic, don't you think? He was most grateful, mind you. Even offered to deliver letters for me when I was in hospital. You were right when you accused Eden of corresponding with me. The Reverend Tombs was our winged messenger, our Hermes.'

Hyde feigned forgetfulness. 'But I digress. Where was I...? Ah, yes, I remember. No, they won't hang us, Captain Hawkwood. We're too damned valuable.'

'Not to me,' Hawkwood said.

Hyde's eyes widened as, in a move almost too fast to follow, Hawkwood raised his pistol and squeezed the trigger.

He heard Carslow gasp. There was a flash, but that was all. In that instant Hawkwood knew the pistol had misfired. Although the flint had struck

474

the frizzen and ignited the powder in the pan, the flash had failed to penetrate the hole in the side of the barrel. The only thing the pistol had discharged was smoke.

And Hyde was gone.

The man was fast. Hawkwood had forgotten how fast. One minute Hyde was there, the next he wasn't.

'Door!' Jago threw his pistol up, brought it to bear. Hawkwood had a glimpse of a darting figure entering a patch of shadow beyond the arc of the candle glow and then it vanished.

'No!' Hawkwood pointed back at Carslow, who was standing open-mouthed, struck dumb by the escalation of events. 'Mind him! Hyde's mine!'

Hawkwood ran.

It was immediately apparent as he plunged through the doorway, that he'd entered a different world. There were no dingy passages here, no dark stairways, no bare boards. What he found instead was a long, portrait-lined corridor, with an open door at the far end. Not stopping to wonder at the contrast, he raced down the darkened corridor. Passing through the door, he found himself in what looked to be a large reception room, devoid of furniture. Neither was there artificial illumination, but the shutters on the tall windows were open, allowing the cold moonlight to pour in. He pulled up. Where was Hyde?

'Sawney said you were a bastard. He was right,' a voice said behind him.

Hawkwood spun. Hyde was standing perfectly still. A sword was in his hand, the point resting on the floor by his foot. He had divested himself of

475

the blood-splattered apron. He looked perfectly at ease. His face was grey in the moonlight. His eyes were black and as hard as stone.

Hawkwood assumed Hyde had taken the sword from one of the racks on the wall. The room was lined with them. It was clear now why there was no furniture. This must have been where Hyde had obtained the sword-stick he'd been carrying the other evening. The selection of weapons displayed around the room's perimeter was hugely impressive and would have done justice to a regimental armoury. There weren't just swords, Hawkwood saw, there were pole-arms, too. Stilettos, sabres and foils vied for space with halberds, glaives, guisarmes and pikes.

'I can see you're wondering where you are,' Hyde said. 'This was Hunter's house, too. He owned both properties. Go through those rooms and out of the front door and you'll find yourself in Leicester Square. He had all this part built on afterwards – the operating room, everything. There was even a museum for his specimens. He welcomed his patrons and his patients through the door in Leicester Square and he took delivery of his bodies in Castle Street. Fascinating, isn't it?

'They used to call this the *conversazione* room,' Hyde continued blithely. 'It was his reception room. Curious that its purpose is now to do with the teaching of combat rather than the art of conversation. From soirees to swordplay, eh? Who'd have thought? They've preserved it rather well, though, don't you think? The paintings aren't the originals, of course. They were sold off with the rest of the contents when Hunter died. That's when the main house was rented out. I'm not sure who was here before, but it's a fencing academy now; a place for the sons of the nobility to learn the noble science. That's what they call it, you know. Hunter would probably find that ironic, too.' Hyde gave a little laugh.

'Fortunately for me, the maître d'armes is indisposed. He's recovering from a rather severe wound inflicted by an over-enthusiastic pupil. By a happy coincidence he is also one of Eden Carslow's patients. We had the place to ourselves until you blundered in.'

Hawkwood watched the blade. He wondered what his chances were of getting to a weapon. He wondered why Hyde hadn't attacked him as soon as he'd entered the room. It occurred to him that it had probably been Hyde's intention to lead him here in the first place.

Hawkwood gauged the distance to the wall. It would be close. The colonel was quick on his feet. He, on the other hand, was still wearing his bloody coat. That was bound to slow him down. There was no button on the point of Hyde's weapon, Hawkwood saw.

'How's the arm?' Hyde said. 'I almost forgot to ask. If it's giving you pain, you should let me take a look at it. The cut on your cheek looks as if it's healing nicely, though.'

Hyde smiled suddenly. 'By the way, did you know – and this really is a most extraordinary coincidence – that I attended the Delancey boy after you'd shot him? Couldn't do anything for him, of course. He was stone dead. A pistol ball to the heart will do that.'

Hawkwood stared at him. Delancey had been the Guards' officer he'd killed in a duel following the battle at Talavera. Delancey had called him out after Hawkwood accused him of recklessly endangering his men. But for Wellington's intervention, Hawkwood would have been cashiered and shipped home. Instead, he'd joined Colquhoun Grant's intelligence unit as liaison with the *guerrilleros*.

'Made me wonder how you might be with a sword instead of a pistol. Ever used a blade, Hawkwood?'

'Occasionally,' Hawkwood said.

'Really? Ah, yes, but you were an officer, weren't you? Eden told me. Well, how about it?'

'How about what?'

'Why, man to man, what else? At least I'm giving you more of a fighting chance than you were willing to give me back there. Tell you what; I'll make it easier for you. Here, catch–'

Hyde tossed the rapier high towards him. Had it not been for the moonlight catching on the turning blade, Hawkwood would have lost sight of it in the air. But the high parabola had been a deliberate ploy, providing Hyde with the opportunity to re-arm himself. By the time the weapon was in Hawkwood's hand, Hyde had turned and retrieved a second sword from the rack behind him. 'You might find it easier if you removed your coat.'

Hawkwood hesitated. *This is madness,* he thought.

'Well?' Hyde said. The challenge in the soft

478

voice was unmistakable.

Hawkwood took off his coat, dropped it to the floor. He heard Hyde chuckle.

There was, Hawkwood discovered, a distinct chill in the room. He looked towards the windows. There wasn't a lot of light coming in. He wondered if the snow that Jago had predicted was finally on its way.

Hyde attacked. His sword arm was a blur as the rapier blade plunged towards Hawkwood's throat.

Instinctively, Hawkwood parried, quarte to prime. The room rang as blade clashed on blade. Hawkwood riposted, drove the point of his sword down towards Hyde's flank. Hyde parried easily, disengaged, and withdrew.

'I see you have *some* knowledge,' Hyde said dismissively.

Hawkwood knew then that Hyde's opening gambit had been merely a reconnaissance to test his reflexes. A good swordsman's strategy was dictated by his opponent's defensive actions. Hyde would have seen how Hawkwood held his sword, how he moved, and the speed at which he had executed his response. The second attack was likely to be more aggressive, but probably still exploratory.

Hawkwood waited.

Hyde's next foray was a strike towards Hawkwood's sword arm. Hawkwood parried, using his *forte* and the curve of his sword guard to deflect the blade. He riposted towards Hyde's flank. Hyde parried and moved in again, his sword blade flickering in the light from the windows.

Hawkwood parried, riposted, and lunged towards his opponent's right side. Hyde brought his sword up and Hawkwood withdrew his feint. As he did so, he turned his wrist palm down and slashed his sword back-handed towards Hyde's belly. He felt the point rasp across Hyde's chest, heard Hyde grunt as the blade raked the underside of his throat. As Hyde twisted, Hawkwood stepped back before Hyde could riposte. Hyde lifted his hand to his breast and chin and stared at the blood on his fingers. He looked up. There was a new understanding in his dark eyes.

Suddenly, he launched himself forward. Hawkwood barely had time to react as the edge of Hyde's blade slashed towards his ribs. Hawkwood sucked in air, brought his sword around and felt the nerves in his wrist jar as his blade caught the full force of Hyde's attack. He heard Hyde grunt. Hawkwood pushed Hyde's blade away and adjusted his grip in preparation for the colonel's next offensive.

Hyde came in again. Sword held high, Hawkwood moved to block the cut, realized, too late, that he'd misread the signal and felt a searing pain lance down his right arm as the point of Hyde's blade sliced across his bicep. He heard Hyde's hiss of pleasure at the contact.

It was time to end it.

Hawkwood snapped a strike towards Hyde's sword arm. Hyde flicked the blade away with contemptuous ease and scythed his sword towards Hawkwood's ribcage. Hawkwood smashed Hyde's blade aside. Hyde counter-attacked. Hawkwood brought his sword across the front of

his body and struck hard on the outside of Hyde's blade, driving it down and away. As Hyde's shoulders began to turn, Hawkwood made his move. Sidestepping left, he spun right, turning into his opponent and locking his left arm over Hyde's sword arm. Hyde was a slender man with a long reach. By stepping forward into Hyde's attack and thus shortening the distance between them, Hawkwood had reduced his opponent's room to manoeuvre. Hyde's cadence was disrupted.

Ignoring the shriek of agony from the wound in his arm, Hawkwood slammed his body against Hyde's shoulder until they were almost back to back. As Hyde fought for balance, Hawkwood reversed direction, using the outside of his rigid left arm as a fulcrum to force Hyde's sword arm away from his body. He felt the wound in his arm open and the warm flow of blood, but continued the turn, straightened, and brought himself back to the vertical. Completely wrong-footed by the speed of Hawkwood's attack, Hyde found himself stranded, his sword arm held adrift, his guard destroyed, and the point of Hawkwood's sword hovering a paper's width from his left eye.

And yet, Hawkwood saw, there was no fear there, only a kind of awe, giving way to respect and then uncertainty.

'There was a fencing master called John Turner,' Hawkwood said. 'His speciality was killing his opponent by putting the point of his sword through the eye. *I* killed someone through the eye once. Pierced his brain with an auger. But there's another attack, supposed to have been

perfected by a French master, name of Le Flamand. He called it the *botte de Nouilles*. The blade enters *between* the eyes...' Hawkwood shifted the point of the blade an inch and a half to the right. 'There's a weak spot, I've been told. Not sure if that's true, though.'

Hyde frowned.

Hawkwood thrust the blade home.

The point went in with very little resistance. Hyde's eyes widened with surprise. They were still open as Hawkwood withdrew the blade and stepped away. He watched as Hyde's corpse pitched forward and hit the floor. He looked down on the still body for several seconds. Then, retrieving his coat, he threw the sword aside and strode out of the room.

Jago looked up with relief as Hawkwood emerged from the darkness.

Hawkwood sighed wearily. 'Go home, Carslow.'

He heard Jago gasp. 'You ain't serious?'

The surgeon stared towards the door through which Hawkwood and Hyde had disappeared. 'You heard, Carslow. Go home.' Hawkwood fixed the surgeon with a steel gaze. 'But be sure to present yourself at Bow Street before midday. I don't want to have to come looking for you. And if I were you, I wouldn't plan on holding any lectures for a while either.'

His composure destroyed, the blood drained from Carslow's face. Hawkwood turned on his heel. 'Coming, Sergeant?'

James Read was standing in front of his fire, staring into the flames. He looked, Hawkwood

thought, more than a little pensive.

'A terrible business, Hawkwood.'

Hawkwood assumed the question was rhetorical. He kept quiet.

The Chief Magistrate turned. 'How is your arm?'

'Mending.'

Read nodded slowly. 'I spoke with Eden Carslow.'

Hawkwood waited.

'He has accepted that his involvement with Colonel Hyde was ill judged.'

'Ill judged?'

'Hindsight has made him realize that he allowed loyalty to his friend to rule his head. Once events had been set in motion, it was too late to retract.'

'Too late for him to step in and save Molly Finn?'

Read pursed his lips.

'Did Carslow say what they wanted with her?'

'Molly Finn was not...' Read paused '...a *specific* requirement. Any female of a similar age would have sufficed. It was her heart Hyde wanted.'

Hawkwood went cold. 'They were going to transfer her heart to his daughter's corpse? Hyde was going to start her heart with his electrical machine?'

'That was his intention, yes.'

'Like John Hunter did with the Reverend Dodd.'

'Dodd?' The Chief Magistrate frowned. 'I'm not familiar with that name.'

Hawkwood explained.

483

'I see. Yes, Carslow said that was Hyde's plan.'

'Is it possible? Could they really have done it?'

'Hyde was convinced it could be done. Carslow confessed he did not know.'

'Didn't know? But he went along with it.'

'He was seduced by the possibility. Carslow had no interest in resurrecting Hyde's daughter per se. His participation was purely, he says, to enhance his knowledge.'

'I doubt he'd have told Hyde that,' Hawkwood said.

'He admitted to sharing Hyde's belief that it will be possible one day to take organs and blood from the dead or dying and use them to prolong the life of the living. He said that if one truly believes in the advancement of surgery, one must be prepared to take risks, to push back the boundaries of science and medicine in pursuit of the greater good, the benefit of mankind. He openly acknowledged that Hyde's abilities and grasp of anatomy were far greater than his own. The skills the colonel had gained treating the wounded on the battlefield had given him a unique understanding of how the body functions.'

'What about the girl?'

'He was deeply contrite.'

'Contrite? That's all? *Contrite?*'

'He told me he felt deep remorse, also shame for his actions, but he did not express guilt and I detected none in his manner.'

'In other words, as far as he's concerned, his only crime was getting caught.'

'Crudely put, but I suspect that may be so.'

'He'll get away with it, won't he?' Hawkwood

said heavily.

'Carslow will certainly not face trial. There will be no precedent set this day. You know as well as I do that no surgeon has ever appeared in the dock as a result of an association with the resurrection gangs. In any case, it would be most unlikely that a figure as eminent as Eden Carslow would be taken to task.'

'He was an accomplice to murder!'

Read sighed. 'The authorities have already decreed that Colonel Hyde was killed by the Reverend Tombs in Bethlem Hospital. A dead man cannot rise up and commit murder.'

'But that's exactly what he did do,' Hawkwood said.

'The girl's death at the hands of Colonel Hyde will go unrecorded,' Read said.

'She had a name,' Hawkwood snapped. 'It was Molly Finn.'

Read's head came up. His jaw was set. Then his face softened. 'You are right. Forgive me, Hawkwood. I cannot say I like this state of affairs any more than you do.'

'Can't you do anything?'

'Some things are beyond the remit of this office.'

The Chief Magistrate steepled his hands. 'As I believe I advised you before, Hawkwood, Eden Carslow moves in privileged circles. He has powerful, influential friends. He attends the Prime Minister and at least two members of the cabinet. Molly Finn was a working girl, of little consequence. His words, not mine, I hasten to say. I found his arrogance a shade irritating, as you may imagine.'

'You mean they're closing ranks?'

'Indeed.'

'So what next – he resumes his rounds as if nothing happened?'

'Not entirely.'

'What does that mean?'

'I understand a knighthood has been mooted. I saw no harm in advising him that such an honour bestows certain responsibilities on the recipient. I told him there could well come a time when he would be reminded of his ... aberration, and his obligations to this office.'

'What does that mean?'

'It means he is beholden to us.'

'So he gets a knighthood while Molly Finn goes to an early grave. Where's the justice?'

'Justice, Hawkwood?' James Read sighed. 'It is the way of the world.'

'It's wrong.'

'Perhaps. But the world turns, there is no stopping it. It is relentless. It is inevitable.'

'It doesn't mean I have to like it.'

'No,' Read conceded. A silence fell between them. The fire crackled in the grate. It was Read who finally broke the spell. 'How is Major Lomax?'

'He'll live. He has more lives than a cat.'

'I am pleased to hear it. And Constable Hopkins?'

'I'll be having words with him about the maintenance of sidearms.'

'And Sergeant Jago?'

'He was his usual efficient self.'

Read's mouth twitched. 'By the way, I'm assuming Twigg told you that he discovered the location of Hyde's daughter's grave?'

'No, he didn't.'

'A very curious state of affairs.'

'How so?'

'It appears that the body was still in situ.'

'What?'

'The grave had not been tampered with. The body Hyde was attempting to resuscitate was not that of his daughter.'

'Then whose was it?'

'I doubt we shall ever know the answer to that question. I suspect, if anyone could shed light on the mystery, it would be Eden Carslow. He told me that Hyde had asked *him* to obtain the corpse.'

'He told you that?'

'In one of his more unguarded moments.'

'He wouldn't have dug it up himself though.'

'No. He did, however, admit to making regular use of one of the resurrection gangs. A porter at St Thomas's by the name of Butler is his liaison. Butler, you will be interested to know, is also a former military man. He was an associate of Sawney's during the war. It would be ironic if Sawney was hired to retrieve the daughter's body. Twigg tells me the grave was constructed of stone and protected by a metal grille. I think it's safe to assume that Sawney and his cohorts, if indeed it was them, would have considered that particular exhumation to be too exacting. They evidently obtained another body instead and kept quiet about it. I doubt Carslow knew. Colonel Hyde, of course, had never met his daughter. He placed his reliance on Carslow to retrieve the body and preserve it until his escape. Carslow stored the corpse at 13 Castle Street...' The Chief Magistrate's brow creased. 'It was fortunate you found that note.'

'What are they going to do with the place?'

'No decision has been made. The contents will most likely be moved to Lincoln's Inn to join the rest of John Hunter's collection. I've yet to receive an explanation as to why they were not removed earlier when the house was closed. It appears to have been an oversight.'

'God Almighty,' Hawkwood said.

'Indeed. The Lord does work in mysterious ways. Which, incidentally, brings me to another mystery. I'm intrigued and not a little concerned to learn of the fire which consumed the Black Dog public house. I understand the owner and his sons died in the blaze, along with Sawney and his associates.'

'So I heard,' Hawkwood said. 'A terrible business.'

'Indeed. So you would have no knowledge of how the fire might have started? It was down to good fortune that it did not spread to the surrounding buildings, though I believe the neighbours were able to offer some assistance. This morning's early snowfall would also have helped to dampen it down.' The Chief Magistrate looked towards the window.

'Probably a stray spark,' Hawkwood said, moving towards the door. 'You know how easy things like that can happen.'

James Read turned and looked down the end of his long nose.

Hawkwood paused, hand on the door knob, and nodded past the Chief Magistrate towards the newly installed fireguard. 'Could happen to anyone, sir...'

Read's eyes narrowed.

Closing the door behind him, Hawkwood smiled grimly at Ezra Twigg, who was seated at his desk in the ante-room, and murmured softly under his breath, '...even surgeons.'

HISTORICAL NOTE

By any definition, body snatching is and was a foul trade, and yet there is no doubt that during the late eighteenth and early nineteenth centuries, prior to the Anatomy Act of 1832, which allowed corpses other than those of condemned murderers to be used in anatomy studies, it played a crucial role in the advancement of medical knowledge. There were very few surgeons who did not rely on the resurrection men to provide fresh cadavers for their research.

Hyde's real-life mentor, John Hunter, certainly made use of them and took delivery of fresh corpses for his anatomy classes at 13 Castle Street, now Charing Cross Road.

Other characters in the story also existed. James McGrigor was Surgeon-General of the Army, Richard Ryder was Home Secretary and both James Norris and James Tilly Matthews were patients at Bethlem Hospital. Mike Jay's book, *The Air Loom Gang*, gives a fascinating account of Matthews' incarceration in Bedlam, as well as great insight into the workings of the mad houses of the time.

Eden Carslow is a fictitious character, though based for the most part on the surgeon Astley Paston Cooper, who was a student of Hunter's and who later became lecturer in anatomy at St Thomas's and senior surgeon to Guy's Hospital. There is no suggestion that Cooper was involved in aiding and abetting murder, though he was in league with the sack-'em-up men, using Thomas Butler, a porter at St Thomas's dissecting room, as a go-between. Cooper often boasted that he could obtain any body that he wished and he paid the resurrection men handsomely for their services, despite referring to them as 'the lowest dregs of degradation'.

In that, Cooper was not wrong, as I discovered during my reading of Ruth Richardson's excellent *Death, Dissection and the Destitute*. The scene in which Hawkwood discovers that human flesh had been converted into soap and candles in the cellar of the Black Dog is not the product solely of my imagination. If anything, I have held back in describing some of the more bizarre uses to which human corpses were subjected. For example, John Sheldon, another of Hunter's former pupils, lived with the preserved body of a beautiful woman in a glass case in his bedroom for ten years, while another, dentist Martin van Butchell, had his wife embalmed by Hunter and kept her in his living room where visitors could view her by appointment. I confess I did try to work a similar scenario into the story but decided to abandon the idea, for fear it would be considered too fanciful.

Equally, while some of the medical procedures I have attributed to Hyde during his service in Spain may seem unlikely, they too are based on fact. Crude blood transfusions had been attempted, including one from a sheep to a man by seventeenth-century physicians Richard Lower and Jean Baptiste Denys. John Hunter also conducted transplantation experiments involving both human and animal subjects.

Lest any readers think it a tad convenient that Hyde should have found himself a bolt-hole equipped with both an operating room and an escape route through an adjoining building that just happened to back on to his hideaway, I can assure them this was not poetic licence. Hunter did indeed own the lease to 28 Leicester Square, the house directly behind the Castle Street property. He had the gap between the houses bridged with an operating room specially constructed to aid his anatomy lectures. Above it he built a museum, in which were displayed thousands of his preparations. Following Hunter's death in 1793, the Leicester Square property was rented out, while the museum remained in place, tended by Hunter's former assistant, William Clift. The museum's contents were later purchased by the Royal College of Surgeons. They are now displayed to splendid effect in the galleries in the Hunterian Museum at the RCS's headquarters in Lincoln's Inn. Sadly, unlike Hunter's specimens, neither his home nor the school building has been preserved, though the plaque placed above his grave in Westminster Abbey can be seen, commemorating him as the 'Founder of Scientific Surgery'. While researching the novel, I referred constantly to Wendy Moore's immensely readable biography of John Hunter, *The Knife Man*. I cannot recommend it too highly. I am also indebted to

Mick Crumplin, Archivist to the Association of Surgeons of Great Britain and Ireland, whose knowledge of general surgical history, in particular that of the Napoleonic Wars, is truly encyclopaedic. He responded to my questioning with great patience and good humour. Any mistakes in the story are mine, not his.

The science of electricity was in its infancy during this period, and yet scientists and physicians were already attempting to harness electrical power as a means to dominate nature. Several experiments were conducted to inject life into human cadavers. The attempt to reanimate the corpse of the murderer George Forster did take place as described, as did John Hunter's efforts to resuscitate the forger William Dodd.

Regarding the latter experiment, there is an intriguing footnote in Wendy Moore's biography. Despite there being a memorial stone bearing his name in St Laurence's churchyard in Cowley, West London, there is no mention of Reverend Dodd's interment in the parish register.

This Large Print Book for the partially sighted, who cannot read normal print, is published under the auspices of

THE ULVERSCROFT FOUNDATION

400   52

793

353

303

903

1316

101

815

900